KATE ELLIS

THE
BURIAL
CIRCLE

PIATKUS

PIATKUS

First published in Great Britain in 2020 by Piatkus
This paperback edition published in 2020 by Piatkus

3 5 7 9 10 8 6 4 2

A CIP catalogue record for this book
is available from the British Library.

ISBN 978-0-349-41832-2

Typeset in New Baskerville by M Rules
Printed and bound in Great Britain by
Clays Ltd, Elcograf S.p.A

Papers used by Piatkus are from well-managed forests
and other responsible sources.

Piatkus
An imprint of
Little, Brown Book Group
Carmelite House
50 Victoria Embankment
London EC4Y 0DZ

An Hachette UK Company
www.hachette.co.uk

www.littlebrown.co.uk

For Alexander James,
the newest member of the family

December 2008

'Where are you going?'

She hesitates. He's good-looking. Dark. Late twenties. Nice smile. And yet his steady gaze reminds her of a farmer assessing livestock at market.

He leans over to open the car door. 'What are you waiting for? Hop in.'

She heaves her red rucksack off her back. The thing's heavy, weighing her down. She needs a lift . . . and if he tries anything, she's sure she can deal with it.

She climbs into the passenger seat, keeping the rucksack at her feet in case she needs to make a swift escape.

As soon as he drives off too fast, she fears she's made a bad mistake, and she clings to her seat belt as if it's a protective shield as he presses his foot on the accelerator.

Once out of the town, the darkness closes in around her. Hedges like walls flash by, looming in like a trap as the roads grow narrower; a labyrinth leading to God knows where.

When he changes gear, she feels his hand brushing against her knee and she moves her leg away fast, telling herself she can cope with this.

'Drop me here.'

'We're not there yet.'

'Drop me here. I can walk.'

He ignores her and carries on driving. But as soon as he stops at a junction, she opens the door and stumbles out onto the lane, falling to her knees before hauling herself upright. The air is cold and her jeans are damp with mud, but she begins to walk, hoisting the rucksack onto her back, determined to ignore the sound of the car engine throbbing slowly behind her.

She can see the signpost. Not far now.

What she doesn't know is that in an hour's time, she'll be dead.

2

Twelve years later

The Reverend Mark Fitzgerald stepped into the gloom of the church and shut the heavy oak door behind him. The place smelled of polish and old books. A comforting smell, unchanged over the years.

He'd always believed that the building should be kept open for members of the community to visit any time they felt the need, even though his wife, Maritia, wasn't happy with the idea of him being alone and vulnerable in there. He told her that she took far too much notice of her brother, who was a detective inspector with the local police. Wesley Peterson was always advising them to take sensible precautions against intruders, because rural crime was on the increase. Mark knew his brother-in-law was probably right, and yet he still preferred to rely on the defence of prayer.

The first Advent candle had been lit the previous Sunday, so there was a lot to do. Soon the Christmas tree would be erected to be decorated by the Sunday school children as it was every year; a comforting ritual of joy and light, a world away from Wesley's crime figures and tales of senseless violence.

Mark hurried into the vestry to check the decorations were ready for their annual outing. They were stored in a huge oak cupboard crammed with the detritus of the past hundred years – old hymn books, tattered Bibles and rusty biscuit tins, the contents of which were a mystery to him – and as he opened the cupboard door, he caught a movement out of the corner of his eye.

The vestry door was opening. Slowly.

'Hello. Can I help you?'

He could see a figure in the half-open doorway, little more than a black outline against the ray of bright winter sunlight pouring through the tall stained-glass window behind. As he shielded his eyes, he saw that the newcomer was wearing a dark padded coat with the hood raised, and a grey woollen scarf concealed the bottom half of his face.

'Hi. Can I help you?' Mark repeated. As he waited for a reply, he arranged his features into the expression of sympathy he used when speaking to the troubled.

After a few seconds, the stranger spoke in a whisper, his voice muffled behind the scarf. 'I want to make a confession.'

Mark hesitated but if this person needed to share something in confidence, he felt it was his duty to help.

'Come into the vestry. There's a kettle there and I can make us a cup of tea.' As he took a step forward, the stranger backed out of the doorway. 'If something's troubling you, I'm here to listen,' he added, hoping his words sounded encouraging and non-judgemental.

All of a sudden the man vanished from sight. Mark assumed he'd lost his nerve at the last moment. He followed him out into the body of the church and saw that he'd slid into one of the front pews, where he sat staring at the altar beyond the ornate rood screen. Outside, the sun had retreated behind a cloud, plunging everything into deep shadow as Mark walked slowly over to the man and took a seat a few feet away.

'There's nothing so bad that God can't forgive, you know,' he said softly.

He saw the man shake his head, but he still couldn't see his face. 'How does your God feel about murder?'

For a few moments, all suitable words fled from Mark's head. The visitor showed no sign of moving, so he waited a while before asking his next question. 'Are you saying you've murdered somebody?'

'It was a long time ago, but I was responsible.' There was a lengthy pause and Mark sensed there was more to come. 'And now it's going to happen again ... soon.'

Mark took a deep breath. The man's words had shaken him, but he was determined not to show it. 'You wouldn't be here talking to me if you didn't want to be stopped.'

'You don't understand. I can't stop it. I don't know how.'

Without warning, the stranger sprang up and dashed out of the church, slamming the heavy oak door behind him. Mark followed him into the porch, rushing past the parish notices and lost umbrellas into the daylight, his heart pounding as the realisation that he'd just been sitting a few feet away from a murderer sank in.

He looked around, searching for his visitor, but the only sign of life in the churchyard was a gang of crows flapping and cackling in the skeletal branches of the surrounding trees.

The murderer, whoever he was, had gone.

Report of Petherham Burial Circle

19 January 1882
Payments received: £13 2s. 9d
Payments made: £6 1s. 10d

The board of the Circle regrets to report the deaths of two members. Mary Tucker passed away on the thirteenth day of July, at the age of seventy-nine. Her funeral took place at the church of St Mary Magdalene followed by interment in the churchyard, paid for by the Circle.

Elizabeth Boden, daughter of John Boden of Church Cottages, passed away from a fever on the twentieth day of July, at the age of nine. She was also buried in the grounds of the church of St Mary Magdalene after a funeral service in the church, paid for by the Circle.

The Circle has the honour of welcoming Dr Christopher Cruckshank onto the board. As our new village doctor, he will be a valued member of the committee. Let it be recorded that the meeting welcomed him in the customary manner.

Dr Cruckshank, formerly of London, is a wise and experienced physician and will be a worthy successor to Dr Smith, who was called to his reward in November after a short illness.

3

DCI Gerry Heffernan seemed to be in a remarkably good mood as he entered the CID office singing 'Good King Wenceslas' in a tuneful baritone.

DI Wesley Peterson looked up from his paperwork. 'You're cheerful today, Gerry.'

'It's Christmas in a few weeks. Besides, everything's been quiet since that farm near Whitely was done over.'

'It won't last. Never does.'

'Know your trouble, Wes? You're a pessimist. We got 'em, didn't we? Remanded in custody till the trial.'

'As long as no one else starts targeting farms.' DS Rachel Tracey's face was solemn as she joined in the conversation. 'I worry about my parents. They're not getting any younger.'

'Are any of us?' said Gerry.

The newly married Rachel came from a family who'd farmed the Devon land for generations, as did her new husband, Nigel Haynes. The marriage had been the union of two dynasties well acquainted with the realities of farming life.

'Hope you've been advising that new husband of yours on security,' said Gerry, wagging his finger.

Rachel looked away. 'He's well aware of it already, boss.'

The phone on Wesley's desk began to ring, and he was surprised to hear his brother-in-law's voice on the other end of the line. As far as he could recall, Mark had never called him at work before.

'Hi, Mark. Everything OK?'

'No, it's not actually. I think I might have just been speaking to a murderer.'

Mark was talking quietly, as though he didn't want to be overheard, and Wesley pressed the receiver closer to his ear. 'What do you mean?'

'A man came into the church while I was alone in the vestry. He said he wanted to make a confession, so I invited him in expecting a heart-to-heart about something that was troubling him. I didn't imagine ...' His words trailed off and Wesley waited patiently for him to continue.

'I thought he'd probably been cheating on his wife or pinching from the petty cash – the sort of sin you come across most days in my job, but ...'

'What did he say?'

'That he'd murdered somebody.'

'Who? When?'

'He said it was a long time ago.'

Suddenly Mark's call lost its urgency

'I wouldn't worry too much. We get people coming into the station confessing to all sorts. Attention-seekers ... or people with problems.'

'I realise that, but I had the impression he was telling the truth.' Mark hesitated, and Wesley knew he had more to say. 'He told me it was going to happen again. He said he didn't know how to stop it.'

'Did you recognise him?'

'No. He had his face covered and his voice wasn't

familiar. He ran out of the church before I had a chance to ask any more.' There was a long pause. 'Trouble is, Wes, I think he was deadly serious. I think someone's going to be murdered.'

4

Come and experience the paranormal in the comfortable surroundings of Mill House, Petherham. Book now
for a ghostly weekend at our luxury B&B in the company
of renowned TV psychic Damien Lee.

As soon as Corrine Malin had seen the advert on social
media, she'd booked right away. It would be good to conduct her research in comfort for a change.

She'd always been fascinated by the paranormal – a
purely academic interest, she assured anyone who looked
as though they were about to sneer at her gullibility –
and when she'd embarked on her doctorate at Morbay
University, she'd chosen it as the subject of her thesis. *The
role of the paranormal in modern-day life and its effects on contemporary thought.* She was pleased with the title; it sounded
scholarly, with no hint of the sensational or the Gothic. It
also allowed her a lot of scope.

She had done her first degree at Exeter. Later, having abandoned work in an insurance office at the age of thirty, she'd
decided to pursue her dream of continuing her academic
career, taking a part-time job serving in a Morbay restaurant
to make ends meet, a necessity of life as a mature student.

After months of counting the pennies, the prospect

of spending a long weekend of luxury at Mill House had proved irresistible. Besides, she had a personal reason for wanting to visit Petherham – something she felt unable to share with anyone else, because nobody would understand.

Mill House had once been home to the owner of the water-powered textile mill on Pether Creek, a tidal inlet three miles north of Tradmouth. The house and mill were reputed to have a history of death, tragedy and misfortune, although Corrine intended to keep an open mind. According to the publicity she'd seen, the present owner had fulfilled his dream of reopening the place as a working mill; a tourist attraction that also produced woollen cloth, mainly for soft furnishings and souvenirs. But this aspect didn't particularly interest Corrine. She'd leave the industrial history of the area to those who appreciated that sort of thing.

She'd paid for the stay upfront, gritting her teeth at the cost, and as she steered her fifteen-year-old Yaris into the parking space, she looked at the other cars in the small paved area outside the house. There was a new BMW sitting beside an Audi – the latest model – along with a flashy car with a personalised number plate whose make she didn't recognise. As she took her case from the car boot, she was conscious that it was worn and tatty, having been pressed into use often since her undergraduate days.

Inside were her clothes, carefully chosen from local charity shops for the stay. And she'd brought with her the most important thing of all – the little wooden box she'd bought at the car boot sale. She wanted to find out the truth about its contents and she hoped Mill House would provide the answers – along with some material that would add originality and sparkle to her dissertation.

A stiff breeze was whipping the leafless trees surrounding

the village into a frenzy, and from the look of the darkening sky, a storm was brewing. It was four o'clock, and in the fading light she could see that Mill House resembled a Georgian-style doll's house, beautifully symmetrical, with a glossy red front door and sash windows already lit up in welcome. A wreath of dried flowers dangled from the lion's-head knocker and a tasteful painted sign beside the entrance confirmed that she'd come to the right address.

She pulled her shoulders back, gathered her confidence and marched up the front path. The email she'd received had informed the guests that their rooms would be available from midday onwards, but she'd worked a lunchtime shift in the restaurant before she set off, so she suspected she might be the last to arrive.

She rang the doorbell, a grand circular ceramic affair bearing the instruction *PRESS*, and heard a distant jangling. The woman who answered the door was tall and blonde. At first, with her slim figure, short denim skirt and long straight hair, Corrine thought she must be in her twenties; thirties at most. Then she noticed the wrinkled neck and the lined skin stretched tight across her cheekbones. The woman was fifty if she was a day. Possibly older.

Her hostess switched on a smile that didn't spread to her eyes. 'You must be Corrine. Come in out of the cold. Welcome to Petherham Mill House. I'm Selina Quayle.' She held out her hand, and when Corrine took it, she found it ice cold and the handshake limp. 'I'll show you to your room. Would you like any help with your case?'

Detecting a note of disapproval in her hostess's voice, Corrine shook her head vigorously, self-conscious about her shabby luggage and reluctant to give a stranger possession of her new treasure, even for a few moments. She followed the woman up the thickly carpeted stairs, resting the case every now and then. The banisters were original, polished mahogany and cast iron, and she knew they must have witnessed the things that had happened here over a century ago – if the contents of her box were to be believed. She'd heard that buildings could absorb emotions and play them back, like a tape. But so far, to her disappointment, the house had given her nothing.

When they reached the landing, Selina Quayle led her to a door at the far end. 'This is you. Do come down and meet the others when you're ready. If you need anything in the meantime, just let me know.' She gave Corrine another smile, no more convincing than the last. 'Damien will be arriving tomorrow. I've heard he's wonderful.'

'I'm looking forward to it,' Corrine replied, suddenly eager to be on her own.

To her relief Selina didn't linger, and once she'd gone, Corrine hoisted her case onto the stand in the corner of the room and looked around. The advert hadn't lied. The room was large and tastefully decorated, with a neat en suite shower room and a view over Pether Creek. The bed was luxuriously large, and she lay down and closed her eyes, relishing a few minutes of self-indulgence before rising to her feet and opening her case.

She'd packed the box between two sweaters for protection, and now she took it out carefully, stroking the highly polished surface inlaid with geometric patterns in different-coloured woods. She opened it and spread its contents on the bed before studying her room, wondering whether this was where the strange photographs she'd found in the secret compartment in the base of the box had been taken. Those carefully posed images of the dead.

13

5

As a farmer's wife, Stella Tracey was accustomed to the vagaries of the Devon weather. Even so, on Thursday night she felt uneasy. She'd heard the dogs barking as the wind howled around the farmhouse. She knew the cattle in the barn were bound to be restless because of the brewing storm, so earlier on she'd asked her eldest son, Tom, who lived with his wife and family in one of the adjoining cottages, to check on them.

Her husband, Jim, had fallen asleep in front of the TV, as he did so often these days, exhausted from rising for the early-morning milking, and she was glad that Tom and his two brothers were there to shoulder the responsibility of making sure all was well. She had told Jim time and time again to start taking it easy and leave the hard graft to the next generation, but he was a stubborn man, which meant there were frequent arguments. Their daughter, Rachel, had inherited her father's determined nature. Although Stella supposed that was a useful trait in a detective sergeant.

Stella had missed Rachel ever since she'd decided to leave home to share a house with Trish, another policewoman. (She knew you weren't supposed to call them policewomen nowadays for reasons of equality, but she often lost track of what you were and weren't allowed to say.) Rachel was her only daughter, and her absence hit Stella hard. However, with the farm to run, she didn't have a lot of time to dwell on it, which, she told herself, was probably a good thing.

The run-up to Rachel's wedding had brought mother and daughter closer for a while. It had been a wonderful day: the sun had shone – a minor miracle for an autumn wedding – and Rachel had looked serene in her plain white gown, her face solemn as she walked up the aisle of St Margaret's church on her father's arm. For a brief moment she had hesitated before saying the words 'I will', but Stella had put the pause down to her daughter being nervous, as brides were meant to be. She knew Rachel would be happy with Nigel Haynes, a solid, reliable young man who owned a large farm a few miles away. How could she be otherwise? And it had been good to see her police colleagues at the service and reception, particularly Wesley Peterson, of whom Rachel had always spoken so highly.

As the bride's mother, Stella had played a major role in the preparations, and now that the wedding was over, she felt empty, as though her part in her daughter's life was over. But you couldn't hold on to your children for ever. Perhaps that was the bitterest lesson any parent had to learn.

She spent a restless night listening to the storm while her husband snored by her side. As the years had gone on, she'd grown to hate the winter months, when they had to rise in the darkness, but she was well used to it, and at 4.30 in the morning she slid out of bed, giving him a nudge.

The livestock had to be attended to first. Then everyone would come in for a cooked breakfast. The routine was the same each day, rain or shine, summer or winter.

Over breakfast, Jim hardly said a word, leaving the talking to his sons, and once the breakfast things were cleared away, Tom made an announcement. 'A tree's come down on the edge of that field we ploughed the other day – the one near the lane. I'm going down to have a look.'

Stella saw that Jim was about to rise from his seat, but she put her hand on his shoulder. 'Hang on,' she told Tom. 'I'll come with you. It's stopped raining and I fancy the walk.' She turned to her husband. 'You stay there, love. I'll see what's what.'

As soon as she'd donned her wellingtons and old waxed coat, they set out, walking over the fields in companionable silence. It wasn't until they'd reached the newly ploughed field that Tom finally told his mother what was on his mind.

'I'm worried about Dad. He hasn't looked well since our Rachel's wedding.'

Tom had put her own fears into words, and she thought for a while before she answered. 'You know what he's like, Tom. If I say he should see a doctor, he'll accuse me of fussing.'

'Always playing the tough guy,' said Tom with a roll of his eyes.

'He won't admit he's getting older, that's all. I'll have another word. Not that it'll do much good.'

The subject was closed. Stella could see the fallen tree a few yards away, a large sycamore propped against the hedgerow.

'It'll be blocking the lane,' said Tom. 'There's not much traffic down there this time of year, but it needs to be moved. I'll go and get the tractor to shift it. Eli can give me a hand. I'm surprised he didn't notice it when he came in this morning.'

'Probably too dark. It was quite a storm last night. Mind you, that trunk was probably half rotten. Could have come down any time.'

Stella strolled up to the sycamore. Lying there, it looked massive, a felled giant. She'd known that tree since she'd arrived at Little Barton Farm as a bride, and she felt an unexpected pang of sorrow.

She glanced down into the crater where the roots had been torn from the earth and saw something lying half buried. She crouched down to tug it out, and as it emerged from the loosened soil, she saw that it was a rucksack.

'Someone must have dumped it,' said Tom, leaning over to see what his mother had found. 'What's that?'

He was pointing to the edge of the hole, where something stood out dirty white against the rich red earth. Stella began to push the damp soil away with her bare hands until the object was partially revealed.

'There aren't any animals buried here, are there?' Tom asked.

'I doubt it,' she said. 'Not that I remember anyway.'

She uncovered more of the thing until she could see it clearly. Then she stood up and brushed the dirt from her hands. 'I think we should call our Rachel.'

'Why?'

'Don't forget I was a nurse before I had you lot. I'm pretty sure this isn't an animal bone. I might be wrong, but I think it could be human.'

Tom took out his mobile phone and called his sister.

6

Rachel Tracey had decided to keep her maiden name at work because she thought it would avoid confusion. So when her brother Tom asked to speak to Detective Sergeant Haynes, he was told by the switchboard that there was no such person working in CID. It took a couple of minutes to clear up the misunderstanding, and he was eventually put through to her extension.

When Rachel broke the news to Gerry Heffernan, he didn't look pleased. 'It's a farm, isn't it? They'll be animal bones.'

'Dead livestock are taken away.'

'Dogs?'

'They're like family, so they have their own little burial ground near the house. As far as my mother knows, nothing's ever been buried in that particular spot. Besides, she used to be a nurse, so she recognises human bones when she sees them,' she added, irritated by her boss's doubts.

Gerry let out a long sigh. 'Skeletons are more Wesley's thing than mine. Have you told him?' Wesley had studied archaeology at university, so Gerry regarded him as the expert on all things long-buried.

'He's downstairs at the moment interviewing a witness to

that theft at the gallery in the high street. My brother says they found a rucksack buried with the bones. It's made of some sort of artificial fibre, so it's well preserved. It's red.'

'You sure?'

'That's what he said.'

Gerry frowned as though he was trying to grasp some elusive memory. Then a look of triumph appeared on his face. 'There was that case years ago – the hitch-hiker who went missing. A couple of witnesses who saw her in the area said she was carrying a red rucksack. But she was last spotted in Falmouth, so the search was diverted to Cornwall. As far as I know, she's still a missing person.'

Rachel took a deep breath. 'Well, if it does turn out to be her, how the hell did she end up buried on my parents' land?'

'That's what we need to find out.'

Breakfast at Mill House was scheduled for 9.15; late to give everybody a leisurely start. The food was good. After fresh orange juice and wholegrain muesli, Corrine opted for smoked salmon and creamy scrambled eggs, her favourite. She was surprised to discover how hungry she'd been as she tucked into the rustic wholemeal toast and home-made jam that followed.

The guests sat around what was the city dweller's idea of a farmhouse table. Scrubbed pine, and spacious enough for some imaginary farmer's wife to prepare a week's worth of wholesome bread and cakes on. Only Corrine suspected this one had originated in some swish London furniture store.

The table easily accommodated eight people, and she tried to concentrate on her food to avoid having to make

19

conversation. She was never at her most sociable first thing in the morning, and she wished everyone had been allocated separate tables. But realising she couldn't avoid the company of her fellow guests, she gritted her teeth and made the best of it.

She had met them all the previous night in the drawing room, with Selina playing the hostess and making the introductions, but had fled upstairs at the earliest opportunity, saying she had calls to make. It had been a lie. She'd wanted to be alone. And she'd wanted to examine the contents of her box again.

She looked up from her toast and saw the man opposite watching her. His name was Brad Percy and he'd told her last night that he owned an IT company. He was in his forties, she reckoned, and he had shaved his head to conceal his incipient hair loss. His clothes were expensive and he had been eager to inform her that he'd just bought a new car: a Tesla, the latest model and so good for the environment. He had monopolised her, telling her all about the new vehicle he clearly found so fascinating – although she hadn't been able to share his enthusiasm. After half an hour, she had been losing the will to live. She was there to investigate people's belief in paranormal activity, not to be lectured on boys' toys.

'You're enjoying that, aren't you?' he said. 'Must say, the food's up to standard. Did you sleep well?'

'Fine, thanks,' she answered, concentrating on buttering another piece of toast.

This wasn't true, but it avoided the need for further explanation. In reality, Corrine had lain in the centre of the big bed, her ears straining for any sound, wondering if the events that had taken place in that house had left any imprint. She wished she knew which room the photographs had been taken in – whether it had been hers or one of the others. Perhaps when the psychic arrived she would find out.

Brad had just opened his mouth to continue the conversation when Selina Quayle cleared her throat. 'Damien's very keen to meet you all,' she said with a forced smile.

Her husband, Jeremy, a tall man with ginger hair and a beard to match, was seated at the other end of the table like a Victorian paterfamilias, but he'd said nothing since his initial morning greeting and was now staring at his empty plate as though fascinated by the pattern of egg stains on the white china. He'd been quiet the previous evening too, leaving most of the talking to his wife. Corrine thought he looked worried about something – perhaps whether the psychic was going to turn up, and what he was going to say if he did.

The other guests were two couples in their fifties. Jacob and Wendy Chalmers were what Corrine's late mum would have called ageing hippies. Wendy wore her greying hair long and favoured floor-length skirts and colourful scarves. Jacob's white hair was gathered back into a thin pony-tail and he wore a collarless shirt and jeans. In contrast, Jennifer and Charlie Taylor appeared conventional and quietly prosperous, although there was an underlying air of sadness around them, as though their lives weren't as comfortable as might be assumed at first sight. Corrine thought they looked out of place at a psychic weekend, unlike Jacob and Wendy, who'd dropped 'auras' and 'energies' into the conversation at every opportunity.

Jennifer Taylor glanced around the table. 'I'm really looking forward to meeting Damien,' she said with an intensity Corrine found surprising. 'I've heard so much about him.' Her accent was Birmingham, and Corrine wondered if she'd made the journey to Devon specially to meet the psychic medium. Perhaps there was somebody she was desperate to contact on the other side – or something she needed to know.

Corrine was finding the effort of making small talk with strangers wearing, so once she'd drained her coffee cup, she glanced at the long-case clock ticking away in the corner of the room, wondering how soon she could retreat up to her room without seeming rude.

'Damien should be here in time for lunch,' said Selina, glancing at her watch. 'But in the meantime, we have newspapers in the drawing room if anybody wants . . .' Muttered thanks followed, then the scraping of chairs. This was Corrine's chance to make her escape.

When she reached her room, she shut the door behind her, feeling a sudden chill. The place seemed colder than it had, but when she touched the radiator she found it was warm, so she put it down to her imagination. There was a Roberts radio on the polished oak chest of drawers, and she switched it on, feeling the need for noise in that silent room. It was tuned to the local station. The 10.30 news.

'Police have been called to a farm near Tradmouth, where human remains are believed to have been discovered. A spokesman said that a statement will be issued later.'

She slumped down on the bed, her heart beating fast. The report had been vague, but she had a bad feeling about it.

Something told her it could be Erica. Funny it should happen now, when she was staying in the village near where she'd been seen. It was almost as though it was meant to be.

From the notebook of
Dr Christopher Cruckshank

29 January 1882

Petherham is as unlike London as it is possible to be.
The houses of the poor are mean cottages. Some are
stone but others, I am informed, are constructed from a
substance called cob, which we would know in London as
mud. This cob is painted and the roofs are made of thatch,
some sparse and leaking after years of neglect.

It is said that my predecessor, Dr Smith, was a
saintly man who treated the poor of the village for little
or no fee, and the vicar of the parish church hinted that
I am expected to continue the tradition, which I am
willing to do. In London I tended to the needs of many
poor families who lived in conditions I would hesitate
to allow a pig to occupy, far worse than anything I have
seen in Petherham. There my wealthy patients always
provided me with sufficient income to continue this
charitable work, and I learned much about the human
body and its diseases through my excursions into the viler
parts of the capital.

The village has a handsome mill at its heart, which, I am told, makes woollen cloth. Many in the village work at the mill and there are several rows of cottages built for the mill workers, although these too are poor dwellings. The village's picturesque nature and the rural character of its inhabitants will undoubtedly prove fitting subjects for my favoured pastime. I have brought my photographic equipment with me from London and I wonder if its use will cause curiosity amongst my new patients.

The owner of the mill, one Josiah Partridge, lives in a fine house within sight of the great water wheel. I understand his family were patients of Dr Smith, so I will, no doubt, make their acquaintance in due course. There are several families of the better sort in the district who I hope will have need of my services. Dr Smith's practice was, I am sorry to say, hardly flourishing, but I have already been called to the home of one of the district's more prosperous farmers, whose wife will soon be brought to bed with her third child, so I have hopes for the future. Had I the means, I would have bought a more lucrative practice, but my family are not wealthy and I must make do with what I can.

I have already been invited to join the Parish Committee for Charitable Works, and last night I attended my first meeting of an organisation called the Burial Circle. Perhaps my stay in Petherham will prove more profitable than I had hoped.

7

Mark's strange visitor had been on Wesley's mind ever since he'd received his call the previous day, although the incident wasn't high on his priority list. Clergy, like the police, were often approached by people who had problems of one kind or another, and the unusual confession wasn't necessarily to be taken seriously. Besides, Rachel's brother's news had taken priority.

Wesley had first visited Rachel's childhood home some years ago, when the Traceys had been the victims of a vicious robbery. As he turned through the gate, his first thought was that little had altered since that time. Apart from the acquisition of new vehicles and machinery and the odd domestic improvement, working farms tended to be unchanging places.

Stella Tracey seemed pleased to see them, greeting them at the door like old friends. When she smiled, Wesley was struck by the resemblance between mother and daughter.

'Good to see you again,' she said. 'I can't believe it's been a month since the wedding. Only seems like yesterday, doesn't it? Tom showed your colleagues where the tree came down. Can I tempt you with some tea? There's scones too – I made them first thing.' She beamed at her daughter's workmates as though their visit was a social occasion. 'Come on. Those bones aren't going anywhere. You've got time.'

Wesley caught Gerry's eye. Stella was right. The crime-scene investigators had already started work down by the fallen tree; half an hour or so would make little difference. Besides, they had a few questions for Stella, and then Wesley needed to make some calls to ensure the bones were lifted from their resting place properly.

'Tell us exactly what happened,' he said once they were settled in the farmhouse kitchen with tea and fresh scones that melted in the mouth. Two dogs, black and white Border collies, lounged by the Aga, taking a break from their sheep-herding duties. The scene looked idyllic, but Wesley knew from Rachel how much back-breaking toil went into keeping Little Barton Farm running smoothly.

'The tree came down in last night's storm and it needed to be shifted with a tractor because it was blocking the lane. When Tom and I went down there to look at it, we saw something where the ground had been torn up by the tree roots. I pulled it out and found it was a rucksack – red. Then I noticed something white in the ground nearby, and when I pushed the soil away I thought it looked like a femur. I didn't think it was an animal, so I told Tom to call Rachel. There's no rain forecast today so I left everything as we found it. I know from Rachel how important it is not to move anything.'

'I know it's hard to remember that far back, but do you recall a hitch-hiker who went missing around twelve years ago?' Gerry asked.

Stella thought for a few moments, dredging the depths of her memory as the dogs roused themselves and came up to her, tails wagging, hoping for crumbs from the discarded plates. She fondled their heads absent-mindedly. 'I remember something. Wasn't she a student? Erica something?'

'I looked up the case before we came out. Her name was Erica Walsh. Aged nineteen. She'd had a row with her mum and said she was coming to Tradmouth to look for a job over Christmas. She was seen not far from here, but a few days later someone saw her in Falmouth and her debit card was used there, so the search shifted to Cornwall.' He paused. 'Witnesses said she was carrying a red rucksack.'

'You think it could be her?' said Stella, her eyes widening in alarm.

'It has to be a possibility,' said Wesley. 'But we don't even know for sure that the bones are human yet, so ...'

'Quite right,' said Gerry. 'We mustn't jump the gun. By the way, Stella, the press have already got wind that something's going on. Someone saw the patrol cars rushing here with all lights blazing, and called the local radio station. Sorry about that. You might get reporters knocking on your door.'

'Then they'll be disappointed,' she said with a wink.

'If you do talk to them, don't mention Erica Walsh, will you? Or the red rucksack. We don't want to get her family's hopes up.'

'Of course not. I understand.'

Before leading them down to the field, Stella put on her coat and wellingtons, and Wesley and Gerry did the same in the farmyard. They always kept wellingtons in the boot of the car, knowing from long experience of working in a rural area that suitable footwear was the key to a comfortable investigation.

Stella left them at the field entrance before returning to

the house, her hands thrust into her coat pockets. She had a farm to run.

The tree had been hauled away from the hedgerow by the tractor and lay waiting to be dealt with by the farm chainsaw. In accordance with Gerry's orders, the CSIs had taped off the area and erected a large white crime-scene tent. The rucksack had been photographed *in situ* before being moved, and as they entered the tent, having changed into the white protective suits that Gerry claimed made him look like a snowman, they saw it lying on a tarpaulin near the gaping hole. Wesley edged forward so he could see into the crater. The white thing protruding from the side was certainly a bone, and a few others had tumbled down into the hole. A shin bone and part of a foot, he guessed from his experience of excavating ancient graves as a student. The rest would still be there in the soil somewhere.

'Think it's human?' said Gerry behind him.

'Looks like it. I take it Colin's on his way?'

'He's in the middle of a post-mortem at the moment, but he'll be here as soon as he can.'

'I'm going to call Neil too. This needs to be excavated properly.'

Gerry nodded in agreement. Wesley's old friend from university had helped them out many times before, and as an archaeologist, he knew how to proceed systematically in order to preserve all the evidence from the burial site. Neil had recently acquired a new job title: Heritage Manager – Archaeology and Historic Environment. He'd joked that it sounded as if he ought to wear a suit to work rather than his disreputable old combat jacket, but he'd assured Wesley that nothing would change. He'd still be available to lend the police a hand whenever necessary.

Wesley eyed the rucksack, longing to tear it open to discover what was inside, but instead he made the call to Neil, who answered almost at once.

Wesley came straight to the point. 'Are you free to excavate some bones for us?'

'Where?'

'Just outside Tradmouth. Rachel's parents' farm.'

'Archaeological?'

Wesley hesitated. 'More likely suspicious.'

'You're in luck. I'm in Petherham at the moment, which isn't far away. We're conducting a survey of historic mills, and the one here dates from the early eighteenth century, possibly on the site of an earlier structure—'

'Can you come and deal with our bones?' Wesley hadn't time to listen to tales of south Devon's industrial heritage, however interesting he might have found it if he didn't have more urgent things on his mind.

'No problem,' Neil said. 'I can leave my team to carry on here and be with you in half an hour.'

The rucksack was about to be carefully wrapped in a large evidence bag ready to be sent to the lab for investigation. But first Wesley wanted to take a quick peep at the contents.

He and Gerry leaned over the bag and the CSIs gathered round to watch. With gloved fingers, Wesley gave a tentative tug on the rusting zip, stiff from years below the ground. Eventually it moved, and the contents were revealed. He examined them gently, disturbing them as little as possible. The clothing inside looked damp but remarkably fresh, and he was pleased to see what appeared to be a small notebook or diary in a plastic bag, which would have to be looked at properly in due course. A leather purse lay on

29

top of the clothes, and he picked it out, careful to leave everything else in place. The rucksack was good quality, which was probably why its contents had remained relatively undamaged. It must have been expensive in its day.

'What's in the purse?' said Gerry, craning his neck to see.

Wesley opened it and found it empty apart from a few coins. But it was the name on the student ID card that interested him.

Erica Walsh had been found at last.

8

Damien Lee didn't suppose it mattered too much if he arrived late at Mill House. It would add to his mystique and make the punters even keener to hang on his every word. Over time he'd learned how to manipulate every situation to his advantage. Smoke and mirrors had become his stock in trade.

During the past years he'd reinvented himself a number of times. A change of name always did the trick, as did a change of history. He'd come a long way since his days as an entertainer in the pubs and clubs of north-west England – and occasionally further afield. He'd become a new man. A respected psychic with an impressive reputation.

He'd first realised he had the gift ten years ago while visiting a Liverpool pub. He had been engaged one evening as the 'turn': a singer of ballads and cover versions to entertain the Saturday-night drinking crowd. But while he was taking his break in what passed for the green room on the first floor – in reality the landlord's spare bedroom – he'd had an experience that had set his life on a different course.

He'd seen a woman, battered, bleeding and semi-transparent, emerge noiselessly from the wardrobe in the corner, materialising through the solid wood and looking at him with pleading eyes. Then, as quickly as she'd appeared, she vanished again. When he told the landlord about it, the man had turned pale, and it wasn't until he'd helped himself to a stiff Scotch from one of the optics behind the bar that he'd revealed that a former landlady had died violently in that very room back in the 1920s.

Surprisingly, Damien hadn't been shocked or frightened by what he saw. Rather he'd experienced a heavy, suffocating sadness after feeling the woman's terror. The following day he'd gone to Liverpool's magnificent central library to look up the story in old newspapers, and had discovered that shortly before her death, she had lost her only son to influenza and at the time of her murder had been in mourning. He had experienced her grief with an empathy he'd never imagined he possessed.

Soon after this incident, he'd left the north-west circuit, abandoned his singing career and become a psychic, first in the resorts of north Wales, and then in Bristol, before heading to the south-west, where he'd had a few singing engagements back in his crooning days.

He began in a small way by holding psychic events in pubs and clubs, the same sorts of places he'd visited as a singer. He was enough of a realist to know that his career singing ballads and cover versions to a handful of drinkers more interested in beer and conversation had never been an unbridled success. His psychic evenings, on the other hand, soon started to pull in the punters, and it wasn't long before, with a fresh name to go with his new career, he was in great demand and playing in larger and larger venues.

He would come on stage and pick out members of the audience; people for whom he'd received messages from the 'other side'. People in need of comfort, advice or warning.

If nothing came through, he'd resort to guesswork – cold reading. *Someone with the initial J is trying to get in touch with a lady sitting towards the front. He passed over suddenly. A heart attack or accident?* There was always somebody who thought the generalised message he delivered was for them; some-one desperate to believe a loved one was still nearby.

But a lot of the time the messages were real enough and the voices of the dead steered him towards individuals. Then there were the people who consulted him privately about strange happenings in their homes. Damien had become adept at diagnosing those kind of problems. Hostile presences; lost, sad souls – he was aware of them all. And, like an expensive private doctor, people paid well for his remedies. He knew things about people and places that he was at a loss to explain, and sometimes his powers frightened him. He'd once been told it was a gift, but at times it didn't feel that way.

Due to a TV producer seeing his act in a small theatre in Plymouth, he'd been offered his own series, and soon he'd become the go-to psychic for celebrities and even the occasional politician. His career, along with his bank bal-ance, had soared in a way he'd never envisaged during his singing years, and now he owned a flat in central London and a historic Devon longhouse on the edge of Dartmoor that he shared with his partner, Sheryl, a former dancer he'd met during his singing years. Sheryl was one of the few people who really understood him. They had been through bad times and good together, and with the recent loss of his TV contract, she feared it might not be too long before the bad times returned. That was why she encouraged him to take whatever work was on offer. That was how he'd ended up at Mill House.

That morning he'd had a well-paid private engagement, which he'd slotted in before the psychic weekend in Petherham where he was to be the star attraction. The money on offer meant Sheryl hadn't minded being left on her own in their Dartmoor home over the weekend, enjoying an evening alone in front of a box set with a glass of Pinot Grigio before retiring to bed in the master suite with the en suite dressing room that had been so handsomely fitted out in the TV years.

His private appointment had been at a grand five-bedroom house on the quayside in Tradmouth. The place had recently been purchased by a man who had made his fortune up north and had decided to retire early to the south-west, something that had always been his dream. His wife, Abigail, fancied there was something amiss with the atmosphere in her new home, claiming that objects had been moved and that there was a chill in the air as well as an inexplicable scent of lavender.

Damien had had an initial meeting with Abigail Watkins in a Tradmouth wine bar and had found her an irritating woman, full of psychobabble and New Age clichés about ley lines and presences. At first he'd suspected she was seeking attention; either that or making her husband suffer for some domestic sin, real or imagined. However, once he'd stepped inside the house, he'd felt a restless, malevolent presence and had revised his initial judgement. Abigail hadn't been far off the mark when she said something wasn't right.

The unquiet soul, he'd told her, was a sea captain's wife who'd waited in vain for her husband's return, only to discover that his ship had been lost at sea with all hands on its return voyage through the Bay of Biscay with a cargo of wine. She was still waiting, he told Abigail, and felt spiteful towards any intruder who dared to trespass in what she still regarded as her home. Once he'd made the diagnosis, he left it at that, knowing Abigail would be in touch again to ask him to deal with her little problem, which would mean another fat fee, though he'd have to be careful to avoid her husband. He'd encountered Brian Watkins before in his previous life, and he had no wish to renew their flimsy acquaintance.

Petherham was just four miles from Tradmouth. The Georgian house had been built for the owner of the neighbouring mill, and the couple who had transformed it into an upmarket B&B had engaged his services for a psychic weekend. This was a new venture for them and, to his surprise, they hadn't haggled about his charge, obviously thinking his celebrity status would be a big draw. In addition to his generous fee, he was to enjoy their hospitality: three nights' luxury accommodation, and meals created with locally sourced organic ingredients by the chef at the Fisherman's Arms, a pub with a growing reputation for delicious food. It wasn't an offer he had felt inclined to refuse.

When he pulled up outside Mill House, he took his weekend case out of the boot of his Lexus, rearranging his features into an expression of concern before ringing the doorbell. As he waited on the doorstep, a chill ran through his body. He recognised the house. He had seen it before many years ago – and he was suddenly afraid that he might be asked to interfere with something beyond his control.

Some things, he knew, should be left well alone.

9

Wesley had booked the weekend off. But because of the discovery at Little Barton Farm, he'd had to change his arrangements.

Not that he and Pam had anything exciting planned. Rather he'd promised to help his mother-in-law, Della, put up some shelves in her new flat in the centre of Tradmouth, conveniently opposite the Star, one of her favourite hostelries. Della had been injured in an accident connected to one of Wesley's former cases and had stayed with them while she convalesced. She hadn't been the easiest of house guests, but because he'd felt partly responsible for her injuries, he hadn't been inclined to raise any objection.

Even so, he'd been more than happy to help her move to her new place. And doing a few odd jobs there seemed a small price to pay for him and Pam having their house to themselves again. However, this time he was going to have to let her down. If the bones did belong to Erica Walsh – and from the contents of the rucksack this seemed all too likely – he was going to be fully occupied for the foreseeable future.

He hadn't fancied hanging around in the cold field until Neil arrived, so he'd returned to the station to supervise the setting-up of the major incident room and to arrange for statements to be taken from the Tracey family and any of their workers who were around at the time Erica Walsh was seen in the area.

Neil called half an hour later to say he'd arrived at Little Barton Farm and that Colin Bowman, the pathologist, had just turned up too. Wesley said he'd join them right away. When he asked Gerry if he wanted to come with him, the DCI shook his head, disappointed, saying he needed to brief the chief super and the press office. The disappearance of Erica Walsh twelve years ago might have drifted out of the public consciousness, but all that was about to change.

As Wesley left the office for the second time that morning, he wondered whether to ask Rachel to come with him, but when he passed her desk she was tapping her computer keyboard, deep in concentration, so he chose not to disturb her.

The drive out of Tradmouth took him up the steep hill past the naval college, then out past the housing estate and the supermarket on the edge of town. He soon found himself in a rolling landscape of patchwork fields dotted with copses of bare trees and the occasional house. He turned off onto a narrow lane with tall hedges rising each side, impenetrable as brick walls.

When he reached the cobbled yard in front of the Traceys' farmhouse, he was greeted by a Border collie, barking and wagging his shaggy tail enthusiastically. Once out of the car, he bent to stroke the dog's head, and the animal leaned against his legs adoringly, depositing hairs all over his suit trousers.

'Is he being a nuisance?' said Stella Tracey as she emerged from the doorway.

'Not at all. I like dogs.' His comment was rewarded by a more vigorous wag from the sweeping tail.

'I wasn't expecting you back so soon, Wesley.' She peered at the car. 'Rachel not with you?'

'Sorry. I would have brought her, but she's busy.'

'She's always busy these days,' said Stella with a note of disappointment. 'But I suppose she's adjusting to married life, and she's got Nigel's farm to see to as well as her job.'

Since her marriage, Rachel had said little to Wesley about her new domestic situation, and he hadn't asked. There had been a time when she'd confided in him; told him things he'd rather not have heard. But once she'd decided to go through with the wedding, that had changed.

'Your friend Neil's arrived. When are you going to take the skeleton away?' There was a hint of anxiety in Stella's question, as though she wanted to get the remains off her property as soon as possible.

'Sorry, Stella. These things take time. I take it Neil's down there already?'

She stepped further into the farmyard, and the dog left Wesley's side to go to his mistress. 'You know the way,' she said. 'We've just let the cows out into the next field, but take no notice of them and they shouldn't bother you.' She sounded concerned, as though she suspected that a man who'd been raised in London might panic at the sight of livestock.

'Thanks,' he said, before opening his car boot to take out his wellingtons again. 'Have you had any press around yet?'

'Oh yes. They've already got wind something's happening, but I sent them away. No comment.'

'Well done.'

Stella was still hovering there as though she had another

question to ask. 'Have you looked inside that rucksack?' For the first time, she sounded worried. 'Is it that hitch-hiker who went missing?'

'I don't suppose it'll do any harm to tell you we've found some ID in the rucksack. It looks as if it is her, but don't mention it to anyone, will you – not until we've made an announcement.'

'Was she killed on our land?'

Wesley could tell that the idea of someone using the land that she'd tended lovingly for most of her adult life for such an evil purpose upset her.

'Too early to say, I'm afraid,' he replied quickly. 'But someone'll be taking statements from you and anyone else who was here twelve years ago. And we'll need details of all the people who were working here back then and have since moved on.'

Stella frowned. 'There were a few. I can give you names, but I don't know where they'll be now.' She shuddered. 'That poor girl's parents. It hardly bears thinking about, does it.'

Wesley couldn't think of any suitable words. As a father himself, the thought of what the missing girl's parents must have gone through made him feel a little sick. He said goodbye to Stella and left the farmhouse, following the route he'd taken before. The cattle looked up as he passed, then returned their attention to the more interesting grass.

Eventually he arrived at the white tent to find Neil in his crime-scene suit hard at work. Colin Bowman was there too, leaning over to see what Neil had uncovered in the shallow trench. Wesley could see white bones standing out against the red soil. The grave was shallow, which suggested that the interment had been a panicked, spur-of-the-moment act; either that, or the tree roots had got in the way. He knew from his days studying archaeology with Neil that roots were the enemy of excavation.

Neil looked up and raised his trowel in greeting while Colin straightened his back and held out his hand. 'Wesley, good to see you again. Gerry not with you?'

The pathologist always managed to make the discovery of a body seem like a pleasant social occasion, and Wesley thought, not for the first time, that his genial bedside manner was wasted on his patients, who were hardly in a position to appreciate it.

'He's been and gone. Things to do. ' He looked from one man to the other. 'What have we got?'

It was Neil who answered. 'I think it's a female, youngish judging by the teeth. Late teens, early twenties. Would you agree, Colin?'

Bowman squatted down to take a better look. 'I don't think I can argue with that. Although I'll be able to tell you more once we get her to the mortuary. You mentioned getting a forensic anthropologist in, Neil.'

'Jemima Baine. She's good,' Neil said enthusiastically. 'She's helped me out quite a bit. Should be here any time.'

Wesley nodded. Jemima Baine wasn't only good at her job, she was stunningly good-looking. As Wesley and Pam had both grown fond of Neil's partner Lucy, he'd always felt a little uncomfortable about the glamorous newcomer. He decided not to mention Jemima's name to Pam when he finally got home.

He watched, breathing in the scent of the disturbed earth, as Neil uncovered more of the bones. The process was slow and painstaking to ensure no fragment of evidence was lost, and as Neil worked, he stopped occasionally to allow photographs to be taken and to bag up small items that might or might not be linked to the remains.

After half an hour, Jemima Baine appeared, driving her Range Rover over the field. When she emerged from the driver's door, Wesley saw that she was already wearing white overalls – and that they looked considerably better on her than on anybody else.

'I got your call,' she said to Neil, who was squatting in the trench, before turning to Colin. 'Well, Doctor. What's the verdict?'

Colin pointed to the skeleton emerging from the soil. Now that Neil had uncovered the skull and part of the torso, Wesley could see fragments of fabric clinging to the ribcage, rotten from years in the ground. 'Looks as though she was buried fully clothed,' the pathologist said.

'Don't suppose there's anything that might tell us the cause of death?' Wesley asked, more in hope than expectation.

Colin gave him an indulgent smile. 'Well, there's no ligature around the neck, if that's what you mean, and no obvious head injury. You'll just have to be patient, but she obviously didn't bury herself, so we're almost certainly looking at murder.'

'Don't suppose you know who she is yet?' Although Jemima's question sounded casual, Wesley detected a hint of nervousness in her voice.

'Keep this to yourself, because we don't want the press getting hold of it yet. A rucksack found with the body appears to have belonged to a girl who went missing twelve years ago – a hitch-hiker called Erica Walsh.'

Jemima Baine smiled. 'You've got an ID then. Good.'

From the notebook of
Dr Christopher Cruckshank

4 February 1882

*This Burial Circle, I have discovered, is run on the
same principles as the burial clubs I encountered
while I was working in London, although I had no
involvement in their workings. For a small weekly sum,
those in straitened circumstances could ensure that any
funeral costs did not push families further into poverty.
I thought this a good and prudent idea but, as always
with the human race, some used the scheme for their own
evil ends.*

*I heard rumours that in poorer districts certain
unscrupulous persons joined several burial clubs at
once, claiming they wished only to cover the expense
of a funeral should a relative pass away. Soon
afterwards, however, an unfortunate member of their
household was poisoned and money claimed from
each club by the relative who had committed the
deed, enough to cover the obsequies and considerably
more, which was, in reality, the profit of murder.*

Some, I am told, ended the lives of their own infants for money.

I trust this degree of wickedness will not be found in Petherham.

10

Damien Lee told his hosts he wanted to stay in his room to prepare for the evening because he needed to accustom himself to the house and its atmosphere. The truth was, however, that being in that house – in that village – disturbed him.

The room he'd been given was spacious and tastefully furnished, with hand-made soaps in the newly refurbished en suite bathroom and a king-sized bed with Egyptian cotton sheets; the best. He thought of all the seedy places he'd had to stay in during his singing years and allowed himself a smile. Fame and money couldn't buy you happiness, so they said, but they could certainly buy you comfort.

There was a view of the mill through the tall sash window. It was a large rectangular building, dating from the same period as the house, with rows of small-paned windows and a decorative clock tower. Selina had told him that she and Jeremy owned the place and that Jeremy had abandoned his former career as director of a large agricultural equipment company to fulfil his dream of turning it back into a working mill powered by a huge water wheel.

Through Jeremy's efforts, the mill now housed a visitors' centre telling the history of woollen cloth production in the south-west; it also produced fabric, which was sold in the mill shop. Selina had once been Jeremy's PA, and since their wedding she'd shared his dream. Her burning ambition, though, was to expand the operation and eventually sell their cloth to exclusive designer brands in London. She thought that using fine Devon wool would be a selling point. It was good, she said, to have a vision; a plan for your life. Damien smiled and agreed. Selina Quayle wasn't a woman he was inclined to contradict.

He was to eat dinner with his fellow guests before the evening began in earnest, and he viewed the prospect with dread. Small talk never appealed to him, and he knew how hard it was to maintain your mystery while you were sharing a meal. He was afraid of revealing too much about himself. One slip-up concerning his past could ruin the whole illusion. Alcohol loosened tongues, and on top of that, it had once been a weakness of his, so he'd have to keep off the wine. However, if it put the others in the mood for confidences, that would work to his advantage. When it was all over, he would treat himself to a drink in the Fisherman's Arms, if he could manage to sneak away unseen.

He'd carried out some research on his fellow guests. That side of things was so much easier nowadays with the internet, and it never ceased to amaze him how indiscreet people could be online. There was one couple, however, he hadn't been able to pin down. He'd found no trace of Jacob and Wendy Chalmers anywhere and this intrigued him. He knew some people objected to living their lives on social media, but even so, he'd exercise caution with the Chalmerses – just in case.

He had wondered what to wear and eventually opted for black shirt and matching trousers. Black seemed right for

45

what he was about to do. Besides, Sheryl said it took inches off his waistline. He planned to be the last down for dinner because he wanted to make an entrance, so he listened for doors opening and closing and the muffled conversations as the others made their way downstairs. Once he was confident that they'd all gone down, he opened his bedroom door and stepped out onto the landing, pausing to take a deep breath, like an actor in the wings preparing to step onto the stage.

Suddenly he heard a door opening to his left. He froze, annoyed with himself that he'd miscalculated. For a moment he wondered whether to shoot back into his room. But it was too late.

He recalled the name of the woman who'd just emerged from her doorway, although he'd discovered very little about her from his researches. Corrine Malin looked shocked to see him but he gave her one of his sincere smiles.

'After you,' he said with exaggerated politeness.

He watched her descend the stairs, waiting on the landing until she was safely in the hallway. If he let her get settled before walking down slowly, he would still be able to make his entrance. As soon as she disappeared into the room below, he made his way to the top of the stairs, but as he passed the small staircase that led to the upper floor, a wave of terror hit him like a hammer blow. When he looked up, he saw the small gap beneath the nearest door on the upper landing glowing with a blood-red light, and a distant moan of pain echoed through his head. Something had happened in that room. Something terrible.

He steadied himself on the newel post, trying to overcome the horror he'd felt. It would pass – it always did – and he had to carry on and do what he'd been paid to do. He concentrated on getting down the stairs, forcing himself to put one foot in front of the other. This was his blessing and his curse and he had to live with it.

During the meal, Damien made no mention of what he'd experienced. Rather he allowed the others to make awkward conversation while he listened and observed. He was tempted to ask Selina what she knew about the history of the house, but there would be time for that later. In the meantime, he had six eager punters, each wanting their own encounter with the spirit world.

After dinner, they retired to the drawing room. It was a comfortable room with deep leather sofas and French windows leading out to the garden, now concealed behind long William Morris curtains. A wood-burning stove glowed in the marble fireplace, and every so often, Jeremy Quayle got up to feed it with the logs stacked in a basket on the hearth. The lights were dim, ideal for Damien's purpose. Atmosphere made his job easier.

The chairs had been arranged in a circle, and he looked round the expectant faces, all willing him to give a personal message, just for them. It was always the same. Contact with the dead brought out the selfish side of people, but he couldn't blame them. If he'd lost someone, he'd be impatient to hear that they were still out there somewhere, waiting.

He closed his eyes, trying to concentrate, but his mind was suddenly filled with the overwhelming terror he'd felt upstairs. Something evil was blotting out everything else.

He put his hands over his ears to stop the screaming, but it was still there in his head. His throat felt constricted, as though he was being strangled. Then the feeling vanished and a woman was there in the room with him, terrified,

47

pleading for mercy for her and her child. The name Diana echoed through his head. Beneath her cries, he heard another woman sobbing weakly and moaning in pain, and he could see a fearful young woman, dripping wet, with dead, staring eyes. When he could no longer bear it, his own eyes snapped open and the noises stopped.

The strong signals he was receiving from the house were overwhelming, but he still had to give everyone what they'd paid good money for. Even though it made him feel like a charlatan, he had no choice but to wing it; to go back to tried and trusted techniques. He'd done his research, so along with a bit of cold reading – gauging the reactions to certain questions – it should be easy enough, though the Chalmerses were still an enigma.

He had the banter and the well-practised sincerity off pat, and soon his little audience was hanging on his every word. Apart from his hostess Selina, who he suspected was a sceptic who regarded the weekend purely as a money-making exercise. Jeremy, on the other hand, sat with his head bowed as though he was hoping he wouldn't be noticed. Damien couldn't see his face, but he could sense his discomfort.

Apart from the Chalmerses, the person who most intrigued him was Corrine Malin. He tried to place what it was about her that made him uneasy, but the answer proved elusive. She wasn't a sceptic, he was sure of that, but neither was she a regular punter. He sensed that she was anxious about someone who had passed over to the other side, and a memory from the distant past flashed through his head. A memory he'd rather forget.

When he looked at her again, he experienced a terrifying constriction in his throat, as though he was being strangled, and he was suddenly afraid for her – and for himself. Then pictures started to fill his head: memories of a fumbled advance and a sharp pain as the red rucksack hit the side of his face; memories of a car door slamming in anger; memories of his own weakness.

He was glad to move on to the others, trying to give equal attention to each. The Chalmerses wanted to know whether Jacob's late sister approved of their plans for a new vegan restaurant in Neston, and the Taylors were trying to get in touch with a lost son who'd died of a drug overdose. Damien felt their grief almost as though it was his own, and the encounter left him drained. Even though he failed to contact their son, he told them he was at peace in the next world, which was what they'd wanted to hear. As for the Chalmerses, he could tell their story was a sham. He didn't think they'd come here to catch him out, but their true motive remained a mystery.

Finally he turned to Brad Percy, but when he tried to read him, all he felt was deceit, as though the man had erected a barrier to hide his inner self. He wondered why Percy had made the effort to come here in the first place. Unless it was to test him in some way; to prove him a fraud. Then all of a sudden he felt a strong sense of danger; not for Percy himself, but for someone close to him. The sensation was there for a second, then gone, elusive as mist.

Once the session was over, he was desperate to be on his own. He needed to block out the pain and fear he felt in that house, and if he hadn't agreed to stay for the whole weekend, he would have fled the place and driven home as fast as the speed limit allowed. But before he could escape, Corrine Malin sidled up to him and asked a question.

'Are you able to tell whether someone's dead or not?'

'I'm not sure what you mean.'

'I had a friend who disappeared,' she said in a whisper, looking around to make sure she couldn't be overheard. 'Vanished into thin air. Can you tell me whether she's still alive?'

He looked into her eyes, certain that she knew the truth. But he needed to stay calm. The last thing he wanted to do was arouse suspicion. He thought of the Fisherman's Arms, somewhere he could be anonymous; somewhere he could get a drink to calm his nerves; somewhere he wouldn't have to answer any questions.

'Sorry, can we speak tomorrow?' he said, ignoring Corrine's look of disappointment.

As he climbed the stairs, clinging to the banisters, he could hear sobbing again. And all he could see in front of him was death.

11

On Saturday morning, Wesley sat in Gerry's office going over everything they knew, which wasn't much so far. Colin Bowman had confirmed that the skeleton was that of a young woman, around the same age and height as the missing Erica Walsh, which meant the investigation into her death had begun in earnest.

The rucksack was the most important piece of physical evidence they had at the moment. After being examined thoroughly for prints and DNA, it had now been removed from the exhibits store and delivered to the incident room so they could take a proper look at the contents.

He knew that Rachel had been living at home at the time of Erica's disappearance, but when he mentioned this, she pointed out that the field where the bones had been found lay some distance from the farmhouse and the band of the Coldstream Guards could have been marching up and down there and the Traceys wouldn't have noticed, adding that in the countryside there was nobody about to hear you scream. It wasn't like Rachel to choose such a dramatic phrase, but he knew she was right. The killer had made a good choice.

Statements had been taken from all the Tracey family

and the workers who'd been there in 2008. One of them, Eli, one of the farm labourers, didn't live far from the spot where the bones had been found, but according to his statement, he was a man who went to bed and rose early, and he hadn't seen or heard anything out of the ordinary.

Colin and Neil thought it likely that the shallow grave beneath the fallen tree was merely a deposition site, and that someone had killed Erica elsewhere then looked for a convenient spot in the middle of nowhere to dispose of her body. If it weren't for the tree falling in the storm, she might never have been found.

'I've asked for all the files on the Erica Walsh disappearance to be sent over,' said Wesley. 'And those officers you requested from Neston should be with us this afternoon.'

'Good,' said Gerry, rubbing his hands together. 'And we can have a shufti at her rucksack while we're waiting.'

The rucksack and its contents now lay in a large plastic tray on top of the bookcase in Gerry's office. When the DCI carried it over to his desk, he swept his paperwork to one side. Some of it fell to the floor and Wesley retrieved it and placed it on a chair. Paperwork was the boss's pet hate, and he found the fact that the powers-that-be considered it a priority a constant source of frustration. It was one of the reasons he had never sought further promotion.

They stood for a few moments staring at the things Erica Walsh had carried with her on her travels. There was a small sponge bag containing toothbrush and toothpaste, a blister pack of painkillers, dried-up soap in a plastic box and what was left of a stick deodorant. Wesley unfolded the clothes: spare jeans, a sweater that had survived intact because it was made from artificial fibres, a couple of T-shirts, a denim jacket and a blue cagoule. There was underwear too: four pairs of socks, a bra faded to grey and three pairs of pants. A pair of unseasonal flip-flops completed the collection along with a pair of worn trainers. As far as worldly possessions went, it wasn't much.

'She wasn't buried naked, was she?' said Gerry, as though the possibility bothered him.

'Neil found fragments of a coat along with buttons, zips and remnants of fabric. She was also wearing what he thought were probably leather boots, mostly rotted away. Looks like she was fully dressed when she went in the grave.'

'There were only a few coppers in the purse, Wes. No cash or bank cards – think the killer nicked 'em?'

'It's likely.'

'What about this?' Gerry pointed to the dirty plastic bag containing what looked to Wesley like a small diary, the kind used to jot down appointments. The plastic had degraded over the years underground but it had done its job of protecting the little book inside. Wesley reached out and picked it up. It felt brittle in his fingers as he slid the contents out.

'Right, Wes, what have we got?'

'It's a diary. Dated 2008.' He pointed to the faded gold numbers on the floral front.

'With any luck the killer's name'll be in there.'

Wesley didn't share the boss's optimism as he turned the fragile pages.

'Well?'

'Looks like the usual. Dentist, lectures, parties, meeting friends, essay deadlines. There are some names that'll need to be checked out.'

'What's that?'

There was something stuck between the pages of the diary, neatly folded. It was a thin envelope bearing an Exeter address in a district Wesley recognised as being popular with students. He unfolded it on the desk and extracted its contents with great care: a single sheet of lined paper covered in neat handwriting.

'What does it say?' Gerry was finding it hard to curb his impatience.

'It appears to be from her mother, begging her to get in touch. She says she's been on her own since Erica's dad died and she doesn't want her to go away to look for a job at Christmas. She says Erica shouldn't resent Barry so much, whoever Barry is. She just wants her daughter there for Christmas. Says Erica's all she's got.'

'Can't say I blame a mum for wanting her only daughter home with her for the festive season,' said Gerry, the father of two grown-up children whose teenage years didn't seem that long ago.

'She says Barry's a good man and Erica's misjudged him. Erica obviously ignored her letter and went her own merry way.'

'The poor woman'll have to be told. Where does she live?'

'Leeds.'

'In that case we'll get the local force there to break the bad news,' said Gerry with some relief. 'Does the diary mention any names?'

'There's someone called Corry, possibly a friend: June eighteenth, Corry's birthday. And there's a Jem too. Think that could be a boyfriend?'

'The file I've read doesn't mention a boyfriend. But there wasn't much in it. The focus of the case soon switched to Falmouth, so it was passed over to the local station there.'

Suddenly Wesley was impatient for the case files to arrive. Erica Walsh had ended up buried beneath a tree a mile from Tradmouth. And he wanted to know how she'd got there.

12

The bed was comfortable enough, with its memory foam mattress and natural down pillows and quilt, but even so, Corrine had lain awake tossing and turning. Eventually she'd given in and put the bedside light on to read the book she'd brought with her. After that, she'd managed to doze off, only to awake in the unfamiliar room with a feeling of dread.

She'd listened to the radio news again, hoping to learn more about the human remains found on farmland near Tradmouth. But when nothing was said in the next bulletin, she told herself it couldn't be Erica. She'd last been seen in Cornwall, so that must have been where she'd vanished.

She was hoping to catch up with Damien after breakfast to ask him about his work. An interview with a renowned psychic medium would add credibility to her thesis. However, to her disappointment, Damien didn't appear at breakfast and she found herself sitting opposite Brad Percy again. Having run out of things to say about his beloved car, he'd been mercifully quiet, and when she asked him what he'd made of the session the previous night, he'd just replied that it was all right. His reticence made her wonder again about his motive for being there, because he didn't strike her as someone who'd take much interest in the paranormal.

Another session with Damien was planned for that evening. She'd watched him closely the previous night, noting the panic in his eyes and the way he'd clasped his hands over his ears as though he was trying to block out something terrifying. It had occurred to her inner sceptic that this might have been part of his act, guaranteed to give the punters their money's worth, and she wondered whether his absence at breakfast was calculated to preserve his air of mystery. In which case, it might not be easy to catch him alone.

As soon as breakfast was over, she returned to her room and locked the door. There was to be a discussion about paranormal phenomena after lunch, but until then her time was her own, and she knew exactly how she wanted to fill it.

She took the box out of the wardrobe where she'd hidden it and spread its contents on the bed. She'd bought it a fortnight before, at a Saturday morning car boot sale near the village of Derenham, after spotting it at the back of a stall filled with household bric-a-brac and long-abandoned plastic toys. It was clearly old, but the stallholder, a harassed-looking young woman in leggings and a shabby fleece, had let it go for a fiver. When Corrine had opened it, she'd found a pile of old sepia photographs inside: images of the Devon landscape and a village she now recognised as Petherham, its quaint cottages shabby and tumbledown in those far-off days, quite unlike their modernised present-day incarnation. There were several pictures of the mill in its heyday, with its water wheel churning up the fast-flowing stream that spewed out into Pether

Creek, turning relentlessly to drive the noisy looms inside the building.

There were people too: young Victorian children with pinched features and men and women whose faces had been wizened by tough lives and harsh weather. There were women in aprons who looked like servants, as well as carefully posed ladies and gentlemen, amongst them a scholarly clergyman and a much younger pretty dark-haired woman with bright, intelligent eyes who may have been his wife – or perhaps his daughter. Some photographs had been taken inside the mill: men with their sleeves rolled up to reveal muscular arms, and thin women in linen caps; workers tending the needy machines.

Once the box had been emptied, she'd noticed that the exterior was larger than the inside, and after some investigation, she'd discovered a hidden compartment in the base. Inside the hollow space she'd found more photographs. Different. Sinister. The subjects were lying down, stretched out fully clothed with hands neatly folded over their chests and eyes closed as if in sleep. But these people weren't sleepers. Corrine could tell they were corpses.

One was a middle-aged woman in a stained nightgown, her death agony still visible on her haggard face. In another, an elderly man lay on a bloodied bed with a dark wound to his head, and a third showed a younger woman lying on a chaise longue, her hair and clothes clearly damp, as though she'd drowned and had recently been pulled from the water. In the fourth photograph, a young woman's dead features were half concealed by a layer of dried blood. She reminded Corrine of the clergyman's companion, although in death she couldn't be sure. She turned the pictures over and saw writing on the reverse: two bore the words *Mill House, Petherham*; the picture of the elderly man was inscribed *Westral Hall*, now a nursing home just outside the village, and the other merely said *Petherham* and the date. All had been taken in 1882.

Her discovery had made her decide to delve deeper into the nineteenth-century obsession with death and spiritualism, and the pictures had given her the perfect excuse to come to Mill House. As for her other reason for visiting Petherham, that was something she wouldn't share with anybody until she knew more about the bones.

After studying the contents for a while, Corrine replaced the photographs in their hidden compartment, placing the innocent pictures back on top before returning the box to the wardrobe, on the shelf above the hanging rail. She was longing to ask Damien what he made of them; she thought they might provide the ideal excuse to request a private interview. Her mother's favourite saying had been 'Seize the day', and the worst that could happen was that he'd refuse to see her. With fresh determination, she put on her coat, scooped up her bag and shut the bedroom door behind her. If anybody asked, she was going for a walk in the fresh air. It was cold, but at least it wasn't raining. It could rain a lot in Devon in early December.

Damien had been allocated a room at the end of a passage, well away from the others, and Corrine walked towards it, feigning a confidence she didn't feel. When she rapped on the door, there was no answer, so she knocked again, but still there was no telltale sound of movement beyond the door.

Disappointed, she made her way downstairs, hoping she wouldn't bump into any of her fellow guests, but as she tiptoed towards the front door, Brad Percy emerged from the drawing room carrying a copy of the *Times*. His eyes lit up when he saw her.

'Going for a walk? Fancy some company?'

'No, it's OK, thanks,' she said, making for the door.

'Where are you going?'

She ignored his question and shot out of the door, closing it firmly behind her. Her actions might have been interpreted as rude, but she didn't care.

She half walked, half ran to the mill across the lane, surprised to see lights in the windows. She'd assumed nobody would be working there at the weekend, but it seemed she was wrong. Some of the pictures in her box had been taken inside the building and she was curious to see the interior.

The entrance was accessed via a small iron bridge that spanned the rushing stream. Her footsteps clanged against the metal as she walked across. She pushed the door open, expecting to hear the clatter of machinery, but the place was silent.

She shouted a wary hello, and when there was no reply, she began to walk past the looms and spinning machines. They now lay idle, but she could see bolts of finished cloth in various patterns and colours lying on steel shelves at the end of the long, tall room. She guessed the mill hadn't changed much since the time her pictures had been taken. Only the silence was different.

Suddenly she heard footsteps, followed by a scraping sound, as though someone was moving something in the next room. She called out again, but again there was no reply.

She could see light through the small windows set into the top of a pair of swing doors in the far corner, and she heard the noise again.

Gathering her courage, she pushed the swing doors open, and almost jumped when she heard a voice.

'Can I help you?'

Standing in front of her was a tall man with fair hair that curled down to the collar of his shabby combat jacket. He wore many-pocketed trousers in a thick camouflage material and what looked like walking boots. He was holding a clipboard, and she could see plans unfolded on a nearby table.

'Sorry to disturb you,' she said.

'That's OK. Do you work here, or ...?'

'No. I'm staying at Mill House.'

'Name's Neil Watson.' He held out his hand and she took it. 'I'm from the County Archaeological Service, as we have to call it now. My team's conducting a survey of historic mills. Archaeology's not just digging holes, you know.'

'Corrine Malin. You're an archaeologist?'

'For my sins.' He looked around. 'This place was built as a woollen mill in the late eighteenth century and converted to a paper mill in 1898. Then it lay derelict from 1960 until eight years ago, when the current owners acquired some machines from a disused mill up in Yorkshire and refurbished the place. It manufactures woollen cloth on a small scale – tourist stuff, but it's nice to see old industries revived. Robert, the guy in charge, said it was best to do our survey at the weekend when the mill wasn't in production. It's an interesting building.'

'I've got some old photographs of this place.'

Neil's eyes lit up. 'I'd be interested to see them.'

'There are some of the village too. And some ... strange ones.'

Neil frowned. 'Strange?'

'Dead people.'

She suddenly wished she hadn't said it. Neil Watson was bound to think she was weird. 'I'd better go.'

She retraced her steps and walked out over the iron bridge, the sound of her footsteps reminding her of the fairy tale she'd loved as a child: the three billy goats gruff trip-trapping over the bridge, harassed by the troll who lived underneath. When she heard Neil's footsteps behind her, she somehow felt safer than she had when she'd arrived.

'Hang on. I'm going to take a look at the water wheel,' he said. 'Interested?'

Without a word, she followed him to the side of the mill, where the water wheel usually swished round and round, scooping up the water that kept it turning and powered the machines inside. It had been working on the afternoon she'd arrived, and when it was in action, the beating rhythm of the water was deafening, but today the wheel sat silently while the water below rushed past into the creek, which in its turn fed the voracious River Trad.

'Must be interesting being an archaeologist,' she said, making conversation as she stood beside him.

'It has its moments. I was helping to excavate a skeleton for the police yesterday.'

His words hit her like a blow. 'Was that near Tradmouth? I heard something on the radio, but there's been nothing since.' She could almost hear her heart thumping as she waited for his answer.

Neil shuffled from foot to foot as though he'd suddenly realised he'd said too much. The only fact released to the local press was that human remains had been found at a farm and there'd be nothing more until the police knew exactly what they were dealing with. He suspected that he'd been trying to impress this young woman with his inside knowledge.

'Was it a man or a woman?'

'I can't say yet. Not until the police are ready to release more details. Sorry.'

'It's just that twelve years ago a friend of mine disappeared . . .'

Neil caught on quickly. 'I know the detective inspector dealing with the case. If you think it could be your friend, he'll want to talk to you.'

Corrine shook her head. 'They said she'd hitched a lift to somewhere near here, but she was last seen in Cornwall so it can't be her.'

'Even so, if you're worried . . .'

She shook her head again. Then she seemed to change her mind. 'OK. Call your friend. I need to know for sure.'

From the notebook of
Dr Christopher Cruckshank

8 February 1882

I have just returned from my first visit to Mill House, where the owner of the mill, Josiah Partridge, resides with his family. I was called to attend Mrs Partridge, who is said to be so hungry for sympathy and attention that she is in the habit of feigning illness. There is a daughter from Mr Partridge's first marriage, and I observed no affection between her and her stepmother. Rather, the daughter rolled her eyes in a most dismissive manner when I arrived at the house, and muttered under her breath that Mrs Partridge was always calling out Dr Smith for no valid reason and had no doubt decided to continue the practice with his successor.

I did not comment on her observation, preferring to see the patient for myself. When the maidservant led me to Mrs Partridge's bedchamber – which, I was told, used to be the old nursery on the upper floor – I noted that she looked concerned and I guessed she didn't share the stepdaughter's opinion. She said that her mistress had moved into that room a year ago, no longer wishing to share her husband's bed and suffer his advances. I caught her meaning at once. The Partridges' marriage was far from blissful.

When I entered the room, I noted that the curtains were drawn, and for a while my patient didn't seem to be aware of my presence. Then, when I leaned over her, she looked up at me with desperation in her eyes.

'Are you in pain?' I asked, and she gave a little nod in reply. 'What have you eaten?'

'Very little,' she said. 'Only Joanna's medicine. It is a tonic given to her by Dr Smith when she felt unwell some months ago.'

I asked her who Joanna was, and she told me it was her stepdaughter. I made no answer while I considered the situation. Then I recommended that she consume nothing for twenty-four hours. And that she should avoid Joanna's medicine.

13

Now that it was almost certain that the bones belonged to Erica Walsh, the police had to rethink all the assumptions about her disappearance twelve years before.

The remains had been taken to the mortuary to allow Colin Bowman to make a thorough examination. Jemima Baine would also have some input, and a full forensic report on the burial site was being prepared. Even though Erica might not have died in that spot, it was hoped her killer had left behind some clues.

All the available material on her disappearance had been brought over from Neston, but when it arrived, Wesley was in for a disappointment. There was one solitary file, and that wasn't particularly thick. As soon as the Falmouth sighting was reported, the focus of the search shifted west to Cornwall, and Neston had no doubt been relieved to pass the investigation over.

Now, however, Gerry reckoned the only reason to involve Falmouth was to try to find out who'd used Erica's bank card to withdraw a hundred pounds from a cash machine four days after she was last seen in Devon. There'd been no CCTV of whoever withdrew the cash because the camera in question hadn't been working at the time, and Wesley could only conclude that the witness who'd claimed to have seen her there had been mistaken. If it hadn't been for the cash withdrawal, the sighting might not have been taken so seriously. In missing persons cases there could be sightings from John o'Groats to Land's End, and most of them came to nothing.

He sat at his desk with the file open in front of him. Another weekend away from his family. Sometimes he wondered how Pam put up with it, although he was grateful that she did.

He began to read, wanting to get the salient facts straight in his mind. Erica had been a nineteen-year-old English literature student at Exeter University, Wesley's own alma mater. On Friday 12 December 2008, the day after her lectures had finished for the Christmas break, she'd left the flat she shared with another student, saying she wasn't going home for Christmas because she hated her mother's new partner – a man called Barry Clegg. Instead she was planning to travel to Tradmouth to look for a seasonal job in a hotel. Her flatmate confirmed that Erica had no job arranged, although she'd been sure of securing some form of employment, even if it was only washing dishes. Her attitude to accommodation had been equally casual: something would turn up.

Wesley found himself envying her carefree confidence. He'd always liked everything neatly arranged before he embarked on any sort of journey because he liked to be prepared for any possible pitfalls. Sometimes Pam teased him for being obsessive, and maybe she was right. But at least it meant he hardly ever found himself in situations beyond his control – apart from at work; there was plenty of scope there for the unpredictable.

Erica had told her flatmate she intended to hitch-hike to Tradmouth, and Wesley's cautious nature, coupled with his police experience, told him this probably hadn't been a wise decision. A lone girl who got into a car with a stranger put herself in a vulnerable position, especially in the Devon countryside, where help wasn't readily at hand.

No hotel in or near Tradmouth had reported that the missing girl had called there enquiring about work, although two people did come forward to admit to having picked her up in their cars. The first was a middle-aged man called Kevin Nash who'd offered her a lift when he'd seen her near Exeter St David's station and taken her as far as Newton Abbot. Nash claimed that he'd been concerned when he'd seen her standing by the road thumbing a lift and had asked her where she was going. Newton Abbot was on her way, she'd said, and she'd hopped into the passenger seat without hesitation. He said he had a daughter around the same age so the situation had made him uneasy, and if he hadn't had an appointment to keep, he'd have been inclined to take her on to Tradmouth. The interviewing policeman had commented on the statement that Nash seemed genuinely upset and frustrated that he couldn't be more help.

According to Nash's statement, Erica had talked a lot during their journey. 'Rattled on', was how he put it. She'd told him how her father had died when she was small and that she hated her mother's partner. That was why she planned to spend Christmas working in a Tradmouth hotel. She'd thought it would be fun, she said; she saw herself partying with her fellow workers after a hard day serving Christmas dinners while the boring guests slept off their turkey with all the trimmings. When he'd dropped her off in the middle of Newton Abbot, she'd seemed cheerful, hoisting her red rucksack onto her back and walking off in search of another lift.

Wesley fetched himself a cup of coffee from the machine in the corridor before rereading Nash's statement, searching for any tiny thing he might have missed. But there was nothing, so he moved on to the statement of the only other person who'd admitted to picking Erica up that day.

It was another man, younger this time, who went by the name of David Leeson. He'd been traced when his registration number was picked up on a traffic camera and had been interviewed at his home near Manchester. He'd been on his way to Morbay, where he'd been booked to sing at a club, when he'd seen her thumbing a lift by a roundabout just outside the centre of Newton Abbot. She'd been quiet, he said, but she'd told him she was going to Tradmouth to work. He had the impression it was all arranged, although he claimed he hadn't been listening very attentively. The interviewing officer commented that Leeson might have been entertaining hopes of a sexual nature, although he hadn't admitted this in so many words. He had no way of proving that his story was true, but he was questioned for several hours and never deviated from it. He'd left Erica on a country lane somewhere near Neston and had no idea what had happened to her after that.

Later a witness came forward to say she'd seen Erica walking down the lane Leeson had described an hour after he said he'd dropped her off. The witness, Florence Valery, a retired headmistress, had been returning to her home in Derenham after visiting a friend in Petherham, driving the ancient Volkswagen Beetle that was her pride and joy. Erica, she'd said, had been heading towards Petherham or she would have offered her a lift. It had been getting dark and she'd been worried at the thought of a girl walking on her own like that.

Miss Valery's sighting was the final one until someone saw Erica in Falmouth a few days later. She had mentioned Falmouth to one of her university friends, so it was feasible that she might have gone there. A seemingly reliable middle-aged woman had seen a girl matching Erica's description with a red rucksack, a sighting backed up by the use of her bank card, so the search had switched from Devon to Cornwall. It was assumed that if Erica had met an unfortunate end, it was Falmouth's responsibility.

Wesley scanned the statements again for anything that might provide the slightest clue to what happened to Erica between the time she was seen by Florence Valery and the discovery of her bones at Little Barton Farm. But there was nothing.

He was about to make for Gerry's office to compare notes when his phone rang. Neil rarely displayed much emotion about anything outside the world of archaeology, but Wesley could tell from the agitation in his voice that something was bothering him.

'I'm at Petherham Mill. There's someone here you might like to speak to.'

14

Wesley stopped at Rachel's desk and she looked up hopefully.

'There's been a new development on the Erica Walsh case,' he said. 'Neil's just met someone who knew her. He's in Petherham and I'm going over to have a word.'

'Want me to come with you?' she said, half rising from her seat.

Wesley sensed she was keen to get away from the office and her paperwork, but he was going to have to disappoint her.

'It might be best if I go on my own. Neil's told her I'm a friend of his so it'll just be an informal chat. I'll let you know if it comes to anything.'

'My mother keeps calling to ask if we've made any progress.' She hesitated before leaning towards him, lowering her voice. 'Everyone at the farm's given statements, but between you and me, I think she's afraid the family might come under suspicion.'

'I suppose being questioned by the police can be worrying if you're not used to it.'

'I've tried to reassure her, but ...'

'You've told her it's likely the body was dumped there?'

71

'Yes, but with all the workers, past and present, being questioned too, she can't help wondering if someone we've employed was to blame.'

There was nothing more Wesley could say to reassure her, so he gave her an apologetic smile and set off.

Petherham wasn't far as the crow flies, but the web of country lanes meandering across the Devon landscape hadn't been designed by crows. The narrow, winding thoroughfares, some little more than tracks, had terrified Wesley when he'd first arrived in the area. Only Rachel, who'd been brought up in the area, drove along them with complete confidence. Wesley always exercised caution, which made every journey longer.

Petherham was a small village with the customary medieval church and stone-built pub. Its houses were clustered around the spot where a small river rushed down to meet the tidal inlet of Pether Creek. At the edge of this hurtling stream stood the mill, a smaller and more picturesque version of mills he'd seen up north, with rows of windows to provide light for those who laboured on the looms inside. This one had originally been built as a woollen mill, making use of the bounty from the white-faced sheep that dotted the landscape of Dartmoor, and he'd heard it was now being used for its intended purpose again, although this time catering for the tourist market.

The woman with Neil had short brown hair and wore jeans and Doc Martens. There were tattoos on her neck and the backs of her hands, elaborate Celtic patterns in muted blue and red. Wesley suspected the patterns extended up her arms, although, being December, they were concealed by her black padded coat. She looked worried, and she was standing close to Neil, as though seeking protection.

Neil introduced her as Corrine Malin, and she shook Wesley's hand feebly.

'Pleased to meet you, Ms Malin.'

'Call me Corrine, please.'

'Neil tells me you're here for a psychic weekend – staying at Mill House, I believe.'

The woman nodded. 'I'm writing a thesis on the role of the paranormal in modern-day life and I'm here to do some research.'

'Do your hosts know that?'

'I thought it best to keep it quiet. They've no idea they have a sceptic in their midst.'

'You don't believe in the paranormal?'

She hesitated. 'I try to keep an open mind.'

Wesley detected an impatience in her voice, as though she had something urgent to say and was anxious to get it said.

'Neil said you have some information for me.'

She nodded. 'I don't know if I'm wasting your time, but … I heard that a body was found on farmland near here and I wondered … ' Her voice tailed off.

'What did you wonder?'

'Is it a man or a woman? They didn't say on the news.'

'That's because we haven't released the details yet.'

There was a lengthy silence, and Wesley waited, watching her expression change from indecision to determination.

Finally she spoke. 'Twelve years ago, a friend of mine went missing. She said she was going to Tradmouth but she must have changed her mind, because she was last seen in Falmouth. After that, nobody saw her again and no one knows what happened to her.'

'You're talking about Erica Walsh?'

Corrine nodded. 'I used to live in the flat below hers. I got to know her really well.'

'The police must have spoken to you at the time.'

'I wasn't in Exeter when she left. My mum was rushed into hospital, so I'd gone home. Nobody bothered asking me about Erica. Mind you, I couldn't have told them anything they didn't already know.'

Wesley glanced towards the pub at the other end of the village. The Fisherman's Arms was an old inn with a reputation for good food. He and Pam had eaten there a couple of times. It would be full of weekend diners, but it was a better place to talk than outside in the biting cold. And he didn't trust Mill House to provide them with much privacy.

'Let's continue this over a drink, shall we?'

Neil nodded eagerly, and they began to walk towards the pub, which overlooked the creek a little further upstream from the mill. The tide was out, leaving behind muddy banks and beached boats.

When they arrived, Neil managed to bag them a seat by the window. It was a cosy pub, with a real fire and sporting memorabilia on the walls: fishing rods, shotguns and a cricket bat hanging over the fireplace surrounded by photographs of various village teams – cricketers in white and smiling footballers. In pride of place above the bar was a large stuffed pike in a glass case, big enough to give bragging rights to any self-respecting fisherman.

'That body they found – do you think it could be Erica?' said Corrine quietly once she had her drink in front of her.

Erica's mother had been informed and was travelling down from Leeds the following day, so Wesley judged it safe to reveal the skeleton's identity, especially as Corrine might have new information for them.

'We found a rucksack with the skeleton. A red rucksack – very distinctive.' He glanced at Neil, who was nodding in agreement. 'There was a diary inside dating from the time Erica went missing. It mentions a Corry. Was that you?'

Corrine's hand went to her mouth and she nodded.

'We found a student ID card in the rucksack too. We're pretty sure it's Erica. I'm afraid she never got as far as Falmouth, which means the sighting must have been false.'

Tears welled in Corrine's eyes, and when one spilled out and trickled down her cheek, she wiped it away fiercely with the back of her hand as though she was cross with herself for losing control of her emotions.

'How did she . . . ?'

'We're not sure yet, but we're treating her death as murder. I'm sorry.'

'You've had a shock,' said Neil quietly, picking up her wine glass and handing it to her. She took a long sip, then put the glass down carefully on the table.

'While I was at home, I kept trying to contact her, but she never replied. Now I know why.'

'I understand she didn't want to go home for Christmas.'

'She hardly ever went home if she could help it. She hated her mother's boyfriend – really hated him.' She took out a tissue and wiped her nose.

'You and Erica were close?'

She nodded and turned her head away so Wesley couldn't see her expression, and there was a long pause before she spoke again. 'We . . . we'd just started a relationship that term, but it was early days. When she didn't reply to my texts or answer my calls, I thought she might have been having problems coming to terms with her sexuality. I thought maybe things had been moving too fast for her and . . . ' She took a deep, shuddering breath. 'She was hitch-hiking. Do you think she got in a car with the wrong person?'

'That's a line of enquiry we're considering,' Wesley replied.

'It horrifies me when I think of the things we used to do when we were students,' said Neil. 'People think they're invincible at that age. Trouble is, they're not.'

Wesley caught his friend's eye and Neil got the message.

'The diary mentions a Jem,' said Wesley gently. 'Who is he?'

'He's a she. Jem was the girl she shared a flat with – Jem Wallace. Don't know what became of her.'

Wesley knew they'd need to speak to Jem in case she remembered something she hadn't thought to mention at the time. Hopefully her details would be somewhere in the original files.

After a while, Neil spoke again. 'You mentioned you had some pictures of the village?'

Corrine looked surprised at the change of subject, and then a little relieved that she'd been offered something to take her mind off her dead friend. 'They're in my room at Mill House.' She looked at her watch. 'I should get back. You can see them some other time if you like.'

'You'll still be here tomorrow?'

'Yes. The psychic weekend doesn't finish till Monday.'

She stood up to leave, and Wesley drained his glass of alcohol-free lager; he was still on duty, and besides, he had to drive back to Tradmouth.

'Inspector,' she said as she put on her coat, 'there is someone who might have wanted Erica dead. She always said he'd like it if she was out of the way for good.'

'Who are you talking about?'

'Her mum's boyfriend – Barry Clegg. She told me he'd threatened to kill her.'

76

15

Wesley wanted to learn more, but Corrine insisted she needed to get back because she didn't want to miss out on a discussion about psychic phenomena with Damien Lee – purely in the interests of research. He didn't press the matter, and in a way he was glad she had something to distract her, because he could tell the news about Erica had hit her hard. He'd looked into her eyes and seen grief rather than simply shock.

He told her he'd send someone round to Mill House to take her statement later, and watched her walk off, experiencing a rare thrill of optimism. They now had the name of someone who had allegedly wanted Erica dead. Perhaps the case would prove straightforward after all.

As soon as Neil left him to rejoin his colleagues, who were still conducting their survey of the mill, Wesley called Gerry, knowing he'd want to be kept up to date. To his surprise, Gerry told him to stay where he was, and half an hour later, Rachel arrived.

'This is a turn-up for the books,' she said as she emerged from the driver's seat. 'Erica's friend, eh? Shall we go and have a word?'

'She's taking part in some discussion connected with her

77

thesis. She seemed upset, so I thought it was best to give her some space. I asked Trish to come over to take a statement from her later.'

Rachel shrugged. 'OK. If you've got that covered, the boss wants us to speak to the last person who saw Erica alive around here. Florence Valery still lives down the road in Derenham, and who knows, she might have remembered something about that night that she didn't think was relevant at the time.'

Wesley couldn't argue with Rachel's logic. Now that they knew Erica had never reached Falmouth, Florence Valery's testimony had suddenly acquired a new significance.

Rachel had Miss Valery's address written in the notebook she took from her coat pocket once they reached Derenham. Wesley parked on the lane leading to the church at the top of the hill. From there he could see the river in the distance, its waters choppy and dark. The pair of them walked slowly towards the village centre, studying the house numbers on the row of small stone cottages to their left. In summer, their little front gardens would be a riot of life and colour, but now, in early December, the remaining flowers had turned brown, while a few mummified roses dangled from straggly bushes. Only the perennials looked green and healthy, a sign that life continued even in the midst of death.

There was a light on in the front room of Florence Valery's cottage, glowing in the gathering darkness behind the little leaded windows. Rachel stood back while Wesley raised the polished brass door knocker shaped like a dolphin.

The woman who answered the door was in her late seventies, but she didn't look as though she was about to let age defeat her. She was stick thin with a straight back and sharp blue eyes, the type who missed nothing.

When they showed their warrant cards and introduced themselves, her face lit up with delight, as though she'd just opened the door to Father Christmas himself.

'Come in, come in. I'll put the kettle on.'

As she hurried out, Rachel caught Wesley's eye. They'd met witnesses like Miss Valery before. The only trouble was, they were sometimes so eager to oblige that they were inclined to embroider the facts and tell the police what they thought they wanted to hear.

Once the bone-china cups and saucers were set out in front of them, Rachel left it to Wesley to ask the first question.

'Do you remember giving a statement to the police in 2008 concerning the disappearance of a student? Her name was Erica Walsh.'

'The girl with the rucksack? I saw her as clearly as I can see you now, walking down the lane as though she had all the cares of the world on her shoulders. I was driving back from my friend Betty's house in Petherham. We still meet once a week for a game of bridge. Keeps us out of mischief,' she added with a girlish giggle. 'Anyway, I saw this girl walking the other way.'

'Towards Petherham?'

'That's right. She stuck her thumb out. Hitch-hiking. I've always thought that was a bit risky myself. You never know who you're getting into a car with, do you? I would have given her a lift if she'd been going in my direction. At least that way she'd have been safe. I slowed down and she peered into the car, so I got a good look at her face. It was the girl in the photograph the constable showed me, all right. No doubt about it. I wound the window down and she asked me where I was going. I said Derenham and she said she was going the other way and trotted off with a little wave. It was dark and I was a bit worried about her, to tell you the truth.'

'She didn't say where she was headed?' Rachel asked.

'I'm afraid not. I wish I'd asked her now, but we can all be wise with hindsight, can't we?'

Wesley took a sip of tea. It had cooled rapidly but he drank the tepid liquid out of politeness. 'She'd told her friends she was going to Tradmouth to look for work in one of the hotels. I would have thought she'd have been glad of a lift towards the main road.'

'That puzzled me as well. Perhaps she knew someone in Petherham.'

'That road branches off for Stokeworthy further up,' Rachel chipped in. 'She might have been going there and found herself on the wrong road. The search for her shifted to Cornwall before we got a chance to organise house-to-house enquiries.' She gave Wesley a meaningful look. Assumptions had been made and they'd screwed up. But this wasn't something they could say in front of Florence Valery.

'You seem like an observant lady, Miss Valery. I bet you know everything that goes on in your friend Betty's village,' said Wesley.

Their hostess blushed at the compliment. 'I like to keep abreast of what's going on locally . . . although I don't listen to gossip, of course.'

'Of course,' said Wesley with a smile. 'When Erica went missing, you must have heard things. Do you know if anyone else saw her that night?'

Florence Valery shook her head. 'It was a cold night in

December, Chief Inspector. Not the sort of night people wanted to be out and about, and no, I didn't hear of anyone else who'd seen her.' She stopped for a moment and frowned, as though she'd suddenly remembered something. 'Do you know, I think it was the same night that poor woman committed suicide. Terrible business. Now what was her name? Diane something – or was it Diana, like the princess? She killed her little boy too. Betty had heard her marriage wasn't happy, but that's no excuse for doing something so wicked, is it?'

Wesley and Rachel looked at each other. 'This happened the same night you saw the girl? Are you sure?'

Miss Valery frowned as though she was annoyed with herself for not recalling every detail. 'I think so. Or was it the following night? I'm not sure. The poor woman had some sort of breakdown and threw herself into the river along with her little boy. Betty said everyone in the village was so upset.' There was a short pause before she spoke again. 'I heard on the radio news that human remains have been found. Is it the girl I saw? Is that why you've come round asking questions again?'

'I'm sorry, we can't confirm anything at this stage.'

'You think it's her, don't you? You think she never got as far as Cornwall.'

There was no fooling Miss Valery. 'All I can say at the moment is that we've reopened the investigation.' Wesley levered himself up from the depths of the saggy chintz sofa. 'Thank you for the tea, Miss Valery. It was very welcome.'

'Any time, Inspector . . . Sergeant,' the woman answered, beaming.

'Do you remember that suicide?' Wesley asked Rachel as they were walking back to the car.

'Only vaguely. I think Neston dealt with it, and as far as I remember, there were no suspicious circumstances.'

'Seems strange that the two things should occur in the same small area around the same time.'

'Coincidences happen. And Erica might have been making for Stokeworthy, not Petherham.'

Wesley sighed. 'The Falmouth sighting seemed so credible. I want to speak to the person who claimed to have seen her there.'

'You think they had a reason for lying?'

'It's got to be a possibility. It might have been a smoke-screen, and we fell for it.'

16

After the discussion on paranormal phenomena had finished, Damien spent the rest of the afternoon alone in his room. He needed to think. Things were happening, bad things he had yet to fully understand. Things that could easily overwhelm him.

Luckily the guests had had a lot to say for themselves during the session, so after initiating the discussion, he'd been able to sit back and listen as they shared stories of their strange experiences and those of their friends – and friends of friends. Although he suspected some had been made up, especially Brad Percy's account of a grey lady in the office where he worked.

The person who surprised him most was Corrine Malin. He'd expected her to join in the discussion, but instead she'd kept silent, and he'd felt a deep sadness about her that hadn't been there before. He knew she was grieving and he couldn't shake off the feeling that her grief was somehow linked to his recent discovery. Although he couldn't think how this could be possible.

He wasn't sure the seance planned for that evening was a good idea, but as it was the main attraction, he felt he had to go through with it, especially as Selina Quayle seemed so keen on the whole thing. He was a little wary of Selina, sensing a ruthless determination about her. He'd come across people like her before and had learned to treat them with caution.

He couldn't shake off the malevolence that seemed to surround Mill House like an aura. When Selina had offered him the booking, he'd done the usual checks on the internet, but all he'd managed to find was the suicide back in 2008, something he'd already known about. He was certain Jeremy Quayle had no idea he was so familiar with the fate of his first wife Diana and his six-year-old stepson Orlando. If he had known, Damien suspected he wouldn't have been invited. Diana's name hadn't been mentioned since his arrival, and that was the way it was going to stay.

It was seven o'clock and he'd already eaten alone, telling the Quayles he needed to prepare mentally for the ordeal ahead. This was partly true, but there was another reason for his self-imposed solitude, and that was the discovery he'd made the previous night. What he'd found out had come as a shock, and he couldn't wait to get away from Petherham and the creeping feeling of evil that engulfed him. He'd texted Sheryl earlier: *Bad place. Need to get out. Back soon as I can.* She hadn't replied.

The thought of the seance was filling him with dread. He had no objection to helping people like the Taylors contact their loved ones, but Selina's set-up had the whiff of show business. He would do his best to ignore the voices that had started to murmur in his head, and go through the motions – like the charlatan so many people assumed he was.

At 7.30, he examined his appearance in the long mirror inside his wardrobe. He was all in black again, since it fitted with the image he wanted to convey. As he studied his reflection, he could see his hand was shaking slightly, but he told himself it would soon be over and tomorrow he could go home to Sheryl.

His phone rang and the unexpected sound made him jump. The number on the caller display was unfamiliar, but curiosity made him answer. It could be another engagement, and Sheryl always told him he should never turn down work, however much he was tempted.

He didn't recognise the voice at first, but when he realised who it was, his heart began to race.

When the call was over, he looked at his watch. It was time to go down and face his audience as though nothing had happened.

They sat around the dining table, hands touching and lights dimmed. Damien had told Selina he couldn't promise anything. Spirits, he'd said, could be elusive. But the sharp look she'd given him told him that she expected him to come up with the goods regardless.

He breathed deeply, resisting the temptation to lapse into cliché and ask if anyone was there. He was just starting to relax into his role when the pain suddenly hit him. He was hot, burning up, and the agony left him gasping for breath. It was the woman he'd sensed before, thin as a skeleton, writhing in agony in stinking, sweat-soaked sheets as poison gnawed at her vital organs. He heard himself let out a moan as he fought for breath – then the pain left him as suddenly as it had arrived.

When he recovered, he looked round to see that everyone was watching him open-mouthed. He wondered how many of them would realise that what they'd just witnessed had been real. He closed his eyes and it hit him again, different this time – perhaps more recent. A feeling of intense terror as he clung tightly to something. He was hiding in an enclosed space – maybe a wardrobe – comforting a child. 'Shh, don't make a sound. Be quiet or he'll hear you.' Something or someone was prowling outside like a predatory beast, and his eyes were stinging with tears.

This time when the feeling left him, he found that he was clinging to the edge of the table and his face was wet with tears. His little audience was staring at him again, but he couldn't find the words to describe what he'd just experienced, so he asked for a glass of wine and gulped it down thirstily. Although he was shaken, he had to resume his act. He was a professional and he was being paid well for the weekend, so he would carry on coming up with anodyne messages for the assembled company; messages he would have to improvise because the only spirits present that night weren't the sort to reassure the needy. Only Corrine Malin was watching him as though she understood what had just happened, and he felt a wave of gratitude.

By ten o'clock it was over, and Damien was desperate to be alone to collect his thoughts before the meeting he'd arranged earlier. An encounter he was dreading, because when it came down to it, the living were far more terrifying than the dead.

Without telling anyone where he was going, he put on his coat and stepped out of the front door into the cold night air. The moon was obscured by thick black clouds, but despite the darkness, he could see the outline of the mill buildings ahead of him, the little clock tower protruding into the dark grey sky. He walked towards the sound of the rushing water, and when he reached the edge, he paused for a few moments to peer down into the inky depths.

An all-encompassing sense of evil made his body shake with fear. Whatever had happened in Mill House more than a century ago hadn't gone away. It echoed down the years, history repeating itself.

The thunder of the mill race drowned out the sound of approaching footsteps, and he only sensed someone behind him a split second before he felt the blow to his back. And by the time he realised he was tumbling into the dark, hungry water, it was too late.

From the notebook of
Dr Christopher Cruckshank

16 February 1882

I was called to the home of the mill overseer to attend his daughter, who had a fever. I assured him the child would soon be well and made discreet enquiries about Mr Partridge's situation. However, he knew little – either that, or he was reluctant to speak freely out of loyalty to his employer. He did say, however, that while Mrs Partridge claimed to be a sickly woman, he'd heard tell that Dr Smith could find nothing amiss with her.

The overseer's house is larger than most in the village and stands near to the Fisherman's Arms public house, which I am told attracts men of the working sort, eager to slake their thirst with ale after a hard day labouring in the mill. I have heard some of the women in the village complaining that their men spend too much time within its walls, but as a doctor, there is little I can do about that.

The mill provides employment for many in the village. The rest work on the farms round about or fish in the

river nearby. The farmers, I have learned, are mostly
prosperous, God-fearing folk, but many of their labourers
lack respectability. There are carters too, and a blacksmith,
who is a large, silent man. When my horse shed a shoe,
he provided a replacement with pleasing readiness, and
I have heard that, for all his taciturn nature, he is a good
man at heart. His wife, in contrast, is a small woman
who loves little more than to chatter with her fellows.
Perhaps she does all the talking for him.

I was invited to dine with the vicar, the Reverend
Stephens, last night. He is a gaunt, cadaverous man,
more suited in appearance to presiding at funerals than
weddings, yet agreeable enough. His wife is related
to local gentry, and over dinner I was forced to listen
to the reverend's tales of her family's noble connections,
although Mrs Stephens herself scolded her husband for
his boastfulness, saying that we are all equal before the
Lord. She is a talkative woman and prone to asking
questions of a personal nature. She is a lot younger than
her husband, and quite handsome.

She listened with great interest to my talk of my
pastime, an interest I developed in London. As I
expected, the art of photography is not yet commonplace
in Petherham, and she expressed a desire to see my work,
which I found most gratifying.

The vicar raised the subject of Mrs Partridge, telling
me that he was concerned for her welfare. Of course my
profession is forbidden to discuss our patients, so I smiled
and said nothing.

17

Robert Farnley, who managed the mill complex for the Quayles, was an amiable man who'd been happy to accommodate Neil's request for access to the premises, even though it was Sunday morning and he'd had to make a special journey from his home in Neston to open up the building. Neil switched his charm to full throttle when he asked to see the water wheel working, and Robert said it was no trouble – just a matter of pulling a few levers to open the sluice and get the wheel turning.

Neil left the mill to see it in action and was halfway across the bridge when he spotted Corrine Malin emerging from Mill House opposite. Wrapped up warmly in her padded coat and a woollen trapper hat in bright tribal colours, head bowed and hands thrust into pockets, she looked as though she was about to embark on a long trek.

There was something he wanted to ask her, so he hurried over to join her. 'Off for a walk?'

'I just needed to get out of that place.'

'How are you?'

'A detective came to take my statement yesterday and that made it seem more ... real somehow. Erica's been missing for twelve years, so I don't know why I feel so ...'

She searched for suitable words to describe her desolation. 'Dead inside.'

'She was your friend. It's natural that you'll be upset.'

'She was more than that – or she would have been if ...'

Neil searched for something appropriate to say, but his mind had gone blank. He'd never been comfortable with the emotional stuff, so he changed the subject. 'How was your seance last night?'

She considered the question for a few moments. 'Not sure, to tell you the truth. At first I thought it was going to be the usual drivel, but when it got going, Damien seemed really rattled. He's either a bloody good actor or there's something bad in that house. He looked terrified.'

'Part of the act?'

'That's the logical explanation, but ... there seemed to be more to it than that.'

Neil hesitated. 'You know those pictures you told me about – any chance of seeing them?'

She shrugged. 'Now's as good a time as any, I suppose.'

'Thanks. I'd like to see the house anyway. It's contemporary with the mill. Built by the owner.' He was on safer ground now. When he was talking about the past, he was never lost for words.

But Corrine's attention was focused elsewhere. He heard her gasp a split second before he saw something that looked at first glance like a bundle of rags caught up on the revolving water wheel. It took him a few moments to realise that the thing being carried up to the top then plunged back down into the foaming stream was a human being, dressed in funereal black.

*

Wesley had to leave for work early on Sunday morning. Erica's mother was travelling down from Leeds later that day, and Gerry had asked him and Rachel to meet her at Neston station and take her straight to the mortuary. Even though her daughter had been reduced to a skeleton, she was insisting on seeing her to say her last goodbyes. It was something Wesley could understand.

As he ate his breakfast, he could hear the children moving about upstairs, and he felt a sudden pang of nostalgia for their younger days, when this time in December meant making lists for Father Christmas. They were growing up fast and time was passing too quickly, but he tried to banish the thought from his head as he ate his muesli. Dealing with the murder of a teenage girl was depressing enough, even though it had happened twelve years ago.

Pam came downstairs wearing her dressing gown and sat down at the table beside him. 'I suppose you'll be late tonight.' There was no hint of reproach in her voice.

'Afraid so.'

'I can't believe those bones have been buried on the Traceys' farm all those years.' She shuddered at the thought. 'How is Rachel?'

'Fine,' he said quickly. Pam's unexpected question suddenly revived memories of the pull of temptation he'd once felt in Rachel's presence. An uneasy conscience could hit you when you least expected it, he thought, thinking of his brother-in-law's repentant sinner.

'At least we haven't heard any more about Mark's strange visitor,' Pam said, as though she'd read his mind.

'It was probably an isolated incident. Some people see the clergy as a soft target.'

'I told you I'm taking the kids over there for lunch today?'

'Yes. Enjoy yourselves.' He glanced at the clock on the kitchen wall. 'Better go. See you later.'

She stood to kiss him goodbye while the cat, Moriarty, ordered her breakfast loudly at the kitchen door. Suddenly he wished he didn't have to face a day dealing with death and grief. He held Pam for a while until she broke away with a final peck on the cheek. 'You should go or you'll be late.'

Even though it was threatening rain, he decided to walk down the steep, narrow roads into the centre of the town, a medieval port that had been as bustling as Gerry's native Liverpool in its heyday. Now, though, it mainly relied on the tourist trade.

He arrived at the station fifteen minutes later to find Gerry already at his desk, frowning as he went through his paperwork.

'Anything come in overnight? Has Barry Clegg been traced yet?'

Gerry looked up. 'And a good morning to you too, Wes. No sign of Clegg so far, but it's early days. I've asked someone to track down that witness in Falmouth and all. Either they were mistaken or they were telling porkies, and if they were lying, I want to know why.'

'I've been thinking, Gerry. What if Erica did make it to Falmouth and then came back to this area for some reason? There's no evidence she died shortly after Florence Valery saw her, is there?'

'Why go all the way to Falmouth and then come back?'

'Maybe when we find the witness who saw her there, we'll find out. And I want to speak to the girl she shared a flat with in Exeter; Jem Wallace, her name was.'

He saw Trish Walton sitting at her desk, deep in concentration as she tapped the keys on her computer. 'Trish, can you see if there have been any other cases that could be linked to Erica's? Hitch-hikers going missing in similar circumstances.'

'Locally or anywhere in the country?'

'Anywhere. Get Paul to give you a hand.' He detected a slight blush on Trish's cheeks. She and Paul had been an item at one time and Wesley was sure Paul still harboured hopes of rekindling their relationship. Perhaps he was doing them a favour, although playing Cupid was hardly in his job description.

As well as tracing Jem Wallace, there was something else he needed to do. He returned to his desk and made a call to Neston police station. After a short conversation, he sat there taking in what he'd just been told. When he and Rachel had spoken to Miss Valery, she'd mentioned a suicide in Petherham, and now he'd just had it confirmed. A woman called Diana Quayle had killed herself and her six-year-old son on exactly the same night Erica was last seen. The twelfth of December 2008 had been a tragic night in Petherham.

His phone rang. He saw it was Neil and was tempted to kill the call. But he answered, and when he heard his friend's voice, he knew that something was very wrong.

18

'I'm at Petherham Mill. There's been an accident.'

Wesley pressed the phone to his ear, blocking out the noise of the busy incident room. 'What kind of accident?'

'A man's been caught up in the water wheel. He's dead. His name's Damien Lee. He's a psychic – or rather he was.'

'Any idea what happened?'

'No. I went back to the mill first thing this morning and we saw the body on the wheel.'

'We?'

'Corrine Malin was with me. I got them to turn the wheel off, then I jumped into the water to drag him out. I hoped he might still be alive. The water was bloody freezing. Corrine called an ambulance, and once the paramedics had pronounced him dead, they carted him off to hospital.'

'You took a hell of a risk. It's not long since you were hurt in that ...'

'I acted on instinct,' Neil said with a note of modesty. 'You would have done the same. I was soaking wet, so the paramedics put one of those foil blankets round me. Wanted to take me to hospital for a once-over, but I said not to fuss. Begged a shower and a change of clothes from the people at Mill House. Next time I play the hero, I'll make sure it's in summer. After the ambulance arrived, a couple of bored-looking constables in a patrol car turned up, but they didn't seem too bothered.'

'CID haven't been informed yet. I presume it's being treated as an accident?'

'They taped off the area, but they didn't confide in me. Archaeologists don't come under the definition of emergency services, I'm afraid. I overheard the guys in the patrol car saying Lee was probably looking at the wheel when he lost his footing and fell in the water.'

'Any idea when it happened?'

'Corrine hasn't seen him since last night, although he wasn't in the habit of joining the others for breakfast so she thought nothing of it. There's no barrier, so it's easy to fall in if you lean over too far.'

Before Wesley could reply, Gerry appeared at his office door, signalling to him as though he wanted him to join him. Wesley told Neil he'd have to go.

'That was Neil,' he told Gerry. 'He's at Petherham Mill with Corrine Malin. Someone fell into the water and got caught up on the water wheel. Neil jumped in to save him, but it was too late.'

Gerry raised his eyebrows. 'Very noble of him. Never struck me as the action hero type.'

'The man was pronounced dead when they pulled him out. According to Neil, it looks like an accident.'

'I already know, Wes. I've just had a call from the patrol who attended the scene.' He thought for a moment. 'But as Corrine Malin's name's come up again, it might be wise to get over there and show our faces. Hopefully it won't take long to establish that it's something we can leave to Uniform.'

'Corrine named the dead man as Damien Lee. He's a psychic taking part in a weekend at Mill House.'

'Bet he didn't see that coming,' said Gerry quickly. The boss's Liverpudlian wit wasn't always in the best of taste, but Wesley knew that gallows humour often helped when the situation was grim.

By the time they arrived in Petherham, the mill entrance had been sealed off with blue and white police tape. Neil was standing just outside the barrier with Corrine Malin, and his account of having begged a shower and a change of clothes from the owners of Mill House explained his attire. Instead of his usual combat jacket and camouflage trousers, he was wearing a quilted coat over a smart sweater and chinos. Wesley found the effect a little unsettling – like the Mona Lisa in a baseball cap, it didn't look right.

After having a word with the uniformed officers standing by the entrance, trying to look busy in front of their superiors, Wesley and Gerry joined Neil and Corrine.

'I believe you've been a bit of a hero, Neil,' said Gerry cheerfully.

'Hardly that. It was too late to save him. Paramedics said he was probably dead soon after he hit the water.'

Gerry grinned at Neil's companion, who had her hands thrust into her coat pockets and was stamping her feet against the cold. 'Hello, love. You Corrine?'

She nodded warily.

'You gave a statement to one of my officers yesterday. Sorry about your mate. Can't be easy to hear something like that out of the blue. I'm in charge of the investigation, so if there's anything else you remember, give us a call, won't you.' He looked round. 'So what went on here then?'

Neil nudged Corrine's arm. 'Tell them what you told me.'

She hesitated for a second before speaking. 'I was looking out of the window last night around ten thirty. My room overlooks Pether Creek and I saw someone heading for the mill. It looked like Damien.'

Wesley waited for her to continue.

'It was dark, and there's only one feeble street light near the mill, so I might have been mistaken. Sorry I can't be more help.'

'Don't be, love,' said Gerry, at his most avuncular. 'You weren't to know what was going to happen. You didn't see Lee fall into the water by any chance?'

'I assumed he'd gone out for a walk to clear his head, so I closed the curtains and got ready for bed. It had been a heavy night – pretty intense.'

'How do you mean?'

'It was strange. I'm still trying to take it in myself.'

'I thought you didn't believe in all that stuff,' said Neil.

She ignored his remark. 'We were supposed to be having a final session with Damien this lunchtime to go over what we'd experienced during the weekend. I was looking forward to seeing how he was going to explain what happened at the seance last night.'

'What did happen?'

She considered the question for a few moments. 'He seemed to . . . see into the past. Experience terrible things. Either whatever it was really shook him, or he was an extremely good actor.'

'Which was it?' Wesley asked.

Corrine shrugged in reply.

They stood for a while, saying nothing. Then Wesley broke the silence. 'I'm sure if we go back to Mill House now, they'll give us a cup of tea,' he said, looking at Neil.

He doubted the wisdom of him standing out in the cold after what he'd just been through.

Gerry's face lit up at the prospect of refreshment. 'I could do with a cuppa. Lead on, love.'

On the way, he whispered in Wesley's ear that he suspected they were wasting time: the unguarded drop into the mill race looked dangerous to say the least. He was surprised that Health and Safety hadn't been on to it years ago.

'But did he fall or was he pushed?' said Wesley, careful not to let their companions overhear.

'If there's any doubt, it'll have to be followed up, but we can pass it over to one of the DCs for the time being. We've got the Erica Walsh case to deal with, don't forget.'

Gerry was right. Investigating Erica's murder, even though it had taken place twelve years ago, was more urgent than an unfortunate accident. But, like Gerry, he needed a cup of tea – and he wanted to see Mill House for himself.

Jeremy Quayle was welcoming, even solicitous, allowing them to use the drawing room and bringing in a tray of steaming mugs and home-made biscuits. The other guests, he told them, had been spoken to by Uniform and they were now out at the Fisherman's Arms. A light lunch at Mill House had been planned, followed by the final session with Damien, but in view of the tragic accident, they'd made the decision to go to the pub for lunch instead. It had seemed like the right thing to do in the circumstances.

Wesley noticed Gerry staring at Jeremy Quayle as though he recognised him from somewhere. Gerry's encyclopedic knowledge of local criminals and their associates was legendary, but Quayle hardly looked the criminal type.

'I spoke to Robert Farnley, the manager of the mill, before you arrived,' said Neil as soon as Quayle had left them alone. 'He's worried in case the mill's held liable for the accident.'

'Depends how it happened,' said Wesley. 'But as far as I can see, the spot where he must have fallen from isn't on mill property.' He was aware that he was beginning to sound like a lawyer. 'I thought the Quayles owned the mill.'

'They do. Robert manages it for them. They bought it eight years ago and renovated it.'

Wesley saw Corrine catch Neil's eye. Neil rose to his feet. 'Corrine's got some photographs she wants to show me. We won't be long.'

As the pair left them alone in the drawing room Wesley saw Gerry frowning, as though he was trying to remember something that lay long forgotten at the back of his mind. From his expression, Wesley suspected it was something unpleasant.

'Anything the matter, Gerry?'

'That bloke, Jeremy Quayle. I've just remembered where I've come across his name before.'

Wesley waited for him to continue, and after a few moments his patience was rewarded.

'My old boss once suspected him of killing his wife.'

19

'I presume you mean his previous wife.'

'That's right. The second's alive and kicking. Wife number one killed herself and her kiddie twelve years ago.'

'I know all about it. Florence Valery mentioned it when Rach and I spoke to her.' Wesley paused. 'I did some checking, and it turns out the first Mrs Quayle died on the same night Erica was last seen – the twelfth of December 2008.'

'Really?'

'I called Neston before Neil rang to tell me about his bit of excitement.'

Gerry raised his eyebrows. 'They confirmed the date?'

'Absolutely.'

'I'm surprised Jeremy Quayle chose to stay here after it happened. If it had been me, I'd have moved well away.'

'Diana Quayle's death was definitely suicide?'

'Oh yes. Bill Irwin used to be my old guv'nor when I was a DC at Morbay back in the olden days, but in 2008 he was in charge at Neston and I remember meeting up with him for a drink shortly after it happened. There were no suspicious circumstances. She left a note and everything. Her coat was found on a rocky outcrop above the river and her car was parked nearby. Coroner said she'd taken her own life and that of her son while the balance of her mind was disturbed, and medical opinion backed him up – she'd been on anti-depressants. Seemed like an open-and-shut case.'

'But your old guv'nor was still suspicious.'

'He had a feeling Jeremy Quayle was involved somehow, even though he was away at the time.'

'Why?'

'Just instinct – the old copper's nose. He had absolutely no evidence to back it up. Quayle had a good job – he was director of an agricultural supply company in Morbay – but rumour had it he got into debt when he started renovating Mill House; spent a fortune on the place. According to Bill, Diana had just inherited a couple of million from her parents, who died in a plane crash in Africa, but she didn't share his obsession with the place. She wanted to move to some posh modern development in Exeter, but he was having none of it. After her death, he inherited the lot, gave up his job, married his secretary and redeveloped the mill with his late wife's money; something he'd dreamed of doing but couldn't have afforded otherwise.'

'Even if he'd wanted the wife dead, surely he wouldn't have harmed the child. Any chance he drove her to kill herself to get his hands on the cash? A touch of gaslighting?'

'There was no suggestion of that at the time. But it's not really our concern. Like I said, it was an open-and-shut case, and Jeremy Quayle wasn't even at home at the time. He was at a conference in London, as I remember. There for the whole week with loads of witnesses and no chance at all of popping back to do in his missus. If he'd been having tea at Buckingham Palace with the entire royal family, he couldn't have had a better alibi. The coroner said it was a tragic case but no one was to blame.'

'So DI Irwin's copper's nose let him down.'

'Certainly looked that way at the time.'

'Good to see Quayle's rebuilt his life.'

Gerry snorted. 'Your faith in human nature is touching, Wes. I've never forgotten Bill telling me how much Quayle inherited – and how he married again so soon after.' He looked at his watch. 'Neil's been gone a long time.'

'They went upstairs to look at some photographs.'

'Is that what they're calling it nowadays?' said Gerry with a wink. 'Time we were off.'

As they stood up, Neil and Corrine re-entered the room. Neil was carrying a polished wooden box, which he thrust into Wesley's hands.

'Look what Corrine found, Wes. Lots of pictures of Petherham, dating to the 1880s judging by the clothes. The visitors' centre at the mill might be interested, so we're going to show them to Robert.'

There were a few pictures still in Neil's hand that he'd kept back.

'These were in a separate hidden compartment in the box.' He passed them to Wesley. 'They look like photographs of dead people. The writing on the back suggests that a couple were taken here in this house. We'd consider it macabre, but it wasn't uncommon to photograph dead loved ones in those days.'

'I'll take your word for it,' said Gerry, nudging Wesley's arm, a signal that he was impatient to be away. Tempted as Wesley was to let himself be sidetracked by Neil's find, duty called.

'Sorry, Neil, got to go,' he said, handing the pictures back. 'I'll have a look another time.'

Ignoring the disappointment on his friend's face, he left

Mill House, trailing slightly behind Gerry, who was striding past the bridge to the mill. There were lights on in the building, but no muffled clatter of machinery from inside. Some CSIs were still taking photographs of the scene, but Wesley knew the accident was probably more a matter for Health and Safety than CID. Besides, they needed to get back to the station and continue the search for whoever had killed Erica Walsh.

'Are you from the police?'

Wesley spun round and saw a man standing on the iron bridge. He was in his forties, tall, with the build of a regular runner, and he was wearing a coat over his suit against the cold breeze blowing in from the creek.

'Can we help you?' said Wesley, retracing his steps, ignoring Gerry muttering impatiently behind him. He stepped onto the bridge, delving in his pocket for his ID. 'I'm DI Peterson and this is DCI Heffernan,' he said, pointing at Gerry, who was approaching slowly like a reluctant child on his way to school.

'Robert Farnley. I manage this place.'

Wesley shook his hand. Farnley had a firm handshake, a useful asset for anyone in business, he supposed.

'When will your people be finished? They've sealed off the area around the water wheel and we can't operate the mill if the wheel's out of action because it powers the machinery. We've got orders to fulfil and the visitors' centre to prepare for the Christmas rush. If we can't get the machines working first thing tomorrow, my staff will be twiddling their thumbs.'

'I'm sorry, Mr Farnley, but the accident has to be investigated. They won't take any longer than necessary.'

'You're detectives,' he said sharply. 'Surely they don't

call in CID for a straightforward accident. What's really going on?'

'It's too early to say yet.' Wesley knew the man was unlikely to be fobbed off with half-truths.

'So it might be suspicious?'

'We're not sure yet what happened, that's all.'

'I heard someone saying the dead man was a psychic.'

Wesley nodded. Gerry was standing by his side now, suddenly attentive. 'You're right. Word gets round fast.' He had the feeling Farnley was going to reveal something important.

'I've been running this place for three years and it's been a bloody nuisance.'

'What has?'

'This ghost business. Someone wrote a piece about the mill around the time it reopened for some ridiculous tourist book. *Devon at its Ghostliest*, it was called. It claimed the mill was haunted by the ghost of a man who killed a local landowner and hid in the clock tower before he was caught and hanged. And there's another story about a girl who was raped and murdered by a wicked mill owner. Then there's a child who was said to have died when he got caught in a loom. Trouble is, at the time that was supposed to have happened, it had been converted into a paper mill. The idiot who made it up got it completely wrong, but that doesn't stop them. We've even had ghost hunters asking if they can spend the night here.'

'Do you let them?' said Gerry.

Robert Farnley swung round to face the DCI as though he'd only just noticed him standing there. 'Health and Safety's always a good excuse,' he said with a smile.

'Did you ever meet the dead man?' Wesley asked.

'Damien Lee, his name was. Did he ever come here ghost hunting?'

'No, I never met him.' Farnley hugged his coat tightly around his body. 'If you'll excuse me, I have things to see to.'

'Did you believe him when he said he'd never met Damien Lee?' Wesley asked once Farnley was out of earshot.

'Not sure.'

'Neither am I.'

From the notebook of
Dr Christopher Cruckshank

20 February 1882

The countryside around these parts is most pleasing, and I have taken to walking in the lanes round about after my visits to my patients, sometimes carrying my photographic equipment with me to make a record of the landscape if the weather permits. People here are in the habit of greeting anybody they meet as though they are a friend or at least a close acquaintance, which is not what I was accustomed to in London.

I often encounter lowly farmhands who will doff their caps in a respectful manner, but earlier today I met a lady walking on her own with an empty basket over her arm. It was Mrs Stephens, wife to the vicar, whose husband had seemed so proud of her family connections when I took dinner with him. Now, out of the vicarage, her manner was different, subdued and rather shy. As she stopped to speak with me, her eyes were focused on the basket she carried, as though it held a fascination for her.

I asked her where she had been, and she told me

she had been visiting some of her husband's poorer
parishioners in a row of farm cottages just outside the
village. She had delivered nourishing food and warm
clothing the churchwarden's wife no longer had use for,
but there was no pride in her voice; rather she seemed
reluctant to boast of her good works.

When she enquired after Mrs Partridge, though, she
raised her eyes to mine.

'I have visited her,' she said. 'And I suspect
her sickness may not be imagined as most in the
village think.'

I asked her what she meant, and she said she had
heard gossip that Mr Partridge had insured his wife's
life for a large sum, and that he was an avaricious man
who was not popular with the men who worked in his
mill. There had also been rumours about his friendship
with his daughter's governess. I said that idle gossip was
no reason to accuse a man of a heinous crime. I confess
I was rather curt with the lady, and she blushed prettily
before changing the subject.

'My husband was most concerned for the poor of the
parish unable to afford a decent funeral,' she said. 'It has
been a source of great distress to many who are forced to
give their loved ones a pauper's burial. He learned that
in some places there are burial clubs where folk put aside
a small sum each week to pay for a dignified ceremony.
I am so pleased that he has established such a club in
Petherham. We call it the Burial Circle.'

I told her it was indeed an excellent idea, as I saw
many families in London forced into poverty to pay for
such things – a double grief, if you like.

She then asked where I kept my photographic

apparatus, and whether it could be carried about. I told her it could, and that I had a mind to capture the lovely scenery round about for posterity.

She smiled at me for the first time, and I saw that she was beautiful.

20

Erica Walsh's mother was due to arrive at Neston station at three o'clock, and Rachel went to meet her. She knew the woman would be exhausted after her lengthy train ride from Leeds, and she imagined that the journey would have given her plenty of opportunity to think about her daughter's fate. Staring out of the window of a speeding train gives you a chance to brood on the realities of life and death at the best of times.

Even wearing her thickest coat, she felt cold as the wind whipped down the platform, chilling her to the bone, and as the train drew up, she watched the passengers alighting. She was certain that she'd recognise Janet Walsh immediately; in her work as a family liaison officer she'd seen enough grieving relatives to know the telltale signs. It never got any easier, she thought. But at least it took her mind off her own problems – problems a newly married woman wasn't supposed to have.

Janet was one of the last people to emerge from the carriage at the rear of the train, and she stood on the platform with her wheelie case looking lost until Rachel approached her.

'Mrs Walsh?' she said with a smile of professional sympathy.

'That's right.'

'I'm Rachel Tracey. I'm a detective sergeant working on your daughter's case. My car's outside. Let's go somewhere more comfortable. You must be freezing.'

She'd noticed Janet shivering in spite of her faux-fur coat. She was an unremarkable woman, with half an inch of grey showing at the roots of her dark hair, and was dressed in unrelieved black, the shade of mourning, which sucked all natural colour from her complexion and made her skin look grey and sickly. Rachel took her arm gently and led her to the car.

'Would you prefer to stop somewhere in Neston for a cup of tea, or shall we go straight to the station? It's up to you. Whatever you feel comfortable with.'

'I'd rather go to the police station. Get it over with. And then ... can I see her?'

'Of course. If you want. But I warn you, she's ...'

'Just bones. I know. They told me. But I still want to see my little girl.'

'Of course. I understand.' Rachel gave her arm a squeeze. 'We've booked a nice B&B for you in Tradmouth. I'm sure you'll be comfortable there.'

'Thank you. You're very kind.'

Rachel didn't feel as though she was being particularly kind. Just human. She was treating the bereaved mother as she'd want to be treated herself if she was unfortunate enough to find herself in similar tragic circumstances, something she prayed would never happen.

As she drove back to Tradmouth, she asked Janet about her journey, trying to take the woman's mind off the ordeal to come. The train had been on time and the trip had been uneventful with no hold-ups. She eventually ran out

111

of small talk, censoring herself whenever a new subject popped into her head. Talking about Tradmouth was out because it would resurrect too many memories, and asking about Christmas plans seemed wildly inappropriate, as did chatting about her own wedding a few weeks before to a woman whose daughter would never be a bride. In the end, she drove in silence until she drew up outside the police station.

When she reached the entrance, with Janet Walsh walking silently beside her, the automatic doors opened with a swish and Rachel gave her companion a reassuring smile. As she led Janet straight to the interview room on the ground floor, she could tell the woman was nervous. Unlike the interview rooms down the corridor, this one, reserved for victims and witnesses, was furnished with armchairs and coffee tables. It also had a kettle, a small fridge and a selection of tea bags. In Rachel's opinion, tea was just what the woman needed.

Once they were settled with steaming mugs of strong brown liquid, Janet seemed to relax slightly, but Rachel was reluctant to hurry her, and she was a little annoyed when she heard a tap on the door. The last thing she needed was an interruption. When the door opened and she saw Wesley standing there, however, her misgivings receded. He was the one person she was glad to see.

'Do you mind if I come in?' he said quietly, looking enquiringly at Janet, leaving it up to her to give permission.

'This is Inspector Peterson,' Rachel said. 'He's dealing with Erica's case.'

Janet gave him an apprehensive nod of acknowledgement.

'If you'd rather talk to Rachel alone, I'll understand.'

'No. It's OK, Inspector. I just want to help you find who did this to Erica.'

'Call me Wesley, please. Is it all right if we have a chat?'

The answer was a nod, and Wesley caught Rachel's eye. He'd leave the questioning to her for now, as she seemed to have developed a rapport with the victim's mother.

'If you want to stop any time, just say,' she began. 'We know the bare facts of the case from our records – how Erica didn't get on with your partner and decided to spend Christmas working in Tradmouth rather than going home. Why did she choose Tradmouth?'

'She'd been there before and she liked it. That's all she told me.'

'There was a letter from you in a rucksack we found with her remains.'

Rachel saw the woman wince, and she glanced at Wesley, wondering if she'd been too brutal. After a few moments, though, Janet spoke.

'I wrote begging her to come home, but she ignored me.'

'She kept your letter with her,' said Wesley gently. 'It must have meant a lot to her.'

'She was angry with me, punishing me for wanting to rebuild my life.' She looked straight at Rachel, as though hoping she'd understand. 'What was I supposed to do? Her dad passed away when she was small, and I was lonely. When I met Barry, he made me feel ...' She searched for the appropriate word, but even though she failed, Rachel understood only too well the need for love and company. 'I fell for him,' Janet continued. 'It was as though he'd cast a spell over me and he became the most important thing in my life. More important than my daughter, who needed me.'

Tears began to form in her eyes. Rachel handed her a tissue and waited for her to continue.

'I can see that now, but I couldn't back then. It was like an obsession. I ignored all the signs.'

'What signs?'

'It wasn't until later that I realised what kind of man Barry was.'

'You're not together now?'

She shook her head vigorously. 'He buggered off soon after Erica disappeared and the police started sniffing around. Said he couldn't stand the pressure. What about me? I had to face everything alone.'

'Erica didn't get on with Barry.'

'That's an understatement. She hated him, and the feeling was mutual. She did her best to break us up. Whenever I spoke to her, she'd make snide comments, tell me how he was cheating on me with other women and that he was just after my money. I thought she was making it up, but . . .'

'Now you're not so sure?' said Wesley. 'What kind of man *was* Barry?'

'Possessive. I was flattered at first, because it made me feel safe, and important. Now I realise it was his way of controlling me.'

Rachel caught Wesley's eye again. It was a story both of them had heard many times before in the course of their police careers. The controlling man, the woman blind to what was happening. It made Wesley angry that so often the law couldn't intervene until it was too late, which meant the perpetrators got away with it. One glance at Rachel's face told him that she felt the same.

'And Erica warned you about him?' he said gently.

'I only wish I'd listened to her. Maybe if I had, she'd still be alive.'

'You can't think like that,' said Rachel. 'You mustn't blame yourself.' She knew her words were futile. This woman would be blaming herself until the day she died.

'I've spoken to a friend of Erica's – a girl called Corrine,' said Wesley.

Janet gave a weak smile. 'Corry. Erica used to talk about her a lot.'

'She told us Barry threatened to kill Erica. Is that true?' Wesley sat on the edge of his chair, sensing that Janet was about to reveal something important.

'Erica came home for the weekend about a month before she disappeared and had a big row with Barry. He said she'd better watch out or he'd make sure she never bothered us again. He said he'd kill her if she kept making trouble.'

Wesley and Rachel looked at each other. Corrine had been telling the truth.

'Did he know she was planning to go to Tradmouth?'

Janet nodded. 'Yes. I told him everything in those days.'

'According to the reports I've read, he was with you at the time Erica disappeared.'

There was a long silence. Then a sob. Rachel walked over to Janet's chair and perched on the arm, putting her own arm around the woman's shoulders. 'It's OK, Janet. Just tell us the truth. Nobody's going to blame you.'

'He said that if I told the police he was with me in Leeds it would save him a lot of trouble. He said he was in the middle of doing an important business deal and he didn't want anything to interfere with it. I believed every word he said.'

'So he *wasn't* with you?' said Wesley, knowing what the answer would be.

'He went away for a few days. Said he'd been to Bristol, and I believed him because I didn't dare not to.'

'Do you know where Barry is now?' Wesley asked.

'I've no idea,' Janet said, before the tears began to flow.

21

Wesley left Janet in Rachel's care and returned to the CID office, knowing that Gerry would want to be informed of this new development right away. They now had a suspect, a man who could easily have followed Erica down to Devon and eliminated the girl who was threatening to come between him and his vulnerable victim. Janet wouldn't be the first comfortably off widow to attract a controlling predator – and Wesley feared she wouldn't be the last.

He found Gerry in his office, catching up on paperwork and looking bored.

'Nothing from Petherham yet,' he said as Wesley entered his inner sanctum, partitioned off from the main CID office by a wall of glass that the boss claimed made him feel like a goldfish in its bowl. 'Looks like Damien Lee's death was an unlucky accident.' He paused, as though something was bothering him. 'But I wonder whether Robert Farnley knows more than he's letting on. He's not keen on ghost hunters, is he?'

'That doesn't mean he'd want to kill Damien Lee. Besides, he's been checked out: he's got no criminal record and he was home all last night with his family in Neston. He's married with two teenage children, and according to his wife, he spent the evening going over some reports and accounts. Looks like we're not the only ones drowning in paperwork.'

'So he's in the clear. Anything else to report?'

'Rach and I have spoken to Erica Walsh's mum, and we have a new suspect.' As he recounted what Janet Walsh had told them, he saw Gerry's face light up.

'Why didn't she tell the police this at the time?'

'Because she was infatuated with Barry Clegg and believed every word that came out of his mouth.'

'But her own daughter ...'

'People believe what they want to believe.'

Gerry sighed. 'I suppose I should know that at my age.' He picked up a biro and began to turn it over and over in his fingers. He sat in silence for a few moments before suddenly looking up. 'I've been thinking about my pension, Wes.'

Wesley sank down into the chair opposite. He and the DCI had worked closely together for years; they were two very different men from different backgrounds, but they were a team. He held his breath, dreading what was coming next.

'It's just an idea, but I think I'd like to spend more time up in Liverpool – maybe get to know Alison better.'

Alison was the daughter whose existence Gerry had known nothing about until a short time ago, the result of a brief relationship back in his native Liverpool. She'd turned up in Tradmouth looking for him after her dying mother had revealed her biological father's true identity. The trouble was that Gerry's other daughter, Rosie, resented her new-found half-sister, considering her very presence in Tradmouth a slur on her late mother Kathy's memory, even though Alison had been conceived long before her parents even met. Gerry's son Sam, on the other hand, had welcomed the news; as far as he was concerned, the more the merrier in the Heffernan clan.

Wesley had known that the day of Gerry's retirement would arrive eventually, but it didn't make the prospect any easier to face.

'Could be good for you, Wes,' Gerry said with a knowing wink. 'I'm sure the chief super will jump at the chance of promoting you.'

Wesley knew he was probably right. CS Noreen Fitton would love to be able to promote a black officer to prove how diverse the force was. That was all very well, but Wesley would prefer to be promoted for his ability rather than the colour of his skin.

'I'll put my two penn'orth in and all – recommend you highly and all that. Just think how chuffed your Pam'd be.' Gerry saw the forlorn look on Wesley's face. 'I only said I was thinking about it, Wes. Nothing definite. I just wanted to know where I'd stand financially if I did decide . . .'

'You've got to do whatever's right for you, Gerry. I'd miss you if you went, that's all.'

'Same here, Wes.' Gerry began to shuffle papers on his desk. Wesley had never seen the man embarrassed by emotion before, but there was a first time for everything. 'Anyway, we'd better try and locate this Barry Clegg character. We need to have a word with him sooner rather than later.'

'If he did have anything to do with Erica's death, he's spent the last twelve years thinking he's got away with it, so let's hope he hasn't been taking notice of the press reports. Wherever he is, we don't want him panicking and going to ground.'

119

'If he's the one who put her in that grave, he'll have been keeping an eye on the news ever since. Skeletons have a habit of turning up when you least expect them, as we well know.' Gerry looked at his watch. 'Talking of dead bodies, Colin says he can fit in Damien Lee's post-mortem this afternoon. The wife's been informed and has already been to make the formal ID. She lives on the edge of Dartmoor.'

'Then perhaps we should go and have a word with her.'

Gerry shook his head. 'If Lee's death was an accident, there's no need for us to get involved. Leave it to Uniform. We've got enough on our plate.'

Wesley was still curious to find out more about the dead psychic, but he knew Gerry was right. Robert Farnley's talk of ghost hunters was intriguing, but it wasn't going to help them catch Erica Walsh's killer.

'Erica's mum wants to see her remains.'

'You told her . . .'

'Of course, but she insists.'

Gerry gave a sad nod. He understood the mother's need to see her child, even though that child was now bare bones. 'Colin's been examining the remains with that forensic anthropologist. What's her name?'

'Jemima Baine.'

'That's the one. Hopefully by the time we get to the mortuary he'll know more about a cause of death.'

Wesley didn't reply. With bones, it wasn't always possible to determine how someone had died. But he harboured a hope that Colin and Jemima between them might have come up with some clue.

The light was fading and a vicious wind had started to blow in from the river, so they fastened their coats before venturing out into the fresh air. As they walked down the embankment, Wesley could see boats dancing energetically on the rough surface of the dark grey river as though they were trying to escape their moorings. The town's decorations were already up and lit, and it wouldn't be long before the festivities began. Many people would be arriving to spend the Christmas season in Tradmouth, attracted by the festive markets and the candlelit processions around the medieval town. Then the hotels, pubs and restaurants would be full to overflowing with seasonal cheer.

They walked beneath the rows of coloured lights the council had strung between the lamp posts on the edge of the quay. The lights were blowing around like the rigging of a sailing ship in a storm. Wesley hoped as he did every year that they'd last until Christmas Day; by some miracle, they always seemed to survive whatever nature threw at them.

Tradmouth Hospital mortuary looked anything but festive. Wesley and Gerry made their way down the sterile corridors and past Colin's office. The pathologist's lair was surprisingly cosy, and he kept a stash of luxury biscuits and teas, something the two detectives always appreciated after witnessing the gruesome spectacle of a post-mortem.

Today they found him already gowned up in the post-mortem room, the body of Damien Lee lying on the stainless-steel table in front of him.

'Hello, gentlemen. I was just waiting for you to arrive before I began.'

'Sorry we're a bit late,' said Wesley. The truth was that his interview with Janet Walsh, followed by Gerry's talk of retirement, had made him lose track of the time.

'I'll forgive you,' said Colin, before turning his

attention to the body. Wesley glanced at it, then averted his eyes. The water wheel had left Damien Lee's remains bruised and battered, with multiple lacerations. Not a pleasant sight.

Colin went about his work with quiet efficiency, speaking into the microphone dangling above the corpse every so often to record his observations. As Wesley watched, it struck him that the whole procedure looked pretty routine. Colin's examination of the lungs confirmed that the dead man had inhaled a lot of water before he died, which made Wesley relax a little. If Lee had fallen in by accident and drowned, then his death wasn't their concern.

But the pathologist's next words made his heart sink.

'There is something rather interesting.'

'What's that?' said Gerry, leaning over as close as he dared to have a look.

'There's a wound on the back. About an inch long. It's almost sealed itself after the immersion in water, so it's not easy to see amongst all the other lacerations. I'm ashamed to say I almost missed it.'

Wesley averted his eyes while Colin inserted an instrument into the wound, his face a picture of concentration.

'Well?' said Gerry with a note of impatience.

'It's about seven inches deep and has missed the heart byless than a centimetre. I hate to tell you this, gentlemen, but I think our man here was stabbed before he went into the water. Just once, in the back. Sorry to add to your workload. I'll send across my full report in due course.'

Gerry stared at the body, lost for words.

'You say it just missed the heart?'

'Only by a millimetre or two. The knife slipped between the ribs, but that could well have been a lucky strike.'

'Not lucky for this poor sod,' Gerry muttered, gesturing at the body. 'Did the stab wound kill him?'

'No, Gerry. The actual cause of death is drowning, but the force of the blow probably propelled him forward into the water.'

'So he's standing there minding his own business and someone comes up behind him and sticks a knife in him, and he falls forward into the water and drowns?' Wesley wanted to get the facts straight in his mind.

'In my opinion that sums it up nicely, Wesley. It seems you've got another murder on your hands.'

Gerry gave a long sigh. 'This is all we need.'

'Just so you're aware, Colin, Erica Walsh's mother wants to see her remains,' said Wesley. 'Rachel'll bring her in as soon as you give the word.'

'Ah yes, our skeleton. I have a bit of news for you on that subject.'

Wesley could tell from Colin's expression that he was about to impart some important information. He held his breath and waited.

'With the help of Dr Baine, the forensic anthropologist, I performed a thorough examination of the bones and made a rather interesting discovery. Your friend Neil made an excellent job of the excavation, and as a result we were able to examine the small bones of the neck and throat, including the hyoid bone. I found it to be fractured, which indicates—'

'Strangulation,' said Wesley.

From the notebook of
Dr Christopher Cruckshank

2 *May* 1882

It is some months now since the inauguration of the Petherham Burial Circle, and it is proving most popular in the village and the surrounding area. Some of the local farmers have joined along with their labourers, and even Mr Partridge is encouraging his workers at the mill to take up membership.

Mrs Partridge claims to suffer still and keeps to her bed, even though I can find nothing amiss with her. I prescribe a tonic and bleed her from time to time, but there seems to be little improvement to her health.

I was surprised when Partridge came to my home yesterday and asked to see me. He said he had spoken to a business acquaintance in London who claimed to know me, and that he wished for my advice on a certain matter. After some thought, I agreed to help him. I felt I could not do otherwise.

22

The following morning, Wesley woke up with a headache. He hadn't slept well. The two cases had churned around in his head as Pam slept peacefully by his side. Part of him, the selfish part he tried to suppress, felt annoyed by her ability to switch off from the problems of the day. But, like him, she had to go to work. She taught at the local primary school, so he wasn't the only one who needed to be alert. He knew that Christmas was always a stressful time for her, and this year she was writing and directing the Year 6 nativity play. She wasn't the only member of the family involved in the world of drama that month: Michael had been awarded the role of the Artful Dodger in his school's production of *Oliver!* Not, Wesley had observed, a particularly suitable role for a police inspector's son.

The night-time rain had stopped by the time he set off for work, so he made the decision to walk down the steep hill into town, hoping the fresh air would wake him up. When he arrived in the incident room, the day shift were trickling in, carrying plastic cups of coffee from the machine in the corridor, but Rachel was already at her desk, tapping on her computer keyboard. She looked up as he suppressed a yawn.

'Don't know why you're yawning, Wesley. I've been up since half four helping with the milking. In farming terms, this is midday.'

The hint of criticism in her voice surprised him, and he couldn't think of a suitable answer that wouldn't make him sound like an effete townie. Instead he asked her whether anything new had come in, but to his disappointment the answer was no.

Before he could say any more, Gerry appeared, looking harassed as he struggled to take off his thick anorak. 'Chilly out there,' he said to nobody in particular before beckoning Wesley into his office.

'Right then,' he said, slumping down in the big leather chair, which creaked dangerously under his weight. 'We now know Erica Walsh was strangled before being buried in a shallow grave on the edge of that field. Unfortunately there's no way of telling whether she was sexually assaulted, but in my opinion it can't be ruled out. Bloke picks up hitch-hiker and tries his luck. Things get out of hand and she ends up dead. Killer disposes of the body and drives off into the night. Maybe we should have another word with the last bloke who gave her a lift – David Leeson. Shouldn't be too hard to trace him, even after all this time.'

Wesley knew the boss could well be right. Leeson had been ruled out at the time because of Miss Valery's sighting and the Falmouth connection, but it was certainly worth speaking to him again. They really needed some luck; a breakthrough. Although he wasn't getting his hopes up.

'Now that we know Damien Lee's death wasn't an accident, we need to speak to his wife,' Gerry continued. 'If we set off now, we'll be there by ten. I'd suggest you take Rach, but she's due to see Mrs Walsh.'

'I'm waiting to hear from West Yorkshire. They promised to let us know if Barry Clegg's still on their patch.'

'Let's face it, he could be anywhere by now,' said Gerry with a sigh. 'He sounds like the kind of bullying bastard who might travel down here to find the girl who was making his life a misery and deal with her. And the fact that he threatened to kill her makes him our chief suspect ... unless I'm right about the hitch-hiking theory. Clegg claimed he was in Bristol, but it wouldn't have taken much effort to drive a bit further down the M5 and the A38. Why the hell did that poor lass's mum lie for him?'

Wesley didn't answer. Who knew what the fear of loneliness and the need to be loved might drive someone to? He wasn't going to judge Janet Walsh.

When they set out to visit Damien Lee's widow at 9.30, the sun was shining and the rain that had fallen overnight glistened on tree branches and hedgerows like diamonds. As Wesley drove towards Dartmoor, he found himself wondering what kind of house a psychic would live in. At one time Damien Lee had been a regular on TV, which he guessed was paid well. However, if he had chosen to take part in a psychic weekend in an obscure Devon village, perhaps business wasn't so good nowadays. Unless the Quayles had paid him very well – or he'd had his own reasons for visiting Petherham.

The Lees' home stood on the edge of a village ten miles from Exeter, on a minor road between the city and Dartmoor. The spot was more isolated than he'd expected, and the house a lot older. Wesley recognised it as a typical Devon longhouse – the kind that had once accommodated a family at one end and their animals at the other. He brought the car to a halt on the lane outside, making sure it wasn't blocking the thoroughfare before getting out and zipping up his coat. The cold was more biting up here, but the wind wasn't as fierce as it had been on the coast.

A woman walking past with a large golden Labrador looked at them curiously but still said good morning. Wesley returned her greeting and Gerry did likewise. It was expected in the countryside.

There was no car parked outside, and Wesley wondered whether Sheryl had gone out. But when he rang the doorbell, she opened the old oak front door. She was small, with peroxide curls cascading to her shoulders, and she wore no make-up, which was probably a wise decision because her eyes were red and swollen from crying. As far as Wesley knew, she still believed her husband's death had been a tragic accident, and the reality was going to come as a shock. Unless she knew more than they supposed.

She led them into a living room furnished in a modern style that jarred with the house's traditional architecture – but then Sheryl didn't look the type to go for antiques. Her leather skirt was short, as was her top, and the outfit was finished off with a pair of UGG boots, her only concession to comfort. She invited them to sit, and after the routine condolences had been given, she offered tea. Wesley thanked her, glad that the slight delay would give him the chance to get his thoughts in order and work out the best way to tell the woman that her husband had been murdered.

She returned with a tray of matching mugs and Wesley took his gratefully.

It was Gerry who spoke first. 'We're sorry to have to call like this, love. I know it's a difficult time for you. You identified your husband's body yesterday, didn't you?'

Her eyes widened and Wesley could see they were glassy

128

with unshed tears. 'That's right. That doctor was very kind –
the pathologist. They said it was a terrible accident . . .' She
shook her head in disbelief. 'I can't think how it could have
happened. Why would he have gone so near the edge like
that?' Her accent was northern; Manchester probably.

Wesley knew they couldn't keep the truth from her any
longer. 'We've spoken to Dr Bowman. Since you saw him,
he's conducted a post-mortem on your husband's body.
He found multiple injuries from the water wheel, as you'd
expect, and confirmed that drowning was the cause of
death. But there was something else.'

Sheryl was sitting on the edge of her seat, her generous
mouth slightly open. 'What?'

Wesley paused for a moment. The news he had to
impart seemed so blunt, so brutal. But she had to know.
'Dr Bowman found another wound. A knife wound in your
husband's back. The other injuries were extensive, so it
wasn't obvious at first. I'm afraid it looks as though Mr Lee
was murdered. I'm sorry.'

For a while Sheryl sat perfectly still, staring ahead in
shock as she absorbed what Wesley had told her. Then she
turned her head slowly to look at him. 'Nobody would want
to kill him. He didn't have any enemies. He wasn't that sort
of person.' She shook her blonde curls. 'He must have been
mugged. It's the only explanation.'

'His wallet was found in his room at Mill House, along
with his phone.'

'His attacker might not have known that.'

'We've never had muggings in Petherham, love,' said
Gerry quietly. 'It's a small place.'

'There's a first time for everything. And you hear a lot
about crime in the countryside nowadays. Drug dealing

and all that. County lines, isn't it?' She sounded desperate, as though she couldn't bring herself to believe that her husband's murder was personal. Tears had begun to trickle down her cheeks; she pulled a tissue from her pocket and wiped them away angrily.

'Tell me about Damien,' said Wesley gently after a few moments of silence. 'When did you meet?'

'Years ago. We've been together since the Millennium.'

'Childhood sweethearts?' said Gerry.

She gave a sad little smile. 'I was twenty when we got together. Hardly a kid. We met in a pub in the middle of Stockport. He was performing at a New Year's Eve party, and I was working behind the bar.'

'Performing as a psychic?'

She shook her head. 'Not then. That came later. He was a singer. He had a day job in an office, but of an evening he sang in pubs and clubs to make a bit extra. In the end he started getting bookings all over the country and gave up the day job. Holiday places and all that. He was good – had a lovely voice.'

'But he chose to abandon singing for seances?'

'He had an experience – in a pub.'

'An encounter with spirits?'

Wesley wished the boss had curbed his natural urge to make a quip at every opportunity, but Sheryl seemed unaware of what had been said.

'Yes. He saw a ghost. An old landlady who'd been murdered there. He didn't know the story, but he sort of knew exactly what had happened to her. He said it shook him, but from then on, he knew he had the gift. It took a couple of years for him to decide what he wanted to do, but eight years ago he changed his name and started doing psychic shows. It paid a lot more than singing, but that wasn't the point. His gift was real. He helped people.'

'I saw his TV programme once,' said Gerry.

'The programme was what really made his reputation. Once that started, he had no shortage of bookings. All sorts of things from shows to psychic weekends like the one in Petherham. He has – had – private clients too.'

'You say he changed his name,' said Wesley. 'What was it before?'

'He used his real name when he was singing. David Leeson.'

The words struck Wesley like a bombshell. 'David Leeson? Did he have any engagements here in Devon in 2008?' He looked at Gerry and saw that his mouth had fallen open in astonishment.

Sheryl sat in silence for a while before she replied. 'You're talking about when he gave a lift to that girl – the one who went missing.'

'Her body's just been found,' said Wesley. 'He told you he'd given her a lift?' Somehow he'd imagined that he might not have admitted to his partner that he'd picked up a young female hitch-hiker.

'He had no choice. The police turned up to interview him – said they'd got his registration number from a traffic camera. I told him he was bloody stupid. Giving a girl a lift like that could lead to trouble – you hear of people being falsely accused of all sorts, don't you?'

'What did he tell you about it?' said Gerry.

'He said he saw her hitching in some town – Newton Abbot, I think it was – and he picked her up. He was on his way to a gig in Morbay – a hotel offering pre-Christmas packages with entertainment thrown in. He dropped her off near Tradmouth and thought no more of it until he heard she was missing. End of story. He had nothing to hide.'

'You trusted him?' Wesley said softly.

There was a slight hesitation. 'Yeah.'

'You don't sound too sure.'

Sheryl stared into the dregs of the tea she'd just finished. 'He swore it didn't mean anything, and I wanted to trust him, but ... I looked on the map. The police said he dropped that girl off on a little lane leading to a village. Hardly the quickest route to Morbay.'

Wesley had noticed this when he'd reread David Leeson's statement, but he said nothing and waited for her to continue. Eventually his patience was rewarded.

'Dave's ex moved to Devon around that time. She was working in some village in the middle of nowhere. I found a message from her on his phone once. I thought he might have been on his way to see her when he picked the girl up.'

'Did you ask him about it?'

'Yes. He said he thought it was a shortcut.'

'You didn't believe him?'

'I knew he was lying. He wasn't very good at it.'

'Do you know the name of his ex?'

'Lynette. Lynette Preston.'

The name wasn't familiar, and Wesley was sure it hadn't cropped up in any of the statements or reports he'd read while he was familiarising himself with the case. 'Is this Lynette Preston still living in the south Devon area?'

'As far as I know.'

'You think David had arranged to see her when he came down here in 2008?'

'I don't have my husband's psychic powers, so I don't

know,' she said with a note of bitterness. 'But it wouldn't surprise me. Don't ask, don't tell. That's always been my motto.'

Wesley detected a spark of jealousy. Her late husband's involvement with another woman bothered her all right. And jealousy was a powerful emotion – powerful enough to make someone take another person's life.

'Do you know where we can find her?'

'No. But I heard she got married and I think she runs a pub. I don't know where; I prefer not to think about her.' She pressed her lips together in a determined line. The subject was closed.

'I'm sorry, but I have to ask this. Where were you on the night Damien died?'

'I was here.'

'Can anyone confirm that?'

'No. I was on my own.' The tears had gone and there was a hint of defiance in the statement. 'I don't mind being on my own. I'm used to it. And before you ask, I don't drive, so I couldn't have gone down there to see him. I did get a text from him on Saturday night, though.' She took out her phone and read, '"Bad place. Need to get out. Back soon as I can." That's all. His last words to me.'

Wesley saw tears forming in her eyes again and he knew they'd learn nothing more, so they took their leave.

As soon as they were out of sight of the house, he called the station. He wanted to speak to Lynette Preston and find out what she knew.

23

In spite of the patient welcome he'd received, Neil couldn't help wondering whether Robert Farnley was beginning to regard him as a nuisance. Neil's team had tried hard to be unobtrusive, but their presence during working hours was bound to get in the way of business to some extent.

When he entered the building, his ears were assaulted by the clatter of working looms. He could see three middle-aged women tending the machines, deep in concentration as they did something deft and mysterious with shuttles and thread that looked to Neil like a conjuring trick.

They didn't appear to notice him as he made his way to the manager's office, where he found Robert making a phone call.

'So if we stick to the delivery date we agreed, that's fine by me.'

He spotted Neil waiting in the doorway and gave him a businesslike smile. As soon as the call ended, Neil stepped into the office and shut the door behind him.

'We've finished the survey of the main mill, but I'd like to take some measurements in the clock tower and have a look at the workings of the old clock if that's OK with you.'

'Shouldn't be a problem, but I warn you, nobody's been up there for years.'

'Thanks. I told you that the unit's publishing a booklet based on the project, didn't I? Glossy cover, fully illustrated.'

'I believe you did mention it.'

'Your mill's been chosen to feature on the front cover, as it's Grade II listed.'

'So it is,' Robert said with a sigh. 'Jeremy's always going on about it.'

'I get the impression he's a bit obsessed with the place.'

Robert smiled. 'It's his baby, so you can't blame him. He had a vision – a dream – and he achieved it.'

'With your help.'

'Only for the past three years.'

'How did you come to take the job?'

'I was involved in the management of a historic mill in Derbyshire run by the Heritage Trust, and when this vacancy came up, I grabbed the opportunity to relocate to Devon. Me and my wife have always loved this part of the world, and it's a great place to bring up kids.' He smiled fondly as though he was remembering happy family week-ends in the countryside. 'This book of yours ... can we sell copies in the visitors' centre?'

'Of course. Have the police been back?'

Robert nodded. 'They've let us start up the water wheel, so we've been able to get the machines working again. They seem to be concentrating on the area on the other side of the mill race, which has nothing to do with us, thank God.'

Neil knew his colleagues were waiting outside, shivering in the cold, armed with clipboards, cameras and draw-ing equipment, so he left Robert in peace and exited the building, clamping his hands over his ears as he passed the clattering looms. He'd heard that before the days of Health and Safety mill workers often went deaf, and developed lip-reading skills. Now that he'd heard the racket made by the machines, he understood why.

Once outside, he instructed his colleagues to make a start in the clock tower. He himself had other plans. He'd already called Corrine Malin to ask whether she'd had a chance to make copies of the photographs she'd shown him, and the answer was yes. They were ready for him to pick up if he wanted to come round to her flat in Morbay. He drove off feeling a small pang of guilt about leaving his team to do all the hard work, but the inclusion of the photographs and the story behind them – if he could find it – might lift *The Historic Mills of South Devon* from a dry factual publication to something with much wider appeal. A spot of human interest, so he'd heard, was worth a hundred facts and diagrams.

The resort of Morbay had enjoyed its heyday as 'Queen of the English Riviera' back in the twentieth century. Now the main street was filled with pound shops and amusement arcades, and the once-glamorous promenade had seen better days. The town still had its fashionable parts, with large and prosperous villas perched on the hillside, but the advent of cheap foreign travel and a lack of investment had taken its toll. Corrine lived in a run-down part of town favoured by students and benefit claimants. Her flat was on the first floor of a Victorian house with flaking stucco and rotting windows. Neil, who had once been a student himself, knew the telltale signs.

The flat itself was surprisingly neat, with a cheerful poinsettia plant in pride of place on the shabby sideboard. Corrine invited him in with an eagerness that told him she was glad of the company. The laptop on the desk by the window was surrounded by files and books; she had obviously been working.

'I know what you're thinking – it's a bit different from Mill House.'

'Everyone's entitled to treat themselves to a bit of luxury now and again.'

'Cost a bloody fortune, that weekend. Now it's back to beans on toast.'

'The psychic falling into the mill race must have put a dampener on things. Do you think he was a fraud?'

'He'd obviously researched us all beforehand. Combined with a bit of cold reading, he was very convincing.'

'The CSIs are still examining the place where they think he went in.'

'Why?'

'Don't know. I haven't seen Wesley to ask. You said you've got those photos of the mill for me ... and the ones of the dead people.'

'Yes. Why are you so interested?'

'I'm always interested in the weird and inexplicable.'

'Is that why you became an archaeologist?'

'Some of my colleagues might be weird and inexplicable, but the work usually isn't,' he said with a grin.

Corrine opened a drawer in the sideboard, took out a cardboard folder and handed it to Neil. As he took it from her, he caught sight of a trio of framed pictures standing on top of the sideboard: a middle-aged couple he guessed were her parents; a wedding group with Corrine as brides-maid. But it was the middle picture that interested him. He picked it up. Two girls beamed from the frame, each holding a pint of beer. They looked happy, carefree.

'That's me with Erica,' she said, pointing at a pretty girl with dark curls. She had her arm around Corrine's shoulder, and was leaning in so their heads touched, their glasses of beer raised in a silent toast. They looked as though they hadn't a care in the world.

Neil stared at the image. The sight of Erica so alive shook him; last time he'd seen her face it had been a bare white skull. 'I helped to excavate her bones,' he said quietly. Then he pointed to another girl, sitting sulkily at a table in the background of the photo, but still just in focus. 'I know her.'

'That's Jem – the girl who shared with Erica.'

'She's not Jem any more. She calls herself Jemima these days. Jemima Baine.'

From the notebook of
Dr Christopher Cruckshank

20 *May* 1882

Mrs Partridge's funeral was an elaborate affair.
Her hearse was drawn by six black horses resplendent
with glossy plumes and jangling harness. All the
village attended, along with many of the better sort
from the district round about. The church of St Mary
Magdalene was full to bursting, and even the servants
wept, although Partridge's daughter, Joanna, sat stony-
faced at the front, unable to feign grief for the stepmother
she despised.

Partridge and his daughter were away from home
visiting relatives in Surrey at the time of his wife's death.
I attended my patient on the day of her sad demise and
certified the cause of death as a gastric upset so severe it
robbed the patient of the strength to fight for life. Her
weakened heart simply gave up the battle.

Mrs Stephens accosted me after the funeral and
asked me if I thought Mrs Partridge might have
consumed poison. I told her I had seen her shortly before

her death and I had no such suspicions, so it was unwise to indulge in such speculation. An hour or so later I saw her talking most animatedly with the blacksmith's wife. In spite of her noble connections, it seems she has no hesitation in associating with those beneath her social station.

24

When Wesley and Gerry returned, they found the CID office buzzing with activity.

'Anyone managed to trace Barry Clegg yet?' Wesley called out as they walked in.

Rachel looked up, her expression serious. 'I took Janet Walsh to the station earlier. She swears she has no idea where he is now, and I believe her. I've spoken to West Yorkshire; they're still looking into his whereabouts. He's got a couple of convictions for deception and a few arrests for violence back in the 1990s, but he's kept his nose clean since 2011 – unless he's just got cleverer and hasn't been caught.'

'He threatened to kill Erica and his alibi's been shot to pieces, so I want him found sooner rather than later,' said Gerry, taking off his coat.

Wesley called for attention and the team stopped work. 'There's someone else we need to find,' he said. 'A Lynette Preston. Possibly involved in the licensed trade. And we've just spoken to Damien Lee's wife. Our latest victim changed his name a few years ago. Turns out his real name's David Leeson. The same David Leeson who gave Erica Walsh a lift on the night she vanished.'

There were a few gasps of surprise around the room.

'It's possible he was involved with this Lynette Preston at the time of Erica's disappearance, so we need to interview her. It's now looking as if Leeson's the link between our two cases.'

DC Paul Johnson put his hand up. 'Does this mean we're looking for the same killer?'

Gerry was standing in his office door, scratching his head. 'I wouldn't rule it out, Paul. I don't believe in coincidences. Right, let's get a move on. We need to find this Preston woman – and Erica Walsh's wicked stepfather, Barry Clegg. Carry on. Keep up the good work,' he added to nobody in particular before retreating into his lair. Wesley followed him in with two sheets of paper he'd just been handed by one of the detective constables.

After scanning them, he sat down beside Gerry's desk. 'Someone's gone through Damien Lee's phone records. He received a call from an unregistered mobile on the night he died. Untraceable.'

'His killer?'

'I'd put money on it.' He pushed the second sheet across the desk. 'And this is a list of Lee's clients – those he saw on a one-to-one basis. It was on his phone; for a psychic, he was very businesslike.'

'They'll have to be spoken to, but I can't see anybody murdering him just because he failed to get in touch with Great-Aunt Betty.'

'He visited a private client in Tradmouth on the morning of the day he arrived in Petherham. You'll never guess where she lives.'

'Don't keep me in suspense, Wes.'

'Baynards Quay. She's a neighbour of yours.'

'What number?'

'Five.'

Gerry raised his eyebrows. 'It was sold recently for almost two million. I know mine's a lot smaller, but it cost me and Kathy peanuts all those years ago.'

'You're sitting on a gold mine, Gerry.'

Gerry snorted. 'I don't feel like a millionaire. I suppose it'll be Sam and Rosie who'll reap the benefit eventually – and Alison, of course.'

'You're not thinking of moving?'

'Away from my view of the sea? They'll have to carry me out feet first. Mind you, the yuppies and millionaire second-home owners are starting to take over. Noses in the air and won't pass the time of day.'

'Does anyone say yuppies any more?'

Gerry gave an exaggerated shrug of his bulky shoulders. 'Who cares? That's what I call 'em.'

'What's the woman at number five like?'

'Long dark curly hair, but not in the first flush of youth. Skinny. I reckon she could do with a good meal inside her.'

'Husband? Partner?'

'Smarmy bugger. Looks like he's just stepped straight out of the hairdresser's. I've seen him carrying golf clubs to his flashy car, and he tries to dress like a sailor but I doubt if his pricey gear has ever seen the deck of a yacht. Probably playing at it like that French queen – Marie whatshername with her shepherdess outfit. Got her head chopped off.'

'Marie Antoinette.'

'That's the one.'

'I take it you don't like your new neighbours then?'

'Never spoken to 'em, so it's sheer prejudice on my part.'

He grinned, showing the gap between his front teeth, something he'd always claimed was a sign of good luck.

'Fancy paying them a neighbourly visit?'

Gerry went to his office door and saw that everyone seemed to be engrossed in their tasks. 'Why not,' he said. 'Let's get some fresh air.'

The day was fine, the fierce wind had died down and the sun was shining, making the rippling river sparkle with light. But Wesley could see clouds gathering like a gang of bullies over the river mouth. The crisp December day would, he suspected, turn wet and miserable before nightfall.

It didn't take long to reach the cobbles of Baynards Quay. Gerry's house stood at the nearest end of the terraced row, smaller than the rest and leaning against its neighbour as if for protection. In the middle of the quayside was a considerably grander house, double-fronted and painted an appealing shade of china blue. Wesley remembered Gerry telling him that sailors and sea captains painted their houses different colours so they could recognise them easily when their ship sailed into port, although it was probably a long time since this particular house had been owned by anybody who made their living at sea.

Wesley knocked at the door and the DCI stood slightly behind him, shuffling his feet impatiently. It was half a minute before the door was opened by a man wearing a pink cashmere jumper over white trousers. He had the prosperous, tanned look of someone who took regular holidays somewhere considerably sunnier than Devon in the winter.

'Mr Watkins?' Wesley said as he held out his ID.

The man's mask of confidence slipped for a brief moment. 'That's right. I'm Brian Watkins. What can I do for you, Inspector?'

'We'd like a word with your wife if she's in.'

'Look, if it's about that speeding ticket ...'

'We don't deal with speeding tickets, sir,' said Gerry. 'We're investigating a murder.'

'In that case, I don't know how Abigail can help you.'

'If we could speak to her ...'

The man was blocking the doorway and Wesley wondered why he was being so protective. Perhaps he considered his wife to be vulnerable in some way – or perhaps he didn't trust the police.

'It's a routine matter,' he said. 'We won't keep Mrs Watkins long.'

After a moment of hesitation, Brian Watkins stood aside to let them in. The decor was opulent, too fancy for Wesley's taste, with an excess of gold and marble. The contrast to Gerry's homely abode a few doors away couldn't have been starker.

Watkins looked at Gerry accusingly. 'Do I know you?'

'We're neighbours. I live in the end house.'

There was no friendly neighbourly reaction; no small talk; in fact there was no reaction at all.

The woman Gerry had described earlier emerged from a door to their right. She had the jittery look of a chain smoker newly deprived of her drug of choice.

'It's the police. They want to speak to you,' Brian Watkins told her. The words 'What have you done?' weren't uttered, but they were certainly implied.

'You'd better come through to the drawing room,' she said, turning her back on them and walking ahead.

The room was expensively decorated and the decor looked fresh, as though an interior designer with grandiose ideas had recently been let loose in the place with an unlimited budget. Wesley noticed that Watkins had vanished into the depths of the house, leaving his wife alone with them. In view of the man's initial display of protectiveness, he was surprised he hadn't hung around.

'What do you want?' Mrs Watkins asked nervously after she'd invited them to take a seat.

'You're acquainted with Damien Lee,' said Wesley, a statement rather than a question.

The woman bowed her head so that it was hard to make out her expression. 'Yes. Why?'

'When did you last see him?'

'Last Friday morning. I had a private consultation.'

'Why was that?' said Gerry.

She fidgeted with the hem of her sweater for a few seconds as though she needed time to consider her answer. 'When we moved into this house, I sensed a ... hostile presence. Things started happening and I felt—'

'What sort of things?' Wesley asked.

'Objects being moved around. Pictures jumping off walls. And I could feel a threatening atmosphere, as though something didn't want us here. Someone else I consulted – a psychic from Neston – said the house stood on a ley line and bad energy was seeping up from the earth. She said the spirit of the river resented us being here, but Damien said that was rubbish. He sensed the presence of a sea captain's wife whose husband died in a shipwreck and never came home. He said she's still here waiting for him and she resents us taking over her home.' She suddenly looked puzzled. 'I don't understand why you're here. What's this about?'

'I'm sorry to have to tell you that Mr Lee was found dead yesterday. We're treating his death as suspicious.'

Abigail Watkins' eyes widened in horror. 'Where did it happen? How did he die?'

Wesley thought they were reasonable questions, the kind of questions an innocent person would ask, so he told her, although he made no mention of the knife wound. They were keeping that to themselves for the time being.

The woman's shock appeared genuine. 'He was fine when he was here. He promised to come back and sort out the problem.' She frowned. 'He said the hostility was very strong and he'd felt the same thing before in places where murders had been committed.'

'He told you a murder had been committed here?'

Wesley saw the expression on Gerry's face and wished he'd kept his scepticism to himself.

'I don't think . . . Well, not in so many words,' said Abigail, suddenly flustered. 'But he seemed really worried about whatever it was. He was quite . . . professional when he arrived that day, but by the time he left, he looked scared.'

'Did he tell you what he was scared of?'

'No. But he couldn't get out fast enough. It's really been bothering me. I've got to live here. I've got to face it day after day.' The pitch of her voice was rising.

'Was your husband here when Damien visited? Did he hear what was said?'

She shook her head. 'He arrived home about ten minutes before Damien left and popped his head round the door, but when he saw Damien was here he left us alone. Why?'

'I just wondered whether it would be worth speaking to him.'

'Brian never said a word to Damien; just stared at him

for a few seconds as though he didn't approve of him being here. He doesn't believe in that sort of thing.' She gave a sly smile. 'He says I spend far too much money on it, although I don't know what he's complaining about. He spends a fortune on his golf trips and that boat of his.'

'You have different priorities.'

'I suppose so.' She looked straight at Wesley. 'Are you married, Inspector?'

'He's spoken for, love,' said Gerry, standing up. 'If you remember anything else, you'll let us know, won't you?'

But Wesley hadn't quite finished. 'Did Damien say anything unusual before he left?'

Abigail frowned in concentration, pointedly ignoring Gerry, who was shifting from foot to foot, anxious to bring the interview to a close.

'He did say something that frightened me. When he was about to leave, he told me the hatred he felt in this house was so strong that if I stayed here, I might be in danger.'

25

'What did you make of her?' Gerry asked as soon as they were out of sight of Abigail Watkins' house. Wesley detected a note of anxiety in his voice.

'Something's troubling her.'

'Probably the captain's wife. I bet Damien told her he could shift her for a large fee, only he died before he could do the deed so she's stuck with her.' He snorted. 'I've lived a few doors down for years and I've never heard of number five being haunted.'

'Do you think our friend Damien, alias David, was a con man who was finished off by a disgruntled client?'

'Would people who consult psychics react like that?'

'A husband who's footing the bill might not be too pleased. I'll get someone to check out Brian Watkins. He struck me as the kind of man who wouldn't tolerate any nonsense.'

'Wouldn't he be more likely to demand his money back than resort to murder?'

When they reached the police station, they found that someone had erected a Christmas tree in the foyer in their absence and the civilian receptionist, who had replaced the traditional trusty desk sergeant a few years ago, was stringing it with lights.

'Just getting into the Christmas spirit,' the woman said when she saw Gerry looking at her efforts with a frown on his chubby face.

'It'll cheer the villains up when we take 'em down to the cells,' he muttered under his breath.

'Keep up the good work,' said Wesley, fearing the boss was about to come out with another Scrooge-like comment. He led the way up to the CID office, where Rachel stood to greet them.

'Janet Walsh called me from the train,' she said. 'She said she's just remembered something. One of Erica's old school friends came to Devon to work as a nanny. Her name was Bella.'

'Why wasn't this mentioned in the original investigation?'

'Because Bella wasn't in Devon at the time of Erica's disappearance. According to her parents, she'd gone away with her boyfriend for a week, so Janet never bothered mentioning it to the police.'

'So if she wasn't here, there'd be no reason for Erica to contact her.'

'That's what Janet thought at first. But now she says Erica might not have known she was away, because she remembers her mentioning that it was hard to get a mobile signal where Bella was living. So if Erica decided to look her up on the spur of the moment, there might have been no way of letting her know she'd arrived.'

'And Janet's only just thought of this?' said Gerry.

'Yes. She said she's been going over things in her mind on the journey and wondered whether it could be important.'

'Does she know where Bella was working?'

'She thinks it could have been somewhere near

Tradmouth, but she isn't sure. This could explain why Erica was wandering about near Petherham that night.'

It was just a theory but Wesley had known cases cracked by less promising leads. 'Does Mrs Walsh know where Bella is now?'

'Her family moved down south and she hasn't seen or heard of them for years.'

'What's the surname?'

'Brown.'

Gerry rolled his eyes. 'Great.'

'I've asked someone to try and trace them,' said Rachel, trying to sound positive. 'It's a long shot, but ...'

'It's worth checking out,' said Wesley. 'Thanks.'

'What do you think, Wes?' said Gerry once they were in his office. 'Has Rach started a wild goose chase?'

Wesley put his head in his hands, deep in thought. Then he looked up. 'There was no mention of a Bella in the diary we found in Erica's rucksack, but we didn't find a phone or an address book, did we? If we had, we might have discovered Bella Brown's details. Maybe the killer took them to stop us finding out.'

'You're letting your imagination run away with you, Wes. If anyone had thought to ask at the time, I'm sure it wouldn't have been hard to find her. Only she was away, so they didn't.' Gerry rolled his eyes again.

'Surely if she'd known anything, she would have come forward when Erica vanished.'

'You'd think so.'

'I'd still like to speak to her.'

'She might have changed her name by now,' said Gerry pessimistically. 'She could be anywhere. She might even be on the other side of the world.'

151

Wesley carried on talking, voicing his thoughts. 'I think this opens up new possibilities.'

'We don't even know if Bella was working in this area. Devon's a big county.'

'True, but it still seems odd to me that she didn't ask David Leeson to drop her on the main road. Why take a country lane?'

'I can think of a reason that has nothing to do with Bella Brown. If Leeson wanted to drive her to an isolated spot . . .'

'Florence Valery saw her after he claimed to have dropped her off.'

'He could easily have gone back to pick her up again. If he dropped her in the middle of nowhere, she'd be pretty desperate to get back on the Tradmouth road.'

Wesley knew that what Gerry was saying made sense. He could visualise the scene: the apologetic would-be attacker assuring the young hitch-hiker that he wouldn't try it on again; promising she'd be safe with him – and lying. 'That would mean that Damien Lee, alias David Leeson, becomes our main suspect. And he's dead.'

'What we need is a psychic.'

Wesley smiled. He was used to the boss's irreverent sense of humour. Others, including Chief Superintendent Noreen Fitton, sometimes didn't appreciate his wit. There were even some people who chose to take offence, but Wesley had no time for the po-faced.

'It might be worth organising a house-to-house in the Petherham and Stokeworthy area to see whether anybody employed a nanny called Bella Brown twelve years ago.'

'Don't forget Auntie Noreen's keeping a sharp eye on the budget.' Gerry rolled his eyes. 'Which reminds me,

I've got to give her an update. And once we release the fact that we're treating Damien Lee's death as murder, the press office is going to have their work cut out. I can see the headlines now.'

At that moment, a young uniformed constable rushed up to them, waving a statement form and wearing an eager expression on his freckled face. 'Sir, can I have a word?'

'Have as many as you like,' said Gerry. 'You look as though you've won the lottery. What is it?'

'I've found a discrepancy, sir,' the young man said, thrusting the sheet of paper into Gerry's outstretched hand.

Gerry fumbled in his pocket for his reading glasses and studied the statement for a few moments before passing it to Wesley. 'Someone's been telling us porkies,' he said with a hint of triumph.

'Jacob and Wendy Chalmers gave the Quayles a false address, and this vegan restaurant in Neston they claimed they were taking over doesn't exist.'

Wesley scanned the statement, then looked up at the young constable, who was hovering there, awaiting their verdict. 'Their car registration – did the Quayles make a note of it?'

'I'll give them a call,' the young man said eagerly.

'Thanks. If we can match their registration number to an address, we might discover exactly what they were up to.'

'What do you think, Wes?' Gerry said once the constable was out of earshot.

'I think the Chalmerses have some questions to answer.'

26

Jacob and Wendy Chalmers weren't the only guests at the psychic weekend Wesley wanted to find out more about. Brad Percy, who according to Corrine Malin had seemed more concerned with cars than spirits, owned an IT company in Exeter. He claimed he'd seen the weekend advertised on the internet and signed up for a laugh, as he put it. But the notion of attending such a weekend alone simply for his own amusement didn't ring true somehow. However, so far they'd found no link between Percy and the dead psychic.

Corrine Malin's story of being there to conduct research for her doctorate definitely checked out, and the other couple, Jennifer and Charlie Taylor, had indeed lost their son to a drugs overdose, a tragedy from which they'd never recovered.

Wesley was deep in thought when his phone rang and he saw Neil's name on the caller display. He answered, tempted by the prospect of a chat about something other than the murders of Erica Walsh and David Leeson.

Neil sounded breathless, as though he'd been hurrying, and there was an urgency in his greeting.

'You'll never guess what I've just found out,' he began.

'Surprise me.' Wesley had no time for guessing games.

'Corrine Malin and I have a mutual acquaintance. Jemima Baine.'

'So?'

'Corrine knew Jemima at university.' He paused like a magician about to reveal the climax of his most impressive trick. 'Jemima shared a flat with Erica Walsh.'

Wesley said nothing for a few moments while he took in this new snippet of information. It was on record that Erica's flatmate had been interviewed at the time of her disappearance, but she'd claimed that all she knew about Erica's plans for the Christmas break was that she intended to go to Tradmouth. He recalled from the file that her name had been Jem Wallace, not Jemima Baine. It was hardly his fault if he hadn't made the connection.

'Have you spoken to Jemima about it?'

'I thought I'd let you know first. Always happy to help the police with their enquiries,' he added cheerfully before the line went dead.

Wesley sat staring at his phone. Jemima Baine had examined Erica's remains; she'd handled her bones with professional calm while all the time she'd known her in life. She'd shared a flat with her and yet she'd shown no emotion, not even once the contents of the rucksack had revealed her identity. Now that he knew the two women had been flatmates, somehow her reaction seemed unnatural. And he needed to find out why.

Gerry had just returned from his meeting with the chief super, so Wesley walked over to his office. This was something he'd want to know.

Wesley didn't tell Jemima why he wanted to see her. He felt it would be best if he kept that as a surprise. He wanted to see her face when he revealed what he knew – and he wanted to hear how she'd explain her silence about knowing the victim.

Reluctantly she agreed to meet him in Exeter at five o'clock, making it clear she was a busy woman and could only spare him half an hour. Wesley didn't argue. He wanted her off her guard.

Rachel asked whether he wanted her to come with him, and after some thought he said yes. A change of scene would do them both good. Besides, he always valued her opinion.

The pub where they'd agreed to meet Jemima overlooked Exeter Cathedral, and as they approached the meeting place, they passed the ornate facade of the magnificent medieval building rising up beyond the expanse of the cathedral green. In the summer, tourists and students crowded onto the grass to enjoy the sunshine, but now in December, the green was crammed with the bustling Christmas market. People with coats firmly fastened against the cold thronged between brightly lit wooden huts in search of food, drink or festive gifts. If Wesley didn't have two murders to investigate he would have been tempted to join the cheerful scene but he knew Jemima Baine would be waiting. As soon as they walked into the pub, Wesley noticed that many of the tables were set for dinner, and the tempting aroma of food in the air reminded him that he was hungry. It wasn't long before he spotted Jemima sitting at a table in the corner, scrolling through her phone impatiently as though she resented the intrusion into her precious time. He felt a stab of irritation, and one glance at Rachel told him she shared his feelings. Wesley was determined to make sure Jemima co-operated, however inconvenient she might find it.

He greeted her before introducing Rachel, who received a cool, assessing look, as though she was a specimen in a lab.

After he'd bought drinks at the bar – orange juice for him and Rachel and a half-pint of bitter for Jemima – he returned to the table and sat down. It was Jemima who spoke first.

'This is about Erica, I take it.'

Wesley leaned forward. 'I can't understand why you didn't say anything about your relationship with her before. How could you have examined her bones and seen that red rucksack without declaring that you knew her?'

'You could have said something,' said Rachel reasonably. 'Even if you were wrong, nobody would have minded.'

Jemima gave her a withering look. 'I don't like being wrong.'

'What about once her ID was confirmed?' said Wesley.

'There was nothing I could tell you that you didn't already know, so there didn't seem much point in complicating matters.'

'OK, we'll leave that for now,' said Wesley, sensing Rachel's patience was wearing thin. 'Tell us about Erica.'

'To be honest, I never found her very interesting. She was always going on about how much she hated her stepfather. I know she had problems, but it did get a bit tedious.'

'You were her friend,' said Wesley. 'Friends usually share their problems.'

Jemima gave a tinkling laugh. Wesley had only met her in professional situations before and had formed no particular judgement about her personality. Now the real Jemima Baine was revealing herself and he didn't much like what he saw.

'I'd hardly describe her as a friend. I shared a flat with

157

her out of convenience and I never had much to do with her. She was far more *friendly* with the girl who lived downstairs.' The words were said with heavy meaning. If Jemima had been the type to wink, she would have done so. 'Her name was Corrine. You should speak to her.'

'We have already. She was very upset about Erica's death.'

'I'm not surprised,' Jemima said before taking a sip of beer. 'They were very ... close.' Some froth stuck to her upper lip, forming a moustache. To Wesley's disappointment, she realised and swiftly wiped it away.

'You called yourself Jem Wallace in those days.'

'Yes. I shortened my name to Jem when I was a student; not sure why now. Baine is my married name – and before you ask, the marriage only lasted a year. I'm divorced.'

Now that little mystery was cleared up, Wesley continued with the questions. 'Did Erica say anything to you before she went away?'

'Corrine had to go home – something to do with her mum having an operation – so there was no way Erica could spend a cosy Christmas with her. She couldn't face going home so she said she was going to Tradmouth to work in a hotel over the holidays. But I didn't take much notice, to tell you the truth.'

'Is there anything else you can remember? Did she mention a friend called Bella who was a nanny?'

Jemima screwed up her face as though she was making a great effort to remember. 'Now you come to mention it, on the morning she left, she said she might try and see an old school friend – she thought she might know somewhere she could stay while she looked for work or something like that. She was wittering on about not being able to get in touch with her – no signal or something – but said she might take

158

a chance and call on her anyway but I don't know if her name was Bella or what she did for a living. She said other things, but by that time I'd stopped listening. She could be a pain. I'm sorry she's dead, of course, but—'

'Why didn't you tell the police about her plans at the time?' Wesley was trying hard to keep the anger out of his voice.

For the first time, Jemima looked embarrassed. 'Maybe I should have done, but then she was seen in Falmouth, so I thought, what's the point?' She hesitated. 'The man I was seeing at the time convinced me it was best to keep out of it. She'd obviously moved on. I didn't think it was important. Why are you asking? Do you think this friend had something to do with her death?'

Wesley and Rachel walked out of the pub without answering.

Neil was satisfied that he'd done his public duty. Jemima Baine was undoubtedly beautiful; she radiated confidence and she was excellent at her job, but he'd never been attracted to her, either as a friend or as a potential lover. There was a coldness about her; a guarded quality that made him choose his words carefully whenever she was around, fearing her disdain should he say the wrong thing. People like that made him uncomfortable. And from the way Corrine had spoken about her, he suspected she'd felt the same when they'd lived in close proximity.

The survey of Petherham Mill was almost completed; the clock tower was the only part of the building left to examine, well away from the working looms and spinning machines. It was getting dark outside, but his colleagues were still up there, working by the light of their torches and a single dusty bulb that dangled sadly from the ceiling.

Although the tower had been painted on the outside during the renovation of the mill, the interior hadn't been touched. There'd been no need: the clock no longer worked and the little gabled tower was purely ornamental, a feature added by the original builders to relieve the uniformity of the mill's functional architecture and to house the bell and the clock that had once summoned the workers to their daily toil.

The rickety flight of steps leading up there was carpeted with dust, and Neil suspected that before the survey, nobody had been up there for many years. He climbed the stairs to join his entourage, and with the four of them in the small room at the top, the space immediately seemed crowded. As the others busied themselves finishing off the measuring, recording and photography, Neil circled the room examining the walls and the rafters above their heads. The workings of the clock were contained in a tall wooden cupboard that took up half of one wall; when he opened the door, he could see the pendulum dangling down and the wheels of the mechanism, rusted from disuse.

'I bet they could get this working again,' he said to nobody in particular, taking his torch from the pocket of his combat jacket. He shone it around the cupboard and saw something scratched on the wooden inner surface of the door.

'Have you read what's inside? We've taken photographs,' one of his colleagues said.

Neil's first thought was that the writing would be a list of the people whose job it was to attend to the clock. But he soon realised it was nothing of the sort.

I, Albert Waring, am an innocent man.

Look to Mill House if you would find the vile murderer.

'Neil, have a look at this.'

He swung round and saw his colleague standing at the far side of the little room, shining a torch beam onto the wall at an oblique angle. Letters scratched into the plaster stood out quite clearly. As he walked over, all activity around him stopped.

'Photograph it, will you,' he said quietly as he studied the words.

There is no escape for those chosen for death.

A curse upon this place and upon the house.

From the notebook of
Dr Christopher Cruckshank

12 June 1882

Yesterday I was summoned to Westral Hall, a
fine house in the classical style that stands just outside
Petherham on the Neston road. The family that lives
there is an ancient one, I am told, and the present
resident, a Mr Fitzterran, is said to be very wealthy. I
felt most gratified that my reputation had reached the ears
of people of such quality, so I saddled my horse and set
off right away.

    I had not been told the purpose of my visit, and I
was surprised to be greeted not by a servant but by a
young lady, handsomely dressed and very beautiful. She
introduced herself as Mrs Susannah Fitzterran, mistress
of the house. Her husband, she informed me, was many
years her senior and she wished me to attend him while
she was away in Bath as she feared for his health. Not
only that, but he had received threats from a gentleman
in Exeter who owed him a great sum of money. Her
husband, she said, was fortunate at the gaming tables,

and this created ill feeling amongst his less desirable
acquaintances.

I asked to see Mr Fitzterran but she told me he was
sleeping. Besides, he would disapprove of her concern for
him as he was a proud man.

I reassured the lady as best I could and noted
the dates when she would be in Bath. A man in my
profession, I told her, would always be a welcome visitor
to a lonely man.

27

Over breakfast on Tuesday morning, Pam told Wesley he was looking tired. He assured her he was fine because he didn't want to worry her. She'd had enough to deal with over the past couple of years, with her cancer diagnosis and her mother's accident. Besides, there was nothing wrong with him that wouldn't be cured by bringing his two murder cases to a swift conclusion and getting a few early nights before Christmas began in earnest.

'I'd better get going,' he said, bending to kiss her.

'It's a bit hard on Rachel,' she said unexpectedly. 'Having to work such long hours when she's only recently married and has a farm to help run as well.'

He was about to say Rachel was fine, but the words stuck in his throat. *Was* she fine? She seemed quieter than usual, and he knew her well enough to suspect something was wrong. But this was something he wasn't inclined to discuss with Pam.

'I'll probably be late home again. Sorry.'

Pam touched his hand just as Michael burst into the room, all clumsy limbs and blossoming hormones. He gave his father a teenage grunt of greeting and helped himself to cornflakes, spilling half the contents of his bowl over the worktop. Wesley ruffled his hair in a fatherly manner, only for his son to brush his hand away. He was getting too old for affection, or so he thought.

Wesley was leaving the kitchen when he heard the boy's voice behind him. 'You are going to come and see me in *Oliver!*, aren't you, Dad?'

He turned to face him. 'Try and stop me.'

As he let himself out of the front door, Amelia was coming down the stairs, neat in her school uniform. He kissed the top of her head and told her to have a good day at school. She responded by giving him a hug and telling him to take care, leaving Wesley with a warm glow that lasted all the way down the hill to the police station.

There was a buzz of excitement in the incident room when he arrived, and Gerry emerged from his office to greet him, stifling a yawn.

'We've found the Chalmerses,' he said. 'Luckily Jeremy Quayle notes down the registration numbers of his guests' cars. The registered owner of their white BMW is a John Camberland, address in Plympton. He owns a private investigation bureau in Plymouth; quite a successful outfit by the sound of it. His wife really is called Wendy, by the way. At least that bit's true.'

'Why join the weekend under an assumed name? And why lie to us?'

'We won't know unless we ask.' Gerry checked his watch. 'You go with Rach and have a word with them. She'll be glad to escape the office for a couple of hours. She's looking peaky.' He frowned. 'I keep thinking about Jemima Baine and the way she examined those bones without batting an eyelid when she knew who they belonged to. Why didn't she say anything?'

'That's the million-dollar question.'

'You spoke to her. Think she knows more than she's letting on?'

'I'm keeping an open mind, Gerry.' Wesley glanced at the clock on the wall. 'Better go and see what the Camberlands have to say for themselves.'

As Gerry had predicted, Rachel was keen to abandon her paperwork for a trip out to Plymouth. They drove in silence for a while before he spoke.

'Can't be easy helping to run the farm and doing this job.'

'I manage.'

'The boss thinks you look tired.'

'The boss should mind his own bloody business.'

Wesley was surprised at the bitterness in her words. He was tempted to ask her what was wrong, but thought better of it. If something was amiss between her and Nigel, it was probably best if he didn't enquire too closely.

She'd chosen to do the driving, and as they hurtled along the A38, Wesley seized the opportunity to get things straight in his head. He still couldn't grasp the link between Erica Walsh's death and the more recent murder of David Leeson, the man who'd picked her up when she was hitch-hiking all those years ago. But there had to be a connection. Coincidences did happen, but not often in his experience.

Camberland Investigations occupied the first floor of a tall modern building overlooking the harbour, with views of Plymouth Hoe where Francis Drake had famously played his game of bowls before sailing off to tackle the Spanish Armada.

'He must be doing well,' said Rachel as she gazed up at

the towering example of modern architecture in front of them. 'A lot of private investigators are ex-cops. Wonder if he used to be in the job.'

'Let's go and find out.'

They took the stairs. Wesley was loath to admit that travelling in a lift made him feel claustrophobic, so he used the excuse that walking was healthier, and Rachel didn't question his decision.

The offices of Camberland Investigations were as sleek and modern as Wesley had expected, but the reception area was furnished with a venerable chesterfield sofa that wouldn't have seemed out of place in a gentlemen's club. The receptionist, a capable-looking middle-aged lady with bobbed blonde hair, sat at an antique oak partner's desk, and a Victorian bentwood hatstand completed the look, suggesting that Camberland had attempted to create a reliably old-fashioned atmosphere amidst the concrete and glass surroundings.

When Wesley introduced himself, the receptionist told him apologetically that Mr Camberland was with a client, but if they'd like to wait ten minutes, he would see them. She offered coffee, which was gratefully accepted. It was hardly appropriate to make plans for the coming interview under the woman's watchful eye, so they contented themselves with studying the magazines on the coffee table in front of them. Wesley selected *Devon Life*, while Rachel opted for *Hello!*, flicking through the pages of flawless glamour but hardly registering the contents.

The ten minutes passed quickly, and when Wesley saw the door behind the reception desk opening, he stood up. He'd heard his colleagues describe Jacob Chalmers as a New Age vegan in jeans and a hand-knitted sweater. But the man who stood in the doorway, shaking hands with a thin, grey woman, had neatly cut hair and wore a sharp suit. Disguises were something he hadn't expected to find outside the pages of the more old-fashioned kind of crime novel, but it seemed they were a tool of this particular private eye's trade. He found himself wishing that CID could have some fun with the dressing-up box occasionally, though it wasn't something he felt inclined to mention to Rachel.

Camberland took his time saying farewell to his client, holding her hand in both of his and murmuring sympathetic reassurances like an old-fashioned family doctor. Once the woman had left, he nodded to his receptionist before inviting his visitors to join him in his office.

Wesley let Rachel go in first, hanging back to study his surroundings. The office, like the outer reception area, was furnished with antiques. Camberland must have picked up on his interest, because his first words were: 'I try to create an atmosphere of reassurance and reliability. The old-fashioned solicitor's office look, although I draw the line at high desks and quill pens. It's set-dressing really, manufacturing emotions. Do take a seat.'

'Very effective,' said Wesley as he sank into a padded leather chair. Camberland's voice was accentless and businesslike, in contrast to the slight cockney whine it had been reported that he'd used at Mill House. Again Wesley was impressed by the man's acting abilities.

'You lied to the police when you were interviewed at Mill House. That's a serious matter,' he said, watching Camberland's face.

The private investigator leaned back in his chair, apparently relaxed. 'I'm sorry about that. The truth is, it would have blown my cover, and as I knew absolutely nothing about that poor man's death, I didn't think it would matter too much.'

'You must have known we'd find out you weren't who you said you were.'

'As far as witnesses go, I didn't think we were that import-ant. I can only repeat that I'm sorry to have misled your colleagues, but wasn't Damien Lee's death an unfortunate accident?' A frown suddenly appeared on his smoothly shaven face. 'Wendy and I won't get into trouble, will we?'

'As my colleague said, lying to the police is a serious matter, Mr Camberland,' said Rachel.

The man bowed his head, the picture of contrition. 'I realise that. I'm very sorry.'

'If you come clean now, it will count in your favour,' said Wesley reasonably, playing good cop.

Camberland thought for a few moments. 'Very well. I was there on behalf of Brad Percy's wife. She'd been checking his emails and saw the booking. She's suspected for some time that he's been seeing another woman, and she hired me to catch him at it. I reckoned it would be more convin-cing to go as a couple, and we thought up our cover story and dressed appropriately. Wendy and I were once in the acting business, you see. We spent many years treading the boards before we decided on a change of career, so role play comes naturally to us. We didn't use our own names, of course.' A smug look appeared on his face. 'Camberland Investigations is rather well known around these parts.'

'Did you find anything untoward?'

He shook his head, disappointed. 'Nothing apart from catching him chatting up that student woman – Corrine – although I don't think she was interested. He was bending her ear about his car, but she didn't look too impressed. As a chat-up line, I don't think it was a winner. However, I did overhear Percy on his phone, possibly to the woman his wife had in mind. He was begging her to reconsider, and I got the impression they'd arranged to meet there but she'd changed her mind for some reason. I thought I'd try and slip the phone out of his jacket pocket if he left it lying around and make a note of the number, but I never got the chance.'

Brad Percy's motive for taking part in the weekend at Mill House had been puzzling Wesley, and now this particular part of the jigsaw was beginning to fit together. It was a lovers' tryst in the last place Percy's wife would suspect.

'That's it, Inspector, Sergeant. I've told you everything I know.'

'We'd like to speak to your wife.'

'She's out on an assignment at the moment. This is a family business. Our daughter's just joined the firm too,' Camberland said with pride. 'You can speak to Wendy if you wish, but I'm sure she won't have anything to add to what I've already told you.'

Wesley suspected he was probably right. But he'd ask someone to have a word with Mrs Camberland just in case.

'Now that you've come clean with us about your reason for being at Mill House, is there anything you can tell us about the death of Damien Lee? Anything at all you might have thought of since you made your initial statement?'

There was a long pause before Camberland leaned forward as though he was about to share a confidence. 'Well, for a start, I don't think he was much of a psychic. He swallowed all that guff we told him about needing my dead sister's approval for opening a vegan restaurant. If he'd really had psychic powers, he would have rumbled us straight away, wouldn't he?'

'I suppose so,' said Wesley, sensing the man still had more to say.

'He kept himself very much to himself – didn't mix with the punters unless it was during one of the designated sessions. He even took his meals in his room. But I was looking out of the window after the session on the Saturday evening and I saw him going outside. It was dark, and the lighting wasn't too good around there, but he was walking towards the mill. He stood there for a while looking at the building, then he walked away. That's it really.'

'You didn't see him being attacked?'

'Attacked? I thought he'd fallen into the water and drowned. If I'd seen anything at all suspicious, I would have said something. Of course I would.'

'The post-mortem revealed that he'd been stabbed in the back. It was definitely murder.'

Camberland took a deep breath, as though the news had come as a shock. 'I'm sorry, I wish I could help you, but I saw nothing. Bit of a professional failure on my part, I'm afraid,' he added with a rueful smile.

'Were any of your fellow guests out of the house at the same time as Lee?'

'I don't think so. I only heard the front door close once, so I don't think it could have been anybody from the house.'

'What about the back door?'

'I didn't hear anything. I'm sorry. But one thing I can tell you: the owners of Mill House – the Quayles – definitely didn't go outside, because five minutes later I went downstairs to fetch something I'd left in the drawing room and they were both there clearing up and getting ready for the next day.' The phone on his desk rang and he picked it up. 'My next client's just arrived, so if you'll excuse me . . .'

Wesley caught Rachel's eye. In spite of the initial deception, he was convinced Camberland had told them everything he knew. At least he'd explained what Brad Percy had been doing there, and possibly cleared the Quayles of suspicion, so their journey hadn't been a complete waste of time. But the question of who had killed David Leeson still remained unanswered.

As they left the office building, Wesley zipped up his coat against the icy wind blowing in off the water.

28

'Petherham should be the sort of place where strangers get noticed,' said Wesley. 'It shouldn't be this hard to catch Damien Lee's killer – or should we be calling him David Leeson?'

The lane had narrowed still further and Rachel switched the windscreen wipers to maximum speed as she peered ahead in the gloom. Eventually they reached a B road, wide enough for two vehicles to pass comfortably, and Wesley saw her hands relax on the steering wheel. There was a long silence before she spoke again.

'My parents are still really upset about Erica being buried on their land. Mum says she can't stop thinking about it. According to Dad, she even cut out a photograph of her from the paper. She rang last night to ask if we've caught the killer, and I couldn't lie to her, could I?'

'We'll get him,' said Wesley with an optimism he couldn't quite feel. 'Maybe something will have come in while we've been out.'

'She's worried about the family being out in the fields alone. Half the work on the farm's done in darkness at this time of year.'

'As far as we can tell, we've found everything that was

deposited at the burial site, so there's nothing for the killer to come back for.'

'That's what I told her, but it makes no difference.'

The rest of the journey passed in silence until they reached the outskirts of Tradmouth.

'A lot of people have got their Christmas trees up already,' Wesley commented, looking at the twinkling lights in many downstairs windows.

'It gets earlier every year.'

'I promised we'd put ours up this weekend, but the way things are going, Pam and the kids are going to have to do it on their own. Have you and Nigel put yours up yet?'

Rachel said nothing, and Wesley guessed her mind was still on her parents – and whoever had buried Erica Walsh on their land. When they reached the police station, they passed the tree in the foyer, and Wesley noticed that some wit had hung a pair of handcuffs from a branch near the top. He knew Gerry would appreciate the joke, but the same probably couldn't be said of the chief superintendent.

As soon as they reached the incident room, Gerry appeared at his office door to greet them. Wesley noticed that he was looking pleased with himself. 'How did it go?'

Rachel returned to her desk while Wesley brought him up to date.

'Why the hell didn't Camberland come clean when he made his statement? Does he think he's above the law?'

'He assumed Lee's death was an accident so he didn't think there was any point. That's what he claims, anyway.'

'Believe him?'

'I think I did. He's also solved the mystery of what Brad Percy was doing there. That was bothering me.'

Gerry grunted. 'Me too. Was he telling the truth when he said he didn't see who killed Leeson that night?'

'As far as I could tell. Why would he lie?'

'Unless he's trying to pull the wool over our eyes.'

'That's not the impression I got, but I always keep an open mind.'

'Mmm. Let's send someone round to speak to Percy, though if Camberland's to be believed, he's probably in the clear.'

'Anything come in while I've been out?'

'We've found an address for Lynette Preston, the woman Sheryl Lee thinks her husband might have been on his way to meet when he gave Erica Walsh a lift. She's running a bar in Morbay. I thought you and I could pay her a visit.'

Wesley glanced up at the office clock. It was coming up to 2.30, and his stomach was reminding him that he hadn't eaten.

'We can grab something to eat while we're out,' said Gerry, as though he'd read his mind. 'My tummy thinks my throat's been cut.'

Wesley drove to Morbay, taking the car ferry rather than the long way round via Neston because the queues were usually short at that time of day. As they chugged across the river, he saw the steam train coming into Queenswear station, all lit up for the festive season and the annual Santa train rides; a reminder that life went on outside the world of crime and death.

The bar Lynette Preston managed stood on Morbay's promenade. Here too the council had strung lights between the lamp posts, but the drizzling rain was doing its best to ruin any festive cheer they might have created.

Beyond the promenade the grey sea churned relentlessly, and Wesley shivered at the sight.

'That chippy's still open,' said Gerry, looking longingly at the steamed-up windows of the chip shop next to Lynette's bar. 'Come on. We're growing lads. We need sustenance.' Wesley didn't argue.

They ate their fish and chips in the car, which Wesley knew would stink for the next few days, before wiping their greasy fingers on tissues and setting off for the unimaginatively named Rose and Crown.

It was the sort of establishment Wesley might have expected to find in a Spanish tourist resort – the quintessential English pub. The interior was covered with fibreglass beams and plastic horse brasses, and the carpet, which had once been red, was now an unhealthy shade of brown and threadbare in places. Some patrons were playing the garishly lit games machines at the edge of the large room, but most were sitting at the scattered tables, sipping sadly from pints of lager. It was hardly Wesley's idea of the perfect pub.

The woman behind the bar looked wary as they approached, as though she recognised them as policemen and expected trouble.

'We're looking for Lynette Preston,' said Wesley.

'You've found her. What's this about?' It was more of a challenge than a question.

She was a big woman, with dyed black hair, and an array of tattoos up her bare arms. Wesley's first thought was that she wasn't the kind of woman it would be wise to argue with. He showed his ID, made the introductions and smiled reassuringly.

'You might have heard on the news that we've found the

remains of a girl who went missing twelve years ago – her name was Erica Walsh.'

Lynette sniffed and picked up a dirty glass that someone had deposited on the bar. 'I heard about it. What's it got to do with me?'

'There's been another death, this time in a village called Petherham,' said Wesley. 'A psychic who was using the name Damien Lee. His real name was David Leeson.'

She put the glass back down on the bar with exaggerated care. 'Yeah. I heard about it on the news.'

'You knew him.' It was a statement rather than a question.

She nodded. 'We were an item for a while – met up north when he was doing the pubs and clubs and kept in touch. Met up the odd time, as you do. He was a singer back then.'

'We know that, love,' said Gerry.

'I was gobsmacked when I saw him on the telly doing his psychic act. Very convincing, he was.'

'When did you last see him?'

'A long time ago. He became too famous to keep in touch with the likes of me.'

'Was it twelve years ago?'

She gave a long sigh. 'Something like that. A lot of water's passed under the bridge since then. Nasty divorce. Three years managing this hole.'

'You haven't heard from David more recently?'

'Like I said, he became a celebrity. And celebrities don't mix with ordinary mortals who work in run-down bars in seaside resorts.'

'Let's get back to the last time you saw him,' said Wesley, fearing she was in danger of becoming maudlin. 'Was it twelve years ago? December 2008?'

'Yeah. Must have been.' There was something guarded about her answer.

'What happened?'

'He was doing a gig in Morbay and he stayed the night at my place on the way. The sex was pretty average. The spark had gone, you see. When he left, he made it quite clear it was over. Said he'd decided to stay with Sheryl.'

'We've heard you were working near Tradmouth,' said Wesley. 'Where was that exactly?'

'In that village you mentioned – Petherham. It's a one-horse place with a church and a pub, you know the sort of thing. There was an old mill there too, but it was closed back then. I hear it's open again now – saw an article about it in a magazine.' She looked Wesley in the eye. 'They said on the news that he got caught up in the water wheel. Is that right?'

Wesley nodded. 'What were you doing in Petherham?'

'Working at the pub, the Fisherman's Arms. The landlord was trying to turn it into a gastropub, without much success. I was doing the lot: waiting at table, serving behind the bar. Bloody slave driver, he was.'

'It's a nice pub,' said Wesley. 'I've eaten there a couple of times.'

'I hear it's thriving now. New landlord took over a couple of years ago – Simon Pussett, his name is. He came from somewhere up north and bought the place outright, did it up and got a decent chef in. Nice if you've got the funds to do it.' She looked round her own sad establishment and gave a shrug of resignation.

'Did David just turn up out of the blue?' Wesley asked, wanting to get the conversation back on track.

'No, he let me know he was coming down so I arranged to take the evening off.'

'You were living in at the pub?'

'No. The landlord back then owned a cottage nearby that he let staff use, so I was staying there. Why are you asking all these questions? Wasn't Dave's death an accident?'

'We don't think so.'

'You're saying someone pushed him in?'

Wesley didn't answer.

'What the hell was he doing in Petherham? I don't understand.'

'He was taking part in a psychic weekend at Mill House. It's a B&B now. You know it?'

She nodded slowly. 'Yeah, though it wasn't a B&B back then. There was some tragedy while I was there. Woman killed herself and her kid.'

'You knew them?'

'Nah. I was working all the hours God sent behind the bar so I didn't get to know anyone in the village apart from the pub regulars. Besides, I was only there over the Christmas season – I took a job in Neston once New Year was over 'cause I couldn't put up with that bloody landlord and his wandering hands any more.'

'People tell bar staff things. You must have heard some gossip about the woman's death,' said Wesley, earning himself a curious look from the DCI.

'Only people saying how terrible it was – woman doing that and taking her little kid with her. I mean, how could anyone do that? Bloody wicked, if you ask me. And just before Christmas and all.' She tutted and picked up another glass, a clean one this time, which she began polishing enthusiastically with a grubby tea towel.

'The woman's husband still lives at Mill House. He married again.'

'Good for him. If it was me, I'd have moved miles away.'

'Me too,' said Gerry quietly. 'Dave gave a lift to a girl on his way to Petherham that night. Did he tell you about it?'

'He said he'd picked up a hitch-hiker – some girl on her way to Tradmouth. She told him she was going to work there over Christmas.'

'Did he say anything else about her?'

'He said she was going to visit a mate she knew from school before she went to Tradmouth.'

'Where did this mate live?'

'Don't ask me. She was going to look for a job but she'd decided to drop in on this mate first. That's all he said.'

'The girl he picked up was Erica Walsh.'

Lynette froze. 'He never mentioned her name. You don't think he had something to do with her disappearance?'

'Do you?'

She didn't answer for a while, turning away to put some glasses on the shelf behind her. Wesley guessed she needed time to consider her reply, and his patience was rewarded when she turned and leaned across the bar as though she was about to share a confidence.

'When he arrived that night, he was ... distant. As though he had something on his mind. When I asked him, he wouldn't tell me at first, but I kept on at him until he finally admitted he'd picked up the girl.'

'You think something happened?'

There was another long silence. 'I wouldn't be surprised if he'd tried it on with her. He said he'd dropped her in the middle of nowhere; why would he do that if she wasn't trying to get away from him?'

'Was he the type who'd behave like that?'

180

She gave Wesley a pitying look. 'He was a man. They're all the type.'

'Someone saw Erica Walsh after he dropped her off.'

'Who's to say he didn't go back and pick her up again? Dave was never one to take no for an answer. I felt sorry for Sheryl, if you want the truth.'

'Do you think he could have killed Erica Walsh?'

'If she'd given him the come-on then turned him down, it wouldn't surprise me if he'd lost his temper and acted on the spur of the moment. Maybe that's why his performance in bed that night wasn't up to standard,' she added bitterly. 'If he had her body in the boot of his car, it would explain a lot, wouldn't it?'

A large man with a shaved head sidled up to the bar and banged down his empty glass. 'Fill that up, my lover,' he said, pointedly ignoring Wesley and Gerry as though he thought they'd been monopolising the barmaid too long.

'If you're done, I'd better get on,' said Lynette, giving the customer a bright smile.

'Thanks, love. We might be back,' said Gerry, making it sound like a threat.

From the notebook of
Dr Christopher Cruckshank

25 June 1882

It is said around Petherham that Fitzterran is an unpleasant man who married a young woman whose family fortunes had waned. Her father insisted on the match and the unfortunate bride has been living miserably ever since.

I met Mrs Stephens outside the church and it seemed that she too had learned of my visit to Westral Hall. There seems to be little that happens in Petherham that escapes her notice. I said I would show her some of the photographs I had taken of the people of Petherham when next we met, and she seemed most interested.

I am beginning to feel at home in the village at last and am growing accustomed to the sight of the mill next to the river, its bulk overshadowing the little cottages round about. The water wheel turns relentlessly and I cannot help glancing at Mill House opposite. News has reached me that Josiah Partridge is to marry again, and his bride is to be his daughter's former governess.

I went walking down by the creek this evening. It would be an agreeable place were it not for the lime kilns on the bank near the village. The men working there touched their caps as I passed, and I nodded to them and carried on. The bank further on is wooded and quiet, with a steep drop to the water. I stood and watched the boats gliding down the river laden with their cargoes, wondering who would be the next to die in Petherham.

29

'Rachel, is that you?' Stella Tracey always asked the same question, as though it was a possibility that her daughter's mobile might be answered by a stranger.

'It's me, Mum. What is it? I'm at work. I'm busy.'

Stella hesitated for a few moments before replying. 'I'm worried about Eli.'

The taciturn Eli had worked as a labourer at Little Barton Farm for almost thirty years, and he lived in one of the Traceys' tied cottages, not far from the spot where Erica Walsh had been buried. He was small and wiry, with a face lined and worn from working out of doors in all weathers. He was a man of few words, and Rachel couldn't remember ever having a conversation with him that went beyond a grunt of greeting. It was hard to guess his age and his past was a mystery, but her father had always said he was a reliable worker; an invaluable asset to the farm.

'Why?' she asked, curious. Eli had been interviewed along with everyone else, but his statement had said little. He'd seen nothing and heard nothing.

'Our Tom was chatting to him and said it was a pity he hadn't seen anything around the time that poor girl disappeared, seeing as how he only lives fifty yards along

184

the lane from where the tree came down. Then Eli said he thought there'd been a car parked in the lane but he couldn't be sure of the date. Tom told him he should tell the police, but he said he thought it was just a courting couple or someone stopping to answer a call of nature.' She paused. 'I wanted to ask you what you thought. He's been behaving a bit strangely ever since those bones turned up.'

'He never mentioned this in his statement.'

'Between you and me, I think the police make him nervous.'

Rachel was surprised by her mother's candour. Her revelation added to the air of mystery that had clung to Eli ever since his arrival at the farm all those years ago.

'Why doesn't he like the police?'

'There are some things people prefer to keep private, my love. He's never told us and we've never asked.'

'Don't suppose he got the make or reg of this car?'

'Not that he told Tom.'

'I'll come over and have a word with him,' she said. 'He knows me.'

When she'd ended the call, she sat at her desk for a while, deep in thought. Eli had been a permanent, if distant, feature in her life from childhood and she'd never given his presence much thought. But now she tapped his name into her computer.

The photograph that appeared was of a young man in his late teens, but even though it had been taken thirty-five years ago, it was still recognisable. Eli Jelkes, then a resident of Bideford in the north of the county, had been convicted of attacking a woman in 1984, and had served four months of an eight-month sentence.

*

Wesley kept thinking about the interview with Lynette Preston. Because of Florence Valery's sighting of Erica, David Leeson had moved to the bottom of the list of potential suspects for her murder. But now they had to face the possibility that he might have turned his car around and picked Erica up again. Perhaps, as Lynette had suggested, his advances were rejected and things got out of hand. Perhaps the solution to the case was simple after all. And maybe someone had taken revenge on David for her death – which meant his killer was someone who knew exactly what had happened that night.

As soon as he entered the incident room, Rachel rose to greet him. 'Wes, can I have a word?'

She looked uneasy, and he wondered what was coming.

'Of course.' He perched on the edge of her desk, and she sat down again, looking around as though she didn't want to be overheard.

'I've had a call from my mum. One of the men who works on the farm told my brother he saw a car on the lane around the time Erica disappeared.'

'Don't suppose he got the registration number?'

'No such luck. But Mum says he's been behaving a bit oddly since the bones turned up. I said I'd go and have a word.'

'You think he knows something about Erica's death?'

Rachel studied her fingernails. 'That's what's worrying me, Wes. I don't know if . . . '

'If what?'

'Eli's worked on the farm since I was a kid, but he's always been a bit of an enigma, if you know what I mean, and my dad's never asked questions because he's a good worker. He's never been in any trouble while he's been working for us, but . . . ' She raised her eyes to meet Wesley's. 'I thought I'd check his name to see if anything came up, and it turns out he has a record for violence – attacked a woman in Bideford in 1984.'

'Do you want me to come with you when you speak to him?'

'It's probably better if I go alone. He knows me.'

'Be careful.'

'I will,' she said. She was glad he cared enough to issue the warning, but she was a married woman now, and those days of mutual attraction should be over. The fact that she found the idea depressing made her uneasy.

The phone on Wesley's desk rang, and when he picked it up, he heard the voice of Janet Walsh, who was now back in Leeds. According to Rachel, she'd been anxious to return because she needed the comfort of familiar people and surroundings, something Wesley could understand.

'What can I do for you, Mrs Walsh?' he asked gently.

'When I got home I decided to sort out some things in the loft. I wanted to keep busy to take my mind off . . . well, you know. Anyway, I came across a letter to Erica from Bella Brown. You remember? Her friend I told you about who was working as a nanny in Devon. It mentions the name of her boyfriend at the time, and I wondered . . . '

Wesley suspected that any relationship Bella had had twelve years ago probably hadn't lasted. Even so, he asked the boyfriend's name.

'It was Carl. In the letter, Bella says they were getting engaged and that he'd just applied to join Devon and Cornwall Police. I don't know if that's any help.'

'It might be a great help, Mrs Walsh. Thank you. Is there an address on the letter?'

'Afraid not. She just said she had no phone signal where she was so she had to write. Sorry.'

'That's OK.'

Despite the lack of address, he felt a glimmer of fresh hope. If he could track down an officer called Carl in the area, he might make some progress.

30

When Wesley asked DC Rob Carter to make a list of all officers called Carl serving in Devon and Cornwall Police, Rob looked at him as though he was mad. The young detective constable had a preference for the flashier side of policing – car chases and stakeouts – so Wesley thought the menial task would do him good. Boredom, so he'd heard, could be therapeutic.

At 4.30, Gerry suggested that they both leave at a reasonable time that evening and get an early night. They'd make a fresh start in the morning. Wesley was looking forward to getting home in time to have dinner with the children when he heard the DCI's phone ring. A short time later, Gerry called him into his office. There was a wide grin on his face, so Wesley suspected the news, whatever it was, was good.

'I've just had someone from West Yorkshire on, Wes. They've found Barry Clegg. We need to go up and have a word.'

'He's still in Leeds?'

'No. They made some enquiries and found he's moved to Liverpool. Shouldn't be hard to track him down.'

Gerry had greeted the news with obvious glee. He

never passed up on a chance to visit his home city; he had a large number of relatives there, not to mention his daughter. But Wesley found it hard to share his enthusiasm.

'I suppose you'll want to go up there yourself. If you stay overnight, you'll have time to see Alison too.'

Gerry's smile widened. 'Didn't I say, Wes? She's agreed to come down and spend Christmas here.'

'Have you cleared that with Rosie?'

'Rosie's spending Christmas Day with her new boyfriend, so it'll be fine.'

'Maybe we can get someone from Merseyside to interview Barry Clegg,' Wesley said hopefully.

'Now that we know he wasn't at home when Erica disappeared, he's got to be our prime suspect. I want to hear what he has to say for himself – look him in the eye and see if he's lying. If Merseyside can come up with an address, we'll set off first thing tomorrow. Tell Pam you'll be spending the night. Rach is more than capable of dealing with things here. We can go and see if they've put a blue plaque on my old house yet,' Gerry added, his eyes glowing at the prospect of a journey to his former stamping ground.

However, his plans were to come to nothing. Half an hour later, Merseyside Police called to say that Barry Clegg was no longer at his old Liverpool address and there was no record of him elsewhere in the area. His last address had been owned by a church in the Dingle area of Liverpool, and the woman the officer had spoken to there had referred to him as the Reverend Clegg and said he'd moved to the Midlands. Was Wesley sure it was the same person?

He replaced the receiver and sat staring into space for a while, turning over the possibilities in his mind. He was starting to suspect that they'd been chasing the wrong Barry Clegg, but they had to make sure.

An hour later, after breaking the news to Gerry, and trying to ignore the look of disappointment on his face, there was good news from the constable who'd been stuck on the phone making calls to various parts of the country. It was the church angle that had provided the break-through. A Reverend Clegg had been found in charge of a church in Gloucester; further enquiries had confirmed that he had formerly been in Liverpool, in an area close to the docks, and before that he'd been a businessman in the Leeds area; something to do with cars. Wesley said they'd travel up to see him first thing the next day.

Although the promised early night hadn't turned out to be quite as early as he'd hoped, he was home by seven. When he broke the news to Pam that he needed to be up at the crack of dawn because he and Gerry were going up the M5 to interview a suspect in Gloucester, she said that at least if he was with Gerry he couldn't get into too much mischief. She'd always had a soft spot for his boss, and the feeling was mutual. He hadn't told her that Gerry had mentioned retirement, partly because it was something he was trying not to think about, and talking about it would make it real.

The next morning he did the driving, as he always did. Gerry claimed he saved his own navigational skills for the water. Wesley had never enquired too closely as to the reason he never got behind a wheel. Gerry had said once that he'd passed his driving test when he was twenty-one, but after that the subject had been closed. Wesley wondered whether it had something to do with his late wife Kathy's death having been caused by a carelessly driven car, but it was something he'd never been able to bring himself to ask.

They set out at 7.30, their journey slowed by a tedious cocktail of roadworks and heavy traffic around Bristol, and because of the delays it was approaching lunchtime by the time they reached Gloucester. Wesley assumed they'd drive straight to Barry Clegg's address, but Gerry had other ideas.

'I'm starving,' the DCI announced as they drove past a row of shops on the outskirts. 'There's a place. Look.' He pointed to a café that had rather optimistically placed a couple of chairs and a small table outside in defiance of the cold. Once Wesley had found a parking space, they filled up with soup, sandwiches and a warming cup of tea before driving on towards the city, following the satnav's imperious directions.

Barry Clegg's address turned out to be on a council estate just past a run-down parade of shops, some boarded up.

'Not the most picturesque part of the city,' said Wesley. 'It's number thirty-two. And it's got a name as well as a number. St Bridget's. I just hope we've got the right man. Maybe we should have sent one of the local uniforms to check him out before we came all this way.'

'And lose the element of surprise, Wes? I'm surprised at you.'

Wesley slowed the car to a crawl, peering at the numbers on the doors. Soon he saw a gap in the houses and realised there was a small church set back from the road behind rusty railings. Built of red brick, it looked considerably older than the surrounding buildings, and there was a cheerful banner over the entrance: *Welcome to St Bridget's. Come unto me all who are heavy laden and I will give you rest.*

'The Reverend Clegg. Is he some sort of con man, or what?' said Gerry as Wesley stopped the car.

'Let's go and find out.'

The church door was shut, but when Wesley tried the handle, it opened smoothly and they found themselves in a small, brightly painted lobby. Ahead of them they saw a pair of swing doors, the frosted glass glowing with light from the church beyond.

They heard the familiar sound of a Christmas carol – 'Silent Night' – and the door swung open to reveal a small church with pine pews, and stark white walls decorated with colourful banners. The choir lined up in front of the plain altar consisted mainly of young people, along with a few pensioners. The woman conducting them didn't turn as they entered, so they waited until the carol was finished before approaching her.

'Excuse me, we're looking for Barry Clegg,' said Wesley.

'You mean the pastor,' the woman said cheerfully. 'That's him over there.' She pointed to a man at the side of the platform adjusting the microphone on a wooden lectern.

He was good-looking, in his fifties, with a shock of black hair streaked with grey. His lithe body suggested that he kept himself fit, and tattoos were visible on his neck and protruding from the sleeves of his sweatshirt. Unlike Wesley's brother-in-law, Mark, he looked nothing like a clergyman.

Gerry allowed Wesley to make the first approach.

'Excuse me, Mr Clegg?' he said tentatively.

The man turned and flashed a beaming smile. 'That's me. What can I do for you?'

'Barry Clegg?'

'Around here they call me Pastor, but Barry will do.' The smile was still there, and Wesley wondered whether it would last once they'd revealed the reason for their visit.

'I'm Detective Inspector Peterson, and this is my colleague Detective Chief Inspector Heffernan. We've come up from Devon. Can we have a word in private?'

The calm smile slipped for a split second, then reappeared as he led them to an office-cum-vestry at the side of the church.

'Do take a seat,' he said, making himself comfortable behind a large desk. 'Devon? You're a bit off your patch, aren't you? How can I help you?'

The innocence of the question suggested that what Wesley had to say would come as a shock. Either that or the man was a good actor.

'I don't know whether you've heard that human remains have been found on farmland in south Devon – near the town of Tradmouth.'

'I don't pay much attention to the news, Inspector. It's invariably bad and I have better things to do.'

'Twelve years ago you were living with a woman called Janet Walsh in Leeds. Her daughter, Erica, went missing in the Tradmouth area. She'd travelled down there to look for a job in a hotel over Christmas.' He paused, watching Clegg's face, but his expression gave nothing away. 'She told a friend she didn't want to spend Christmas at home because she didn't get on with you.'

Clegg nodded sadly. 'I believe that's what she told her mother, too.'

'I understand you threatened to kill her.'

Clegg swallowed hard. 'I was a different person in those days, Inspector, and when I remember some of the things I did, it makes me cringe with shame. Five years ago I had a heart attack – a near-death experience, you could say – and the man you see before you now isn't the man Erica hated. I found the Lord – or rather He found me – and I made a new beginning. If I were to come face to face with Janet now, I'd beg her forgiveness . . . if she could find it in her heart to see me.'

'I think that might be pushing it,' muttered Gerry. It was clear to Wesley that he hadn't swallowed the man's account of his miraculous conversion.

'You became a pastor,' said Wesley.

'I wanted to serve in any way I could, and I discovered that I had a gift for leadership.' The words were humble, but Wesley thought he could detect a hint of pride behind them; and pride, he knew from his Sunday school days, was one of the deadly sins.

'Can we talk about Erica's disappearance? I was told you were away from home around that time.'

For a moment the man looked uncomfortable, then the half-smile reappeared on his lips. 'I really can't remember. It's a long time ago.'

'We've spoken to Janet. She remembers. You see, Mr Clegg, the human remains we found belong to Erica. She was murdered and buried in an isolated spot. That's why we need to establish your whereabouts so we can eliminate you from our enquiries.'

The smile vanished. 'Poor Janet must be devastated. I'd always assumed that Erica chose to disappear. She was seen in Falmouth, so I told Janet she must have chosen to make a new life for herself in Cornwall, and not to worry.'

His words reminded Wesley that they still hadn't made any progress with the Falmouth connection. Who had been using Erica's debit card? And who had claimed to have seen her? This was something he needed to follow up when he got back to Tradmouth.

'We're working on the assumption the Falmouth sighting was false. Can you produce an alibi for the time of her disappearance?'

'Surely your lot checked it out at the time.' Clegg's manner was changing now; there was a new note of aggression in his voice. So much for peace and love.

Gerry looked him in the eye. 'According to your statement, you were at home in Leeds, and Janet Walsh confirmed your story. Only now she's saying different. She says you were away. Bristol was mentioned, and you only have to carry on down the M5 from there to get to Devon.'

There was a long silence before Clegg spoke again. 'OK, I admit I was in Bristol on business. I sold cars in those days – the luxury end of the market. I had a good customer in the area and I decided to stay a couple of days. He was a very generous man – invited me to a party while I was down there. They say the rich are different, don't they? Well, I can confirm that they are. He threw a pre-Christmas bash on board his yacht. Amazing.'

'His yacht was moored in Tradmouth?' said Wesley, making a wild guess.

'I never said that. You're putting words into my mouth. The yacht was in Bristol. I never saw Erica, and I'm ashamed to say I was relieved when she didn't come back and I had Janet to myself. Until she started pining for her daughter and everything went pear-shaped.'

'You're all heart, aren't you, Reverend?' said Gerry with heavy sarcasm.

'Like I said, I was a different man back then. I regarded Erica as an inconvenience, but if I was in the same situation now, I assure you things would be completely different.'

'Tell us about Erica.'

'She was a student, little more than a sulky teenager really. She'd been close to her mother since her dad died and she resented me. That's all there was to it.'

'All?' Gerry growled.

'OK, she hated me. She even threatened to tell her mother I'd been touching her . . . inappropriately.'

'And had you?'

'No. She was a vindictive little bitch, but I never harmed her.'

Wesley wasn't sure whether to believe him.

'We'll need the name of the man you went to see in Bristol.'

Clegg looked uncomfortable. 'That was in another life. I don't want to go back there.'

'Nobody's asking you to go back. We need to confirm your story in order to eliminate you from our enquiries.'

Clegg nodded slowly. 'Very well. I'll have his details in my old contact book. It's at home somewhere, although it might take some time to find. I live in the flat at the side of the church. My wife's there now if you want to come with me.'

'You're married?'

'I am indeed. Best thing I ever did, Inspector.'

'Rich widow, was she?'

Clegg's face reddened at Gerry's suggestion. 'She was a widow, yes. But you'll see that we hardly live in the lap of luxury.'

Wesley caught Gerry's eye. He still had one more question to ask. 'Where were you last Saturday night?'

'Here.'

'Can anyone confirm that?'

'I'm afraid not. My wife's mother's just come out of

197

hospital and she needed someone with her, so Sarah stayed over.'

'Did you see anyone else?'

'Sorry. I had a quiet night in preparing for the services the following day.'

They left the church building, and Barry Clegg led them across a yard separated from the street by spiked railings to a small house. Wesley guessed from the pair of bell pushes by the front door that it was divided into two flats. Clegg's was on the ground floor, and when he unlocked the door, he called out a cheerful hello that sounded forced.

A woman came out into the cramped hallway to greet them. She was plump and homely in her Christmas apron. Her brown hair was tied back and the rosiness of her cheeks was due to nature rather than make-up. She had the contented look of a woman in a happy marriage. Perhaps Clegg's insistence that he was a changed man had some substance after all.

'You're back early,' she said, giving her husband a quizzical look. She smiled at Wesley and Gerry. 'Aren't you going to introduce us?'

'These two gentlemen are from the police. It's just routine. About one of the women from the hostel.'

Wesley said nothing, but he couldn't help wondering why Barry Clegg hadn't told his wife the truth about why they were there. Perhaps there were things about his past he didn't want her to know about – like his relationship with Janet Walsh and the threats he'd made against Erica.

He asked them to wait while he went off in search of his alibi's details. Sarah Clegg offered tea and mince pies, which Gerry accepted gratefully on behalf of them both. The mince pies were home-made. It seemed Barry

Clegg had landed on his feet, although Wesley still wasn't absolutely sure whether his conversion to the path of righteousness was genuine.

Sarah seemed convinced by the lie her husband had told her and chatted about the good work the hostel did. Wesley and Gerry could only nod in agreement, glad that at least they hadn't been called upon to tell a direct untruth. Once Barry Clegg returned, his wife left the room, saying she had things to do, and Clegg handed Gerry a sheet of paper bearing a name and address.

'I don't know whether he'll still be at that address, although the business is still up and running. I saw an advert for it on the internet only the other day.'

Gerry showed Wesley the address. It was in Clifton, a desirable area of Bristol.

'I didn't kill Erica,' said Clegg. 'I'll swear that on a stack of Bibles.'

'We have to eliminate all possibilities, sir,' said Wesley stiffly.

'I know they say that if you've nothing to hide, you've nothing to fear. But that's not always the case, is it?'

'And what have you got to hide?' Gerry asked, a hint of threat in his voice.

'A man in my position – someone who becomes a spiritual leader – is bound to have things in his past he'd rather didn't become common knowledge.'

'Like how you treated Janet Walsh and her daughter?'

He looked down at his feet. 'A man shouldn't be judged by what he used to be, only by what he's become.'

'You've already admitted that Erica threatened to tell her mother you abused her,' said Gerry. 'In my book that gives you a whopping great motive for killing her. She couldn't even bear to be in the same house as you over Christmas.'

'She resented me for taking her father's place, that's all.' Clegg didn't sound convincing.

Gerry caught Wesley's eye and gave him a small nod. 'Someone from the local station'll be round to take a fresh statement from you, Mr Clegg. And we'll check out your alibi for the time of Erica's death.'

'Of course, Chief Inspector.' Wesley thought he saw a momentary flash of fear in Clegg's eyes, there for a split second then gone. 'With Christmas coming there are a lot of people around here who are struggling, so if you'd like to make a contribution to our work . . . '

Wesley delved into his jacket pocket and pulled out a ten-pound note. Gerry hesitated before doing the same.

'Thank you, gentlemen. If you have any more questions, I'd be happy to answer them.' Clegg looked Wesley in the eye: the honest citizen.

'What did you think?' Wesley asked as they left the flat.

'Must say I'm surprised he's found religion. Sounded a nasty bit of work from what Janet Walsh told us.'

'People can change.'

'I know that, Wes, but I can't make up my mind if he's genuine. It's just a pity he'll have a chance to call up his mate in Bristol to warn him we're on our way before we get his side of the story.'

Wesley knew the boss was right. He wasn't sure whether to trust Barry Clegg either. He'd known enough convincing con men in his time, and he was well aware that the worst of human nature could be hidden behind the mask of virtue. On the other hand, the man's discovery of faith might be genuine. His own church upbringing had taught him that even the worst of sinners could be saved, so he felt a little ashamed of his suspicions. Perhaps he'd been in the job too long.

'Let's pay his old mate in Bristol a call on our way home,' said Gerry.

Wesley was curious to discover what the man whose name Clegg had given would have to say. Would he too be surprised that the former car salesman had become a pastor?

He checked the time. 'Traffic permitting, we should still be back before close of play.'

Rachel hadn't told her mother that the police were checking on Eli Jelkes – and she certainly didn't intend to share what she'd found out about his criminal conviction. Eli had worked for the Traceys for so many years that her suspicions seemed almost like a betrayal, and yet she couldn't dismiss the nagging fact that he'd had the perfect opportunity to bury Erica Walsh's body beneath the tree on the edge of the field just fifty yards from his cottage, well away from the farmhouse.

She was sitting at her desk, staring at her paperwork and lost in her own thoughts, when DC Rob Carter sauntered up to her looking pleased with himself.

'The boss asked me to trace all the Carls in the local force. I've found one around the right age. Carl Pritchard – based in Ilfracombe. Want me to give his station a call?'

'Good idea, Rob,' she said, trying to hide her impatience.

With any luck, they'd have some good news to give Gerry Heffernan on his return.

From the notebook of
Dr Christopher Cruckshank

3 August 1882

All the district is shocked by the dark events I shall now describe. Mrs Fitzterran being away in Bath, I called upon her husband as she had requested. I had not expected a good welcome, for I feared Fitzterran would resent his wife's interference, but I was quite unprepared for what I discovered when I arrived at Westral Hall.

I was surprised when no servant answered the door to me. The place seemed deserted, and it appeared as though Mr Fitzterran had decided to accompany his wife on her visit to Bath and had closed up the house while they were away.

Then I saw that the heavy oak front door was standing slightly ajar, and when I pushed it, it opened with a loud creak. I stood for a while in the grand hall with its chequerboard floor under the painted gaze of the family portraits that lined the walls, then slowly began to ascend the stairs, fearing what I might find, for I could smell the dreadful odour of decay.

I went from one room to the next, pushing open the doors. I reached a feminine room I assumed belonged to the mistress and found it empty. When I tried the room next door, the scent of death became overpowering, and from my experience as a physician, I knew what I would find in there. Mr Fitzterran was lying upon the bed, curled up like a babe in its mother's womb. His head was a mass of blood and brain, and he was well and truly dead.

31

As a courtesy Wesley and Gerry informed Barry Clegg's old business contact's local police station in Bristol what they intended to do, and the officer on the other end of the line sounded grateful that he hadn't been landed with the job. With the build-up to Christmas, things were busy everywhere.

When they pulled up outside James Warrington's elegant Georgian house in Clifton, they saw that it was already dressed for Christmas, with an impressive wreath on the door and a tastefully decorated real Christmas tree occupying most of the front window. It was almost dark, and the tree lights glittered to welcome them as they stood on the doorstep. It was the sort of door that would have been answered by a servant in days gone by, and Gerry shifted from foot to foot like a tradesman waiting for his Christmas box.

The door was eventually opened by a slightly overweight man, his shirt open at the neck to reveal a thick gold chain. He had the lined face of a habitual smoker and his dark hair showed no hint of grey, which made Wesley suspect it was dyed. When they showed their ID, he looked worried.

'What's this about?'

'We'd like a quick word, if that's OK.' Wesley gave his most reassuring smile, and this seemed to work, because Warrington invited them in, although no tea was on offer.

They spoke in the tastefully decorated hallway. It was as though the man feared the encounter might be prolonged if he made his visitors too comfortable.

'How long's this going to take? I've got to be somewhere in an hour.' He examined his watch ostentatiously, sending out the message that he was a busy man.

'We won't keep you long, sir. You might have heard that the body of a girl called Erica Walsh has been discovered near Tradmouth in south Devon.'

'No.' The monosyllabic reply held a note of impatience.

'Erica went missing twelve years ago, in December 2008. She'd been hitch-hiking just before she disappeared.'

'I never pick up hitch-hikers. It's asking for trouble.'

'Nobody says you did, sir. At the time she went missing, you had a meeting with a man called Barry Clegg, who came down from Leeds to see you. He was the girl's mother's partner.'

'If you say so.'

'You know Barry Clegg? He says he sold you a car.'

'Yeah. A Merc. Nice motor. Top-of-the-range. He did me a good deal on my fleet cars as well. I did quite a bit of business with him back in the day. Haven't heard from him recently, though.'

'Can you confirm that he was here in Bristol on the twelfth of December 2008, the date Erica went missing?'

'How should I know? It was a long time ago.'

'Is there any way of checking? A diary, perhaps?' As Wesley said the words, he feared they'd had a wasted journey. It had been a long shot.

But to his surprise, James Warrington nodded. 'I always keep my old diaries. They'll be in my office. Hang on.'

Neither man said a word while they were waiting, still standing in the hall like a pair of supplicants. Several minutes later, Warrington returned holding a desk diary, which he brandished in triumph.

'What was that date again?'

Wesley repeated it, and Warrington flicked through the pages, eventually finding the right one. 'Here we are. I had a meeting with Barry at lunchtime on the twelfth. Went to a nice little restaurant I know.' He handed Wesley the open diary. Barry Clegg's name was in there all right.

'How long did the meeting last?'

'Can't remember.'

'Only he says he was still here that evening. He says you invited him to a party aboard a yacht you owned. Is that true?'

'Could be. I'm a sociable guy. If he'd come a long way, I would have shown him a bit of hospitality. Why not?'

'Would anyone else remember him being here that evening?' It was the first time Gerry had spoken, and Wesley could tell he was losing patience.

'Doubt it. There are always a lot of people at my parties. Like I said, I'm a sociable guy.'

'Where's your yacht moored?' Gerry asked.

'Here in Bristol.'

'It's never been in Devon?'

'That wouldn't be very convenient, would it?'

Wesley thanked him and prepared to leave. It looked as though their detour had been fruitless. Barry Clegg had definitely been there on the day Erica vanished, and if he'd stayed on for the party as he'd claimed, he had the perfect alibi.

Then Warrington spoke again, turning the pages of the diary with a puzzled frown on his face. 'Hang on, he can't have stayed for the party that year. I think he did the year before, but not that year.' He handed Wesley the diary. 'I thought I must have forgotten to write it in, but I remember now. The wife's dad had to go into a care home, so we decided to postpone it while we got him settled in. I did put it in. It's here.' He pointed to an entry on the following Friday. 'We had it a week later, so Barry can't have stayed on for it.'

'Thank you, sir,' said Wesley, handing the diary back. 'You've been a great help.'

Barry Clegg had just shot back up to the top of their suspect list.

It was eight o'clock by the time Wesley and Gerry arrived back in Tradmouth, calling into the station to check whether anything new had come in while they'd been away. Rob was still at his desk, keen as ever to impress and hungry for promotion when a suitable vacancy arose. He stood up as soon as he spotted his two superiors and rushed over to them before they could take off their coats.

'I've found the Carl who married Erica Walsh's old school friend – the nanny. He's stationed in Ilfracombe. He married a girl called Bella in 2009. I didn't think it was likely that two Devon and Cornwall officers called Carl had married women with the same name around that time.' He sounded pleased with himself.

'Have you spoken to him?'

'Yes. He says he's not on duty tomorrow so he'll come into the station to have a word.'

'It's really his wife we need to speak to,' said Wesley.

'I know, but they had a big row and she walked out. She said she needed a few days on her own to sort herself out. Space, she said.'

'So where is she?'

'He's tried all her friends and relatives and they haven't seen her – or they say they haven't.'

'Did he say whether she'd mentioned Erica at all?'

'He said she heard about her on the news and soon after that she left.'

Wesley watched the expression on the detective constable's youthful face. Sometimes Rob was so eager to play the action cop that he missed the subtleties; detail wasn't really his thing. 'Anything else we need to know, Rob?'

'He said she didn't take the news well. In tears, he said. And he said something about her wanting to talk to someone.'

'Who?'

Rob suddenly looked crestfallen. 'Er . . . I didn't ask.'

32

Corrine had agreed to meet Neil first thing in the morning. She was fifteen minutes late. He checked his watch impatiently. He had things to do back in the office: a couple of post-excavation reports to finish and a dig to arrange for the spring in conjunction with the university. Not to mention writing up the mill survey and trying to put it in decent English. The deadline for publication of the booklet would soon be looming. He hated deadlines.

She'd chosen a café overlooking the promenade in Morbay for their meeting because she said she liked the view of the sea from the front window, and Neil had already consumed one coffee before she joined him, wrapped up in a heavy tweed coat with a colourful woolly hat hiding her brown hair. When she spotted him, she gave a wave before taking off her coat and draping it over the back of her chair.

'You're late.'

'Yeah. Sorry about that,' she said with a disarming smile. 'I'd kill for a coffee. Just a flat white for me. I'm not into all this fancy stuff.'

Once Neil had placed the order, he returned to the table and saw a small battered book lying beside his empty coffee cup.

'I found it in a second-hand bookshop,' Corrine said as he picked it up and flicked through the pages. 'It's about four deaths in Petherham in the 1880s. A man was hanged for one of them.'

Neil began to read. The frontispiece of the book bore the title *The Petherham Curse*, and the date of publication was 1897. As he scanned the pages of the thin volume, he learned that in 1882, the wife of mill owner Josiah Partridge had died, possibly from poison, although the coroner's verdict was natural causes. Partridge had married again shortly afterwards, his new wife being a much younger woman who'd been his daughter's governess. Soon after the wedding, the second wife also died, this time from drowning, which was said to be a tragic accident. Both women's lives had been heavily insured, although Josiah had been away from home on both occasions so no suspicion had fallen on him.

A couple of weeks after the death of Josiah Partridge's first wife, a local landowner called Fitzterran was attacked in his home, Westral Hall, apparently during the course of a robbery. Some of the stolen goods were found in the possession of a local man with a reputation for violence, who was subsequently hanged for the offence. The victim's widow remarried less than a year after her husband's death, although this aroused no suspicion at the time. Life was short back in the nineteenth century and remarriages were often hasty.

The fourth death was that of the vicar's young wife, who suffered a fall in the churchyard and died from her injuries. There was no apparent connection between the four deaths, apart from the fact that all the victims lived in or near the same village, but this didn't stop the rumours that there was a curse upon the place.

Gossip had it that the curse had begun when a young female mill worker was raped and murdered by a wicked overseer in the 1820s, and that her spirit haunted the place seeking vengeance. It was the type of tale people loved, and the current owners of Mill House had exploited it to the full when they'd advertised their psychic weekend. The weekend hadn't ended well, but Neil doubted whether any curse was responsible.

He put the book down, pleased that he might have found the sensational material he needed to add some spice to his publication. 'Those photographs you found – the ones of dead people. There were four of them. A man and three women.'

'And the dates and locations on the backs of the pictures match the victims of this so-called curse.'

'Maybe they were taken by the police. They photographed victims of crime in those days. Think of Jack the Ripper.'

'But apart from Fitzterran, none of these deaths were regarded as suspicious. Unless the photographer, whoever he or she was, knew otherwise.'

'Is it OK if I borrow the book? I might be able to use some of these stories in the booklet I'm working on. The public enjoy a good murder.'

He saw a look of horror pass across her face, there for a moment then gone, and he cursed his tactlessness. Then she took a deep breath, recovering her composure.

'Keep it as long as you like. I'm going back to the car boot sale on Saturday. I want to see whether the woman who sold me the box of photographs turns up again. I want to know how she came by it.'

'OK if I come with you?'

'You'll need to be up early. You lose out if you're not there by seven.'

The idea of getting up at that time on a Saturday morning when he wasn't involved in a dig hardly appealed to Neil. But he heard himself agreeing against his better judgement. He'd be there.

As Wesley made his way to work on Thursday morning, there was a thin veil of mist over the river. He zipped his coat to the neck against the chill air as he ran through the cases in his mind. Barry Clegg's claim to have been partying in Bristol had been a lie, which made him the chief suspect for Erica's murder. But could he also have killed David Leeson? He had no alibi for last Saturday night – but then how many innocent people thought they'd ever need one?

He reached the bottom of the hill. From now on the going was flat, and by the time he neared the river the mist had dispersed and the weak morning sunshine was poking through the clouds. It was forecast to be a perfect December day, although the possibility of snow later in the week had been mentioned on the radio that morning.

As soon as he reached the police station entrance, he received a call from Neil, who wanted to know whether he'd managed to get in touch with Jemima Baine. Wesley answered in the affirmative, although he didn't feel inclined to share the details of their conversation. Jemima had denied knowing anything about Erica's death, but her lack of emotion when she'd handled her friend's bones still played on his mind. She might be good at her job, but if he needed the services of a forensic anthropologist again, she would be the last person he'd call on.

'We've finished at Petherham now,' said Neil. 'Moving on to the old mill near Tradington next. I'll give you a copy of our publication when it's out.'

'Thanks,' said Wesley, trying to sound as though a booklet about the historic mills of the area was going to be top of his Christmas present list.

'I've just met Corrine Malin for an early-morning coffee. She's found a book about the history of Petherham – and she's got a plan.'

Wesley was in the station foyer now, making for the stairs leading up to the CID office. He stopped walking and saw the civilian receptionist give him a curious look.

'What kind of plan?' he asked warily. The last thing they needed was an amateur interfering with their investigations.

'Something to do with those weird photographs of dead people she found. I think she's upset about Erica and is throwing herself into her work. Displacement activity.'

'Better than brooding,' Wesley said with some relief. 'Sorry. Got to go.'

He found Gerry waiting for him in the CID office, pacing up and down.

'I'm not late, am I?' said Wesley as he shed his coat and hung it on the stand in the corner.

'No, Wes. I got here early. Couldn't sleep. We're expecting a visitor. PC Carl Pritchard's driving down from Ilfracombe first thing.'

'If his wife hasn't turned up, he's bound to be worried.'

Gerry sighed and returned to his desk, slumping down in the chair, which groaned under his weight. 'We need another word with Holy Joe and all.'

'Barry Clegg? Don't you believe in his miraculous conversion then?'

'Do you?'

'I suppose dog collars can hide a multitude of sins.'

Gerry drummed his fingers on the surface of the desk, deep in thought. 'Now that we know Clegg wasn't at his posh mate's yacht party, we need to find out what he was really up to. He could easily have been down here strangling his girlfriend's daughter, and he's got no alibi for David Leeson's murder. Although I can't for the life of me think of a motive for that one – unless Leeson saw him with Erica.'

'We should bring him in for questioning under caution.'

'It'll ruin his carol service,' said Gerry with a grim smile. 'But that can't be helped. I'll arrange for someone to pick him up. Give him a taste of Devon hospitality.'

'Anything come in from Falmouth yet?'

'They need a kick up the backside. Get Rach onto it. She's good at things like that.' He hesitated. 'She hasn't been her usual bouncy self recently. Is she OK?'

'She hasn't said anything to me,' said Wesley quickly.

'She hardly looks like an advert for newly wedded bliss, does she?'

To Wesley's relief, they were interrupted by a tentative knock on Gerry's open door, and when he looked round, he saw one of the young DCs brought in from Neston to help with the inquiry standing there nervously.

'Excuse me, sir, there's a Carl Pritchard to see you.'

Gerry glanced at the clock on the wall. It wasn't yet nine o'clock. 'He's an early riser. Show him in, will you?'

The man who entered the office was wearing a thick black puffa jacket and a trapper hat that flopped over his ears. If his car had broken down in the wilds of Dartmoor on the way here, he'd have been dressed for the occasion.

'Take your things off. Make yourself comfortable,' said Gerry before moving to the door and shouting for three cups of tea, aiming the order at nobody in particular. 'Sit down, Carl. We weren't expecting you so early.'

Once Carl Pritchard had removed his outer clothing, Wesley saw that he was medium height, prone to middle-age spread and losing his hair. But he had a pleasant, even-featured face and there was worry in his grey eyes.

'I couldn't sleep, so I thought I might as well set off before the sun was up – beat the morning traffic.'

'I'm DI Peterson and this is DCI Heffernan,' said Wesley, realising that introductions hadn't been made. 'Thanks for coming. I understand you're worried about your wife.'

'She's been out of sorts ever since she heard about that skeleton. When it was first on the news she seemed a bit ...' He searched for the word. 'On edge. Then when they released the name – Erica Walsh – she became really upset.' He bowed his head. 'I wanted her to tell me what was bothering her, but all she'd say was that she and Erica had been good friends when they were kids and that she felt responsible for what happened to her.'

'Responsible? How?'

Carl shook his head vigorously. 'She wouldn't say. You can't interrogate your wife like you would a suspect, can you? I thought she'd tell me in her own good time, but I admit I got frustrated and shouted at her. I was worried, you see. I've never seen her like that before. How could she have been responsible? She didn't kill her.'

'Do you know where she is?'

When Carl looked up, Wesley could see he was on the verge of tears. 'I've called all her friends and nobody has the faintest idea. I'm worried sick.'

'Of course,' said Wesley sympathetically. 'Can you think of anywhere she might have gone? Or did she say anything that might provide a clue? Something you might not have thought significant at the time?'

Carl gave him a feeble smile. 'I'm in the job, Inspector. I know all the questions, but I've got no answers. I've racked my brains but all I can think of is something she said before she went: that there was someone she wanted to speak to.'

'Who?' said Gerry, leaning forward.

'No idea. I asked her, but she said it probably wasn't important.'

At that moment, the tea was delivered by the young DC who'd shown Carl in. They sat in silence while the plastic cups were placed on Gerry's desk, and once they were alone, Gerry spoke again.

'Did she give you the impression she needed to go far to see this person?'

'No. But her car's gone. I've provided all the details, although my boss says she's a grown woman and not in any category that's considered vulnerable. He says that because we had a row, she's probably gone off to teach me a lesson. He's not happily married, my boss.'

'Are you?' Gerry's question was blunt, but Wesley knew it had to be asked.

'I'd say we were until ...'

'Her car hasn't been spotted?'

'I don't think anyone's made much effort to look. Besides, there might be cameras on a lot of the main roads around here, but there are so many smaller rural roads she could have taken that it wouldn't necessarily have been picked up.'

'We'll check anyway.'

'Thanks. Her bank card hasn't been used – or her credit card. I've been checking online. Because she's only been missing since Tuesday, my boss says it's far too early to start panicking.'

'He's probably right,' said Wesley, feeling sorry for the man, who had the stunned look of a child who'd lost its mother in a supermarket. 'What did she tell you about Erica Walsh?'

'She said she was an old school friend who disappeared in Falmouth but she didn't like to talk about it. Mind you, I'm not surprised she was upset. I mean, if your friend's been raped and murdered—'

'Did she mention rape?' Gerry said sharply.

'No, but I assumed … I mean, Erica Walsh was hitch-hiking. Some men would take that as an invitation. These girls never learn.'

'It's the perpetrator who's to blame, not the victim,' said Wesley.

Carl blushed, as though he knew he'd been caught out. 'Of course. I'm just saying what some people think. Not everyone's a saint, are they?'

'You're not wrong there,' said Gerry. 'What else did she say about Erica?'

'When she first went missing, Bella said she felt guilty.'

'Why?'

'They said Erica was seen near Tradmouth and she thought she might have been coming to see her. There was no mobile signal in those days where Bella lived, so if Erica had decided to turn up to see her on the spur of the moment, she couldn't have let her know. She said if she'd been there instead of with me, it might not have happened, but I told her that was rubbish.'

'Where was Bella when Erica went missing?'

'We'd taken a break in Cornwall, just the two of us. I'd booked us a little hotel for a week and the family she worked for said it'd be OK. I used to wonder whether Erica had found out Bella was in Cornwall somehow and come looking for her in Falmouth.'

'Where did Bella work?'

'At a big house in a village near Tradmouth. After Erica disappeared, she left suddenly and got a new job, but she never said why. She changed the subject whenever I tried to ask – just said she fancied a change – but she's not a good liar.'

'You must have gone to the place where she worked.'

'No. We always met at a pub.'

'Remember the name?'

'I think it was something like the Angler's Arms. She said her employers wouldn't like her bringing a boyfriend into the house. The village had a big mill – derelict place.'

Wesley and Gerry looked at each other.

'Could the pub have been the Fisherman's Arms, in Petherham?'

Carl nodded. 'Yeah. That rings a bell.'

'What was her employer's name?'

'She referred to them as his lordship and her ladyship. They had a little boy she called Shrimp. That was his nickname. She was fond of the kid, but she didn't like his parents much, which was probably why she left.' He hesitated. 'I thought at the time that something had happened to upset her.'

'What?'

'I think it was something bad, but she never talked about it. Always clammed up whenever I tried to ask, so in the end I gave up.'

'You've never had children of your own?'

Carl looked away, and Wesley immediately regretted asking the question. 'We decided against it. We see enough terrible things in our job, don't we? It's no time to bring kids into the world.'

Wesley, with his knowledge of history and archaeology, knew that there'd never been an ideal time to grow up, but he made no comment. Instead he said gently, 'You think your wife's disappearance is connected with the discovery of Erica Walsh's remains, don't you?'

Carl Pritchard shifted in his seat and took a sip of tea. 'The timing fits, and like I said, she started acting strangely as soon as they released the victim's name.' He looked Wesley in the eye. 'I'm wondering whether she knows who killed Erica. In which case, she could be in real trouble.'

From the notebook of
Dr Christopher Cruckshank

7 August 1882

The Fitzterrans' servants all swore that their mistress
had instructed them to shut up the house so that she and
her husband could take the waters in Bath. She said
they were to leave the day after she departed and she told
them Mr Fitzterran would follow her to Bath shortly
afterwards. The coachman received a note to say that
a friend was sending a carriage for the master, so his
services would not be required. Several of the servants
saw their master alive and well on the night before their
departure and had no suspicion that anything was amiss.

After my terrible discovery, a quantity of silver was
found to be missing, so it is assumed that the unfortunate
owner of Westral Hall fell prey to robbers shortly after
his servants' departure. The constables are searching for
the felons, but no arrests have been made as yet.

I paid a visit to Mrs Fitzterran earlier today to
express my condolences, and she requested that I prescribe
a sleeping draught. I acceded to her request and assured

her that it was unlikely the evil men who killed her husband would return. I asked whether she'd informed the constable about the man from Exeter who had made threats against her husband, but she said that the man was in Bristol so he could not have been responsible.

On my return from Westral Hall, I found that my housekeeper had admitted Mrs Stephens, who was waiting for me in the drawing room.

'My housekeeper's daughter is maidservant to Mrs Fitzterran,' she said as soon as I entered the room. 'I was asked to speak to the girl because she is most distressed. You found Mr Fitzterran, I believe. What exactly did you see?'

I told her I saw nothing amiss apart from that unhappy gentleman's corpse; I added that it was not seemly for a lady in her position, the wife of a vicar, to become involved in such unsavoury matters. I would take it upon myself to make enquiries.

I asked if she wished to see the photographs I had taken of the village, but she said she had no appetite for such frivolities at that moment. A man had died and the whole district was upset by the horror of it. I knew she was right and I felt corrected.

33

Carl Pritchard left the police station and sloped off down the street past the arts centre with his hands thrust into his pockets, the picture of misery. Wesley and Gerry had seen him to the entrance, where they'd shaken his hand and thanked him for coming, adding that they hoped for positive news soon. Wesley could tell that Gerry's thoughts matched his own. They were both worried about Bella Pritchard, née Brown, the friend Erica Walsh might have been heading towards Petherham to see on the night she was murdered.

Gerry said he needed some fresh air, so he walked off through the Memorial Gardens towards the embankment. He always claimed that being by the river helped him think, and Wesley sensed he wanted to do his thinking alone, so he returned to the CID office.

As soon as he reached his desk, Rachel hurried over. She looked anxious, and Wesley wondered what was troubling her.

'Can I have a word?'

'Have as many as you like.'

'The boss has asked Rob Carter to go round and take another statement from Eli Jelkes, but I'd rather do it myself. Eli knows me, and Rob ...'

'Might go in like a bull at a gate, to use a farming cliché.' He looked across at Rob Carter's desk by the window. Rob was on the phone, frowning and twirling a pen round and round in his fingers impatiently.

Rachel didn't respond to the feeble joke. 'Now that we know about Eli's conviction, I feel we should tread carefully. He's bound to be nervous of the police.'

'Want me to come with you?'

She considered his offer for a few moments. 'To tell the truth, I wouldn't mind the company. But it might be best if you leave the talking to me. I've known Eli since I was a kid.'

'Agreed.'

He walked out of the station beside Rachel and they made straight for her car; she reckoned it would reassure Eli if he saw a familiar vehicle drawing up.

'He'll have finished work for the morning,' she said as she negotiated the narrow lane leading to Little Barton Farm. 'My dad always grabs a break around this time as well.'

'Hard work, farming.'

'It'd be tough if you hadn't been brought up with it, but my brothers wouldn't choose anything else.'

'And your Nigel?'

She hesitated. 'It gets into the blood. Bit like police work.'

'You're happy with that?'

She took a deep breath. 'I suppose I've got to be. Here we are,' she said, suddenly businesslike, as she slowed the car and came to a halt outside a small brick cottage down the lane from where Erica Walsh's skeleton had been discovered.

The fallen tree had now been moved, but drooping blue and white police tape still cordoned off the area, even though the forensic work had long been completed.

'It's a straight stretch of lane so he would have had a good view if he'd been up and about when the killer came to bury her,' said Wesley.

'If you're in Eli's job, you don't tend to stay up late, not when you've got to start the milking by five the next morning.'

There was no doorbell, so she rapped on the flaking wooden door with her knuckles.

'Does Eli own this place?' Wesley asked as they waited.

'It's a tied cottage. My parents could do it up and sell it to incomers, but my dad thinks Eli's need is greater and he seems quite happy with the arrangement,' she said with a hint of defensiveness, as though she thought Wesley was about to criticise the conditions the Traceys provided for their workers.

Eventually the door opened and a weather-beaten face peeped out.

Rachel took a deep breath and forced herself to smile. 'Hi, Eli. Only me. I know someone's already had a word about those bones we found, but I'd like to have another little chat if that's OK. Nothing to worry about. This is Wesley,' she added, omitting to mention his rank.

Wesley could tell Rachel was nervous, which surprised him considering the number of years she'd known the man. Perhaps after discovering his history of violence she was starting to see him as a suspect rather than a witness – which was exactly what Wesley himself was doing.

'You'd best come in.' Jelkes's voice was gruff, as though he wasn't used to conversation.

'You told my brother you saw a car parked on the lane around the time that girl disappeared.'

His eyes widened in alarm. 'I only mentioned it. I didn't

know he was going to make a big thing of it. I only said people sometimes stop there – courting couples and people wanting to relieve themselves. He said did I see anyone around that time and I said I might have done. That's all.'

'And did you?'

There was a long silence before he spoke. 'Yeah ... I think it was around then.'

'It's probably nothing, but I still need to take a statement.'

Eli bowed his head meekly, like a man facing his execution.

Rachel had brought the statement forms with her, and she wrote down Eli's account of what he'd seen, such as it was. The information was vague. He'd looked out of his bedroom window and seen a car parked down the lane near the tree where the body had been found, although he couldn't be sure of the time or even the date. It had been dark, but there'd been a full moon, so there was enough light for him to tell that the car was a saloon, probably dark in colour. He'd thought it might be someone stopping there for the usual reasons, so he'd drawn the curtains and gone to bed. It was none of his business. There'd been no chance of him seeing the registration number because the driver had switched the headlights off as soon as he or she pulled up. He hadn't heard anything. No screams, no shouts for help. It was a quiet night. Still and frosty. That was all he knew.

She asked him to read the statement through to see if there was anything he wanted to add, but he asked her to read it to him, which made Wesley suspect that he found reading difficult. Then he signed it slowly in block capitals, as though he'd learned to write his name but little else. As he handed the statement back, he looked frightened.

'Is that all?' he asked Rachel as she stood up to leave.

If it had been up to Wesley, he would have replied, 'For now', but Rachel spoke first. 'Of course, Eli. Thanks for your help.'

'What did you think?' he asked as they climbed into the car.

'I think he was hiding something,' Rachel answered quietly.

'Me too. I've never seen anyone so terrified.'

34

One of the officers drafted in from Neston to help with the case had been given the job of going through TV footage of Damien Lee's psychic act. A couple of years ago he'd had his own programme on Channel 4, which had run for two seasons until it had been replaced by something more cutting-edge. The DC had watched five of the programmes, paying particular attention to the shots of the audience and the volunteers he'd used to show off his skills. The young woman's eyes had been glazing over with boredom until she'd spotted a face she recognised from the photographs stuck on the huge whiteboard on the far wall of the room.

Brad Percy had been in the front row of the studio audience and Damien had picked him out, telling him there was somebody he'd injured and that he should make amends. Percy had sat there, head bowed so his reaction couldn't be seen, while the woman next to him was obviously seething with fury. He'd lied when he'd said he had no connection with the psychic, and Wesley wanted to know why.

An officer had already been up to Percy's place of work to speak to him after Camberland's revelation, and he'd confirmed the private detective's suspicions that he'd used the psychic weekend as cover for an assignation with a woman.

He'd claimed she had an interest in the supernatural and had encouraged him to book the weekend – then, much to his annoyance, hadn't turned up. He refused to give the name of his absent lady friend, saying it wasn't relevant. Besides, she had a partner, who might turn nasty if he found out what was going on. According to his statement, he'd decided to stick it out, mainly because Mill House offered good food and accommodation; not only that, but he'd fancied his chances with Corrine Malin. Somehow his explanation rang true, but Wesley wasn't going to leave it at that.

It was coming up to three o'clock and he calculated that Brad Percy would still be at work; he didn't seem like the sort of man who'd be anxious to get home to his wife. He decided to ask Rachel to go with him. Corrine Malin had described Percy as a ladies' man, so with any luck, he'd respond better to a female presence. Besides, he sensed Rachel needed someone to confide in, and the journey would provide the perfect opportunity. Given their past history, he knew this might not be wise, and yet he couldn't help worrying about her.

During the drive, however, the conversation didn't stray far from work, and before he knew it, they'd arrived at the premises of Brad Percy's IT firm, a single-storey brick and glass office building, part of a brand-new business park on the outskirts of Exeter. The development hadn't been there when Wesley was a student in the city. As far as he recalled, the area had once been open grassland.

They showed their ID to the receptionist, a young Chinese woman with an immaculate black suit and an aura of efficiency. When she rang through to Percy's office, Wesley noticed that she had a beautiful speaking voice. She was certainly an asset to the company, and he hoped her boss paid her accordingly.

Percy stood to greet them, looking confident now that he was on home territory – although Wesley suspected that confidence was about to be shattered.

'I don't know what else I can tell you,' he began, his gaze focused on Rachel. 'I was interviewed at Mill House and then someone else came to speak to me here. It's been rather embarrassing, to tell the truth.'

'You don't often do that, do you, Mr Percy – tell the truth, I mean.'

It was Rachel who spoke, and Wesley wished she'd resisted the urge to display her prejudice against the suspect so blatantly. He knew it was up to him to smooth the situation.

'You claimed you'd never met Damien Lee before that weekend in Petherham. Is that right?'

'That's what I said.' A momentary flicker of uncertainty appeared in Brad Percy's eyes, there for a second, then gone. He gave Rachel a smile and Wesley noticed that his teeth were unnaturally perfect.

Wesley took out his phone and found the footage of Damien Lee's psychic show. He passed it to the man on the other side of the desk. 'Recognise anybody?'

Percy's face turned an unhealthy shade of red. He handed the phone back to Wesley as though it was a live grenade.

'Care to explain?' Wesley steepled his fingers and waited, leaning back in his chair with his legs crossed, the picture of relaxation.

'I ... I'd forgotten all about it.'

'If I went to a TV filming and a psychic picked me out, I don't think I'd forget. Who's the lady next to you?'

'My wife,' Percy said almost in a whisper.

'Thought it might be. Why did you really go to Mill House?'

'I told you. I went to meet a lady friend, only she never turned up. Her partner made other arrangements, and she's bloody scared of him.'

'Did your wife know about your plans?'

'She does now. I didn't know the bitch had set a private eye onto me. Luckily she didn't turn up in person or the shit would have really hit the fan.'

'Why go if you knew Damien would be there? He might have recognised you.'

'All I was told was that it was a psychic weekend. The lady I've been seeing is into all that supernatural rubbish. I didn't ask the name of the psychic because I wasn't really interested.'

'You were just after a romantic weekend.'

'Exactly. I told my wife I was going to a conference in London. Got Sally, my receptionist, to back me up.'

'She agreed to lie for you?'

'All she had to say was that she'd arranged a place at the conference for me. It was no big deal.'

'Bet you got a hell of a shock when you saw the psychic was Damien,' said Rachel with inappropriate relish.

'Double whammy, as they say. My, er ... friend couldn't make it and then there was this bloke standing in front of me who'd read me like a book at that show.'

'What did you do?'

'Nothing at first. But I saw him watching me and I thought he might have recognised me, so I thought I'd have a quiet word with him – ask for his discretion and all that. If it ever got back to my wife ... She's been saying I'm on my last warning.' He bowed his head. He was a different man now from the one who'd greeted them a few minutes earlier. 'She holds the purse strings, and if she pulls the plug on the business, it could ruin me.'

'So you had no idea she'd hired a private detective?' said Wesley.

He shook his head. 'They were good, I'll give them that. Although I should have known they weren't vegans when they started tucking into the cheeseboard.'

'When the police began asking questions about Damien Lee's death, you must have known your wife would find out,' said Rachel. Her voice was gentler now, as though she knew the man was on the ropes. Defeated by his own deceptions.

'Once I knew they were treating it as suspicious, I hoped I'd be able to ... distance myself. I asked for my statement to be taken at work so with any luck she'd never find out.'

'Keeping things from the police is never wise, Mr Percy,' said Wesley. 'Your sins will always find you out.'

'Don't I know it.' He flashed Rachel an apologetic smile.

Wesley suspected that charm had allowed this man to get away with all sorts over the course of his adult life – and probably his childhood too. However, he'd met psychopaths who could be remarkably charming when it suited them.

'We'll need the name of the lady you planned to meet – just to corroborate your story.'

A look of panic appeared in Percy's eyes. Then he took a deep breath. 'It was Sally Chen, my receptionist. But I'd rather keep her out of it.'

Wesley looked at Rachel, wishing she wasn't making her disapproval so obvious. 'We'll need to confirm your story, but I promise we'll be discreet.'

Percy gave a meek nod.

'Did you manage to speak to Damien while you were at Mill House?' Wesley asked.

There was a long silence. 'The first night, the Friday, I saw him sneaking out after the session and I followed him. He was heading for the pub and I thought, "Got you, mate. You're just like the rest of us." I hoped I'd be able to buy him a drink and have a quiet word, man to man. I doubt if he would have said anything, but I had to be sure. I lost sight of him, then about ten minutes later I saw him shooting out of the pub door as though the hounds of hell were after him. I stayed for a drink anyway, but it was pretty packed; that's probably why he decided to leave. After that, I never got another chance to speak to him. He didn't mix with the rest of us; ate in his room and only emerged for the sessions.'

'What about the Saturday – the night he died? Did you try to follow him when he went out?'

'No. Absolutely not.'

'He never mentioned your previous encounter?'

'He never actually said anything apart from a load of general stuff at the seance. He told me I should be truthful and said there were people I was hurting – more or less what he told me last time.'

'Maybe you should have listened to him,' said Rachel.

'So you never did get to see him on his own?' Wesley was watching the man's face. He could tell a confession of some kind was imminent.

Percy began to fidget with a paper clip on his desk. 'It was still bothering me that he'd recognised me, so once the Saturday-evening session was over, I decided to knock on his door, but there was no answer. I wasn't there long before I realised it was a bad idea.' There was a pause before he spoke again. 'I'll tell you one thing though. I had the impression he was scared of something.'

'Or someone?'

'Possibly.' He thought for a moment. 'When he was doing that TV show, he was a real performer, but at the seance on the Saturday night, he was like a nervous rabbit. I'll swear he was a frightened man.'

Wesley hardly said a word on the way back to Tradmouth. He was thinking about David Leeson. At Mill House, he'd been so frightened of something – or someone – that he'd shut himself away in his room. Had the thing he'd feared been spiritual or flesh and blood? His money was on the latter. It hadn't been a ghost who'd plunged a knife into Leeson's back.

'Is Percy still in the frame?' Rachel said, breaking the silence as they reached the outskirts of the town.

'Well, Ms Chen backed up his story and he admitted that he followed Leeson out on the Friday night.' Wesley thought for a moment. 'The man can't keep his trousers on and he's terrified of his wife, but that doesn't make him a murderer.'

'What if he's lying and Leeson threatened to tell his wife after all? He didn't know the Camberlands were private detectives.'

'There's never been any suggestion that Leeson went in for blackmail, even of the subtle kind. Besides, people like Percy use charm and persuasion to get what they want.'

'I still think that angle's worth looking into. Leeson must have been privy to a lot of sensitive personal information in his line of work.'

Rachel had a point, but there'd been no suggestion that any of the clients on the list they'd obtained had been victims of blackmail. Rather they'd spoken of the psychic in glowing terms, saying how much he'd helped them. Or maybe the officers sent to interview them had been asking the wrong questions.

As soon as they arrived back in the incident room, Gerry stood to greet them, his face glowing with satisfaction.

'Two pieces of good news, Wes,' he said as Wesley took off his coat. 'First of all, I've been asked to play Santa at the station Christmas party; even better, Barry Clegg's made a confession to the officers who paid him a call – couldn't shut him up, they said. He's coming in tomorrow and he says he wants to tell us everything.'

From the notebook of
Dr Christopher Cruckshank

II *August* 1882

The constable has made an arrest. He received an anonymous note saying that Albert Waring, who works at the mill, was seen near Westral Hall on the day of Mr Fitzterran's murder, and when Waring's cottage was searched, a silver cup was found. Mrs Fitzterran has identified it as having been stolen from the hall.

Waring is a ruffian, notorious for fighting and violence, and it seems all Petherham is glad he will face justice at last. It is said the constable ran him to ground in the clock tower of the mill, where he chose to hide from the vengeance of the law. He was hauled from his hiding place by the constable, helped by Waring's workmates, who had no liking for him, and taken away in chains.

The prisoner says he received a note from Mr Fitzterran telling him to attend him at the hall, but the document he produced was clearly a forgery written by his own hand.

He is to stand trial at the Assizes in Exeter, and then he will no doubt face the hangman.

35

Wesley had lain awake all night again, turning their cases over and over in his mind. Eli Jelkes was certainly hiding something – he wasn't a good liar, and besides, he had a history of violence against a woman. Wesley had looked up the case and it had been more serious than he'd first assumed. After pub closing time one Saturday evening, he'd lain in wait for a barmaid who'd refused to serve him because he'd had too much to drink. He'd beaten her so badly that she'd been left with cracked ribs and a broken nose. There'd been previous incidents too. As well as two convictions for affray when he was sixteen, he'd been arrested on suspicion of pushing a girl down some stairs after she'd rejected his advances. Wesley wondered whether Rachel's parents would have employed the man and given him a home so near to their growing children if they'd been aware of his record.

According to the statements taken from the owners and guests at Mill House, nobody could have gone outside without being seen on the evening David Leeson died, with the possible exception of Brad Percy, who'd admitted to leaving the others in the drawing room to knock on the psychic's door. They only had his word for it that he hadn't followed him out as he'd done the previous night, but somehow Wesley had believed him.

Then there was Bella Pritchard's disappearance. She had been working as a nanny in Petherham at the time of Erica Walsh's murder, and Erica might have made a detour in her journey to Tradmouth to visit her, unaware that she was away in Cornwall with her boyfriend, Carl. They still didn't know the identity of Bella's employers in Petherham – his lordship, her ladyship and little Shrimp. He doubted they were actually a titled family; the names were most likely a comment on their attitude towards their staff. However, he could be wrong, and he'd already asked someone to check.

He couldn't help wondering if Bella's absence was linked to the Erica Walsh case, or whether she'd simply left the marital home after a domestic tiff. According to Carl, she'd been behaving strangely since Erica's remains were found, but he might have said this to mislead them. Perhaps he didn't want to admit they'd quarrelled, or that she'd gone away to punish him in some way.

With everything that had happened, he'd forgotten all about his brother-in-law's encounter with the self-confessed murderer in his church, but he was briefly reminded of the incident when Pam told him over breakfast that she was going to the church's annual Christmas fair the following day. She said the words 'Christmas fair' with a smile and a roll of the eyes, as though she considered the quintessentially English ritual clichéd and embarrassing but felt obliged to go there to support Mark and Maritia. She said she hoped Michael and Amelia would agree to go with her, and Wesley wished her luck with that. At their age, the lure of friends usually proved more powerful than family duty. She asked him whether he'd be able to make it, more in hope than expectation, but he had to disappoint her. Even though she didn't utter a word of criticism, he felt bad about it.

The day was crisp and cold, and after his walk to the station, he felt alert and ready to conduct the interview with Barry Clegg, who was due to come in that morning.

He wondered whether the shock of committing cold-blooded murder had caused Clegg's sudden conversion to the path of righteousness. As he checked the messages and emails that had come in overnight, he was impatient to find out, hoping they were about to obtain a confession that would clear up the murder of Erica Walsh once and for all so they could concentrate on finding David Leeson's killer.

Gerry was in a good mood, as though he was expecting at least one of his cases to be wrapped up and ready to hand to the CPS before close of play. Wesley, however, was more cautious by nature. They spent an hour planning their strategy for the interview, and when the message came that Barry Clegg was waiting in the interview room, Gerry sat back in his chair with a smug grin on his face.

'No hurry, Wes. We'll get more out of him if we let him stew for a while.'

'The clock's ticking. We should get a move on.' Wesley checked his watch. He didn't want to waste time.

Gerry, however, stayed where he was. 'Any news on Bella Pritchard yet?'

'Trish called Ilfracombe first thing and there's still no sign of her. I'm getting worried.'

'Me too. Her car hasn't been spotted.'

'If it wasn't for her connection with Erica Walsh, we'd be looking more closely at the husband. Carl seemed worried, but I've known husbands who've killed their wives put on

Oscar-winning performances for the police and press, so we can't rule him out – even though he is one of us.'

Gerry gave a deep sigh and hauled himself out of his seat. 'Let's go and see what Barry Clegg has to say for himself.'

Clegg was waiting for them in a bare, functional interview room with no natural light, a half-finished cup of tea in a polystyrene cup sitting on the table in front of him. The uniformed constable standing by the door looked relieved that the two detectives had arrived, as though he'd been afraid he'd be obliged to make polite conversation if he remained alone with the suspect any longer.

'Mr Clegg,' Gerry began after switching on the recording machine and announcing their names. 'I understand you have something to tell us.'

'That's right.'

'I take it you've been offered the services of the duty solicitor. Do you want to wait for them to arrive?'

'I don't need a solicitor.'

'Are you sure?' said Wesley, worried about the possible implications for any future trial.

'Absolutely. I've come here to be honest with you and I don't want someone twisting my words or trying to make excuses for what I've done in the past. I need to come clean and face the consequences.'

'As long as you're sure.' Wesley glanced at Gerry sitting beside him. The DCI had the look of a hungry man who was preparing to devour a good meal.

'I'm ready to admit I lied to you about being in Bristol at the time Erica disappeared. I kept my appointment with James Warrington; that bit's true. But there was no party on board his yacht the day after our meeting. I left Bristol the same day – the twelfth of December – and drove straight down here to south Devon. I kept quiet about it because what I did was illegal. A man I knew in Leeds paid me a lot of money to pick up a consignment of cocaine and bring it back up north for him.'

'Where did you pick up this consignment?' Wesley asked.

'Place called Millicombe. Pretty little town on the coast. Very lively in the summer, I believe, but it was December so it was like the grave. My mate couldn't go down himself because he had a lot on, so when I mentioned I had business in Bristol he asked me to make a detour to Devon. In those days I'd have done anything for money.'

'What happened?'

'He had a yacht moored down here. Some contacts of his took it out to meet a trawler, and that's when the delivery was made. I stayed in Millicombe for a couple of nights till the business was done, then took the stuff back to Leeds and handed it over to him.'

Wesley knew it was time to ask the most important question of all.

'Millicombe's not a million miles from Tradmouth. Did you see Erica while you were down here?'

'No. I swear I didn't.'

'Janet Walsh must have mentioned she was coming here.'

'True. But there was no way I wanted to bump into her. Why would I? We didn't get on.'

'You might have seen it as an opportunity to get her out of the way once and for all.'

For the first time, Clegg looked agitated. 'I admit I've been a bad boy in my time, but I've always drawn the line at murder. I'm not a killer, Chief Inspector. I'll swear that on the Bible.'

'We'll need details of the drugs operation. Names.'

'I forget,' he said quickly. 'It was a long time ago.'

'I'm sure your memory's not that bad. Try.'

'His name was Jezza. He owned a club in the centre of Leeds. I sold him a flash car and we sometimes drank together. He moved to Spain shortly afterwards. No idea where he is now.'

'Surname?'

'Can't remember.'

Wesley and Gerry exchanged a look. Wesley suspected that Barry Clegg was lying, possibly because he was scared of reprisals. On the other hand, he could have been telling the truth. As he said, it was a long time ago.

'What about the people you dealt with in Millicombe? That's on our patch,' said Gerry.

'They were just blokes in a yacht.'

'How did you contact them?'

'Went down to the harbour. The boat was called something like the ...' He frowned. 'I think it was the *Costa Lot* – or the *Costa Packet* – or maybe the *Costa Fortune*. Something funny.'

'Think harder.'

Clegg put his head in his hands as though he was praying for guidance. He looked up. 'It was one of those new boats without any sails. Big and sleek like a speedboat on steroids.'

Gerry wrinkled his nose in distaste. As a keen sailor, he didn't have a high opinion of gin palaces.

'We'll check it out. What about where you stayed?'

'Some B&B a few streets away from the harbour. I was the only guest, so they might remember – if they're still in business. It was a big red-brick house. Victorian terrace. Can't remember the name or the address.'

Again they would check it out, but Wesley didn't hold out much hope of finding any record of Clegg's stay.

'Did you do any more little jobs for this Jezza?'

'No. That was the only one.'

'Are you sure you didn't call into Tradmouth on the way back – just to see what Erica was up to?'

The answer was a vigorous shake of the head.

'And you can't think of anything that might help us find her killer?'

'It must have been someone who picked her up while she was hitch-hiking. You hear about these things happening, don't you?'

As they left the interview room, Wesley knew that Clegg could well be right. Someone might have picked Erica up after David Leeson had dropped her off near Petherham. Leeson might even have seen her killer, and that was why he'd had to die.

36

Neil was surprised that the car boot sale taking place in a freezing field early on a December Saturday morning was so well attended. The field overlooked the river outside the village of Derenham, and the farmer who owned the land was earning a bit extra by charging both stallholders and shoppers for the privilege of attending. Many of the customers circulating around the stalls looked like dealers; easy to distinguish from ordinary punters by their swift and single-minded examination of the goods on offer as they kept a sharp lookout for anything valuable – or merely saleable.

Scouring the cluttered tables was an addictive pastime, and Neil was soon sucked in. He strolled around, picking up anything that caught his eye, while Corrine walked on ahead like a woman on a mission.

She stopped and waited for him while he examined an Anglepoise lamp with a broken mechanism. Eventually her patience wore thin.

'Come on. We're supposed to be looking for this woman.'

Neil gave the stallholder an apologetic smile and followed her, walking fast to keep up. 'Don't you want to look round?' he said to her back, but either she hadn't heard or she was ignoring him.

She turned her head. 'She was around here last time, but I can't see her,' she said impatiently. 'I don't think she's come.'

'If she's got more to sell, she'll be wanting to get some cash together before Christmas. She'll be here some-where,' said Neil. 'We should be systematic. We've already done this side of the field, but there are more stalls over there.'

Corrine couldn't argue with his logic. She pulled her coat tightly around her body against the chill wind blowing in from the river and trudged past another row of folding tables set up behind the parked cars. There were vans there too, selling new goods: DIY items and mobile phone covers. These were dealers who went from sale to sale, but they were of no interest to Corrine and Neil.

It had rained overnight and wellingtons weren't the warmest footwear. As they walked on through the field, Corrine trod in a patch of mud with a resounding squelch. Her left boot was sucked into the ground, and when Neil stopped to steady her so she could extricate it, he heard her give an excited cry. 'There she is!'

She was pointing at a small plump woman in her forties, well wrapped up in a thick black coat and fingerless gloves, with a woolly hat concealing her hair. She was stamping her feet on the ground to keep warm and rubbing her hands together. Corrine began to march towards her with Neil trailing behind.

'Hi. Remember me?' she said when she reached the stall. 'I bought an old box from you a couple of weeks ago.'

The woman suddenly looked wary, as though she feared Corrine had come there to make a complaint about her purchase.

'There were some photographs inside the box and I was wondering where you found it.'

'I didn't nick it if that's what you're thinking. She gave it to me. She'll tell you.'

Neil immediately stepped in. He'd dealt with a lot of awkward people in the course of his archaeological career, landowners and developers in particular, and was adept at smoothing over difficult situations.

'Oh no, you misunderstand,' he said, switching on a charming smile. 'I'm an archaeologist, and some of the photographs were taken in a village where I'm working, so I wondered whether anyone knows more about them. My friend here's doing a doctorate and it might help with her work.' He wasn't going to mention the subject of Corrine's thesis. Why complicate matters?

The woman's defensiveness suddenly vanished. 'Look, the stall's quiet at the moment, so why don't we get a cup of tea at the van? I could do with one. It's bloody freezing.'

'Good idea,' said Neil.

She asked the man on the neighbouring stall to keep an eye on her things before leading the way to a little refreshment van that was doing a roaring trade.

Neil bought the drinks – his treat – and a few minutes later they were back at the woman's stall, warming their hands on the flimsy plastic cups.

'Do you know where the pictures came from?' he asked.

'Like I said, she gave me the box.'

'Who did?'

The woman took a deep breath. 'I'm a carer. I go round to old people's houses, helping them get dressed and eat and all that. I enjoy it, but the agency doesn't give you

245

enough time these days. The old dears need someone to talk to, but we're always rushing them. It's not right.'

'No, it bloody isn't,' said Corrine. She sounded indignant and Neil suspected she had some interest in the problem – an elderly relative who'd been short-changed by the cash-starved system perhaps.

The woman gave her a grateful half-smile, as though their previous misunderstanding had been forgiven, and introduced herself as Greta Moss, single mother of two girls who were staying with their grandma for the weekend.

'Anyway, I visit this lady, Miss Cruckshank, three times a day. She's quite a character and we get on well,' said Greta, now relaxed and ready to share the details.

'Miss Cruckshank gave you the box?'

'She said she'd had it for years – since her mother died. She's got a lot of other stuff too. Lives in a big house in Neston. Like an Aladdin's cave, the place is. I've no idea what's up in those bedrooms, but if you ask me, it could be worth a fortune. She's got a stairlift, so she goes upstairs to have a root around from time to time, and one day she brought the box down. I said it was pretty and she told me I could keep it if I liked it. I never knew there were photos inside – not at first. I said she shouldn't be giving me things, but she insisted and I didn't like to say no.'

'You sold it.'

'What was I going to do with it? Christmas is coming and the kids are asking for all sorts from Santa, so if I can make a bit extra flogging stuff I don't need . . . Besides, she said to do what I liked with it. The past is the past and best forgotten, that's what she said. You can't take it with you, can you?'

'So they say,' said Neil. 'Did she tell you where it came from?'

'Only that it had been in her family.'

'We'd like to speak to her. Do you think that's possible?'

Greta smiled. 'Possible? I think she'd love it.'

Wesley was conscious that they still hadn't made much progress on the Falmouth angle. All they'd had was a promise from the local station that they'd try to dig out the relevant statements, and he thought it was high time they followed it up.

He looked around the incident room. Some of the team looked as tired as he felt, but they owed it to Janet Walsh to bring her daughter's killer to justice. Then there was David Leeson. Every aspect of his life was being examined in detail. His days of fame as a psychic were easy to unravel, but delving into his years spent entertaining in pubs and clubs had proved more difficult. In the course of his varied career, he would have mixed with an awful lot of people, not all of them honest and upright citizens. But they needed to keep digging into the past, because Wesley was as sure as he could be that his murder had been no random attack. The crime rate in rural areas might be on the increase, but motiveless stabbings were fortunately still a rarity.

As he scrolled through his emails, he had the fleeting thought that this investigation was like the archaeological excavations he'd taken part in as a student – a lot of work that produced absolutely nothing, then, if you were lucky, the sudden discovery of something that would turn all previous assumptions about the site on its head. It was just a matter of digging in the right place.

To his delight, he found the message he'd been waiting for from Falmouth. It had taken a while to dig out the material about the claimed sighting of Erica Walsh, the email began apologetically, and Wesley held his breath, telling himself not to get too excited. The final paragraph read: *Unfortunately, one of the witnesses passed away a couple of years after the date of the sighting, but her brother had been with her and he'd also made a statement – both attached.*

Wesley opened the attachment and saw that the officer had scanned the statement forms that had probably been lying in the bowels of the police station for years. The handwriting of the officer who'd taken down the words of the two witnesses was neat and easy to read, but to his disappointment, the woman's statement didn't say very much. She and her brother, who had been visiting her for the day, had been walking down a road near the harbour when they saw a young woman with a red rucksack. When the police appeal was made, they remembered the exact time and date because she didn't see her brother very often and they'd visited the Maritime Museum that afternoon. She'd come forward to make a statement and it had been backed up by the discovery that Erica's bank card had been used in Falmouth the same day – four days after the last sighting of her near Petherham.

He selected the second statement, again in the officer's well-formed handwriting. It mirrored that of the woman, almost as though brother and sister had agreed to say the same thing. But it was when he reached the witness's signature at the bottom that his heart leapt. This was the find – the glint of gold against the soil.

Eli Jelkes had printed his name on the statement he'd made a couple of days ago – and he had printed it at the foot of this older statement too. Clear as day.

37

'Are you sure Miss Cruckshank will be up for visitors?' Corrine's former confidence seemed to have evaporated during the journey, and her question sounded uncertain.

'Greta said it was OK,' said Neil. 'And she seems to know her well.'

'I still think it's a bit much to turn up without any warning and ask if we can go through her things.'

'Greta promised to call and tell her we were on our way. Don't panic.' He smiled and suddenly felt like a conspirator. He was enjoying being with Corrine, following the trail that had begun at Petherham Mill. Those Victorian photographs had touched a nerve. He knew that the Victorians had loved to wallow in death and mourning, but he couldn't shake off the feeling that those images of the dead were evidence of some terrible wrongdoing; a crime perhaps. He hoped Miss Cruckshank would be able to throw some light on the mystery.

'She lives in Neston. It's not far away.'

Neil looked at his watch. It was almost midday and he was hungry. 'Let's have lunch there. Most of the cafés do a mean vegan menu if you're into that sort of thing.'

'I'm a stony-broke postgrad student. I'll eat anything.'

Neil drove into Neston, soon reaching the town's steep and narrow high street with its Elizabethan buildings and independent shops, many with a New Age flavour. It was a lot quieter now than it was in the tourist season, but a sign on the railings outside the sandstone parish church told them that a Christmas fayre was taking place, and he could see people milling around, chatting and laughing.

Miss Cruckshank lived down a side street in a substantial double-fronted terraced house with cream stucco walls. The paintwork had seen better days and the house looked too large for one elderly lady. There was no doorbell, just a large brass lion's-head knocker. Neil picked it up and let it fall three times.

'I hope Greta's phoned her like she promised,' Corrine muttered behind him.

The lack of response made Neil suspect that she hadn't. And if they weren't expected, he knew explanations might be awkward. He waited a minute or so before he knocked again, and this time he heard a shuffling inside the house.

The woman who opened the door was tall, around five foot ten, and very thin, with sparse grey hair, piercing blue eyes and a straight back despite the fact that she was leaning on a Zimmer frame.

Neil gave her a hopeful smile. 'Did Greta call to say we'd be coming? Dr Watson and Ms Malin?'

'Dr Watson. I rather hoped you'd bring Mr Holmes with you,' she said with a hint of mischief. 'But I suppose this young lady will do. Come in, please.' She turned her walking frame before heading slowly towards the open door on the left-hand side of the hall.

Neil ushered Corrine ahead of him, shutting the front door behind him. The wallpaper in the hall had faded to a pale sepia, although he could still make out the flowers entwined in the printed trelliswork. He followed Corrine into a front parlour cluttered with the keepsakes of a long life: ornaments and paintings crammed together in a gloomy room heated only by the old-fashioned two-bar electric fire standing in front of an elaborate marble fireplace.

'Greta mentioned something about a box I gave her,' Miss Cruckshank said as she lowered herself stiffly into a shabby winged chair near the fire.

'That's right. There were some photographs inside.'

'Yes. Some old pictures of people and villages. They were of no interest to me but they might be worth something to somebody.'

'There were also some ...' he searched for an appropriate word, 'some strange pictures hidden in a separate compartment in the base.' He hesitated. He didn't want to distress this elderly lady with talk of death and corpses. On the other hand, he'd sensed a toughness to her character and guessed that she must have dealt with worse things in the course of her long life.

'Were there? I hadn't realised.'

He was about to speak, but Corrine got in first. 'They're pictures of dead people and there's writing on the back saying where they were taken and when.'

'I had no idea there was anything like that in the box,' Miss Cruckshank said quietly.

There was a long silence as she stared at the electric fire, glowing brilliant orange in the gloom.

'My great-grandfather was a doctor, and at one time he worked in the village of Petherham, not far from here. When my parents died, I discovered a lot of his things

251

amongst their possessions, including that box. I sold some of the things – the heavier furniture and the old medical books – but most of it I kept.

'There are still a lot of items upstairs in one of the rooms I never use – five bedrooms is far too many for me, but I can't face moving at my age. When Greta admired the box, I said she could keep it. I told her to sell it if she wanted. I know she struggles financially and she's told me she sells things at car boot sales. Not that I've ever attended a car boot sale,' she added sadly, as though this was a cause of regret.

'That's where I bought it,' said Corrine. 'I chose it because it was pretty, then when I saw what was inside ... I'm studying for a doctorate, you see, and I think the pictures might help with my research.'

'Very impressive, I'm sure,' Miss Cruckshank said sharply.

'According to the writing on the back of the photos, some of the pictures of dead people were taken at Mill House in Petherham – two women, one young and one older.' Corrine paused. 'The house is reputed to be haunted.'

'Nonsense.' Miss Cruckshank hesitated. 'Wasn't someone murdered near there recently? Some famous psychic. I heard about it on the local news.' She nodded in the direction of the large flat-screen TV sitting in the corner of the room, her sole concession to contemporary living. 'The man was probably a charlatan charging people a fortune to listen to his nonsense and somebody took exception.'

She'd clearly formed her own theory, and Neil wondered whether Wesley would agree with her. His friend hadn't discussed the case with him, so he had no way of knowing.

'I met Damien Lee, the man who died,' said Corrine. 'I think he might have been genuine – about some things anyway.'

Miss Cruckshank gave her a disdainful look, and Neil feared Corrine had just gone down in the old lady's estimation.

'We were hoping there might be something amongst your great-grandfather's things that would explain how the photographs came to be there. I'm an archaeologist,' Neil added. 'I've been conducting a survey of local mills, and as the photographs could be linked to Petherham Mill, they might be useful in my research too. I'm always interested in the characters who've lived and died in buildings. Archaeology tells their story.'

'I thought archaeologists dug holes,' Miss Cruckshank said suspiciously, as though she suspected he was an imposter.

'Out of the digging season we get up to all sorts of things – surveying historic buildings, processing finds and writing reports.'

'I'll take your word for it, Dr Watson. I take it you want me to have a look upstairs to see if there's anything else that might interest you.'

'We can do it if you like.'

'Oh no you won't.' Her words were sharp, as though the offer had offended her. 'I'm quite capable. Besides, I know where everything is. It might look like chaos up there, but it's organised chaos. I'll let Greta know if I find anything,' she added firmly.

Neil knew they were being dismissed and he caught Corrine's eye. There was no way they'd be allowed to search through the long-dead doctor's things themselves, however much they longed to see what was up there.

They'd have to be patient.

*

Wesley was reluctant to take Rachel with him when he picked up Eli Jelkes. The man was now a suspect and she was too involved. He wondered how her family would react to the arrest; whether Stella Tracey, who was an astute woman like her daughter, had always harboured nagging suspicions about the farm labourer; feelings of unease she'd suppressed for years because there had never been any indication he'd done anything wrong.

When he broke the news about the Falmouth statement to Gerry, the DCI suggested he take DC Paul Johnson with him. Paul had been working long hours on the inquiry with his lanky frame hunched over a computer. It would do him good to get out of the incident room and into the fresh air.

Wesley let Paul drive to Little Barton Farm, and as he sat in the passenger seat watching the landscape roll by, he contemplated calling at the farmhouse first to inform the Traceys that their employee was about to be taken in for questioning. In the end he decided against it. It was probably best to get the whole thing over and done with as soon as possible.

Even at the weekend, the work of the farm continued, and Wesley knew that Jelkes would have been up and about since before dawn to attend to the milking. As it was now almost lunchtime, he hoped the man would be in his little tied cottage. If not, it would be a case of traipsing through fields and outbuildings until they found him.

When Paul parked the unmarked car outside the cottage, Wesley climbed out and knocked on the door.

'Don't think he's in, sir,' said Paul behind him.

Wesley knocked again, and when there was still no answer, he pushed at the door, which swung open.

He told himself it meant nothing; that many people

didn't bother locking their doors in quiet parts of the countryside, especially when they had little worth stealing. Yet as soon as he stepped into the cottage, he felt something was wrong.

He opened the door to his left and found the room empty, the only sign of life a tall clock ticking away relentlessly in the far corner. They made their way into the kitchen, where a faint smell of cooked cabbage hung in the still air.

'No one here, sir,' said Paul in a whisper.

But before Wesley could reply, he heard a sound, a faint creak as though someone was creeping about upstairs. The two men looked at each other.

The staircase was steep and narrow, and Wesley went up first, his heart beating fast, unsure of what he'd find at the top. There were three doors off the tiny dark landing, all shut. He opened the nearest and found it was a bathroom, with cracked green tiles and a stained cast-iron bath. The second opened onto an empty and unfurnished room. That left the third door, which he guessed would lead to Eli's bedroom.

As he opened it, he heard Paul let out a gasp behind him. Eli Jelkes was slumped in an armchair next to the bed with a shotgun steadied between his knees. His finger hovered by the trigger and he appeared to be trying to fit the barrel into his mouth; with some difficulty, because the weapon was too long.

'Stop!' said Wesley, rushing forward. As soon as he reached the man, he knelt down and gently removed the weapon from his hands. He met no resistance. Instead, Jelkes slumped forward with a shuddering sob. Wesley handed the shotgun to Paul, who made it safe, removing the two cartridges and placing them on a nearby table. Wesley wondered fleetingly why he'd loaded it with two when one would have done the job perfectly well.

Squatting in front of Jelkes, he looked him in the face. The man was crying now, tears streaming down his weather-beaten cheeks, his shoulders shaking. Wesley and Paul waited. Eli Jelkes was going nowhere for the moment.

Once the weeping had subsided, Wesley put a hand on his arm. 'Would you have done it, Eli?'

'Dunno.'

He caught Paul's eye. He suspected the suicide attempt might have been a half-hearted gesture; a moment of despair Eli would have later come to regret . . . if he hadn't succeeded.

'Why?'

'They'll send me to prison. Can't face being shut in.'

'Why do you think you'd be put in prison, Eli? What have you done?'

'It's my fault. It's all my fault,' he said. Then the sobbing began again.

From the notebook of
Dr Christopher Cruckshank

20 August 1882

The constable says that much of the silver stolen by Albert Waring has been found by one of the Fitzterrans' tenant farmers hidden beneath a hedgerow, no doubt left there to be retrieved by the thief once the hue and cry died down. Mrs Fitzterran is still in shock and I attend her regularly.

I am distressed to report that another tragic death occurred in the village yesterday. Josiah Partridge's new bride, his daughter's former governess, was found drowned near the lime kilns. Nobody knows what happened, but when I examined her body, I saw no sign of violence.

Mrs Stephens and her sisters in gossip say that the new Mrs Partridge was seen in the village dressed in finery worthy of London, and rumour has it that her husband scolded her for her extravagance. Word also has it that her life was heavily insured by her husband shortly before her death.

I assured the reverend that it was a tragic accident

and that it was not fitting for his wife to utter such slander against an upright man. Besides, Partridge was away from home at the time of the tragedy. The reverend merely smiled and said his wife was a determined and clever woman who pursued injustice wherever she found it, and he was proud of her spirit. I told him that I shall give my evidence at the coroner's inquest, which is to be held at the Fisherman's Arms in two days' time, and that will be the end of the matter.

I understand that Mrs Stephens also has doubts about the guilt of that ruffian Albert Waring. She is inclined in my opinion to think too well of those less fortunate than herself. She says that Waring went to the hall and, having found it empty, then went to visit his mother, who says there was no blood visible upon his person and his manner was calm. A mother will always lie for her child, and I wish most heartily that Mrs Stephens would leave justice to take its course.

38

Gerry had persuaded the chief super to allow them more time to question Barry Clegg, but he knew the clock was ticking. He'd contacted the drugs squad in the hope of finding something that would confirm or disprove Clegg's story about the drugs delivery, though after all this time he wasn't holding out much hope.

Eli Jelkes was looking increasingly promising as a suspect. Since the discovery of the Falmouth statement, Gerry was pinning a lot of hope on this particular lead, but Wesley said he couldn't see Jelkes being involved with the death of David Leeson, although he acknowledged he could be wrong.

Gerry wasn't convinced that Bella Pritchard's continuing absence was connected to the Erica Walsh case. However, he agreed with Wesley that they needed to find her and make sure she was safe – and to see what she had to say about Erica's journey to Petherham.

He was sitting at his desk, mulling things over in a rare moment of peace, when his phone rang. It was Wesley, telling him they were bringing Jelkes in for questioning. He'd explain all later, he added, which made Gerry suspect the arrest hadn't been altogether straightforward. He left his office to break the news to Rachel, and when she made a call to her parents to inform them of this latest development, he saw her mask of professionalism slip for a moment.

After she'd finished the call, she hurried out of the incident room. When she returned ten minutes later, her eyes were red, as though she'd been crying, which made Gerry wonder if she'd been fonder of Eli Jelkes than she'd admitted.

An hour later, Wesley arrived back with the suspect, and soon the two detectives were sitting in the interview room where they'd spoken to Barry Clegg the previous day. Eli Jelkes sat opposite them looking stunned, with the duty solicitor hovering at his elbow.

'Eli,' Wesley began. 'Can I call you Eli?'

The man nodded. He looked uncomfortably out of place; a creature of the open countryside in a concrete cage. For a brief moment Gerry felt sorry for him.

'You say you want to tell us the truth about what happened.'

Jelkes nodded again. 'I didn't kill that lass and that's God's honest truth.'

'So why did you try and kill yourself?'

'I knew you'd think I did it. I know how you people work – you get a bloke like me who's got a record and you twist everything he says until you make him admit to anything.' He spat out the words, and Gerry suspected he'd had some bad experiences with the forces of law and order in the past.

'That's not going to happen here,' said Wesley. 'We can promise you that. Just tell us what happened from the beginning.'

Jelkes took a deep breath. 'I found her lying at the side of the lane all limp. I knew she was dead 'cause her eyes were staring and her tongue was sticking out. I couldn't leave her like that, could I?'

'You could have called the police.'

'I knew I'd get the blame. I've got a record, you see. I attacked a woman in Ilfracombe when I'd had too much to drink. I lost my temper.' He bowed his head. 'I used to drink a lot in those days, but I swear I haven't touched a drop since then.' He looked Wesley in the eye. 'The dead lass was near my cottage so I knew I'd be the first one you'd come for.'

Gerry gave Wesley a sideways glance. Both men would have liked to deny it, but they knew there was some truth in what Jelkes was saying. A man with a history of violence towards women, living so close to where a body was found, would have been subjected to intensive questioning if nothing else.

'So you found her; then what did you do?'

'I buried her, decent like. I put her in a nice spot on the edge of the field in the shade of that tree – the one that blew down in the storm.'

'You buried her rucksack as well.'

'I didn't want to be found with it – not if anyone came looking for her.'

Gerry leaned forward. 'But you took something out of it first.'

Jelkes gave a little nod. 'I saw her purse and . . . I took her bank card and some cash. I know I shouldn't have done it, but she wasn't going to need it, was she?'

'What about her phone?'

'I didn't find no phone. She didn't have one.'

'You sure?'

'Yeah, I'm sure.'

'You used her bank card in Falmouth.'

'That wasn't my idea. I was going to throw it away, but I went to see my sister who lived there, and she said if we used it it'd make everyone think the girl had been there. Put them off the scent like.'

'It worked. Tell us what you did,' said Wesley.

'There was a piece of paper in the purse with numbers on it. It came out with the card and my sister said it'd be her pin number. She tried the card when I met her in Falmouth. She got a hundred quid out.'

'Must have seemed like blood money,' said Gerry quietly.

'Suppose it did, but it meant they didn't start looking for her around here. My sister gave a statement saying she'd seen her. Said she'd recognised her from the news.'

'She could be prosecuted for perverting the course of justice,' said Gerry.

'Good luck with that. She's been dead two years.'

'So you admit to concealing the body and stealing the bank card?' said Wesley.

'Yes, but I didn't kill her. I'm no murderer.'

'Did you see who did?'

'I saw a dark car, like I told Tom Tracey. That's the truth. But I didn't see who was driving it.'

'How long was the car parked there?'

'Couple of minutes, no more. Just long enough to shove her body out onto the lane, I reckon. I went out to see what was going on and I think he must have seen me, 'cause he drove off fast. No lights or nothing.'

'Did you find anything else by the body? Something you might have taken?' Wesley asked gently. He could see the man's gnarled hands fidgeting with the fabric of his well-worn woollen sweater.

It was a few moments before Jelkes answered. 'Only the tie. It was round her neck, so I took it off – just in case she wasn't dead. The knot was tight, so it wasn't easy.'

Gerry noticed that even the duty solicitor was holding his breath.

'Where's this tie now?'

'At home. Do you think it's important?'

Rachel offered to go to the cottage to look for the tie, and Wesley didn't try to stop her. He knew she felt she owed it to Eli; better that she intruded on his privacy rather than some random stranger.

She returned to the police station with the tie in an evidence bag and handed it to Wesley before making for her desk without a word.

He put on a pair of crime-scene gloves and took it out of the bag. He'd been expecting a chain-store tie and had feared it would take the team months to track down the exact place it had been bought. But the tie he was holding had green, blue and brown stripes, quite distinctive. And on it was embroidered the initials SMNCR.

It looked as if their luck might just have changed.

39

Abigail Watkins always dreaded Sundays, the stale conclusion of the weekend when all you had to look forward to was another Monday morning. But if she drank enough on Saturday night, she wouldn't have to think about it, and at least this week Brian wasn't there to tell her off for opening a second bottle of wine to numb the frustration.

She hated Tradmouth. She missed her friends up north and she hated seeing the river every time she looked out of her front window. They'd first seen the house in the summertime, when the sun was shining on the water and the quayside thronged with tourists, sitting on the benches enjoying drinks from the pub on the far corner while they gazed like sheep at the boats gliding to and fro. Brian had said it would be lovely when the tourists had gone. But it wasn't. It was just cold, and the river had turned grey and angry as it slapped against the sea wall at high tide. It was as though the water was threatening her. *Come near me and I'll get you.*

Somebody had strung festive lights between the old-fashioned lamp posts on the quay, and as she gazed out of the window with her wine glass in her hand, she could see them shaking in the wind, their spots of light reflected in the dark water beyond like dancing fireflies. She'd thought that once Brian had sold the business, he wouldn't go away so often, but now the endless conferences and business journeys had been replaced by golfing trips. She was alone again, left with only a hostile ghost for company.

She sometimes saw the captain's widow in the shadows, glimpsed her out of the corner of her eye, a slight, gloating malevolence, as though she was glad of someone to share her grief and pain. Damien Lee had promised to come back to deal with the situation, but now he was dead. She'd heard on the news that somebody had killed him, but she couldn't imagine why, unless it was a robbery gone wrong. Brian had said a place like Tradmouth would be peaceful and safe, but he'd been lying. And she wanted to go home.

Unable to bear the sight of the heaving river any longer, she took the wine bottle into the drawing room at the back of the house and switched on the TV. At least it provided instant company of a sort, and she flicked through the channels looking for something to take her mind off her situation. She finally settled on an antiques programme. She didn't like antiques, but at least it was cheerful. She filled her glass again. Three quarters of a bottle gone, but there was nobody there to monitor her consumption. The previous evening Brian had texted to say he'd arrived safely in Spain for his golfing break and that he'd be back on Monday. She wasn't sure she could last out until then.

She increased the volume on the TV before kicking off her shoes and putting her feet up on the white sofa. She didn't hear the drawing room door opening quietly, and the sudden tightening of the scarf around her neck took her completely by surprise.

As Abigail struggled against death, the glass tumbled

from her hand, and red wine spread like a slick of blood over the pristine white leather.

The Christmas fair at Belsham church had gone well, and the takings were up on last year, which was a positive sign. Mark's sister-in-law Pam had been there, but Wesley was fully occupied, as were his children, who'd chosen to spend the day with friends. Rivalries amongst the volunteers of the parish had been dealt with and ruffled feathers smoothed, so all in all, Mark thought, it had been a good day – although he was glad it was over for another year.

He usually spent Saturday evening preparing for Sunday, the busiest day of his week, but all he wanted to do after the strain of being nice to everyone at the Christmas fair was to wind down in front of the TV with Maritia. The last thing he needed was a phone call, but then clergy were never off duty.

'Want me to answer it?' Maritia asked, putting down her glass of wine. 'I can tell them you're busy. Or out visiting a sick parishioner.'

'Better not. It might be urgent. If it isn't, I'll be tactful.'

Maritia returned her attention to the programme, a rather good costume drama, even if it was nothing like the book she'd enjoyed. She too needed an early night, but the open bottle was standing there temptingly, so she told herself another glass of wine would do no harm – in spite of what she preached to her patients.

She could hear Mark answering the phone out in the hall. 'Belsham Vicarage.' Then silence.

Her instincts told her it wasn't a call from a fussy church-warden or a plea for help from a parishioner in distress, and when her husband re-entered the room a couple of minutes later, he looked shaken.

Maritia stood up, her glass still in her hand. 'What's the matter?'

'I'm going to call Wesley. I think it was that man who came into the church the other day. This time he told me there's been a murder.'

40

'Mark thinks the caller might have been the same man who came into the church. He thought he recognised the voice.'

Wesley sat down opposite Gerry. It was Sunday morning, and Barry Clegg had been released on bail. Eli Jelkes, however, was being held for further questioning, and according to Rachel, her family were reeling from the shock. She herself had said little on the subject, and Wesley assumed that the events of the weekend had shaken her too. Although he wondered if there was something else – something she didn't want to share with him.

There was a quiet intensity in the incident room as the team worked on tracing the origins of the tie that, if Jelkes was to be believed, had ended Erica Walsh's life. Gerry reckoned it could be the breakthrough they'd been waiting for. Wesley hoped he was right.

'There've been no reports of any suspicious deaths, Wes.'

'Bella Pritchard still hasn't turned up. Think we should get the call traced?'

Gerry looked at the paperwork on his desk in despair. 'Crank call to a clergyman. Hardly counts as a priority ... unless a body's found. Know your trouble, Wes? You're a pessimist.'

Even though Wesley knew Gerry was probably right, he still felt uneasy. Mark had phoned at ten the previous night, and Wesley had been unable to get to sleep for thinking about it. He'd lain there listening to Pam's soft breathing, envying her ability to slumber whatever the situation. It had taken two cups of strong coffee with his breakfast to make him alert enough to face another long day.

The sound of Trish Walton's voice made him jump.

'Sorry, did I startle you?' She sounded slightly amused.

'Deep in thought, that's all.'

She placed the sheet of paper she was holding on the desk in front of him. 'They've found Bella Pritchard's car.'

'Where?'

'In the car park of the Fisherman's Arms at Petherham.'

Wesley picked up the message. The patrol who'd called it in ten minutes ago were awaiting instructions. He looked at the paperwork piled up on his desk. It wasn't a difficult decision. 'I'd better get down there – find out what's happening.'

He walked over to Rachel, who was tapping something into her computer. When she looked up, he could see the dark rings beneath her eyes and he guessed she hadn't slept much either. As soon as he broke the news about Bella's car, she reached for the coat on the back of her chair as though she too was longing for a distraction.

It wasn't far to Petherham. Before David Leeson's death, Wesley had only visited the village a few times, to sample the food at the Fisherman's Arms on the rare occasions they could persuade Della to babysit. Now, however, the winding road was becoming only too familiar.

Eli Jelkes had just been charged with preventing the lawful burial of a body and perverting the course of justice, and the tie that had killed Erica had been sent off to the lab for examination. But although Eli still appeared to be their best suspect for the 2008 murder, Wesley's gut instinct told him to hold off charging him with the more serious offence until they had further evidence.

Rachel was clearly still upset by his arrest, and as she drove to Petherham in silence, the tension made Wesley feel uneasy.

'I'm sorry about Eli. It can't be easy for you or your parents.'

'I'll cope.'

'I'm sure you will, but . . . Look, is something else bothering you?'

There was another long silence. Then, 'I think I might be pregnant.'

'Congratulations,' he said, an automatic response.

'Don't congratulate me. I don't know whether . . . '

'It's a big adjustment. Everyone feels apprehensive at first. I remember when Pam—'

Her hands tightened on the steering wheel. 'Will you stop going on about Pam. I'm not Pam.'

Wesley was stunned by the bitterness of her outburst; temporarily lost for words. Eventually he broke the awkward silence. 'What are you going to do?'

'I don't know. You're the first person I've told.'

'Nigel doesn't know?'

'Nigel's more interested in his prize heifers.'

The anger in her statement shook him, and when he looked at her, he saw tears flowing down her cheeks.

'Want me to take over the driving?'

She steered the car to the side of the road and they swapped places.

'Don't tell anyone. Please,' she said as Wesley pulled out into the traffic.

'Not if you don't want me to.' He was tempted to say she was bound to feel differently soon, and to give herself time. But he knew she wasn't in the mood for advice.

'It's our secret, Wes.'

He opened his mouth to say that it might not be a secret for long, but one look at her expression told him the subject was closed. She took a deep shuddering breath and wiped her eyes with her sleeve.

'Sorry about that,' she said.

'Don't be.' He touched her hand in a gesture that was meant to be reassuring, and she gave him a grateful smile.

'Don't worry. I'm fine. Let's forget it.'

Wesley pulled up in the pub car park. Mill House wasn't visible from there, but he wondered how the Quayles were getting on. He'd seen adverts for a grotto at the mill's visitors' centre, complete with Santa, elves and live reindeer, and he was surprised it was going ahead after the recent tragedy. A few years ago his own children would have been nagging to go to the grotto, but they were far too old for that sort of thing now. Sometimes he missed those days of innocence.

'Is that her car?' he said, pointing to a solitary red Toyota parked in the corner.

'The reg matches. Pub's not open yet.'

'In that case, we'll have to knock loudly.'

When they reached the front entrance of the Fisherman's Arms, they found the door ajar. The bar was empty apart from a woman with a mop and bucket who was cleaning the stone-flagged floor.

'Is the landlord about?'

'Simon!' she shouted in the general direction of the bar. 'Someone asking for you.'

A wiry man with a shaved head, a small beard and a mouth that formed itself into a permanent smile popped up from behind the bar like a jack-in-the-box. 'What can I do for you?' he asked cheerfully. 'I presume it's about that poor bloke who got caught up in the water wheel. Bad business.' He tapped the side of his nose. 'But not bad *for* business, if you know what I mean. We've had a lot of reporters hanging round, and they like their booze and bar meals.' He held out his hand. 'Simon Pussett, landlord.' His accent was northern; west of the Pennines rather than east.

'I'm sure they do, but that's not why we're here. Have you ever seen this man in here?' He produced a photograph of David Leeson, and the landlord studied it intently before shaking his head.

'One of your lot's already been round asking, and sorry, the answer's still no. Although if he came in when we were busy, I probably wouldn't have noticed. Sorry.'

Wesley pointed to the cricket bat hanging above the fireplace to their right. 'Do you play?'

Simon shook his head. 'Not any more, but the punters like a bit of sporting memorabilia.'

'How long have you been here?'

'Bought the place two years ago.'

'So you weren't in Petherham when that hitch-hiker went missing?'

Another shake of the head. Wesley knew it was time he concentrated on the purpose of his visit. 'There's a red Toyota in your car park. Do you know who it belongs to?'

'One of our guests. We have a few rooms here – not that we get many visitors this time of year.'

'Name?'

'Hang on.' He reached beneath the bar and took out a large book. 'It's a Ms B. Brown.'

Wesley and Rachel exchanged a look. Bella had reverted to her maiden name. The marital tiff must have been more serious than Carl Pritchard had made out.

'You wouldn't happen to know where she is now?'

'In her room, as far as I know. I served her at breakfast and I haven't seen her go out.'

'Can we have a word with her?'

'Help yourself. Room four, at the top of the stairs. Just through that door.'

Wesley followed the directions. Upstairs, the Fisherman's Arms was old-fashioned, with a richly patterned carpet on the floor of the narrow corridor. He felt uncharacteristically nervous about coming face to face with another of Erica Walsh's friends, especially one who'd actually grown up with her.

When he knocked, he could hear sounds inside the room: a toilet flushing, followed by approaching footsteps. The woman who opened the door looked at them enquiringly. Her pleasant face was framed by fair curls and he noticed that her skin was covered in freckles. She wasn't beautiful in the conventional sense, but she was attractive.

Her expression changed when they showed their ID. 'I can't believe he's done this. He's sent you to fetch me, hasn't he?' She glared at Rachel as though she thought she was a traitor to her sex.

'I presume you're talking about Carl,' said Wesley. 'In which case I can assure you he's not the reason we're here. We're investigating the murder of Erica Walsh. We understand she was a friend of yours.'

Bella sighed. 'I'm sorry. You must think I'm paranoid. It's just that when I left, he said he'd track me down, and when I saw you were from the police . . . '

It looked as though Carl Pritchard's version of events had been rather skewed, but at least they now knew that the discovery of Erica's remains had nothing to do with Bella's disappearance.

'That's OK,' Rachel said with a sympathetic smile.

'Come in. Please.'

As they followed her into the bedroom, Wesley looked round. It was a pleasant room: old-fashioned like the corridor, but clean and comfortable, with an en suite shower room and a king-sized bed. When Bella invited them to sit, Rachel made herself comfortable on the only chair and Wesley perched on the arm.

'It must have been a shock when you heard Erica had been found,' he began.

'It was. I used to hope she was still alive somewhere. She was seen in Falmouth, so I thought she might have run away to escape her mother's fancy man. She really hated him.'

'She was at university. She wasn't living at home.'

'Last time I saw her up in Leeds, she said she was fed up with her course, so when she disappeared, I thought she'd decided to throw it all in and start again. She'd always been impulsive . . . ' Her words trailed away. 'I hadn't seen her for a while and I presumed things had just got worse. People do vanish, don't they? Cut themselves off from the past and start new lives.' A faraway look appeared in her eyes.

'Tell us where you were at the time Erica disappeared,' said Rachel.

'I'd gone away with Carl. Romantic break. He could be romantic in those days,' she added with a note of sadness.

'But you were working here in Petherham?'

She took a deep breath and nodded. 'I wish to God I'd never gone with Carl. If I'd stayed here, it might never have happened. At the very least I'd have been able to save the little boy I was looking after, Shrimp – that was what everyone called him.'

'You referred to your employers as his lordship and her ladyship. What were their real names?' Wesley had a feeling he already knew, but he needed her to confirm it.

'Jeremy and Diana Quayle. They lived in Mill House, overlooking the creek. Shrimp's real name was Orlando. Diana had called him Shrimp when he was a tiny baby, and it sort of stuck.'

Wesley heard Rachel gasp behind him.

'You were the little boy's nanny?'

'That's right. To tell you the truth, I've never really got over what happened. Jeremy used to say Diana was highly strung, but I guess he should have called it something kinder – more medical. She was a nervy sort of person, but she'd seemed a lot better in the weeks leading up to her death. The doctor had given her some new pills, which seemed to be working. She said she was looking forward to Christmas. She'd ordered a tree from the garden centre and we were all going to pick it up when I got back from my break. I hadn't seen her so happy for ages, so I was really shocked by what happened.'

'What exactly did happen?' Wesley knew the bare facts, but he wanted to hear the story from Bella's point of view.

'While I was away, Jeremy went to some conference in London. I offered to postpone my break with Carl so Diana wouldn't be left by herself, but he said she'd be fine. He said she was a lot better and was looking forward to a bit

275

of peace and quiet while Shrimp was at school. He reckoned I deserved a few days' break. He even gave me some spending money.'

'But while you were away, Diana killed herself and her son.'

Bella nodded, and Wesley could see tears forming in her eyes. 'He was a lovely kid. I don't know how she could have done such a wicked thing.'

'Jeremy must have been devastated,' said Rachel. 'His own son . . . '

'Oh, Shrimp wasn't Jeremy's. Diana had him before they met. I never did find out who his father was, but I don't suppose it's important.' Bella thought for a moment. 'There were times when I wondered whether Jeremy resented him, but I could have been wrong.'

'How was Diana when you left? Did she show any signs of . . . ?'

'Like Jeremy said, she seemed a lot better, otherwise I'd never have left her alone.' She shook her head, tears glistening in her eyes. 'I should have been there to stop her.'

'You weren't to blame,' said Wesley, feeling sorry for the woman. He paused. 'I believe Jeremy inherited a lot of money when she died.'

'I don't know anything about that. Anyway, he was away, so he couldn't have had anything to do with it, could he?'

'I'm surprised you want to come back to a place with so many bad memories,' said Rachel.

Bella hesitated. 'Perhaps that's why I did come back – to exorcise some ghosts. I thought a few days here would help me to put things into perspective. Jeremy still lives at Mill House. I saw him passing the pub with his new wife.'

'Carl said there was someone you wanted to speak to.'

'I came here intending to ask Jeremy if he knew anything about Erica – whether she'd called at the house looking for me – but as soon as I saw him, I knew it was a stupid idea. He wasn't even here when she disappeared.'

'Jeremy and his new wife run a B&B at Mill House now, and they've renovated the mill. It's producing cloth again, and there's a smart new visitors' centre.'

She nodded slowly. 'I recognised her. Selina. She used to be his PA – called at the house a few times, but she always looked down her nose at me, so I never took to her. That was another reason why I decided not to speak to Jeremy. Simon, the landlord here, told me about the psychic weekend and the man who died.' She hesitated. 'Diana used to say Mill House was haunted – that bad things had happened there. She used to say she saw things.'

'What sort of things?'

'Orbs of light. Shapes in the shadows. I never saw anything myself, but there was something about that house. It sounds stupid, but I was never comfortable there and Shrimp – Orlando – used to wake up with nightmares. He said there was a lady in his room, a wet lady, but of course there was nobody there.'

'Do you think Erica might have come here looking for you, not realising you were away?'

She considered the question for a few moments. Then she nodded. 'If she'd tried to call me when she arrived, she wouldn't have succeeded, because there was no signal round here in those days. A black spot, they called it. Did you find her mobile?'

Wesley shook his head. 'No phone was found with her body. If she had one with her, someone must have taken it.'

'If she'd called at Mill House, only Diana would have

been there – unless she'd already ... done what she did.' Tears began to flow down her cheeks. 'I'm sorry,' she said after a few moments, wiping her eyes with the sleeve of her jumper.

'Don't be,' said Wesley. 'It was a terrible thing to have happened.'

'I couldn't go back to working with children after that, so I got a job in an office. I never wanted children of my own either, even though Carl did.'

Wesley nodded. He understood. Little Orlando Quayle's death had blighted this woman's life. Nothing had ever been the same for her since.

'Thank you for talking to us,' he said as he stood up. 'If you remember anything else about Erica – anything at all – please call me.' He handed her his card.

'You won't tell Carl where I am, will you?'

'Not if you don't want us to,' said Rachel. 'What will you do now?'

'My sister lives up north. I'll go to her for Christmas. It'll give me a chance to think things through.'

'Good luck,' said Wesley.

'Poor woman,' Rachel whispered when they reached the car.

Wesley didn't answer. There was something he wanted to check once they were back at the station.

The journey back to Tradmouth was uneventful, and even though they made small talk, nothing more was mentioned about Rachel's revelation. It was as though she'd put it out of her mind.

The house on Baynards Quay was June Marshall's third port of call that day. Monday was always busy because her people – she always thought of them as 'her' people – liked everything spick and span after the weekend.

June's own weekends were dull affairs. The telly and a takeaway pizza with her hubby if she was lucky and he didn't disappear off to the pub. But her people lived more glamorous and exciting lives – that was why they employed her to clean their homes instead of clearing up after themselves.

She'd done the solicitor's office in Tradmouth High Street first thing, then driven to Belsham vicarage. Such a nice couple, the Reverend Fitzgerald and his wife, who was black and a doctor. Their little boy was a sweetie too. She liked them because they treated her almost as one of the family, not like some. Dr Fitzgerald had even examined the funny lump on her wrist, even though she didn't have to, and she always chatted when she had the time. She'd once told June how her parents had come over from Trinidad to train as doctors. Medicine was in the family, she'd said, although her brother, Wesley, was the odd one out because he'd become a detective inspector. June liked the chatty ones. She didn't like the snobs – people who looked down on you just because you cleaned their toilets.

She wasn't sure whether she liked the Watkinses, who owned the house on Baynards Quay. She'd only seen the husband once; he'd been on the phone, studiously ignoring her as she dusted round him. The woman – Abigail – was the type who lived on her nerves; June thought she was shy and probably lonely. She watched June as she cleaned, not critically, but as though she was longing to start a conversation but didn't quite know where to begin. The one time she'd opened up was when she got onto the subject of ghosts. She'd said a psychic had been round and told her the place was haunted. June didn't really believe in such things, but she could tell Abigail did – and that she was frightened of something.

She knocked on the Watkinses' door, and when there was no answer, she put her key in the lock, thinking Abigail must be out. From her clothes, June suspected she did a lot of shopping, although she was usually at home on a Monday.

When she stepped into the hall, she could hear the faint sound of voices coming from the back of the house. Perhaps Abigail had company. She stood for a few moments expecting the woman to emerge from the drawing room, but after a while, she realised that the voices had the artificially hearty note used by daytime TV presenters.

She took off her coat and hung it up, calling out in case Abigail was upstairs or in the bathroom. When there was no reply, she made for the utility room, where the cleaning things were kept. On the way, she peeped into the drawing room to see how many empty wine bottles had been left on the coffee table. Whenever Brian Watkins was away, Abigail's alcohol consumption increased. June always noted her people's weaknesses.

As she pushed the door open further, she could see that the TV was on and that there was a bottle of wine on the table, but no glass. She wouldn't have put it past Abigail to take the glass to bed with her if her husband wasn't there to complain.

She edged her way further into the room, assessing how much time it would take to return it to the pristine condition Brian Watkins expected. He was the fussier of the pair; some men were, she'd found.

All of a sudden she caught sight of the slick of dried red wine on the soft white leather sofa. She stared at it in despair, wondering how on earth she was going to get the stain out. Then she noticed the glass lying on its side on the rug, and beside it, Abigail Watkins, slumped on the floor. She couldn't see her face, but she could see the scarf wound tightly around her neck.

June had never seen a dead body before, but there was a first time for everything.

41

DC Trish Walton knocked on Gerry's door. It was a bold knock, the type that demanded attention. Gerry looked up and favoured her with a gap-toothed grin.

'Hi, Trish. What can I do you for?'

Trish forced herself to smile at the feeble joke. 'They've traced the firm that made that tie – the one Erica Walsh was strangled with.'

'And?'

'Luckily they've kept records going back fifteen years. That tie was a special order – only fifty made.'

'Who ordered them?'

'Someone called Jack Tanthwaite. Address in a place called Cheadle Hulme, near Stockport. I've been in touch with Greater Manchester.'

Gerry raised his eyes to heaven, sending up a silent prayer that the answer to his next question would be yes. 'And is Mr Tanthwaite still in the land of the living?'

'He's still at the same address. GMP have offered to send someone round to take a statement. Or do you want someone from here to go?'

'We'll see what GMP come up with before we decide on that. It's a long way, so I'm inclined to let them do the legwork. Did the manufacturer tell you the name of the company the ties were made for – this SMNCR?'

'Oh yes.' Trish paused as though she was about to make a dramatic revelation. 'It wasn't a company. It was a cricket club.'

Since his meeting with Bella Pritchard, an idea had been forming in Wesley's mind. He'd already done his best to follow it up, but he hadn't made much progress, and he hoped he'd have more luck at the beginning of the working week. However, when a call came into the incident room, all that had to be put on hold. There'd been a suspicious death in Tradmouth. Address on Baynards Quay – a few doors down from the chief inspector's home.

The report had been made by a cleaner who'd discovered the body when she arrived at the house as she always did on a Monday morning. According to the cleaner, June Marshall, the dead woman was a Mrs Abigail Watkins, and her husband was away in Spain on a golfing trip.

As soon as Wesley broke the news, Gerry put his head in his hands and gave a deep sigh. This was all they needed.

He was unusually quiet as they walked side by side under the dark grey sky to Baynards Quay. Wesley hoped this latest death would turn out to be accidental, or due to natural causes. At that moment, he felt overwhelmed.

When they arrived at their destination, they saw that the CSI team had got there before them. The house had been converted swiftly and efficiently into a crime scene, with metal stepping plates dotting the thick carpets.

'Deceased is in the lounge at the back, sir,' a uniformed constable with a clipboard told Gerry cheerfully. 'Her cleaner's indentified her as Abigail Watkins, the householder. Says she heard the TV on and went to investigate. Looks like she's been strangled, but we're waiting for Dr Bowman to arrive and confirm it.'

'What have we done to deserve this just before Christmas?' Gerry mumbled to nobody in particular.

But Wesley's mind was on the case. 'We interviewed Mrs Watkins about David Leeson's murder. She was the last person he visited before he went to Mill House.'

Gerry scratched his head. 'I realise that, and if I was a betting man, I'd put good money on the two deaths being linked. Although I can't for the life of me think how.'

Wesley had been sure that Abigail had told them everything she knew about the psychic's visit – unless there was something she hadn't thought important enough to mention at the time; something Leeson's killer had hoped she wouldn't reveal. Or had Leeson died because he'd found out somebody was planning to kill her? The possibilities whirled through his brain as he made his way to the back of the house, to the room the constable had called the lounge but that Abigail had referred to during their last visit as the drawing room.

The woman's body lay sprawled on the rug in front of the sofa, as though she'd been sitting and had slithered down after losing consciousness. Wesley could see a large red stain on the white leather, wine rather than blood, and the glass that had tumbled from Abigail's hand lay on the floor beside the body. He guessed that somebody had crept up behind her, leaning over the low back of the sofa, which faced away from the door, and taking hold of the colourful scarf around her neck to strangle the life out of her.

Or perhaps the killer had found the scarf in the hall and brought it into the room with him. The constable had mentioned that the TV was on when the cleaner found the body so Abigail might not have heard her assailant entering the room. If that was the case, perhaps it had been a blessing that she hadn't known what was coming.

Careful not to disturb anything, he bent down so he could see her face. Last time he'd met the woman, she'd seemed troubled, and now her bulging dead eyes stared straight at him, challenging him to bring her justice.

'Well, I don't think we need Colin to tell us the cause of death,' said Gerry.

As soon as he'd said the words, Colin himself arrived, carrying the bag containing the tools of his trade. Wesley and Gerry stood back while he conducted his examination of the body.

'Time of death?' Gerry asked hopefully.

Colin looked up and wagged his finger in the DCI's direction. 'Now, now, Gerry, you should know better than to ask that one. We're not in a TV cop show, you know. I can only be approximate.'

'Go on then, Colin, be approximate.'

'Dead more than twenty-four hours – possibly since Saturday night. When was she last seen alive?'

'Apparently her husband's away, so we don't know for certain,' said Gerry.

'There's only one glass, so it doesn't look as though she had company,' said Wesley. 'And Saturday's paper's there on the coffee table, so she can't have died before then.'

Colin nodded slowly. 'She's a neighbour of yours, Gerry. Did you know her well?'

'They've only moved in recently, and they were hardly the type to pop round and borrow a cup of sugar. In fact, I only spoke to her for the first time a couple of days ago. She was a client of that psychic who was stabbed in Petherham.'

Colin raised his eyebrows. 'Connection?'

'Seems too much of a coincidence if there isn't,' said Wesley. 'In which case, I'm wondering whether someone killed her because she knew something about his murder.'

'Thankfully that's your department,' said Colin before continuing his examination. 'Post-mortem at four suit you?'

'We can probably rule out the husband,' said Gerry with a sigh as he arrived back in his office. 'He's been in Spain since Friday afternoon and isn't due back until this evening. He's been playing golf with his mates all weekend and there's no way he could have sneaked back to murder his wife, unless he can pull off the trick of being in two places at once.'

'So we can cross him off our list, but I don't think it was a random assault. And there doesn't appear to be anything missing from the house.'

'None of the neighbours saw or heard anything, and that includes me and Joyce. Everyone hunkers down with the curtains shut in the winter, and both the neighbouring houses are holiday lets and are unoccupied at the moment. Our killer certainly chose the right time of year. In summer, the quay's like Piccadilly Circus.'

Wesley wandered back to his own desk, his mind working. The crime-scene people had found no sign of a break-in, which meant Abigail Watkins must have let her killer in; either that, or whoever strangled her had a key. A lover was Gerry's favoured theory at the moment. And yet a lover would surely have been sharing the bottle of wine. Unless he'd washed up his own glass and put it away. Someone was examining Abigail's phone records and bank account, and Wesley was clinging to the hope that the answer would be found amongst the contacts on her phone.

There was something else he wanted to check. The call Mark had received on Saturday evening was nagging away at him like a troublesome tooth. The caller had said there'd been a murder, and now somebody had actually been killed.

When he contacted Mark, he was pleased to learn that his brother-in-law had made a note of the anonymous caller's number as a precaution. An hour later, Wesley had his answer. The call had been made from the old-fashioned red phone box on the embankment in Tradmouth – a couple of minutes' walk away from Baynards Quay.

From the notebook of
Dr Christopher Cruckshank

29 August 1882

When I arrived home after visiting a patient yesterday, I found Mrs Stephens waiting for me. She was in a state of agitation and it wasn't long before I learned the reason.

'Do you not think it strange, Doctor, that so many people have died unexpectedly in this village?'

I replied that death was always with us, but she carried on.

'Three deaths, all most convenient for those left behind. I am convinced of Albert Waring's innocence, and it was common knowledge that there was nothing amiss with the first Mrs Partridge apart from a desire for attention. And do you not think the drowning of the second Mrs Partridge was a little odd, especially as I understand all was not well between her and her new husband, who had insured her life heavily? Even if I am wrong, which I acknowledge I could be, I do not think these things can be ignored. You are in a position to raise your suspicions with the authorities. I think some action must be taken.'

I told her firmly that the coroner had given his verdict in all cases and refused to discuss the matter further.

I was surprised when the vicar called at my home this morning to tell me that his wife had gone out early to visit a woman from the cottages at the other end of the village who had just been delivered of a new baby and that she had not returned. As he was becoming concerned, he had visited the new mother, who told him that Mrs Stephens had left her cottage more than an hour before. He asked me if I had seen her, but I had to disappoint him. I offered to help him search for her, and he accepted my offer gratefully.

He said that his wife suspected there was wickedness abroad in Petherham – a serpent in our little Eden, as he put it. I told him that Mrs Stephens had already shared her fears with me, and although she seemed to be an impulsive woman, I had no doubt of her good intentions.

We called upon the blacksmith's wife and several others Mrs Stephens visited regularly, but there was no sign of her. Then we saw the sexton hurrying towards us, out of breath.

'Come quickly, Reverend. Something terrible has befallen your missus.'

The man led us into the churchyard and up to an open grave, recently dug to be the last resting place of an elderly man from the farm cottages, his funeral to be paid for by the Petherham Burial Circle. I looked into the grave and saw Mrs Stephens lying at the bottom, one hand above her head as though she was sleeping, blood drying on her pale temple.

'She must have missed her footing and fallen,' I said, staring down at the woman I had once thought beautiful. It was a tragic accident. Nothing more.

42

Greta Moss washed up Miss Cruckshank's breakfast things and left them on the side to drain. She would put them away when she visited again later. When she'd finished, she looked in on the old lady and found her dozing by the fire.

Corrine and Neil had been so interested in her box and its contents that for a short while Greta had felt she was part of their world; a world more glamorous than her own. Or at least it seemed that way.

Surely there was something else up in those junk-filled bedrooms to interest them. She saw herself making the call, and imagined their excitement when she produced a clue to solve the mystery of those strange photographs.

Miss Cruckshank had said she wanted to look through the things herself, but if Greta did it, she'd be saving her a job. She'd been quick enough to give her the box, so she was sure she wouldn't mind. Besides, she wouldn't take anything valuable. That wouldn't be right.

After checking that Miss Cruckshank was still asleep, she crept upstairs and opened the door at the end of the landing.

*

Neil was in his Exeter office, watching the clock and wishing he was somewhere else. He'd just been reading through a draft chapter one of his colleagues had written about the mill at Tradington, making changes here and there, and now he had to choose the photographs and illustrations to go with the piece. As he sat there staring at the words swimming before him on the computer screen, he knew he wasn't cut out to be an author, especially when he wanted nothing more than to get out and about, seeing what was going to turn up in some muddy trench.

He already had the old book Corrine had found about the Petherham Curse to liven up the publication, and he hoped that Miss Cruckshank would produce some material to throw more light on the mill's long and scandalous history. He needed to discover the true story behind those strange pictures of the dead; a story guaranteed to get the book flying off the shelves in the tourist information office.

His phone rang and he answered it, grateful for any distraction from his task. He was glad to hear Corrine's voice.

She came straight to the point. 'Have you heard any more from your friend in the police?'

'He's been working long hours, so I haven't seen much of him.'

There was a pause, and Neil suspected she'd just called to find out whether there was any news about the investigation into Erica Walsh's murder.

Then she spoke again. 'Greta rang to say she's found something we might be interested in at Miss Cruckshank's house. I said I'd pick it up from her place at five. Do you want to meet me?'

Neil agreed with alacrity. Perhaps this would be just

what he needed to make *The Historic Mills of South Devon* a best-seller.

Wesley and Gerry attended Abigail Watkins' post-mortem. The results were more or less as expected. The victim had been attacked from behind, taken by surprise, and although there was a suggestion that she'd tried to pull the scarf from around her throat, there were no other signs that she'd put up a fight. The absence of skin under her well-manicured fingernails suggested that she hadn't defended herself by clawing at her attacker. Neither was there any indication that she'd been restrained. Her murder had been quick and efficient.

It was almost six o'clock when the station's front desk informed Gerry that Brian Watkins had arrived. He'd been shown into the comfortable interview room where they'd spoken to Janet Walsh, and after a brief discussion with Gerry about the approach they should take, Wesley and Rachel hurried down to conduct the interview.

Watkins seemed considerably more subdued than he'd been at their last meeting. He sat with his head in his hands while the tea Rachel had made grew cold on the table in front of him.

'We're very sorry for your loss, Mr Watkins,' Wesley began. He waited for the man to speak. Grieving relatives shouldn't be hurried.

'I still can't believe it. It doesn't seem real.'

'Can you think of anybody who'd want Abigail dead?'

He shook his head. 'She could be a bit ... flaky with all that stuff about ghosts and seances, but she didn't have enemies. She wasn't that sort of woman. It was a robbery, surely?'

'We don't think so. Is there anyone who might have a grudge against *you*? You were a businessman, I believe. Is there anyone you got on the wrong side of?'

The man looked offended. 'Of course not. I've never mixed with those sort of people. Can I go home? There are things I need to do.'

'I'm afraid your house is being treated as a crime scene at the moment. Is there anyone you can stay with?'

'No. We're new around here.' He thought for a moment. 'I can book into the Marina Hotel, but I'll need some things.'

'Someone will go with you to get them,' said Wesley quickly. He knew the routine.

'Thanks.'

Wesley cleared his throat. The next question was a sensitive one. 'Would you like to see your wife?'

'To identify her, you mean?'

'Your cleaner's already done that.'

'In that case, no. I'd rather remember her how she was.' There was a short pause. 'As long as you're sure it is her.'

'We're sure. I'm sorry. Detective Sergeant Tracey here will act as your family liaison officer, so if there's anything you need, anything at all . . .'

Brian Watkins turned his head to look at Rachel. 'Thanks, but no thanks. I don't need a family liaison officer. All I ask is that you catch the bastard who killed Abi.'

The words were half-hearted, and Wesley was sure that Watkins was holding something back. There was a long and awkward silence, and he hoped it wouldn't be long before the newly widowed husband felt the urge to fill it.

'I said she didn't have an enemy in the world, Inspector, but . . . It's not an easy thing to say . . .'

'In this job, we've heard it all, Mr Watkins . . . Brian.

Nothing you say will surprise or shock us, and if it's not relevant, it won't go beyond this room.' Wesley saw Rachel nod in agreement.

Brian's thick lips formed a sad smile. 'Seal of the confessional and all that. You would have made a good priest, Inspector.'

Wesley caught Rachel's eye and saw her lips twitch upwards in amusement. He'd never considered the priesthood as a career option. Rather he'd started life wanting to be an archaeologist, which he supposed had a lot in common with his present job: digging deep until he got to the truth. 'What do you want to tell us, Mr Watkins?'

Watkins steepled his fingers and leaned forward as though he was about to share a confidence. 'I think Abi was having an affair. She'd been distant recently.'

'Are you sure it wasn't something to do with the house? She called in a psychic, so she must have been worried.'

'All in her head.'

'A cover for unhappiness?' Rachel said softly.

'Maybe. Probably my fault – the move was all my idea. I took her away from her family and friends up in Alderley Edge. Perhaps I was wrong to move south when I sold my business. I did very nicely out of the sale and I thought we'd have a better life down here. She used to love coming to this area on holiday – all the yachts and that – but living here full time's a different matter, I guess.'

'You think she'd met another man here in Devon?'

'It was just an impression I got. She became very secretive. Restless.'

'Any idea who he was – or where she might have met him?'

Watkins shook his head.

'You say you've been in Spain on a golfing weekend.'

'I don't just say – I was.'

'I know. We've checked with the airline. Who were you with?'

'Some old mates from where I used to live. We get together from time to time. Used to be cricket, but now it's golf. The old competitive spirit's still alive and kicking,' he added smugly.

'Is there another woman in your life, Mr Watkins?' Wesley asked the question casually, as though he was making friendly conversation.

Brian Watkins' face turned an unattractive shade of red. 'I don't know where you got that idea from.'

'Is there?'

There was a short silence, then, 'No comment.'

Wesley took that for a yes.

'Are you sure you've no idea who your wife was seeing?' Wesley repeated the question. It was something he needed to know.

'No. But with my boat and the golf club, she had been on her own a lot. Plenty of opportunity,' he said, with a knowing nod.

Wesley got the picture: a lonely woman whose husband had tired of her company. It was hardly surprising that her unoccupied mind conjured malevolent ghosts in a historic house.

'I'm sure Abigail's death must be linked to David Leeson's murder somehow,' he said to Rachel as they walked back to the incident room after seeing Watkins off the premises. 'If it isn't, it seems a coincidence too far. Did Leeson reveal some secret to her during their consultation – a secret that turned out to be deadly for both of them?'

'It's possible,' said Rachel. 'But as they're both dead, we can't ask them,' she added, ever the realist.

As soon as they walked through the door of the CID office, Rob Carter hurried over holding an evidence bag containing a mobile phone. 'This was found in Abigail Watkins' bedroom. She didn't share with her husband,' he added meaningfully. 'It was hidden in her underwear drawer.'

'Bet you had fun sorting through that.' Gerry had just emerged from his office. 'Didn't we find her phone by the body?'

'That's right,' said Rob. 'But this one was hidden. A second phone. You know what that means.'

'Get the calls traced,' said Wesley. 'You know the routine.'

Rob nodded and scurried off to his desk. Rachel returned to her paperwork and Wesley followed Gerry into his office.

'How did you get on with the grieving widower?' Gerry asked.

Wesley considered the question for a moment. 'I don't think the marriage was particularly happy, and I think she resented being moved away from her support network up north to come down here. He also thinks she had a lover. Let's hope Rob can identify him from that second phone. And I want someone to look into Watkins' background and financial interests. He says he sold a successful business and everything was going well, but ... '

'You think he might be telling us porkies?'

'Wouldn't put it past him.'

Ten minutes later, Rob hurried into Gerry's office. Only one number had made calls to and from Abigail Watkins' secret phone. Now he was just waiting for a name.

*

The stairlift glided silently upwards, carrying Esme Cruckshank towards the landing.

Perhaps it had been a mistake to give Greta the box, but she'd thought the photographs inside – those rustic images of the village and the mill – hadn't mattered. If she'd known about the others, she wouldn't have been so hasty in her generosity, but they'd been stashed away in a hidden compartment, and her desire for the company of someone young enough to make her feel alive again must have clouded her judgement. If her great-nephew found out that she'd been so free and easy with the family secrets, he'd call her a stupid old woman, and he'd be right. There were some secrets you should never share with anybody.

When she'd been dozing by the electric fire earlier, she'd heard sounds from upstairs and assumed that Greta was tidying her bedroom. But now she wondered whether the noises had come from the room where the things were kept. She was certain Greta was no thief, but what if she'd taken something she thought had no monetary value to impress her new acquaintances, the archaeologist and the young woman with the tattoos?

She needed to find out, so she made her way slowly and painfully to the room at the end of the landing, where she opened the cupboard. When she found it wasn't there, she felt panic rising in her chest.

Then she remembered that some of the pages had been removed many years ago. Greta and her new friends would never discover the whole story. That was special. That was just for family.

43

Wesley and Rachel were still at the station when most people were settling down for an evening with their feet up in front of the TV.

He called Pam at 8.30 to apologise for the fact that he'd probably be very late again, but she sounded remarkably relaxed about the prospect of not seeing him until almost bedtime. And when he asked her about her day, the answer explained her cheerful mood. When she'd arrived home from work, she'd found Neil on the doorstep. He'd brought with him an old notebook someone had given him, and she was reading through it because he wanted her opinion. Wesley might be interested, she said, because it contained references to Mill House at Petherham, the scene of David Leeson's murder.

At the mention of Petherham, Wesley was suddenly eager to learn more. He was as sure as he could be that Erica had been intending to call there to see Bella on the night she vanished, so he couldn't dismiss anything about the village or its history out of hand.

He arrived home at 9.30 and found Pam transcribing the contents of the handwritten notebook onto her laptop. Neil needed it for his publication, she explained, although she hadn't got very far.

He picked up the notebook. It smelled musty and its pages were foxed, but the handwriting was quite legible. He turned to the first page and saw the words *Report of Petherham Burial Circle* printed neatly at the top.

'Have you got time for this after a day at school?'

'I got all my marking and preparation done earlier, and I've even rewritten the Angel Gabriel's speech for the nativity play. A bit of history makes a welcome change,' she added, setting her computer aside. 'The notebook belonged to a doctor who was new to Petherham. He made a lot of calls to Mill House; the owner's wife was a hypochondriac, by the sound of it.' She grinned. 'I think Neil's hoping I'll find him a bit of scandal – something that'll make sense of those weird photographs. He says he needs a bit of human interest for this publication of his.'

'Have you found any scandal?'

'Not yet, but it's early days. I don't think much of this Dr Cruckshank's bedside manner, especially as his patients must have been paying through the nose for his services. How's Rachel?' she asked unexpectedly as the cat leapt onto Wesley's knee and dug her claws into his flesh. 'Must be awkward for her with that man who works for her parents being arrested.' She was looking him in the eye, almost as though she'd guessed something was amiss. But Rachel's secret wasn't his to share.

'She's upset about it, but that's only to be expected. She's known the guy since she was a kid.'

'You think he killed the hitch-hiker?'

'He's admitted to burying her body, but there's no

evidence that he actually killed her.' He felt a sudden urge to change the subject. 'Have you heard from Maritia?'

Pam shook her head and started tidying away her things.

'Gerry mentioned retirement the other day,' he said to the back of her head.

She turned round, suddenly interested. 'Will that mean promotion for you?'

'Possibly.'

'You don't sound too happy about it.'

'Gerry and I are a team – Holmes and Watson, bacon and egg.'

'You'll still have Rachel,' she said innocently.

Wesley gave her a sad smile. 'He only said he was thinking about it – checking his pension and doing the sums.'

'Chief Inspector Peterson. Sounds good.'

Wesley didn't answer. He said he was going to bed to get an early night, and when Pam joined him half an hour later, he pretended to be asleep.

As Wesley sat at his desk the following morning after Gerry's daily briefing, he scrolled through the messages that had come in overnight. One in particular caught his attention. This was something Gerry needed to know.

'We've got a name,' he said, poking his head round the DCI's office door. 'It's the only contact number on Abigail Watkins' second phone.'

'Who's the lucky man?'

'Would you believe, it's Brad Percy.'

Gerry sat back in his chair and scratched his head. 'Let's bring our local Lothario in then. Think he's in the frame for David Leeson's murder as well?'

'He was on the spot, so we can't rule him out. We need

him picked up as soon as possible – before he knows we're on to him.'

It was just before lunch when Brad Percy arrived at the police station in the company of a pair of constables. He'd seemed confident last time they'd spoken to him. This time he looked frightened.

'Look, I want to be straight with you,' he said once they were in the interview room with the tape running.

'That'll make a change,' said Gerry. 'It wasn't Sally Chen you were intending to take to Petherham. She backed up your story, but she was lying for you, wasn't she?'

'Sally's very loyal.'

The statement annoyed Wesley. Percy had used his employee to cover for him without considering the possible consequences for her.

'You were going to Mill House to meet Abigail Watkins,' Gerry continued. 'She was your mystery woman.'

Percy didn't answer.

'Abigail's dead, Brad,' said Wesley, playing good cop. 'She was murdered the night before last. Strangled.'

A look of shock passed across Percy's face, but Wesley found it hard to tell whether it was real or fake. 'That's … Oh God.' He put his head in his hands and sat like that for a while before he looked up. 'You should be questioning her husband then.'

'Why?'

'She was bloody petrified of him. He'd just insured her life for a fortune – put pressure on her to sign the documents. And she was sure he was having an affair. A thirty-year-old blonde at the yacht club, she said. She'd found texts from her on his phone. She was scared. She thought he might arrange an accident for her if he ever got the chance.'

'What kind of accident?'

'She became terrified of the river. She thought he might push her in one dark night. Drown her. I told her she should leave him, but she said she had nowhere to go. Besides, she said he'd find her.'

'But she was still willing to go to Mill House with you.'

'She wanted to go there to see Damien, but in the end, she couldn't come. She'd thought her husband was going away, but he decided against it at the last minute. I went there in case he changed his mind and she was able to join me after all.'

'You lied to your wife and you lied to us,' said Gerry sharply.

'That was because I'd promised to keep her name out of it. I didn't know what that bastard husband of hers might do if he found out. Even though he was playing away himself, he was still possessive. One law for him and another for her. We kept a special phone; took every precaution.'

'We found the phone. That's how we traced you. How did you and Abigail meet?'

'At an art exhibition in Tradmouth. I was looking for a present for my wife – she's not the easiest person to buy for, but she likes paintings. Abi was there on her own, looking lost, and we got talking. She said she'd just moved down here and I offered to show her the sights. I was genuinely fond of her, Inspector. You've got to believe that. I'd never have harmed a hair on her head. Why would I?'

'Where were you on Saturday night?'

'At home with my wife,' he said with confidence. 'We had people round for dinner.'

'You didn't drive to Tradmouth?'

'No way. And you can't prove I did. Like I said, you

should be questioning that husband of hers. She said he was capable of anything.'

'There's just one problem, Mr Percy. Abigail's husband was in Spain at the time of her murder, with lots of witnesses to vouch for him. Any more bright suggestions?'

Brad Percy put his head in his hands again and said no more. Interview ended.

The killer of Abigail Watkins waited for the phone to be answered. Murder was easy. Too easy perhaps. Committing murder made you a monster, set apart from others while living there in plain sight amongst the rest of humanity. Unsuspected. Ordinary.

There was a slight tremble in the voice on the other end of the line. 'Look, I'm not sure I can—'

'We have an agreement.'

'Please. I need time to get it together. It's not that straightforward.'

The killer could hear the fear. Fear was good. Fear made the whole thing more exciting.

44

As soon as Wesley and Gerry returned to the incident room, they headed straight for the DCI's office.

'I can't stand all this waiting around, Wes.'

'Greater Manchester have promised to get back to us the moment they have anything on that tie.' Wesley sat down on Gerry's visitor's chair and leaned across his cluttered desk, pushing aside a heap of overtime forms. 'Let's go over what we've got.'

Gerry looked like a child who was expecting a present but was being appeased with promises.

'Abigail Watkins was having an affair with Brad Percy and we now know she was the woman he was expecting to join him at Petherham Mill House for the psychic weekend. Mind you, he has a cast-iron alibi for her murder, and he claims she was scared of her husband, who had insured her life for a considerable sum and was seeing another woman. But Brian Watkins couldn't possibly have killed her because he was in Spain at the time. That means we're left with the mystery man who called my brother-in-law from the phone box on the embankment claiming there'd been a murder.'

'Who may or may not be the same person who accosted

Mark in Belsham church.' Gerry thought for a moment. 'If he chose Belsham church, that suggests he lives there, don't you think?'

'Mark said he didn't recognise him, but he's priest-in-charge of a few village churches round about – a number of rural parishes sharing one vicar is very common these days. If our man thinks of Mark as his local vicar, he could equally be from one of his other parishes.'

'Which are?'

Wesley frowned, embarrassed by his ignorance. 'I'm not sure, but I can find out.'

'What about David Leeson's murder? Stabbed in the back. Different MO. Different killer?'

'In view of his connection with Abigail, I think that's unlikely.'

'You think Abigail knew something about his death?'

'How could she? She wasn't there. Besides, she was a client rather than a friend, so I can't see him confiding in her if he was afraid of someone.'

'What about Erica Walsh?'

'We're pretty sure Little Barton Farm was just the deposition site and she was strangled elsewhere. If Eli Jelkes is to be believed, he disturbed the killer before he could remove the tie from around her neck.'

'If I was the killer, I'd come back to get it. It's a thumping great clue.'

'But if he did come back, he'd have found the body wasn't there, because Jelkes had buried it.'

The two men sat back, satisfied that they'd started to get things clearer in their minds.

Wesley left the DCI to the paperwork he knew he hated and returned to his own desk to call Mark. 'I know you've probably told me already, but can you just remind me which parishes you're responsible for?'

Mark answered patiently, listing his churches, and when he came to St Mary Magdalene, Petherham, Wesley almost felt like punching the air. 'Thanks. That's very helpful.'

'That phone call I had – do you think it was the person who killed that woman in Tradmouth?'

'We're still working on it,' said Wesley, anxious to end the call and discover what Gerry would make of his new piece of information.

But before he could return to the DCI's office, Rachel appeared at his desk, waving a sheet of paper and looking pleased with herself.

'Message from Greater Manchester. Someone's spoken to Jack Tanthwaite, and it turns out he was the secretary of the cricket club that ordered the ties. When I say cricket club, it was more a group of businessmen and assorted drinking buddies than a serious sports club. It was called the South Manchester and North Cheshire Rogues – hence SMNCR. They played friendly matches against local clubs, but it was disbanded after a couple of years because half the team lost interest. Tanthwaite had club ties made for playing and social members.'

'Social members being the ones who joined them in the bar after matches?'

'Got it in one. Fortunately Tanthwaite's an organised man and he thinks he kept a list of club members. GMP said they'll email it through once he locates it. Apparently it's somewhere in his shed.'

'You can't hurry a man in his shed; we'll just have to be patient,' said Wesley.

There was something he wanted to find out; something

that had been nagging at the back of his mind for a while. He'd been too preoccupied to deal with it, even though the information had only been a couple of clicks away. He felt annoyed with himself for not checking it before, but he'd only just realised its potential relevance.

He called Greater Manchester again, and after that he contacted Neston, because there was something else he needed to know, although it was a long shot.

An hour later, Gerry lumbered out of his office like a bear emerging from hibernation and made for Wesley's desk. 'I've just had an inspector from Neston on. He tells me you've asked for details of that suicide case at Mill House – Bella Brown's employer. He asked me what was going on.'

'Diana Quayle killed herself and her son on the same night Erica Walsh was seen on the road to Petherham, but nobody ever made the connection. The officers who investigated the two cases weren't even aware that Erica knew the Quayles' nanny, and as Bella wasn't there when Diana died, her name never came up. I think Erica called at Mill House that night looking for her friend and was killed because of something she saw.'

Gerry slumped down in the chair opposite Wesley and looked him in the eye. 'You think the suicide could have been murder?'

'I don't know, Gerry. The child was killed as well, so . . .'

'It's not unknown for children to be murder victims, nasty though the thought is. Look, I told you about Bill Irwin, the inspector who dealt with the Quayle suicide case. I know where he lives; let's go round and have a word.' Gerry stood up, filled with fresh enthusiasm. 'I'll give him a call.'

*

An hour later, they were pulling up outside a neat bunga-low on the outskirts of Morbay. It was on a hill with a view of the bay; the kind of house many people dreamed of living in during their declining years.

'Bill's a nice bloke,' Gerry said as they walked up the neat gravel path. 'Old school. He was good to me when I was a green new DC.'

Wesley took this as a recommendation, and he watched as Bill Irwin greeted Gerry like a long-lost relative. He stared at Wesley for a split second as though he was surprised by the colour of his skin – Gerry had said he was old school, after all – then shook his hand politely and invited both men in. When his wife appeared, Bill asked her meekly whether she'd mind making them a cup of tea.

'Am I glad to see you, Gerry,' he said, rubbing his hands together with glee as soon as his wife had vanished into the kitchen. 'How are you keeping?'

'Not too bad, Bill. Yourself?'

'The boss keeps me busy,' he said glumly, nodding in the direction of the kitchen, where Wesley could hear the clattering of cups. 'And I've taken up bowls.'

'All go then,' said Gerry with an uncertain grin. 'Wes here is hoping you can help us with one of our cases.'

The former inspector looked at Gerry as though he'd just rescued him from a sinking vessel. 'Yes, of course. What do you want to know?'

Wesley leaned forward. 'We'd like to talk to you about a case in 2008 – a woman killed herself by jumping into the river near Petherham, taking her six-year-old son with her.'

Irwin's face suddenly clouded. 'It's not something you forget in a hurry. Even if that woman wanted to do away with herself, taking the poor little kiddie with her was a wicked thing to do.'

'I understand you weren't entirely happy with the suicide verdict.'

Bill Irwin seemed to freeze, not even acknowledging his wife when she bustled in with a tray. It was up to Wesley to thank her and help arrange the cups, keeping one eye on the former DI, who showed no sign of moving.

Eventually Irwin emerged from his trance. 'Now you come to mention it, I did have a few doubts . . . '

Wesley waited for him to continue.

'The post-mortem said she died from drowning, and she had multiple injuries consistent with a fall from the high ground above the river onto rocks at low tide, including severe head injuries that probably rendered her unconscious. The likelihood was that she had jumped holding on to the kid and they both sustained the head injuries on the way down. There was nothing to suggest otherwise. Nobody had any reason to want her dead, and the husband – who's usually the main suspect in such cases – was away in London at a conference. His alibi checked out and we had no evidence that anything was suspicious. She left a note – typed it on her computer and printed it out. It seemed cut and dried.'

'But your gut instinct told you otherwise,' said Wesley.

Bill Irwin looked at him and nodded, as though he was glad that someone understood at last.

Wesley noticed a forlorn look on Irwin's face as they left. And Gerry, unusually, didn't say a word on the journey back to Tradmouth.

From the notebook of
Dr Christopher Cruckshank

5 September 1882

The Reverend Stephens summoned me to the vicarage
last night, for it appears Mrs Stephens left a journal in
which she wrote that the deaths of Josiah Partridge's two
wives and the murder of Mr Fitzterran were connected.
Somebody in Petherham, she claimed, had entered
into a terrible pact to rid people of those they deemed
inconvenient while they themselves were far from home
and would come under no suspicion.

I told him this was mere fantasy, but he insisted
his dear late wife was not a woman given to wild
imaginings.

I then told him that Mrs Stephens had revealed to
me that she believed the mill to be haunted, which was
hardly the statement of a rational soul. He shook his
head sadly and admitted that I could be right. He told
me that she had been much agitated in the weeks leading
up to her death, speaking of a circle within a circle
with one whose evil was cleverly concealed at its centre.

Whenever the reverend questioned her about the matter, she told him she was still seeking the proof.

I told him that such hysteria was not uncommon in women of gentle breeding, and left him to his sorrow.

45

Wesley found a message waiting on his desk. In 2009, the drugs squad had found half a million pounds' worth of cocaine on board a yacht called *Costaloadadosh*, moored in Millicombe harbour. The owner, who was said to have contacts in the Leeds area, had served seven years in jail, but his present whereabouts was unknown. This revelation appeared to support Barry Clegg's alibi for the time of Erica's murder. Even so, they weren't ruling him out just yet.

Before Wesley could let Gerry know, Trish appeared in the doorway with a triumphant look on her face. 'This has just come through,' she said, presenting him with a print-out as though she was handing him an award. 'It's the list of SMNCR members. Mr Tanthwaite found it in his shed. Look at the name halfway down.'

Wesley studied the paper. 'Do we know where he was at the time of Erica Walsh's disappearance?'

'We never had any reason to ask him, did we?'

He knew she was right. The name had never come up in that inquiry, and as far as they knew, there had been no connection.

He passed the list to Gerry, who let out a gasp. 'This is

313

a turn-up for the books. We know where he is. I'll send someone to fetch him.'

Half an hour later, Gerry received a message telling him that the suspect had been brought in and was waiting for them in an interview room.

'How do you account for your tie being found around the neck of Erica Walsh?'

Brian Watkins squirmed in his seat. 'I can't. I didn't know her. Never met her. What makes you think it's my tie?'

'The South Manchester and North Cheshire Rogues. You were a member.'

'So? We were just a bunch of mates who got together for a game of cricket and a few drinks.'

'You had a club tie?'

'So did a lot of people.'

'Where is that tie now, Mr Watkins?'

'How should I know? It was years ago. We've moved house since then; it was probably binned or given to a charity shop.'

Wesley knew that this line of questioning was going nowhere. The CPS was hardly likely to prosecute on the basis of such flimsy evidence. They had nothing to put Brian Watkins in Devon at the time of Erica Walsh's murder and the man knew it. He was sitting back in his chair, arms folded, with his expensive solicitor sitting beside him like a smug guardian angel.

'Shouldn't you be out finding the bastard who killed my wife? You haven't made an arrest, have you?' He glanced at the solicitor. 'I think you're floundering and that's why you've brought me in. There were loads of those ties around; why pick on me?'

'Where were you when Erica Walsh disappeared? The twelfth of December 2008.'

'Do you know where you were twelve years ago? I chucked all my old diaries away when we moved.'

'Your company up in Manchester might have a record of your business trips.'

'Doubt it. I sold it for a very large sum and they've moved to flashy new premises. Sorry.'

He didn't look sorry at all. One look at Gerry's face told Wesley that the chief inspector was fighting the urge to grab Watkins by the lapels and shake a confession out of him. But that sort of interrogation belonged to distant history.

'Where were you on the night Damien Lee was killed?'

'At home. If my wife was still alive she'd have vouched for me, but as it is . . . ' Watkins gave a melodramatic shrug.

'Did you know him before he visited your house at your wife's request?'

There was a moment of hesitation. 'No. Of course not.'

'He used to live in Manchester.'

'Manchester's a big place.'

Gerry gave Wesley a nudge, and he announced for the benefit of the tape that the interview was over for now.

When they returned to the incident room, Wesley emailed Greater Manchester Police again. He had another question to ask.

He then called Colin Bowman. He needed some information, and a lot would depend on Colin's answer.

46

Wesley had requested details of any unsolved murders that had taken place in the Manchester area a couple of years either side of 2008. He thought it was a long shot, but in the end an email arrived in his inbox. The officer from GMP had come up trumps.

The murder that grabbed Wesley's particular interest had taken place in July 2008. A businessman had been attacked in an alley in central Manchester – a knifing that had been put down to a mugging gone wrong. The murder weapon had never been found and neither had the perpetrator. It was just another unsolved crime on GMP's books. The death of James Markham had become a statistic.

Wesley would have disregarded the tragedy if it weren't for the fact that Markham had been Brian Watkins' business partner. According to the police files, there had been a long-running dispute between the two men that had become increasingly bitter. It had begun with a disagreement about how the company should expand, but it had soon become personal. According to a member of staff, Markham had accused Watkins of doing dodgy deals with company funds to line his own pocket, but no evidence was ever found, possibly because the police hadn't followed this line of enquiry too closely.

Watkins had been away on business at the time of his partner's death, and his contacts were investigated, just in case he'd paid someone else to do his dirty work for him. But nothing untoward had been found, and he had played the shocked colleague to perfection.

Wesley sat at his desk studying the files with an increasing sense of excitement.

He'd called Jack Tanthwaite again, hoping the man wasn't getting sick of his requests. He needed to ask him another question, and luckily Tanthwaite seemed only too happy to oblige, making Wesley suspect he was pleased to be useful.

Watkins was still being held downstairs, but they didn't have much time before they had to decide whether to release or charge him. Wesley knew the smug solicitor was likely to block the latter. They needed more than suspicions. Even Gerry thought his theory was far-fetched, and the more Wesley studied the printouts in front of him on his desk, the more he began to doubt himself.

Eventually Gerry decided to let Watkins go and Wesley had to bow to the inevitable. All he had was his instinct that the man was involved in some way. There was so much more of the jigsaw that needed fitting into place.

As there was little more they could do that day, Gerry suggested they both go home to get some rest, and make an early start in the morning. The night shift would alert them if anything urgent came in.

Pam seemed delighted to see him back at what passed for a reasonable time during a major investigation, and when he suggested a takeaway pizza, she didn't argue – and neither did the children. Pizza always went down well in the Peterson household.

Once the family had eaten, the children vanished upstairs to their rooms, and Wesley was helping Pam clear away when he heard the doorbell ring. Neil had arrived with Corrine in tow.

Wesley gave her a cautious greeting, wondering whether it was wise to be entertaining a possible witness in a murder inquiry. She'd been close to Erica and had been at Mill House at the time of David Leeson's death. On the other hand, she'd never been regarded as a suspect, so he decided to say nothing.

'Pam emailed me her transcription of that doctor's notebook,' Neil began. 'Have you read it?'

'I've been busy,' Wesley said pointedly. 'What's so interesting about it?'

'Mill House at Petherham features heavily. No wonder people say it's haunted. Corrine came across an old book that claims the place is cursed. And we found some graffiti in the clock tower at the mill that looks like a curse of some kind.'

'Really?' Although curses had no place in modern policing, Wesley was intrigued.

'And what have you been saying to Jemima Baine? She bit my head off this morning when I went to ask her something about a skeleton we have in storage.'

'Let's just say she hasn't been entirely honest with us,' said Wesley, sorely disappointed in the woman he'd previously respected for her professional abilities.

'I did wonder,' said Neil. 'You're not charging her with anything, are you?'

Wesley shook his head.

'I suppose this means you won't be using her in any future cases?'

'Probably not. You were telling me about this curse,' he said, anxious to change the subject.

'I've printed out Pam's transcription,' Neil said. 'I can read you the interesting bits if you can't be bothered.'

Wesley ignored his friend's implied criticism. He was too tired for socialising. Tired and frustrated. The solution to his case seemed to be dangling just out of reach, and every new lead opened another avenue that led to a dead end.

'Go on then.' He felt Pam touch his hand as though she felt his despair.

Neil proceeded to read edited highlights. When he'd finished, Pam cleared her throat. 'Neil, did you notice that some pages have been torn out of the notebook?'

Neil raised his eyebrows. 'In which case, we may never discover the whole truth. That vicar's wife, Mrs Stephens. I'm wondering whether she was killed to stop her enquiring too closely into the deaths at Mill House and the murder of that landowner. Her death feels odd to me. What if the deaths at Mill House were murders too? What if someone took those photographs Corrine found as souvenirs? What do you think, Wes?'

Wesley was only half listening. The talk of Mill House had set his brain racing. There was something he needed to do – but it would have to wait until the next morning.

47

Wesley had called Colin Bowman the previous day to request a meeting, a call that Colin said had been timed to perfection because he had no post-mortems booked for the next morning. Wesley hoped this was a good omen.

He called in to the incident room first and spent some time studying an old file Neston had sent over. Then he told Gerry he'd be out for an hour and left before the DCI could ask any questions. He didn't want anyone with him. He needed to do this alone.

He switched off his phone before driving out to Petherham because he didn't want to be interrupted, and when he reached the village he parked near the mill, next to the area still cordoned off with police tape. He'd brought the file with him, and he checked it before setting off again, steering the car down the narrow lane, little more than a track, that led to the place where Pether Creek met the River Trad. The going was rough, making him fear for his suspension, and when he reached the end of the track, he brought the car to a halt in a little clearing.

His first thought was that the scene had changed little since the photographs in the file were taken: the trees were taller, perhaps, and the bushes more overgrown, but the place was still recognisable. He climbed out of the car and pulled on his wellingtons. The going from now on would be muddy at this time of year. He could see the little path leading through the trees that fringed the river. He was about to follow Diana Quayle's final steps before she ended her life and that of her son, and he felt a sudden chill, as though she was watching him from the trees.

As he walked, he heard no birdsong. This was a desolate place in December. A place of death and despair. When he reached the water, he stood on the rocky outcrop where the creek met the river. The place where Diana had jumped to her death. It was a sheer drop, fifty feet or more, and when he leaned over, he could see the vicious rocks jutting out on the way down. According to the original post-mortem, these, together with the riverbed, were responsible for Diana and Orlando's multiple injuries. Wesley knew from the file that there had been a storm brewing that night, and he wondered what had gone through the woman's mind as she stood here.

He retraced his steps, but instead of getting back into his car, he started to walk towards the village. It wasn't as far as he thought. Only three quarters of a mile. Easily walkable even on a stormy night.

Once he'd learned all he needed, he returned to the car and switched his phone on again, pleased to find a message from Colin. He was waiting at the mortuary if Wesley wanted to call in for a chat. Wesley said he'd be there in half an hour, ignoring a voice message from Gerry asking where he was.

When he arrived at the mortuary, Colin was waiting for him, tea already brewing in a china pot and a selection of biscuits on a dainty plate.

'I've taken a look at Diana Quayle's post-mortem report, as you requested,' he began once they were settled. 'I can see why Dr Benson reached his conclusion. The injuries were indeed consistent with a fall from a considerable height.' He paused. 'However, they were also consistent with a beating from the traditional blunt instrument. Very blunt – not a lead pipe or a hammer, which would leave distinctive marks. There was water in the lungs, so the injuries didn't kill her but they were severe enough to render her unconscious.'

'I've just visited the scene. If you're right, someone could easily have knocked Diana and her son out, then driven them to the spot, thrown them over the edge into the water and walked back to the village. It was always assumed that because her car was found there, nobody else was involved, but . . .'

'You might be on to something, Wesley. I certainly wouldn't rule out a murder dressed up as suicide – although who would want to kill the child?' Colin said with a shudder.

Wesley thanked him and returned to the station. There was still a lot to discover.

'Where have you been?' Gerry asked accusingly as soon as Wesley walked into the incident room.

Wesley followed the DCI into his office and sat down. 'I've been talking to Colin Bowman. I don't think Diana Quayle killed herself. I think she was murdered.'

'Who by? It couldn't have been her husband, because he was in London when it happened. I've been trying to get hold of you. I've heard from Greater Manchester. Brian Watkins was away when his business partner was killed in

July 2008. He was down here seeing someone in Morbay. What do you make of that?'

'Not sure.'

Gerry looked round furtively. 'I need your opinion, Wes. Draw the blinds, will you.'

Wesley was puzzled, but he did as he was asked, and when Gerry opened a large package that was lying beneath his coat stand, he saw that its contents were bright red with touches of white here and there. After a few seconds, he realised what it was.

'Aren't you going to try it on?' He suddenly felt glad of a spot of levity to relieve the recent gloom.

Gerry held the Santa Claus costume up against him. He looked as though he was fighting temptation.

'You need to make sure it fits. You don't want to disappoint all those kiddies, do you?'

'Guard the door. Don't let anyone in.'

Once the DCI had been transformed, Wesley started laughing.

'What's so funny?'

'It suits you.'

'I know a lot of villains who wouldn't agree with you,' Gerry said, donning his long white beard.

Suddenly Trish Walton burst in. She clapped her hand over her mouth, stifling a giggle. 'Sorry, sir. Wesley, there's a video call from a Mrs Ventris. She said GMP asked her to call you.'

Wesley hadn't expected his request to bear fruit so quickly. 'I'd better take it, Gerry. It's Brian Watkins' former PA – thought it might be worth having a word with her.'

Without waiting for Gerry's reply, he rushed from the room. After the brief comic interlude, it was back to reality. He sat down at his computer and saw a woman's face looking straight at him. She was probably in her sixties, with glasses and short grey hair.

'Inspector Peterson?'

'Thanks for agreeing to speak to me, Mrs Ventris.'

'I understand it's about the murder of James Markham. I was his secretary at the time of his death.'

'It must have been a great shock for you when Mr Markham was killed.'

'It's dreadful to think that he met such a violent end.'

'Did you know Mr Watkins well?'

'Oh yes. I worked for both bosses, Mr Markham and Mr Watkins.'

Her manner was alarmingly efficient, and Wesley guessed that not much would get past her. 'I've familiarised myself with the details of Mr Markham's death. It was treated as a mugging gone wrong.'

'So the police said, and I've no evidence to contradict that. What did you want to ask me?' A puzzled frown suddenly appeared on her face. 'Is that ... Father Christmas?'

Wesley swung round to see that Gerry had come up behind him to listen to the conversation. He swiftly dodged out of camera range, but Wesley could see him out of the corner of his eye. He tried to ignore the distraction.

'Sorry, Mrs Ventris. It's the station Christmas fair next weekend ...'

Her lips twitched upwards in a smile. 'Of course.'

'What can you tell me about Mr Markham?'

'Of the two men I worked for, I much preferred James Markham. Brian Watkins was always on the lookout for some shady deal. Only interested in making a fast buck rather than building the business.'

'Did you know his wife?'

'Abigail? I met her a few times. Nervous little thing. They didn't seem suited at all. Mind you, I understand the money was hers. I suspect he had other women; he was always making secretive phone calls, closing the office door so I couldn't overhear.'

'Can you remember where Mr Watkins was when Mr Markham was killed?' He already knew from the information GMP had sent through that Watkins had been in Devon, but he hoped his PA would have more details.

'I remember very well, Inspector, because the police questioned me at the time. I was rather surprised, to tell you the truth, because we'd never had dealings with anyone in that area before. Most of our business was in the north, although there was a firm near London—'

'Where exactly did he go, Mrs Ventris?'

'He said he was going to visit a potential customer in Devon; said he'd made the contact through someone he'd met at a conference the previous month ... but I did wonder whether he'd gone down there to see a woman.'

'Could he have been lying about where he was?'

'Oh no. I saw the receipts he put in for his expenses. He was in Devon all right. After that he seemed to develop a bit of an obsession with the place. He even said he wanted to move there – had this dream about living by the sea and messing about in boats. I believe that's exactly what he did once he sold the company.'

'Do you remember the name of this contact?'

'No. But it was an agricultural supplier in a place called Morbay.'

'Does the name Jeremy Quayle mean anything to you?'

The silence lasted a few seconds. 'Yes. That name sounds familiar. Why?'

'Could he be the contact in Morbay?'

'I can't know for sure without seeing the correspondence, and I've no idea where that is. But it does ring a bell.'

'The conference where he met this contact – where was it?'

'Here in Manchester in June 2008.'

'Can you tell me who organised it?'

'As a matter of fact, I can. A friend of mine still works for the company.'

'I know it's a long shot, but do you think there might be a list of delegates somewhere?'

She looked doubtful. 'I can ask. I'll call her and get back to you.'

'Thank you. Do you know where Brian Watkins was on the twelfth of December 2008?'

'That's a long time ago, Inspector,' she said. She clearly thought he was pushing his luck.

'Is it possible he came down to Devon again?'

She hesitated. 'I don't know, but I can't rule it out. He said he'd fallen in love with the place. Why don't you ask him?'

'Thank you, Mrs Ventris. I'll do that.'

An hour later, Mrs Ventris called again. With remarkable efficiency, her friend had managed to lay her hands on a list of delegates to the Manchester conference in June 2008. And when Wesley broke the news to Gerry that both Jeremy Quayle and Brian Watkins were on it, Gerry gave a low whistle.

'Nice work, Wes.'

48

Wesley drove to Petherham on autopilot, thinking of the old book Pam had transcribed for Neil. Terrible things had happened in that village more than a century ago. Were some places just bad, he wondered, or was it simply that they attracted bad people? Petherham looked so innocent, even idyllic, with its eighteenth-century mill, its pretty pub, its cottages and its quaint stone church. A village from a tourist poster. The parish of Petherham was one of four that Mark was responsible for, and because he took a service in the church of St Mary Magdalene each Sunday, he was known to the villagers – possibly including the man who'd gone into Belsham church to make a confession but had lost his nerve at the last moment.

By the time they reached their destination, it was dark, and the lights were on in Mill House. Gerry marched up to the front door and knocked loudly while Wesley looked around. From where he was standing, he could see the mill wheel turning relentlessly, and somebody had strung cheerful lights around the little iron bridge leading to the mill entrance, dots of colour in the gloom. He could make out an illuminated sign by the door that said *Grotto this way*.

Gerry knocked again. In spite of the recent tragedy of

David Leeson's death, there was a tall Christmas tree in the front bay window, and a holly wreath hanging on the door. The scene looked so cosy and normal that Wesley's discoveries suddenly seemed fantastical.

'Nobody at home.' Gerry's words came out in a disappointed grunt.

'Let's try the mill.'

Gerry looked unsure of himself. 'Isn't there a kiddies' grotto in the visitors' centre? We don't want to go barging in scaring the little darlings.'

Wesley ignored his boss's misgivings and crossed the lane to the mill. As he hurried across the metal bridge, he was relieved to find that, according to a notice by the entrance, the grotto was only open at weekends. He hadn't relished the idea of making an arrest in front of a group of terrified children and their outraged parents. From outside he could hear the clatter of machinery, and when he pushed the door open, the sound grew louder, almost deafening.

They hurried past the busy looms to the office, where Robert Farnley was typing something into a computer.

'Can we have a word, Mr Farnley?'

The manager looked up and smiled patiently. 'Yes, of course. What is it?'

'We're looking for Jeremy Quayle. Know where he is?'

'Your guess is as good as mine. I was expecting him half an hour ago, but he hasn't turned up yet. We're working late tonight to get an order out in time for Christmas, so if that's all ...' He glanced at the clock on the wall meaningfully.

The two men walked back to the car in silence. They could do nothing but wait, but the longer they delayed, the more likely it was that someone else would die.

Wesley turned and stared into the rushing water where David Leeson had been found. The little clock tower was outlined against the clouds that scurried across the dark grey sky, and he could see his own breath emerging from his mouth like a writhing ghost in the icy air.

As they were considering their next move, they saw a woman approaching. She was wearing a woolly hat and her hands were thrust into her coat pockets against the cold. It took Wesley a few moments to recognise her.

'Hello, Bella. Not gone home yet?'

'Not yet. To tell the truth, it makes a pleasant change to stay in the pub and have my meals cooked for me. Besides, I needed time to think.'

'Have you come to a decision?'

'Like I said before, I'm going to stay with my sister. I'm going to look for a place up there and make a new start.'

'And Carl?'

'I think that ship's sailed,' she said with a sad smile. 'I'll see a solicitor once I get to my sister's.' She paused. 'I passed Jeremy Quayle earlier. He was walking towards Mill House with his wife, but I don't think he recognised me and I didn't let on to him. Some things are best forgotten, don't you think?'

When Gerry pounded on the door of Mill House, it took Selina Quayle a few minutes to answer. She looked surprised to see them.

'We need to speak to your husband, Mrs Quayle.'

'He's just gone out for a walk. He said he wouldn't be long.'

'Which way did he go, love?'

The woman bristled with indignation. 'I'm not your "love", Chief Inspector.'

Wesley knew it was up to him to defuse the situation. 'I'm sure no offence was meant.' He was tempted to say that the DCI came from Liverpool, where it was the usual form of address, adding that cultural differences could be a minefield, but one look at the woman's face stopped him.

Determined not to be sidetracked, he repeated Gerry's question. 'Where did your husband go?'

'Towards the lime kilns. Said he wanted to clear his head,' she said, hugging her cardigan more tightly around her body.

'Something wrong, Mrs Quayle?' said Wesley.

'No. Why should there be?'

Once Selina had slammed the door on them, they retraced their steps to the front gate. 'I think Jeremy Quayle could be in danger,' Wesley said.

He knew the path to the lime kilns. He and Pam had walked that way one day in the summer after a good lunch at the Fisherman's Arms. They took the track that ran alongside the creek, dry gravel until it reached the lime kilns. After that it became muddy in winter, fit only for walking boots.

He could see the disused kilns ahead, set into the river-bank, but everything was in shadow, lit only by the full moon that reflected silver on the heaving water to their left.

Suddenly he saw a flicker of torchlight, there for a moment then gone. When he flashed his own torch, he caught a figure in the beam. But whoever it was vanished swiftly into the archway of the kiln.

'Police! Show yourself!' he shouted. Pointing his torch at the kiln, he walked forward, glad that Gerry was there behind him. 'Come out. We need a word.'

The silence seemed to last for ever, and Wesley began to

fear they'd arrived too late. He reached the third lime kiln in the row and saw a man inside bending over a figure on the ground. This was something he hadn't expected.

'Mr Watkins. Fancy meeting you here,' said Gerry behind him.

The figure on the ground hauled himself up as Wesley took his handcuffs from his pocket and snapped them onto the other man's wrists.

'You've got this all wrong,' Brian Watkins said with a slight smile on his face. 'Jeremy fell. I was helping him up.'

'It's true.' Jeremy Quayle's voice was hoarse.

'You're making fools of yourselves, Officers,' added Watkins. 'I haven't done anything wrong.'

'Found that cricket club tie yet?'

He looked surprised by the sudden change of subject, and after that, the only thing he said was 'I want my solicitor.'

49

'He might be telling the truth. Quayle's backing him up.'

'I suspect they'd had some kind of disagreement, but what it was about I've no idea.'

'You've got a smug look about you, Wes. What's going on?'

'Since we got back to the station, I've been speaking to our Manchester colleagues again. You agree that Erica Walsh might have stumbled on something by accident on the night of Diana Quayle's death?'

'I agree it's a possibility.'

'Where was Jeremy when it happened?'

'At a conference in London. It was checked out at the time. He was there all right.'

'The previous June, Quayle was at a conference in Manchester with Brian Watkins. And we know from Watkins' former PA that he was here in Devon in July when James Markham, his business partner, was killed. Who's to say he didn't come back in December and kill Jeremy's wife for him? And who's to say Jeremy wasn't in Manchester when Markham died?'

Gerry's eyes suddenly lit up with realisation. 'You're saying they swapped murders? I'll do your dirty work if you do mine? You think they met at the conference in Manchester and arranged it all?'

'According to Mrs Ventris, Watkins was definitely down here in Devon at the time Markham was murdered, and we assumed he was visiting Quayle in Morbay. But what if he was actually meeting with someone else from the company?'

'While Quayle was up north knifing James Markham in a Manchester alleyway on Watkins' behalf.'

The phone on Wesley's desk rang and he rushed over to answer it, hoping for good news. He was pleased when he learned it was the lab with the DNA results for the tie that had killed Erica Walsh. As expected, they'd found traces of Eli Jelkes's DNA along with Erica's – and that of a third person; someone who must have worn that tie many times. The woman on the other end of the line paused as though she was about to make a dramatic revelation.

'The interesting news is that this third DNA is a match for that found at another crime scene – in Manchester this time. A man called James Markham was killed in July 2008 and the same DNA was found at the scene. Unfortunately, there's no match on our records.'

Wesley thanked her and returned to Gerry's office.

'You're looking pleased with yourself.'

'I've just had the lab on.' He broke the news, and Gerry gave a long whistle.

'In that case, the tie can't belong to Brian Watkins. His DNA's on record. It was taken when he was done for drunk driving in 2012.'

Wesley put his head in his hands, despairing that his new pet theory had just been shattered. Then he suddenly looked up, his eyes bright with realisation. 'What if there's more to this than a simple murder swap? What if there's a third party involved – someone who's never been arrested so his DNA isn't on file; someone who also had access to a SMNCR tie? What if this person's behind it, pulling the strings? Killing inconvenient people for a fee.'

Gerry looked sceptical. 'How did you come up with that one?'

'Those Victorian murders I told you about – the vicar's wife suspected somebody was killing inconvenient people, possibly for money. Her husband and the local doctor said it was nonsense; then she had a very convenient fatal accident.'

'So she could have been right all along?'

'The village bobby in those days wasn't up to solving anything more complicated than a punch-up in the Fisherman's Arms or a spot of light poaching. A man was hanged for the only obvious murder, but he always protested his innocence. He even left a statement carved into the wall of the clock tower, where he hid from the authorities. According to Neil, there could have been more deaths that were assumed to be accidental or natural. He also thinks the killer might have taken photographs of his victims and kept them as souvenirs. That's his theory, anyway.'

'Has he found any real evidence?'

'No, but the people who benefited from the deaths were always far away at the time. What if they were contract killings?'

'A hired assassin in Victorian Petherham? I think Neil's letting his imagination run away with him.' Gerry sighed. 'But if you're right – and I'm not saying you are – how does David Leeson fit in?'

'I've spoken to Jack Tanthwaite again, and he told me something interesting. David Leeson was a regular singer at the bar where the SMNCR met. Very popular, he said. What if he recognised the killer when he came down to Petherham twelve years ago and gradually put two and two together? Perhaps he threatened to voice his suspicions all these years later and the killer couldn't take the risk of him talking.'

'What about Mark's repentant sinner?'

'I think that could have been Jeremy Quayle. What if he knew Brian had arranged for Abigail to be murdered while he was away in Spain and his conscience got the better of him? He wanted to stop it but he couldn't come and tell us because he'd be incriminating himself for his first wife's murder. That means if the real killer recognises him as the weak link – the one who's likely to lose his nerve – he might be in danger.'

'His meeting with Brian Watkins in the lime kiln didn't look too friendly.'

'I think Watkins was trying to persuade him to keep his mouth shut.'

'So he's the killer?'

Wesley shook his head.

'Then who is it?'

Wesley took his phone from his pocket. 'I'm calling Neil. I want him to visit an elderly lady, and once I have the answer to one particular question, we'll find our missing link.'

Neil answered right away and seemed surprised by Wesley's request. He said he'd call him back.

The wait seemed interminable. But when the call came, Neil gave him the answer he was waiting for.

He returned to Gerry's office with a smile on his face. 'I've spoken to Neil. I've also made another call to Jack

Tanthwaite. He confirmed that some of the people who were given those ties weren't necessarily on the list he sent us.' He paused. 'He gave me one name I didn't expect, and now everything's starting to make sense. I think it's time we went for a drink.'

'It's too early for celebrating yet, surely.'

'Bear with me, Gerry. I'll tell you on the way.'

'OK, but you're paying, Wes. I'm skint.'

The Fisherman's Arms was comfortably full as Wesley and Gerry made their way to the bar.

'Sometimes I love this job,' Gerry said as he stood there waiting to catch the barmaid's attention.

Eventually the young woman came over to him. 'What can I get you?'

'A word with the landlord, love. Is he around?'

'I'll see.' She opened a door at the back of the bar and shouted through. 'Simon! Someone to see you.'

She waited a few moments before calling again, but there was still no reply. At that moment, a young man appeared with a tray of glasses. He wore the black shirt that appeared to be the Fisherman's Arms' staff uniform.

'Do you know where Simon Pussett is?' There was a note of urgency in Wesley's question.

'He said he was going into Tradmouth. The candlelight procession's on tonight.'

Wesley caught his breath. The town would be packed with families enjoying the festivities – parents taking their children to see the arrival of Santa, who would board a light-festooned boat and sail across the river to the steam train. The presence of so many innocent bystanders was bound to make their task more challenging.

'Did he say whereabouts in Tradmouth he was going?'

'Said he was going to see someone who owed him big-time. He's going to collect a debt, then he's going to watch the procession.'

'I don't think we can wait,' said Gerry. 'Let everyone know. I want him found, and quick.'

From the notebook of
Dr Christopher Cruckshank

I *July* 1886

*I am leaving Petherham to establish a practice in
Neston. The town is fashionable, with many wealthy
inhabitants. In Petherham, there are several prosperous
families dwelling in the countryside round about, and
Josiah Partridge pays me a fee each time I treat one of
his workers, but there are few people of the better sort in
the district, unlike in the town.*

*My work as a physician has earned me little here,
but there are always ways of making extra money. Apart
from the vicar, the doctor in a village is the nearest
the small-minded folk have to a god. He is above all
criticism and suspicion and his patients obey his advice
without question. At first this amused me, but one
grows accustomed to power. I fear it is not good for the
immortal soul – if such a thing exists.*

50

On Gerry's orders, every available officer and PCSO was on the streets of Tradmouth. There were bound to be pickpockets and punch-ups on a night like this, but Wesley had more serious matters on his mind. He and Gerry wove their way through the crowds by the boat float, scanning every face for the one they wanted. A tiny needle in a large and thronging haystack.

The band from the naval college played Christmas carols in the Memorial Gardens beneath the strings of coloured lights, and the alluring scent of cooking wafted across the air. Crowds clustered around the stalls in search of gourmet burgers and Indian street food. Their quarry could be anywhere, and Wesley was beginning to despair.

Then he saw some familiar faces. Pam was waiting by a pizza stall with Michael, Amelia and Della, the latter leaning on the crutches she still had to use at times. The children were both tapping something into their phones. Wesley often wondered what they had to communicate that was so compelling. For a moment he was tempted to go over to greet them, but Pam hadn't seen him and he didn't need distractions.

He noticed that Neil had just joined his family, greeting

Pam with a kiss on the cheek and giving Michael an avuncular high-five. Corrine Malin was with him, but she hovered impatiently, as though she had better things to do than hang around with people she didn't know.

Wesley was about to follow Gerry into the crowd when Corrine spotted him. She left Neil's side, rushing in his direction with a look of determination on her face. This was the last thing he needed.

'Inspector. What's happening?' she said once she was within earshot.

It was Gerry who answered. 'Nothing that need concern you, love. If you don't mind, we're busy.'

But Corrine wasn't giving up. 'Neil said you'd asked him to call on Miss Cruckshank. Why?'

'Just routine,' said Wesley, knowing he wasn't a good liar.

'You're after the man who killed Erica, aren't you? Take me with you.'

'Absolutely not,' said Wesley firmly. 'We'll keep you informed, I promise.'

He followed Gerry, who'd started to edge his way through the crowd, heading for the embankment, where the procession was due to pass any moment. The uniforms had cleared the road, and Wesley could see the flickering lights in the distance.

Another band headed the procession, and the young children at the front of the crowd danced in time to the music. The vessels on the river were all lit up, the lights reflected in the water that churned, black as oil, beyond the embankment. The procession was snaking along the waterfront, with Santa's brightly illuminated sleigh at its centre pulled not by reindeer, but by a tow truck from a local garage decorated with fairy lights. Soon Santa would do a circuit of the boat float, and once he was safely aboard his craft, the procession would end up in the Memorial Gardens for communal carol singing followed by general festivities in the pubs and the streets. It was the same every year, and Wesley used to love it when the children were small.

'Where do you think he'll go?' Gerry asked, raising his voice to be heard over the band.

'He's meeting someone who owes him.'

'Brian Watkins?'

'I'd put money on it. Our friend will want paying for getting rid of Abigail.'

All of a sudden they spotted a familiar figure.

'Talk of the devil. There's Watkins over there. Looks like he's heading for home.'

Wesley began to barge his way through the crowd, muttering excuse me's and earning himself hostile looks, while Gerry followed in his wake. Soon they saw Watkins hurrying down a side street where the crowd had thinned to a few stragglers guzzling fish and chips from cardboard containers. The narrow thoroughfare leading to Baynards Quay was thronged with drinkers spilling from the Tradmouth Arms, pints in hand. Gerry's little house at the end was in the thick of it, as drinkers braved the cold to sit on the quayside benches and watch the train with its array of coloured lights chug into the station on the far side of the river to await its important passenger. If Wesley hadn't been so used to the spectacle, the effect would have been quite magical.

Keeping Watkins in sight, they passed Gerry's house, where they saw a figure in the front bedroom window. In Gerry's absence, Joyce had chosen to watch the festivities in the warmth. Gerry waved, but she didn't see him, her attention focused elsewhere as a cheer went up in the distance, echoing over the water. Santa's boat was setting off, and the band was playing 'Santa Claus Is Comin' to Town'.

The two men continued along the cobbles, expecting Watkins to make for his own house, still cordoned off by police tape, tattered in places after several days exposed to the elements. But instead, he hurried past and vanished into the archway leading to the little fortress at the end of the quay, the small round tower built by Henry VIII to defend one of his most important ports. Only the outer walls of the fortress were still standing, and its entrance lay in deep shadow. In the past, Gerry had caught kids drinking and taking drugs in there, and he'd asked for the interior to be lit. But now the bulbs were out of action. Vandalised probably.

Wesley wished they had backup, but the budget wouldn't stand for extra expenditure on a hunch. As far as the chief super was concerned, hunches belonged firmly in the crime fiction section of the public library. And yet this wasn't really a hunch – more an educated guess.

He ran towards the archway, relieved when Gerry caught up with him so he wasn't alone as he crossed the threshold. When his eyes adjusted to the gloom, he saw Brian Watkins to his left, holding a small package and staring nervously at a pinpoint of glowing red light at the far side of the circular space: a cigarette. It took Wesley a few seconds to make out the shape of its owner.

'We need a word, Mr Pussett,' he called out.

Watkins let out a gasp and retreated as the figure turned slowly, the face still in shadow.

Wesley recited the words of the caution, his voice echoing against the ancient stone walls. Hoping this was going to be easier than he'd anticipated, he stepped forward, handcuffs at the ready. Then, unexpectedly, he saw a movement to his right, a small figure rushing in like a Fury, hurtling towards Simon Pussett.

'You killed Erica!' screamed Corrine.

As she flew at him, hands outstretched like the claws of a vengeful cat, Wesley leapt forward to drag her off. But she slipped from his grasp and Pussett darted towards the only other entrance – a smaller archway leading to a set of worn steps down to the water, closed off with a metal barrier to deter the more adventurous visitor. The landlord of the Fisherman's Arms vaulted over the barrier, skidded on the slimy top step and disappeared from sight, pursued by Corrine. She wasn't giving up.

'Don't be a fool, love,' Gerry shouted after her as Wesley raced towards the steps. There was only one way their quarry was going to escape, and that was by water. He could hear Gerry's voice behind him calling for backup, barking orders into his phone. But he wasn't going to let the killer get away.

He found himself outside the fortress, standing at the top of the short flight of steps, which were coated with rotting seaweed. There was no sign of Corrine or the man who'd just eluded them.

Suddenly he heard a splash and saw something moving in the water. He knew it to be cold, dangerously so.

'They're both in the water!' he shouted up to Gerry. 'Call the river patrol. Tell them to head for the fortress steps.'

'They're escorting Santa over the river.'

'Santa can manage very well on his own. We need them.'

Gerry retreated to make the call, leaving Wesley standing on the bottom step, scanning the water for signs of

343

movement. He didn't know how long the message would take to reach the river patrol, and if Simon managed to escape, there were still witnesses to his crimes around. He had plenty of reasons to kill again. Corrine was in there somewhere too. He had to find her.

Suddenly he spotted her, floundering, vanishing beneath the surface of the water then bobbing up again. On impulse, he kicked off his shoes, shed his coat and jumped in. He was a strong swimmer, but even so, he gasped as the cold knocked the breath out of him. He felt himself sinking, struggling beneath the waves, and he'd swallowed several mouthfuls of salty river water before he managed to fight his way to the surface and gulp in a lungful of air.

Disorientated, the chill paralysing his limbs, he began to tread water, his sodden clothes dragging him down and the blood pounding in his ears as he summoned all his strength to stay afloat. It took him a few moments to get his bearings; then he spotted a disturbance on the water's surface a few yards away: a swimmer making for a rowing boat moored nearby. Wesley was beginning to feel drowsy. The cold was sapping what little energy he had left, but he knew he had to stay alert. His life depended on it. And so did Corrine's.

Suddenly the swimmer ahead of him stopped, his head bobbing like a seal's. At the same moment, Wesley spotted Corrine a few feet away, splashing frantically and gasping for breath. Remembering his childhood life-saving lessons in his local swimming baths, he gathered all his strength and swam towards her. When he grabbed her, she began to struggle, but as soon as she realised what was happening, she relaxed, allowing him to keep her head out of the water while he paddled her towards the steps, where Gerry was waiting anxiously to haul her out.

As he swam, he could see that Simon had hoisted himself on board a rowing boat moored between him and the shore. Wesley wasn't sure if he could speak – or whether he'd be heard – but he tried anyway.

'The river patrol's on its way. Give yourself up, Simon. It's over.' But the cold water robbed him of breath and his words were lost in the night air.

He was feeling much weaker now, and the burden of supporting Corrine made every movement a painful effort. He realised he'd been foolhardy and that his attempt at heroics could kill him.

He was vaguely aware of an oar swinging in his direction as Gerry's anxious shouts from the shore carried across the water. 'Wes, where are you?'

The oar swung towards him again, appearing like a missile out of the darkness, and connected with the side of his head. Temporarily stunned, he felt his body weakening, and was overcome by an overwhelming temptation to abandon the fight; to allow both of them to sink beneath the waves and feel nothing more. He swallowed another mouthful of water. It tasted foul, and he could hear Corrine spluttering.

He opened his eyes. The steps were a few feet away now, and he made one last effort to reach them. Then, without warning, someone grabbed Corrine from his grasp and hauled her from the water like a landed fish. But before he could follow her, Pussett was there to his right, swinging the oar towards him again. This time Wesley summoned what little strength he had left to make a grab at it. Pussett lost his balance and tumbled into the water with a mighty splash.

They were on equal terms now – close as two boxers in a ring – and Pussett launched himself forward, intent on finishing what he'd started. Wesley went under again, but when he bobbed back up to the surface like a cork, he saw something in the water to his left. Someone, possibly Gerry, had thrown him a life belt, and he made a grab for it as Pussett prepared for another assault.

Then he felt the water churn and saw the welcome sight of the police launch bearing down on them. Pussett froze for a second, then started to swim away. But there was nowhere to go.

51

The police launch was draped in fairy lights, with a Christmas tree standing proudly on the bow. But despite its festive appearance, the officers aboard were soon hauling Pussett from the water, ready with a foil blanket to wrap around his shoulders.

Gerry had summoned an ambulance, and the paramedics insisted on taking Wesley to the hospital to get checked over, along with Corrine, who seemed to have recovered quickly from her ordeal. The prisoner was taken there too under police guard. Swimming fully clothed in the River Trad on a chilly December evening wasn't regarded as being good for the health.

The doctors suggested that Wesley stay in overnight for observation, but all he wanted to do was go home for a bath and a change of clothes. Pam had been contacted, and she'd left the festivities to hurry home and get some dry things, leaving the children in Della's care. They'd become bored with all the Santa business anyway, saying it was for kids. She met him at the hospital entrance, looking at him as though she wasn't sure whether to treat him as a hero or a headstrong idiot. She threw herself into his arms and hugged him tightly before taking a step back.

'What the hell were you thinking?' she said in a furious hiss. 'Why did you have to play the bloody hero? What about me and the kids?' She hit his chest with her fists, once, twice, before turning away as though she could no longer bear to look at him.

He could see tears in her eyes and put his arms around her gently, whispering, 'Sorry' in her ear.

'You're always sorry. Sorry you're going to be late home. Sorry you're risking your life.'

'I'll be more careful in future. Promise.'

'*I'll* make sure of that.'

They looked round and saw Gerry standing there, a look of concern on his face.

'You should be proud of him, love. He's been a hero today.'

'A dead hero's no good to me,' she said before marching off.

Wesley was about to follow, but Gerry put a hand on his shoulder. 'She was worried, that's all. Give her time to calm down. I'll get a patrol car to take you home.'

Wesley was grateful for the lift. When he arrived home, he said little. As Gerry had predicted, Pam's anger had subsided, and she diagnosed delayed shock. He felt exhausted, and there was a contusion on his temple caused by the blow from the oar. A nurse had provided a large white dressing, which made his injury appear more serious than it was; it would come in useful if he wanted to get some sympathy at the station.

Pam gave him a weak smile. 'You're a bloody fool.'

'I'm a bloody fool who needs a bath,' he said, taking her hand to kiss it.

After a long soak in a hot bath, he spent the rest of the

348

evening on the sofa, with a glass of wine in his hand and the cat, Moriarty, purring on his knee. Della brought the children back at nine, but to Wesley's relief, she didn't stay. He couldn't face having to be polite and answer questions just at that moment.

Pam rang Maritia to tell her what had happened, and ever the doctor, Maritia told her to make sure his tetanus jabs were up to date. When Pam offered him the phone, he waved it away. He was in no mood to talk. He just wanted to rest and stare at something mindless on TV. He ended up watching a detective series, amused at the speed the forensic results came back and the fact that the pathologist appeared to do most of the police officers' jobs for them. If only Colin Bowman was so obliging.

He slept remarkably well and awoke the following morning feeling refreshed. Pam hovered anxiously as he ate his breakfast listening to the children squabbling and complaining about their homework. She pointed at their father's dressing and told them to be quiet, but he assured them it was fine to carry on. Things were normal and that was how he liked them.

Against Pam's heartfelt advice, he insisted on going in to work. He needed to see the case to its conclusion. Simon Pussett was being held in one of the cells in the bowels of the station, and the clock was ticking.

As soon as he arrived, he headed straight for Gerry's office. Rachel was already in there. She looked pale and tired. Wesley wondered whether she'd told Gerry her news. But the DCI looked deadly serious, so he thought not.

'Brian Watkins has made a confession, in spite of his solicitor advising him to say "no comment", and Jeremy Quayle's given a very detailed statement,' Gerry said as

Wesley took a seat, ignoring his boss's initial question about his wounds. 'If he hadn't been so forthcoming, we might not have had enough to make the charges stick. In my opinion, he was relieved to tell the truth at last. Being charged with conspiracy to murder doesn't seem half as terrifying as the hold Pussett had over him.'

'I take it it was Quayle who spoke to my brother-in-law?'

'It certainly was, and once he started talking to us, it was difficult to shut him up.'

'So he did arrange his first wife's murder?'

'They didn't get on and it solved all his financial problems, even after he'd paid Pussett, allowing him to fulfil his ambition of reviving the mill. Diana had thought it would be nothing but a money pit, so she refused to let him use any of her inheritance for the project. Poured cold water on his dreams was how he put it. He said Simon seemed to enjoy the killing part. He got a kick out of holding the power of life and death.'

Gerry stretched out in his seat with his hands behind his head and a satisfied smile on his face. 'Good job you thought to check Simon's background, Wes.'

'It was when Jack Tanthwaite told me Pussett managed the bar at the cricket club where David Leeson used to be a regular turn that everything fell into place. When David saw him in Petherham, coming out of Mill House on the night Pussett killed Diana Quayle in 2008, he recognised him right away, but he didn't say anything for years. It wasn't until Erica was found that he worked it out. He asked to speak to Pussett when he saw him in the Fisherman's Arms on the Friday night. According to Tanthwaite, there are still people up in Manchester who remember David Leeson's crooning days – and Simon the bar manager, who was friendly enough but who gave some of the punters the creeps with his obsession with serial killers and his auntie in Devon.'

'Pity we didn't discover the Devon connection before.'

'There was nothing to connect Simon Pussett with Erica Walsh – or Diana Quayle. He didn't even run the Fisherman's Arms in those days, so his name never came up in the investigation.' Wesley smiled. 'I've become new best mates with that inspector from GMP, and he told me he's got a few unsolved murders on his books – cold cases from years ago. They linked the cases, but all their enquiries came to nothing. Now they're going to look at them again to see if Simon Pussett might be involved. I suspect James Markham wasn't his first victim. But it was the tie around Erica's neck that nailed him. Jack Tanthwaite told me some of the bar staff were given ties too – and guess whose name came up.'

'Simon Pussett.'

'That's how Simon met Brian: he used to moan in the bar about his business partner, and Simon offered to get rid of him. Brian thought he was joking at first, then it became clear he was deadly serious. Brian went along with it, making sure he was far away when it happened. He had some business in Devon with Jeremy Quayle's company, so he timed his visit to fit in. Once the deed was done, Pussett demanded payment for his services and Brian paid up, assuming that was the end of the matter. But Pussett never forgot. He always kept a hold over the people he'd killed for.'

'How did Quayle get involved?'

'He met Brian at a conference in Manchester. Drunken confidences and all that. Brian told him about the arrangement he'd made with Pussett and offered to put Quayle in touch with him. Diana's fate was sealed. It had to be while Jeremy was away, of course. That was part of the deal. Jeremy must have got a hell of a shock when Simon took over the Fisherman's Arms.'

'What about little Orlando Quayle?'

'Quayle says he never wanted the kid killed. He's putting the blame for that firmly at Pussett's door. He claims he was horrified when he found out, but I'm not sure I believe him.'

'The scheme was so cold-blooded,' said Rachel, who'd been listening in silence, as surprised as the rest of the incident room when Pussett had been brought in. 'He's down in the interview room now, sir.'

Gerry pulled a face. 'I've got a meeting with the CPS. Rach, do you want to sit in on the interview with Wes?'

Rachel nodded. She'd come across a lot of murderers in the course of her career, but never one who'd made murder into a business.

'Funny,' said Wesley as he stood up. 'Neil thinks something similar was going on in Petherham in the nineteenth century. His theory is that people paid someone to kill their inconvenient relatives for them while they were away so they couldn't possibly come under suspicion. There's an account written by the local doctor at the time, but some of the pages are missing, so the killer's identity is never revealed. I'm wondering if Pussett knew about the case, and that's where he got the idea from.'

Gerry looked puzzled, but he didn't enquire further. 'How's Corrine after her ordeal?'

'Fine, according to Neil. She's pleased she's going to get justice for Erica at last.'

Gerry pointed at the dressing on Wesley's temple. 'Feeling up to this?'

'Try and stop me.'

Wesley went to the mirror hanging on Gerry's wall. He'd never been quite sure why it was there, because Gerry was one of the least vain people he'd ever met. He studied his reflection for a moment before removing the bulky dressing carefully, relieved to find that the wound underneath was held together with steri-strips. After throwing the dressing into the bin, he followed Rachel out into the main office.

He was about to face one of the most calculating killers he'd ever arrested, and he didn't want to do it alone.

I December 1912

My dearest wife,

It grieves me to write this, but the truth must be told. Perhaps when you read it you will understand why I have been so engulfed by melancholy this last year, for in the past I have done terrible things for which I must now pay dearly.

It is many years since I practised medicine in Petherham, and were it not for the terrible deeds I committed there, I would not have become a wealthy man. I never believed in hell in those days. I didn't even believe in the Almighty. From my youthful observation of the human body, I believed that people were merely machines, to be mended or disposed of at will.

Yet now my own body begins to betray me, and feelings of remorse fill my sleepless hours. I have taken lives for monetary reward; rid the avaricious of those they deemed inconvenient. And as soon as I suspected that a good, honest woman, the wife of Petherham's vicar, had guessed the truth, I ended her life as well. At the time, I wrote all in a notebook I kept, but when I met you and proposed marriage, I tore out the pages that revealed the true story, lest you should happen to find it. But now I must make the full confession my conscience demands. I know this will shock you, but you deserve to know the truth about the man who has been your loving husband for so long.

My career of wickedness began many years ago when I was in London and a man asked me to provide a strong sleeping draught for his unwanted wife. I did so without question when he offered me double my usual fee, and the woman died as I knew she would. I was not faced with further temptation until I moved to Petherham.

It began with the wife of Josiah Partridge. When I spoke with Partridge, he hinted that his wife's death would be most convenient for him. Although I could find nothing wrong with her, he claimed she was suffering greatly and he wished to see an end to it. He said that he and his daughter were going away, and I understood that were the woman to die in his absence, no suspicion would be attached to him. I called upon her and administered the fatal dose. I was in the habit of photographing many things in those days. I had brought my equipment from London, and it had become quite a pastime of mine. The notion of capturing her in her subsequent repose appealed to me greatly. A memento of my work, you might say.

Mrs Fitzterran too wished to be rid of her husband, and a similar arrangement was made – only this time, as he habitually refused the services of a physician, I made his death appear to be the work of robbers, and sent word to Albert Waring to attend the scene, knowing all would think him guilty of the crime. No suspicion was ever attached to Fitzterran's wife or servants, who were all absent at the time, and I took an image of the dead man

355

to remind me of the power I had over life and death. It gratified me to look upon those images back then.

When Waring was hanged for the crime, I felt no regret, for the ruffian was of little use to the world and his unfortunate wife was, I think, relieved that she no longer had to endure his blows.

A while later, Partridge wished to dispose of his second wife, having insured her life heavily and the mill being in financial difficulty. She was a healthy young woman, so I performed the deed while her husband and stepdaughter were away from home, inviting her to walk with me then holding her head beneath the waters of the creek until she breathed her last. When her lifeless body was returned to the Mill House, again I recorded my handiwork. I certified the cause of death, and as ever, the coroner never questioned my judgement. I thought I was God – but now I know I was more akin to Satan.

Afterwards, when Partridge paid me handsomely for the deed, he jested that while the poor had their burial circle, we had our own circle – a dark inner circle known only to a select few. The thought brought a smile to my lips.

I confess I felt a strong attraction to Mrs Stephens, the vicar's young wife, but she was a woman of great intelligence and I knew it would not be long before she guessed my secret. My action was necessary, yet killing her distressed me greatly, and after that I could never bring myself to kill again. For the first time, the act of violence, the look in her eyes when she realised I was about to send her to meet her maker, appalled me. I recorded her image as she lay in repose in the mortuary to remind myself that power can hurt as well as reward. I found then I wanted only to forget.

And now I look at the noose I have made for
myself, dangling from the beam in the attic. I am to pay
the proper price for the sins I have kept to myself all
these years; the sins not even those closest to me suspect
me of committing. I leave you this letter, my love,
and whether or not you reveal its contents will be your
decision. I am not the man you thought I was. I am
a murderer, and perhaps my sickness and the loss of our
beloved daughter to consumption is my punishment.

I will put my head into the noose and trust the Lord
will have mercy on a repentant sinner. Farewell.

Your loving Christopher

357

52

Wesley could tell Rachel was nervous as they walked together down the corridor to the interview room where Simon Pussett was waiting under police guard.

'Are you all right?' he asked in a hushed voice, unable to think of anything more suitable to say.

She didn't answer.

'Have you told Nigel about the baby yet?'

'Let's get this over with, shall we?'

When they entered the room, the prisoner looked up, a slight smile on his lips as though he was enjoying some private joke.

The interview had been delayed while Wesley called Neil to arrange for a piece of additional evidence to be delivered to the station; something he hoped would encourage the accused to throw some light on his crimes. It hadn't yet arrived, but Neil had made a promise and Wesley knew his friend would keep his word.

As he flicked the switch on the machine that would record the interview, he saw Simon staring at him, no longer the amiable pub landlord but a cornered killer – one who'd enjoyed his work.

'Twelve years ago, you killed Diana Quayle and her son Orlando. Tell me what happened.'

'No comment.' Simon looked at his solicitor for approval, but the young woman sat stony-faced. She looked uncomfortable, which Wesley took as a good sign.

Simon had turned his attention to Rachel. He was staring at her hungrily, and Wesley saw her push her hair back from her face. After their years of working together, he recognised this as a nervous gesture.

'We've been speaking to our colleagues in Greater Manchester,' he said. 'They have a number of unsolved murders on their books – and some DNA at the scenes that they've never been able to identify. You've been careful to keep your nose clean over the years, so your DNA's never been on record. After all, who'd ever suspect you? The friendly landlord always ready to help the police. You knew David Leeson while he was up in Manchester.'

'No comment.'

'He used to sing regularly at the sports club bar you managed, and he recognised you when he came to Petherham on the twelfth of December 2008. He saw you leaving the Quayles' house in Petherham on the night of Diana's supposed suicide, and I bet he wondered what you were doing there. Erica Walsh called at the house that night too. She was looking for her friend when she stumbled on your crime, so she had to die. You strangled her with your cricket club tie and dumped her body on an isolated lane, but you were disturbed before you could remove the tie from around her neck. That turned out to be your big mistake. The wearer of that tie left their DNA all over it.'

Pussett stared at him, his expression blank. 'You can't prove it was me who was wearing it at the time.'

'Jeremy Quayle's had a fit of conscience and has made a full statement,' Wesley continued. 'Brian Watkins took a little more persuading, but he told us everything eventually – including how you killed his wife for him while he was away in Spain on a golfing trip. You might as well come clean, Simon. Do yourself a favour and co-operate.'

There was a long period of silence, broken when a uniformed constable entered the room. He handed Wesley a plastic evidence bag containing an old book, the paper brown with age and the writing a faded copperplate. This was what he'd been waiting for. There was a note with the package too. He read it, then handed it to Rachel.

'I think you've seen this before,' he said, pushing the book towards the prisoner. 'For the benefit of the tape, I'm showing the suspect a nineteenth-century notebook containing an account of several murders that took place in the village of Petherham in the 1880s. I asked for it to be examined for fingerprints as soon as it was delivered to the station. Turns out your prints are all over it. What have you got to say to that?'

'No comment.'

'Until recently, the book was in the home of a Miss Cruckshank, who lives in Neston. According to Miss Cruckshank, it never left her premises until her carer took it without her permission and gave it to Corrine Malin, a PhD student, and Dr Neil Watson, the county's Heritage Manager for Archaeology and Historic Environment. There is no way you could have had access to it while it's been in their possession, so how come your prints are on it?'

Simon Pussett shifted in his seat.

'What is your relationship to Miss Cruckshank?'

The accused took a deep breath. 'She's my great-aunt.

I used to stay with her a lot when I was young. My parents thought the holidays in sunny Devon would do me good. Either that or they were glad to get rid of me. I still visit her sometimes.'

'While you were at her house, you found this book and learned about the Petherham murders. That's where you got the idea from. Murder as a business. And foolproof because you had no connection to your victims and your DNA wasn't on our database. Clever.'

'If you say so.'

'According to the book, the killer was never caught.'

'That's true. He was a man who was above suspicion. Well regarded. Respected,' Pussett said proudly. 'People are divided into two sorts, Detective Inspector. Predators and prey. It's the predators who come out on top. How's the head?' The question was casual, as if they were chatting over a drink.

'OK.'

'You had a lucky escape. I would have killed you if I could.'

'How did you meet Jeremy Quayle?'

'Through Brian Watkins. He met Jeremy while he was up in Manchester for a business conference. It was one of those drunken conversations – how he had a dream of doing up Petherham Mill. His wife had just inherited a fortune from her parents but she was making sure he didn't see any of it. He told Brian she was a neurotic bitch who wouldn't give his idea of reopening the mill the time of day. Brian said that if he wanted to be rid of her, he knew someone who could help. I'd already agreed to deal with Brian's business partner, who was making life awkward for him. Jeremy had a conference booked in London just before Christmas. I said that would be the perfect time – if he could wait that long. We kept in touch in the meantime.'

'How did you kill Diana Quayle and her son?'

'With the cricket bat that hangs above the fireplace in the pub. You commented on it, as I recall,' Pussett said with a smile. 'Their injuries were put down to the fall from the cliff.'

'But something went wrong.'

'You mean the girl who called at the house just as I was about to dispose of them – said she was a friend of the nanny or something. The nosy little bitch peered into the hall and saw the woman and kid lying there. She started to scream, so I took off my tie and strangled her. Left her body there while I got rid of the others. After I'd driven the woman and the kid to the cliff in her car to make it look like suicide, I walked back to Petherham, where I picked up my own car and the girl's body.'

'You were disturbed when you dumped the body in a quiet lane, and when you went back for your tie, she'd gone. Bet you wondered if she'd got away.'

Wesley wondered whether to reveal Eli Jelkes's deception, but decided against it. This man didn't deserve an explanation.

'I admit it did occur to me. I lay low for a while, then, when nothing happened, I thought I'd got away with it. I put my little business on hold when I took over the Fisherman's Arms . . . until Brian Watkins moved down here and asked me to get rid of his wife for him. He'd overreached himself financially and had just insured her life for a fortune. He'd also met a new lady, so I thought, why not resume my little sideline. Then that girl's body was found.'

'And David Leeson came to Petherham and recognised you.'

He shook his head as though he was annoyed with himself. 'I'd no idea he'd seen me on the night the woman and her kid . . . ' He hesitated, as though he was reluctant to put the fate of Diana Quayle and her son into words. 'He'd been visiting a woman who wasn't his wife, and that's why he never said anything about it at the time. She was a barmaid when the last landlord was at the Fisherman's, and I saw him going into the staff cottage. At least the fact that he was cheating on his wife meant he kept his mouth shut.'

'Then he came back for the psychic weekend, and there you were running the local pub.'

'He came in on the Friday night and recognised me right away. He hadn't realised I'd bought the place, so it gave him a hell of a shock. We had a quick chat and he said something was worrying him. He told me he'd seen me at Mill House that night twelve years ago – said he hadn't given it much thought until the girl's body was found. He'd been interviewed at the time because he'd picked her up in his car, and he was scared he was going to come under suspicion again. Then he asked me what I'd been doing there and if I'd seen the girl at all. I couldn't risk him talking, could I? It had been OK when the police thought she'd gone to Cornwall, but . . . Anyway, I told him the bar was busy and I couldn't talk so he gave me his mobile number. I said I'd slip out of the pub the following night to meet him.'

'You killed innocent people in cold blood,' said Rachel, as though she was unable to stop herself.

'I provided a service. I allowed people to pursue their dreams. What's wrong with that?'

Wesley couldn't find the words to answer. After announcing to the machine that the interview was terminated, he stood up and touched Rachel's arm gently. He could almost feel her pent-up fury as she sat, every muscle tensed, ready to spring. After a few moments, she looked up at him and nodded.

They had enough to charge the suspect. It was time to go.

53

Corrine Malin stood beside Neil at the entrance to Petherham Mill. The sky had turned a dark, ominous grey and the only sound they could hear in the still, heavy air was the rushing of water beneath the iron bridge. They stood silently for a while, watching the water wheel turning, both thinking of the body they'd seen caught up in its workings – the man who'd claimed to have psychic powers but had failed to predict his own end.

Neil broke the silence. 'I'll send you a copy of the book when it's finished. The story of those murders should make it a best-seller.'

'Amongst those who get excited by industrial archaeology,' Corrine said with a wry smile. 'Shame we still don't know the killer's identity.'

'Don't we?'

'Who was it?'

'I can't be a hundred per cent sure, because some of the pages of the notebook are missing. But I have my suspicions.'

'I feel so sorry for Miss Cruckshank. Her own great-nephew . . .'

'I know.'

'My supervisor at the university suggested I include the Victorian case in my thesis. I don't claim to be psychic, but there was definitely something about that house. Something ... unhealthy.' She looked in the direction of Mill House and shuddered.

There was a long silence while they both stared down into the rushing stream.

'I'm sorry about Erica,' Neil said suddenly. He knew his words were inadequate. He wasn't good at the emotional stuff, but he felt he had to say something, however clumsily it came out. Corrine's loss couldn't just be ignored. 'You must miss her.'

She turned her head towards him and gave him a sad smile. 'Every day. Our relationship had only just started, but I think I loved her ... whatever love means.'

There was another long silence before Neil spoke again. 'You need cheering up. Let's go and check out the grotto. Robert Farnley's keeping the place going. Business as usual.'

'Aren't we too old for the grotto?'

'You're never too old,' Neil said.

Corrine smiled. 'I suppose this is the last time we'll meet.'

'Not necessarily. My department will need a fresh pair of eyes to read through the proofs of the book. Check the facts about the Petherham case.'

A pair of mothers passed them, with toddlers in tow.

'I think I'll give the grotto a miss,' Corrine said. 'It was a daft idea. This place only reminds me of Erica.'

'You're right. We're far too big for Santa's knee.'

As they walked away from the mill, the first flakes of snow began to fall from the sky.

*

The case against Simon Pussett was wrapped up and the CPS was satisfied with all the charges. The evidence, combined with his confession and those of Brian Watkins and Jeremy Quayle, would ensure a conviction. But Wesley had a nagging feeling that there was still a loose end that needed to be tied up.

So far, he hadn't spoken to Pussett's great-aunt, Miss Cruckshank. He knew she'd been informed about the arrest, but he hadn't wanted to cause her further distress without good reason. And yet there was a question he wanted to ask; something that had been lurking at the back of his mind ever since Simon had made his confession. He'd had a feeling the man was keeping something back; almost as though he was protecting someone.

He had obtained Miss Cruckshank's address from Neil, but he hadn't told his friend what he was planning. He suspected Neil might not have co-operated if he'd known.

After driving to Neston alone, he knocked on the old woman's door. When there was no reply, he went to the back of the house and let himself into the yard. Unlike at the front, there were no net curtains at the windows, and after a few moments' hesitation, he stood on tiptoe to peer in through the dusty glass.

The room beyond was lit by the winter sun, and inside he saw an elderly woman lying on a shabby chaise longue, her arms crossed across her chest. Her wizened face was peaceful, as though she'd lain down and yielded happily to death. Her pose reminded Wesley of the photographs Neil had shown him. A corpse laid out to be recorded for posterity.

His heart was pounding as he put his shoulder to the back door, and when it gave way, he stumbled into the room and knelt beside the woman, feeling for a pulse, only to find that her flesh was ice cold. He could see an empty bottle of pills beside her on a small table.

The envelope lying beside the pill bottle was addressed to *Greta or whoever finds me*. He remembered Neil saying that Greta was her carer, who came in several times a day; he was glad it had been him who'd found her rather than someone unfamiliar with the sight of death.

He opened the envelope and found that it contained a handwritten letter along with two sheets of paper that looked very different. They were brown and foxed with age, and covered with neat copperplate writing – the same handwriting that had filled the old book he'd seen Pam transcribing, the notebook of Dr Christopher Cruckshank. He walked over to the window to read the letter in the light.

I apologise to whoever finds me for the inconvenience. Throughout my life I've never wished to inconvenience anybody. Even when I conspired to commit murder, I ensured it was done neatly and with as little pain as possible. My dear great-nephew Simon stands accused of killing for his own gain, but I'm afraid I must take the blame, because it was I who started him on this path through my own desire to escape a disagreeable situation.

When I found my great-grandfather's confession amongst the family papers, I read and reread it time and time again because it described a way out of my plight – a way out I was too cowardly to take myself. When Simon came to stay with us – my father was alive in those days, but an invalid – I shared the letter with him even though he was only sixteen and little more than a child. Eventually we came to an agreement. He would hold the pillow over Father's face – something I could not bring myself to do – and I would give him a share of my inheritance. I confess that the eagerness with which he went about the task disturbed me, but I can only think that his ancestor's murderous blood ran in his veins.

I had previously found Christopher Cruckshank's notebook, but some pages had been removed, so it did not tell the whole sorry tale; it was not until I came upon the confession he left for his wife after his death that the truth was finally revealed. This letter's contents were known only to myself and Simon, and I hid it well. But I enclose it here, and when it is read, the full story will be known at last.

I am sorry for my actions, borne of desperation, for my father was a monster who controlled my every move and subjected me to the most vile ordeals throughout my life – these days the newspapers would call it abuse. It ensured that I found the male sex so repellent that I could never contemplate marriage. He deprived me of love and the possibility of children. I had only Simon, my brother's grandson, and now that I know he will spend the rest of his days in prison, I cannot face the future.

Forgive me.

Esme Cruckshank (Miss)

Once Wesley had read Dr Cruckshank's confession, he reported the death, then returned to Tradmouth to break the news to Gerry.

His spirits were low as he drove back in the gathering darkness. It had begun to snow again, and as his wipers swished to and fro, he felt the last piece of the jigsaw was finally in place. The whole picture, albeit a bitter one.

To his surprise, he was greeted by Rachel in the corridor outside the CID office. She looked troubled, as though she was wrestling with some intractable problem, and suddenly he longed to see her smiling again.

He told her about Esme Cruckshank, glad to share his grim discovery with somebody at last.

'That explains a lot,' she said after listening patiently.

'I'd better tell the boss. Everything OK?'

'I suppose it'll have to be.'

He waited for her to continue.

'I've told Nigel.'

'What did he say?'

'He's over the moon. Hoping for a boy.'

He reached out and touched her hand. 'I knew he'd be pleased.'

Before she could answer, there was a sudden gale of laughter from inside the office.

'What's going on?'

'See for yourself.'

As he walked into the CID office beside Rachel, he heard more laughter. The hilarity seemed to be centred around Gerry's office. He wormed his way through the little crowd that had gathered by the boss's door, and the sight that greeted him made it impossible not to smile.

Gerry was sitting behind his desk in full Santa Claus get-up, beard and all, no doubt a dress rehearsal for his role at the station Christmas fair the following day.

'Now then, children, what's on our Christmas list? A larger police budget?'

'All our villains to go on strike,' one of the DCs piped up.

Wesley left them to it and returned to his desk. He'd given Miss Cruckshank's suicide note to the officers who'd attended the scene, but he'd kept the old letter – Dr Cruckshank's confession to his wife. Neil would need it to ensure the accuracy of his new publication. It was about time the village of Petherham learned the truth about its past.

Once he'd cast off his cheery alter ego, Gerry emerged from his office and beckoned Wesley in.

'I've just got back from Neston,' Wesley said as he took a seat. 'Simon Pussett's great-aunt has killed herself. She left a note explaining everything. Seems Pussett's murderous career started earlier than we realised.'

Gerry nodded, but it was clear he had other things on his mind. 'I've got some news myself and all.'

Wesley sat down with a sense of foreboding. He feared this was the moment he'd been dreading, but Gerry was grinning, delighted at what he was about to say.

'Me and Joyce. I'm going to make an honest woman of her. Asked her last night and she said yes. Haven't set a date yet, but . . .'

'What about retirement?' The question almost stuck in his throat.

'Oh, I abandoned that idea when we visited old Bill Irwin. Did you see how pleased he was to see us? Poor man's bored silly. If I wasn't here, what would I do with myself all day?'

'What indeed,' said Wesley, his heart suddenly lighter.

54

Four months later

Selina Quayle looked at the space where the grotto had once been and smiled to herself. She'd always dreamed that one day she'd be in total charge – the former assistant who'd always been one step ahead of the boss. Although she hadn't expected it to happen this way.

She suspected the publicity had actually been good for business. It had put Petherham Mill on the map, and Robert Farnley was in the process of employing more staff. She'd even asked him to apply for charitable status. Heritage was popular, and there was a possibility that they'd be able to recruit volunteers to take on some of the work, which would save on wage bills.

Dr Watson's newly published booklet had also given the business an extra boost, especially the section outlining the colourful history of Petherham in the nineteenth century, and the so-called curse. It had been flying off the stands in the mill shop.

She was employing help at the B&B too, although if the mill started making real money, she'd be able to stop that part of the enterprise. It would be good to have Mill House all to herself.

She hadn't visited Jeremy in prison. He'd served his purpose. When they'd started their affair, he'd complained non-stop about Diana and her brat, saying his marriage to her had been a huge mistake. Diana had been wealthy, but she'd been so mean with her money that he'd never seen any benefit. It had been Selina who'd sowed the seed in his mind during their after-work rendezvous in her small flat. What if Diana was no longer a problem? What if she could just vanish one day and leave them alone together?

They'd made crazy plans, which had been pure fantasy at the time since Jeremy was reluctant to give up the security Diana's fortune provided. Fantasy until he met Brian Watkins at the Manchester conference. After that meeting, the seed had grown and flourished and she'd tended it carefully. Brian knew somebody who'd do the job for a fee – an assassin who could never be traced back to Jeremy. It was Selina who'd banished his doubts; Selina who'd been behind him every step of the way. Needling. Encouraging. Showing him what life would be like once he'd achieved his dream.

He'd become obsessed with the derelict mill he saw from his window each day, and finally he'd been given the chance to own it and restore it to its former glory; to escape the corporate cage and be his own boss. With Selina's help.

The plan had worked perfectly. Until everything unravelled. How was she to know the assassin had a relative in the area and would decide to take over the local pub? Simon Pussett's presence in Petherham had terrified Jeremy, and since he'd acquired the Fisherman's Arms, her husband had never set foot in the place. And how was she to know that the psychic she'd hired had a connection with the killer?

Now, however, she was safe in her new position and confident that Jeremy would never betray her part in it all. She'd convinced the police that she knew nothing about her husband's activities, and the police were notoriously stupid, so she'd heard.

She'd ignored Jeremy's pathetic pleas for a visit; she intended to have nothing more to do with him. And when her divorce came through, she'd make sure she got the lot.

She left the mill, letting the doors swing shut behind her, and was about to cross the road to Mill House when a car drew up.

She recognised its occupants as the two policemen who'd interviewed her at the time of Jeremy's arrest: the well-spoken, attractive black one and the uncouth Scouser. She stopped and waited, wondering what they wanted.

It was the black inspector who spoke first. 'Selina Quayle, I'm arresting you on suspicion of conspiracy to murder Diana Quayle and Orlando Quayle ...'

After he'd recited the caution, the DCI opened the passenger door. 'Get in, love,' he said.

'What's going on? I haven't done anything. I didn't know Jeremy had anything to do with their murders. He fooled me completely. I'm an innocent victim here.'

'That's not what your husband says,' said the big Liverpudlian. 'He's been very chatty since he's been banged up. I blame the porridge. In you get.'

Selina glanced across and saw the mill wheel turning relentlessly, as it had done for almost two centuries. They couldn't prove anything. She'd be back.

Author's Note

The definition of archaeology in the *Oxford English Dictionary* is 'the study of man's past by analysis of the material remains of his cultures', and sometimes those material remains aren't just found in the ground. As in this book, examining historic buildings (including mills) can be part of an archaeologist's job.

Living in the north of England (dark satanic mills territory), I'm fairly familiar with industrial archaeology. I've attended talks about historic mill surveys and I'm fortunate enough to live near Quarry Bank Mill in Cheshire, a large textile mill, lovingly restored by the National Trust, that was originally powered by a water wheel (before steam engines helped out). My many visits there have been invaluable while I've been researching *The Burial Circle*, giving me an insight into the noise and atmosphere of a working mill.

You might wonder what this has to do with the beautiful county in the south-west of England where my Wesley Peterson novels are set, but Devon also has an impressive industrial history. Because of the abundance of sheep on Dartmoor, the cloth trade thrived until the nineteenth century, and the fine houses built by many wealthy cloth merchants can still be seen in the county's historic towns.

Woollen mills were established in the eighteenth century, but due to the wars with France and the development of new technology, the industry fell into decline throughout the nineteenth and twentieth centuries. Some mills, however, survive today as heritage attractions (rather like Petherham Mill in this book) – although without my fictional mill's murderous history.

My inclusion of a supernatural element in the story reflects the Victorian interest in spiritualism and contacting the 'other side'. This fascination with death became quite an obsession, and ostentatious mourning was made fashionable by Queen Victoria herself, who spent many years grieving for her late husband, Prince Albert.

Death would have been a constant and familiar companion to the people of the nineteenth century, and keeping souvenirs of the dead, such as jewellery made from the hair of a dead relative, was commonplace. This was a time of great innovation in photography, and there was a fashion for taking photographs of dead loved ones, sometimes alone and sometimes posed with living relatives, something we would find macabre today. I couldn't resist adding a twist to this practice by having a killer keep such pictures as a reminder of his crimes.

Queen Victoria's reign saw the rise of the burial club. Such clubs were founded at a time of high death rates, especially amongst children, and were set up for poor families who feared they wouldn't be able to give their loved ones a decent funeral. In return for weekly payments, the club would cover funeral expenses, regardless of how long the deceased had been a member. These schemes were generally a great success, relieving people of the fear of seeing their loved ones buried in a pauper's grave. However, human nature being what it is, the system was sometimes abused. Knowing a sick child was unlikely to survive for long, some people enrolled them in several clubs at once, all of which would pay out with no questions asked. One man was said to have put his child in nineteen clubs, thus making a large profit when the unfortunate infant died. This gave rise to the suspicion that people were enrolled in clubs before being murdered. Perhaps my imaginary secret burial circle in Petherham might not be so far-fetched after all.

Acknowledgements

I'd like to thank my agent, Euan Thorneycroft, along with my excellent editor at Piatkus/Little, Brown, Hannah Wann, and everyone else at my publisher who helps to get Wesley Peterson's investigations out to my lovely readers. I'd also like to thank my husband, Roger, who's had to take over as my first reader since the death of my dear friend Ruth Smith, and who's helped so much with my research into mills and water wheels.

Finally I'd like to say a big thank you to Robert Farnley, who allowed me to use his name in this book in aid of a very good cause (CLIC Sargent – helping children with cancer and their families).